ACT
OF
GOD

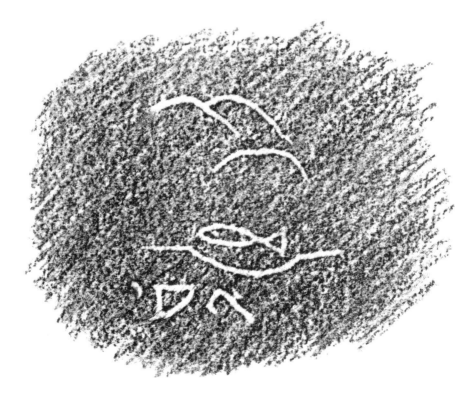

ACT OF GOD

A NOVEL BY

Charles Templeton

McCLELLAND AND STEWART

The principal characters in this book
are fictitious and are not derivative of
anyone living or dead. Some of the
people and organizations referred to
exist, but any words, actions or
attitudes attributed to them are entirely
the product of the author's
imagination.

Portions of the scriptures quoted in
the book are from the Jerusalem Bible,
the Revised Standard Version and the
King James Version.

The Canadian Publishers
McClelland and Stewart Limited
25 Hollinger Road, Toronto

CANADIAN CATALOGUING IN PUBLICATION DATA

Templeton, Charles B., date
  Act of God

ISBN 0-7710-8549-4

I. Title.

PS8589.E46A38   C813'.5'4   C77-001435-6
PR9199.3.T42A38

Printed and bound in Canada

To Laura Beatrice Berton
– who unwittingly sowed the seed

Love with care – and then
what you will, do.

St. Augustine

Prologue

The box had been three days in the belly of the Pan Am 707 cargo aircraft, having been shipped from Amman Jordan to John F. Kennedy airport but being delayed in Amsterdam by reason of the need to replace an engine in the aircraft. In the freight warehouse, a cargo-handler picked it up and dumped it onto a long steel-sheathed table.

"Goddammit!" the supervisor snarled, "It's marked fragile. Can't you read?"

"I can read."

"Then read, for Christ's sake."

The box, three feet long and a foot wide, was made of unpainted half-inch pine. It had been securely nailed and was bound with metal strapping. A bill of lading, glued to the rough surface of the wood, yielded the information that the box had cleared customs at Amman and weighed 11.4 kilograms. A rectangular piece of paper, also glued to the wood, read:

SHIP TO: Dr. Herman Unger
Curator, Department of Anthropology
HOLD FOR: Dr. Harris G. Gordon
Museum of Natural History
Central Park West at 79th St
New York City, 10024, USA

Carefully hand-lettered in red ink on the wood itself were the words: FRAGILE! HANDLE WITH CARE, and beneath them the neatly printed injunction: *Contents archaeological artifacts. Not to be opened except in presence of addressee. Avoid extreme cold, heat or humidity.*

The cargo-handler pivoted the box on the table, picked it up and placed it on a wooden pallet. A forklift truck thrust its tines beneath, wheeled and trundled away. On a long aisle of open-shelved racks the driver spied a space. He stopped, raised the lift, dismounted and slid the box onto a shelf alongside a carton containing a computer keyboard, a box of pharmaceutical supplies, a crate of Jensen automatic rifles and a metal container for motion picture film bearing the label, *Sex Practices in Sodom.*

The cargo-handler made a note of the coded digits on the shelf, mounted his machine and drove off.

Part One

Chapter One

That late afternoon in Rome the setting sun was gilding towers, cupolas and crosses, and impatient traffic contended in the streets as a small black Fiat bearing the distinctive SCV licence plates of the Vatican State separated from the flow of traffic at the lower end of the Via Venetto and turned in at the entrance to the United States embassy. An enormous flag over three wrought-iron gates waved an indolent welcome and two marines in dress-blues drew themselves taut to snap and sustain a salute as the car moved the length of the building, made a 180-degree turn and drew up before the bulletproof glass doors within the security of the inner courtyard. The driver leaped from the car to open the door, and the Very Reverend Michael Cardinal Maloney, Bishop of the Archdiocese of New York, his frame less suited to Fiats than to limousines, emerged. As he approached the doorway, the ambassador strode swiftly down the broad sweep of the marble staircase, hand outstretched.

"Good afternoon, Your Eminence," he said, his voice sepulchral in the vaulted vestibule. "Right on time, but then you always are. Good to see you."

"And you, Mr. Ambassador."

The ambassador was a very tall man, taller by inches than Cardinal Maloney's six feet two, and lean to the point of gauntness. He had a narrow, bald head and lank hair hanging in spikes down the back of a long neck. Not wanting to intimidate by his height, he compensated by thrusting his head forward. Michael never saw him without recalling the great blue herons that stilted solemnly about in the stony shallows near The Cottage in summer.

"You had a good flight from New York?" the ambassador asked, pumping Michael's arm as though trying to draw water.

"Couldn't have been better."

"The Holy Father, he's well?"

"I'll tell him you were asking."

The ambassador flicked a glance at his wristwatch. "I think perhaps I'd better get you to the telephone. It's going on five and Mr. Lieberman . . . " He left the sentence dangling, and cupping Michael's elbow lightly, disdained the tiny elevator and turned him toward the staircase. "I've put you in the conference room," he said, "There's a scrambler on one of the phones there."

The conference room was high-ceilinged, perfectly proportioned and finished in natural oak paneling. On an end wall, bracketed with flags, was the Great Seal of the United States. Ranged around the wall were framed portraits of the presidents, the more recent in color. On the far end of a great oval rosewood table was a red telephone and arranged neatly beside it a supply of pens and pencils and a pad of legal-size foolscap. The ambassador ushered Michael to a chair, seated him and picked up the phone.

"Smitty," he said, "His Eminence is ready." He replaced the receiver. "I'll leave you now," he said. "You'll probably want to collect your thoughts."

"Thank you," Michael said, and was alone.

What could be on Josh Lieberman's mind to cause him to take the most extraordinary measure of having him come to the embassy? As Michael had descended the stairs from the first-class cabin of the Alitalia 747, a uniformed driver had stepped forward and handed him a sealed envelope. It was a request that he go immediately to the embassy to receive a telephone call from the United States Secretary of State on a matter of urgency. There was only one likely explanation: Lieberman had heard about the Holy Father's illness. But why the embassy; could he not talk more easily and as safely – and certainly, more appropriately – at the Vatican? Perhaps, for all the recently intensified security measures, the telephone system there was not invulnerable.

On the telephone a light flashed. He picked up the receiver and said, "Hello."

"The Secretary of State calling from Washington, Your Eminence. Will you hold please?" There was a sustained buzz, a series of automated beeps and the line cleared.

"Are you there, Eminence?"

"Yes, I am," Michael said, his voice cordial. He held a particular affection for Joshuah Lieberman. They had met often and had spoken on the telephone daily during the period just before and after the Communist party took power in Italy.

"Good to hear your voice," Lieberman said, the hint of a chuckle in his tone. "I won't ask how you are because virtue must reward its possessor with a serene mind and a—"

Michael feigned a groan: "Beginning like that you must want an enormous favor."

He could imagine the moon face in the cluttered Washington office swollen in the smile that showed his crooked but astonishingly white teeth. Lieberman was a singularly ugly man. He had a sallow complexion, puffed slits for eyes, black jowls and hair not unlike a monk's tonsure. Standing only five feet eight he weighed almost three hundred pounds, waddled rather than walked and wheezed rather than breathed. He was the joy of political cartoonists: when the government embarked on troubled waters *he* was the inflated raft; when he flew on peacekeeping missions the plane was rendered with a bulge at mid-fuselage; when he managed to get all the Middle East antagonists together for a conference on a neutral ship in the Mediterranean, the ship was depicted low in the stern.

"Sorry to have brought you to the embassy," he said.

"Am I to take it that our switchboard leaks?"

"The way things are I wouldn't be surprised. But if you have bugs they're not ours." He laughed. "At least not that I know of. It's just that I feel more confident on this line."

"I understand," Michael said.

The Secretary's manner changed. "Three things on my mind: Number one, I hear the Holy Father is ill."

Michael's hesitation was so brief as to be undetectable. In that microsecond he balanced the wisdom of admitting the truth against the risk involved and knew that the secret would be secure. "You have good sources," he said.

"How serious is it?"

"He's had a stroke."

"I'm sorry to hear that. A bad one?"

"He's been in a coma off and on for days."

"I *am* sorry." He paused a moment. "My second question is a somewhat indelicate one but I think you'll understand. If the Holy Father should pass away . . . "

"Who will succeed him?"

"Yes."

"It's not a matter about which there can be any certainty. We like to believe that God takes a hand in the choosing."

"Let me put it another way: there must be certain men who are more likely to be selected than others."

"There will be perhaps five candidates."

"Would you be among that five?"

"It would mean a radical break with tradition, but to answer your question, yes."

"Good."

"Why?"

"Because it'll make things a hell of a lot simpler at this end." He was silent for a moment and Michael could hear his wheezing over extraneous sounds in the background. "Sorry to leave you hanging but I wanted to put my hands on a report here. The reason for my chasing you down – beyond my concern for the Holy Father, of course – is that I've just learned that the Italian government is about to take steps that may seriously affect your church and I thought I'd better get the information to you while you're in Rome. Our people over there tell me that, after a bit of kite-flying to test the wind, Premier Gordini has plans to . . . "

When, ten minutes later, Michael put down the telephone, his face was grave.

The summons to Rome had come in an early morning telephone call from Paolo Cardinal Rinsonelli, Dean of the Sacred College of Cardinals and one-time visiting Professor of New Testament at the North American College in Rome with whom Michael had done graduate work after his conversion to Roman Catholicism. At eighty, straight as a pillar and with the vitality of a man half his years, Rinsonelli was the terror of the Vatican bureaucracy. He suffered fools not at all, was intemperate with temporizers, impatient with mediocrity and disdainful of subtlety. He was a man of patrician tastes and often earthy language, whose seamed and craggy face, beneath a mane of purest white hair, suggested a relief map. A Sicilian, he delighted in intrigue, and when he had occasion to telephone Michael long distance – seeking his counsel or relaying messages from the Holy Father – often used the name Giovanni, employing an elaborate code and speaking exquisite Italian in what he fondly believed was a perfect simulation of underworld argot. He was indifferent to the six-hour difference in time between Rome and New York City and as a consequence often broke Michael's rest. On this morning, when the private telephone beside the bed jangled him from his deep sleep, Michael had glanced at the illuminated face of the clock beside his bed, noted that it was just past four, and on hearing Rinsonelli's organ tones identifying himself as Giovanni (double fortissimo because it was long distance), muttered a sleepy, "Damn."

He was soon fully alert. Rinsonelli spoke of "your pal Tony in Genoa" – his code name for the Holy Father – and despite the convoluted ambiguity of his sentences, it quickly became clear that the pope was seriously ill and that Michael was to come immediately.

The secret had been well kept. Only the members of the Sacred College of Cardinals, fewer than a dozen other clergy, the editor of the *Osservatore Romano*, four physicians, a member of the Swiss Guard – and, it now appeared, the United States Secretary of State – knew that the pope lay gravely ill. Gregory XVII, Vicar of Christ on earth, Supreme Pontiff, Bishop of Rome, successor in the See of Rome to its first bishop, Peter, Servant of the Servants of God, spiritual leader of five hundred million Roman Catholics around the world, Patriarch of the West, wearer of the Fisherman's Ring, ruler of the Vatican City State, successor to such as Benedict XV, Pius XII, John XXIII and Paul VI, but for all that, mortal, was nearing the end of his days.

He had been stricken, not as he would have wished, at prayer or standing on his balcony at the open window blessing the throng in St. Peter's Square, but bent over a marble basin, retching, in the bathroom off the library from which he had hastily withdrawn in the midst of a meeting with Valerio Cardinal Benedetti, Prefect of the Holy Office and Vatican Secretary of State. Benedetti, becoming alarmed when after fifteen minutes the 78-year-old pontiff didn't return, had knocked on the door, had tried it and found it locked, had called out, and receiving no response had summoned one of the Swiss Guard posted outside. The guard, unnerved by the circumstances and reluctant to enter the papal bathroom, had finally to be ordered to kick in the door. There, his face as white as the marble on which he lay sprawled, was the pope. Benedetti, with the help of the guard – the corpulent cardinal's face as scarlet as his robes, puffing and in terror at the thumping of his heart – carried the sagging slender body to a brocaded Medici divan and telephoned a doctor.

The prognosis was not reassuring. Gregory, after only five years in office, had been stricken by an embolus that had lodged in the left side of the cerebrum, rendering him paralyzed on the right side of his body, producing aphasia and making his speech sometimes unintelligible during those few moments when he struggled back to consciousness. Three other doctors were bound to secrecy and brought to the papal apartment by a circuitous route. Disguised in furniture cartons, X-ray and various life-support systems were moved in. Consultations were held and consensus was reached: the Holy Father might linger for days, weeks, months ("Who can say but our Blessed Lord himself?") or expire without a word within the minute.

A highly confidential memorandum went out to the members of the Sacred College informing them of the pope's illness and instructing them to so prepare their affairs as to be ready to leave for Rome immediately on call. Telephone messages went from the Secretary of State to an even dozen of the most influential prelates summoning them immediately, among them Michael Maloney. They came to Rome and remained five days – during which time Cardinal Syzbysko of Hungary suffered a heart attack and died – discussing behind the tightest possible security the immediate ramifications of Gregory's incapacitation and measuring the impact his death would have on the beleaguered church.

There was no reason to discuss the arrangements to be made should he die: they had been established by long tradition and specifically in the Apostolic Constitution of 1945. Those cardinals resident in Rome – the Curia Roma – would meet in "preparatory congregation" on the day of his death to choose a *cardinal camerlengo*, a chamberlain. He would immediately decree that the papal apartment be sealed, take charge of the properties of the Holy See, require that the Fisherman's Ring and all other papal seals be brought before the Curia and the seals defaced in its presence, set in motion the complex preparations for the burial and name a date for the beginning of the conclave to elect a new pope.

Gregory, his body having been prepared for public viewing by the embalmers, dressed in full pontificals, a mitre on his head, would be borne to the Sistine Chapel to lie between gigantic white candles beneath Michelangelo's fresco of *The Last Judgment*. With the Holy City draped in black and Rome itself solemnized by the tolling of bells from every tower, they would mourn him with nine funeral masses, give him nine absolutions and, his face covered with a purple veil and his body with an ermine blanket dyed blood-red, bury him on the third day in the sacred grotto beneath the Basilica close to the tomb of Peter: bury him in three coffins, one of cypress within one of lead and both within one of elm, to make him in death kin to the humblest of men borne to their graves in a plain wooden box.

Chapter Two

Lt was an unlikely January evening, the wind soft from the south and smelling of freshly turned earth. Walking in the Vatican gardens with Paolo Rinsonelli, Michael, warmed also by friendship and memories of other nights and of other times on these same paths, has shucked off his topcoat and pressed his host to stay out a few minutes longer. He felt enveloped in a glow of timelessness and history and wanted to sustain it. The moon was a red balloon on the ancient wall enclosing the garden. St. Peter's loomed luminous against the outer darkness, far lovelier from this vantage point than from the square. The pines were black silhouettes against the gray of lawn and bush and sky. The museum had closed, the last tourist had gone, and the only reminder that the sprawling city surrounded like a sea was an occasional muted horn and the distant chime of a belltower.

Despite a difference of nearly twenty years in their ages and centuries in the worlds from which they'd sprung, the two men had become each other's best friend. They were walking idly now across the spongy turf, shoes gleaming with dew and with the musk of night in their nostrils. Michael had just finished recounting the burden of his conversation with the Secretary of State: specifically that the Italian government was about to withdraw all tax exemptions and privileges granted the Vatican State, not only in Rome but from all Catholic churches, schools and monasteries throughout the country, and after testing the wind, would so announce.

"In effect, tear up the Lateran Treaty," Rinsonelli rumbled.

"Lieberman says the economy is in worse shape than outsiders dream. Their balance of payments is away out of line and the probability is they'll have to devalue the lira again. Probably raise taxes."

"So much for election promises."

"So much for the workers' paradise."

"They need a scapegoat, and who better than the church?" Michael imitated the intonations of a public speaker: "No longer should a wealthy church get a free ride on the backs of the workers. *Their* rhetoric."

"The rhetoric of all our enemies," Rinsonelli gloomed. "Little do they know."

"Let's face it, Paolo, it's an argument they can sell."

"Our wealth!" Rinsonelli snorted. "In real property we are as Croesus; in cash-flow we approach beggary."

For all his commitment, Michael had never quite become comfortable with the apparent wealth and sometime ostentation of the church, nor been able to rid himself of the self-consciousness that overcame him when, accoutered in full ecclesiastical regalia, he went among others. His attitude was undoubtedly a residue of the Calvinism of his forebears who had made frugality almost an article of faith. It was not that he hankered for a hair shirt and a life of barest subsistence; he was a sensuous man who enjoyed bodily comfort, good food, good wine and good music, but he regarded such things as life's fringe benefits, to be enjoyed but not coveted. Indeed, he preferred to drink from a glass than a chalice, to sleep between linen than satin, to wear a suit until it shone and shoes until they were scorned when dropped in the parish poor box. Although he had lived for the past ten years in the home of the Archbishops in midtown Manhattan, he lived simply ("Too simply," some of the more worldly priests in the archdiocese grumbled), refusing the gleaming black Custom Imperial the president of the Chrysler Corporation had offered him at his investiture (as had been offered his predecessors) preferring to ride in taxis, or when occasion required it, to rent a limousine and driver from Fugazy, or for those precious weekends in the Poconos, to have his aging Mercedes brought around so that he might drive himself.

Rinsonelli was fuming: "I wonder what those tongue clacking critics of our wealth would have had us do? Would they have had

Michelangelo and Leonardo use their gifts only for emperors and princes? Would they have had Bernini render unto Caesar that which is God's?"

"That's hardly the point, Paolo—"

But Rinsonelli wasn't listening. He pressed on, tugging at the dewlap beneath his chin with brown spatulate fingers. "Where would they have placed the *Pieta*, these critics? In the parliament which now has an atheist majority? Should Michelangelo have painted the *Creation* on the ceiling of an army barracks?"

"I agree, I agree," Michael said. "But will you not in turn agree that that same conspicuous wealth in a world in which millions have hunger as their daily companion is to many a reproach? I almost said a scandal."

Rinsonelli shrugged and turned up his palms. "The trouble with you, Michael, is that you're an American. Not enough centuries flow in your veins. The poor you have with you always; are they advantaged if the church also is in rags?"

They walked on in silence for a moment. "I keep remembering that summer in Ethiopia," Michael said softly. "Thousands of people literally starving to death; old and young, mothers with babies like bundles of sticks at their dry breasts, children without the energy to cry." His voice thickened in the memory. "I saw a skeleton draw his last breath before an altar plated with gold."

Rinsonelli stepped in front of him, tilted his massive head and peered at him over his half-spectacles. "But suppose," he said pianissimo, "suppose, as some would have it, that that altar had been taken to the smelters and sold to buy bread. There would only be more poor tomorrow, and in the meantime something of infinite value lost. That supplicant of yours came to die at the altar because it was the one place he encountered God. Swords into plowshares, perhaps, but altars into bread . . . ? Your man would have been fed but empty."

Michael drew breath to respond and then was silent. "Contradictory as it seems," Rinsonelli went on, "we must all strive to remember that the pomp, the vestments, the ritual, the altar, the very cathedral itself are poems about the infinite. They give sustenance to the impoverished imagination. It's *hard* to keep His face before you in our kind of world, and the ambience of worship, the formalized acts by priest and people, the music, the chants, the very majesty and beauty of it all are hints, auguries of a glory to come. They keep the spirit from starving. It may to some seem far removed from the Galilean but it speaks of God as authentically as he did."

He lowered his voice which had risen in his fervor. "And, Michael," he said gently, "don't we, too, have our poor – the Franciscans, the Trappists, the priests and sisters on the mission fields and in ghetto parishes? We don't all sit on thrones of gold."

Michael smiled at him affectionately. "To quote King Agrippa," he said, " 'A little more, and your arguments would make a Christian of me'." Rinsonelli let out a great whoop of laughter and threw his arms about him.

Though he and Rinsonelli had talked late into the night, Michael had risen to go to an early mass at St. Mary Magdalene. Now, returning, the driver swept through the Via della Reconciliazione, turned right at St. Peter's Square and followed the wall of Vatican City to the gate. The Swiss Guard saluted as the car moved without hesitation through the massive romanesque archway that breached the wall and plunged immediately into the gloomy street of a medieval city. The ancient walls reared high on either side and met above to cover the cobbled street. In a moment they broke out into sunlight, where there were more salutes, turned sharply left, passed beneath another archway, and suddenly the Court of St. Damasus opened before them. As the driver cut diagonally across the courtyard, Michael saw Rinsonelli, tall and tented in a great black cape, waiting in the doorway to the palace.

An elevator took them to the fourth floor where a subdued Paolo, not far from tears, ushered him without a word along the loggia to the entrance to the papal apartment and past the guards to the bedroom, leaving him there.

For all his friend's demeanor and despite the briefing of the night before, Michael was not prepared for what he saw when he tapped lightly on the door and entered. The Holy Father lay at the center of the great four-poster canopied bed, a plastic tube snaking from a suspended bottle into his right nostril. The skin of his face seemed draped over the skull and was so transparent that every follicle on the clean-shaven chin was visible. The eyes were closed and sunk in their sockets and the lids were dark and veinous. The mouth was agape and, the dentures having been removed, was a wrinkled aperture through which pale gums gleamed. The silver hair had been brushed back from the high brow and carefully arranged on the satin pillow. *He was dead!* Michael dropped to his knees, a groan issuing from his throat.

Now, having gone to stand by the bed, he realized it was the hands, one placed atop the other, that had created the illusion of death. Life was there: pulsing in an artery at the temple, evident in a fluttering of the flaccid lips as breath was exhaled, and in the rising and falling of the frail chest beneath the ornate counterpane.

Michael had not seen the doctor when he entered; he had been seated in the shadow beside the door. Now he approached and stood with Michael by the bed: a swarthy man of fifty with a hound's face, stooped and cadaverous but with an inappropriate paunch. "I'm Dr. Sabatinni," he said in a whisper. "You're Cardinal Maloney?"

Michael had to clear his throat. "Yes."

"I'm glad you're here. The Holy Father was asking for you again this morning, but I don't know . . . " He sounded dispirited. "He hasn't moved now for three hours."

Michael looked down at the waxen face, blotched with liver spots. "Perhaps it would be better if I didn't stay," he said.

He had seen death often, but a primeval fear was on him, a dread that the man on the bed would convulse and die before his eyes, that he would be there when the wrench from earth to heaven happened. He thrust the thought away with a flash of anger at himself, but it remained.

"No," Dr. Sabatinni said, "he wants to see you. I told him it was unwise, that he must save his strength, but he looked at me in that way he has . . . " Sabatinni spread his hands in a gesture of impotence. "Who am I to instruct the Holy Father?"

"Is he sleeping?" Michael asked.

"Sleeping . . . ? In a coma . . . ? Who can tell much of the time?"

"Will he recover?"

Again the noncommittal shrug. "The first forty-eight hours we were sure he would never come back to us. Some of us stayed with him right through, expecting the end. But now he seems stable."

"I'll stay awhile and pray," Michael said.

As he put a hand on the bed to lower himself to his knees, the frail figure stirred. As they watched, it seemed he summoned his spirit from far off and brought it to the room. There was a quiver, a sudden shuddering intake of breath, a slight flushing of the skin and the eyes opened slowly. It was a moment before they were drawn into focus. They rested first on the doctor and then moved to Michael's face. The voice when it came was not much more than a breathy whisper. "Michael . . . "

Michael forbade the tears that blurred his eyes. "Holy Father," he said.

This was the man, this fragile figure in the great bed, who had loved him, had seen the possibilities in him, had encouraged him. This was the man who, when he was himself a cardinal, had singled him out and set his feet on the ecclesiastical ladder, who had intervened with Paul VI to have him made a prince of the church and who had helped him with his vestments before the Consistory in which he had received his cardinal's biretta. This was the man who, when he became pope, had taken him into his counsel, with whom he used to meet privately and correspond and speak to at length on the transatlantic telephone, explaining the attitudes of presidents, the vagaries of Congress, the mood of the American people. This was the man who had set his faith in the papacy to soaring after the difficult years of Paul VI. Antonio Giulio d'Annunzio, son of a Genoese pharmicist, trained as a lawyer, member of the Society of Jesus, specialist in foreign affairs, papal nuncio to France, named a cardinal by John XXIII and elected Pope Gregory XVII on the first ballot. And this man was his friend.

The fingers of a hand fluttered like a broken butterfly. "Come closer," the voice whispered. Michael kneeled by the bed. Gregory's eyes turned toward Sabatinni. "Leave us alone," he said.

Dr. Sabatinni hesitated. "Your Holiness . . . "

"Enrico," the pope said. "I shall leave this world when I decide to."

The doctor went off quietly, drawing the door closed behind him. The slightest smile touched Gregory's lips. "Doctors," he said. "They understand the body; they know little of the spirit."

Though some of his words were blurred, he seemed to be gaining strength and Michael's hopes began to rise only to plummet with the next words: "Michael, come closer. This may be the last time we'll speak . . . " Michael began to remonstrate but Gregory shook his head slowly. "We must all die," he said. "My time is not far off. Don't fret, it doesn't trouble me." The breath suddenly caught in his throat and he was racked by coughing. It was a minute before he could continue.

Michael asked, "Are you all right?"

It was as though Gregory hadn't heard. He ran the tip of a dry tongue over his lips and swallowed hard. "Michael," he said, "Our Lord may call you to succeed me . . . "

"Holy Father . . . please."

"No, no. Hear me out." Again he paused to gather his resources. "It will be you or Benedetti or Della Chiesa, and I want a last word with you. These are difficult times. They'll be worse. You must be strong." There was a pause, a frown, and a wandering of the eyes as though the thought was a bird that would not alight. "Yes. . . . Be strong, but be wise. Try to avoid confrontation. . . . . God can use you with your countrymen. Perhaps he has raised you up for such a time as this." His breathing grew shallow and pain drew the corners of his mouth into a grimace. "No time . . . " he said, "No time."

Now the tears would not be forbidden. They inundated Michael's eyes and fell unnoticed to the floor. He lowered his head. "Bless me, Holy Father," he said.

Gregory began to raise a hand but it faltered and fell back. He opened his mouth; the lips worked, trying to form words, but the only sound was a dry exhalation. The concentration that earlier had enabled him to summon his strength ran out as sand in an hourglass and he slipped again into a coma. Michael remained on his knees, his mind numb. He thought he should pray but couldn't; he was empty. There were no words in him. He struggled erect but didn't look again at the motionless figure on the bed.

When he opened the door, Dr. Sabatinni looked past him. "Good morning, Eminence," he said, and went into the room. Michael closed the door.

At Rinsonelli's quarters there was a note. Michael tore open the envelope. In a script as precise as hieroglyphic were the words:

Madame Ovary has lost her Bee – or does the memory-bank of a cardinal retain such trivia? Spotted you at the airport but you were gone when I got through customs. I'm at the Hotel Lombardia. Can we have dinner? It was signed, *Harris Gordon.*

Harris! – the name exploded in his head and each fragment was a memory. Harris! The irrepressible, the zany! Best friend of his undergraduate years at Princeton, roommate in his senior year, fellow member of the track team, fellow graduate *magna cum laude,* he in philosophy and Harris in archaeology. After the ceremony in the chapel there had been pledges, soon forgotten, to keep in touch. Later, as Michael had gleaned from newspapers and periodicals, there was celebrity: Harris Gordon, discoverer of the lost city of Horan, Dr. Gordon with the Leakeys at Olduvai Gorge, Dr. Gordon with Yigdal Allon in Israel. . . .A half dozen times Michael had made a mental note to be in touch and each time had procrastinated. And now here was Harris in Rome.

He rang the hotel and gave the operator his name. There was nothing familiar about the voice that came on except the note of banter.

"Mike Maloney, I presume," the voice said, "or do I call you father, Father?"

"Harris! How marvelous to hear from you."

"So you *do* remember Madame Ovary."

The film, *Madame Bovary,* starring Jennifer Jones, had played the Princeton Playhouse and the ribald comments of the undergraduates at each line of dialogue had kept the theatre in an uproar. Afterwards, Michael had boosted Harris onto his shoulders and he had removed the letter *B* from the title. For the remainder of the run the marquee read, MADAME OVARY. They had mounted the battered metal trophy in a place of honor on the wall of their rooms in the dorm beside a STOP sign in French and English smuggled from Canada.

"I remember *all* the crazy things we did," Michael said.

"Even that blind date at Mingles?"

A slow smile moved on Michael's face. "I refuse to answer on the usual grounds," he said.

"You're one hell of a correspondent," Harris grouched. "You were going to send me your address. We were going to get together at least once a year."

"I presumed you were too busy digging up somebody's mummy."

"Or you, kissing somebody's ring."

"Believe it or not, I've followed most of your adventures through the newspapers, even the honorary doctorate at Oxford. Then you dropped out of sight."

"Been in Israel the past four years," Harris said. "On digs with Freeling and Allon. Spent about six months at Hazor Tell. I was getting ready to head home at the end of my sabbatical when I got . . . " a slight tension entered his voice even as it continued lighthearted . . . "how shall I put it? – waylaid by history."

Michael wasn't sure how to respond so he said, "Uh, huh."

" I was planning to come see you about it back home, and here you are. What are the chances of our getting together?"

Michael was apologetic. "I'd love to," he said, "but it's impossible. I'm here only till Thursday and there are a thousand things to do. But why not in New York? I stop off in London on the way back but —"

"Could we have dinner in London?" Harris asked. "I'll be there from tomorrow."

"Perfect. I have to see a lady about a hospital but otherwise I'm free."

They refined the arrangements and chatted on tangentially for another five minutes, each relishing the resurrection of the past, both discovering that nothing of their old camaraderie had altered.

"Question," Harris said.

"Ask away."

"I thought your old man was a Presbyterian."

"He was."

"A preacher."

"Right."

"So how come you're a dogan? Nobody was about to nominate you altar boy of the year when I knew you."

Michael laughed. Harris's irreverence pleased him. He was so accustomed to sychophancy and formality that his old friend's impudence gave delight. "Happened during the war," he said lightly.

"I even hear talk you may make pope. Mike Maloney, pope! Boggles the mind."

"I wouldn't hold my breath."

"No, I'm impressed. I really am. In my line of work you don't get to meet many of the Almighty's Mafia. When I finally buy it, can I use you as a reference?"

There was more of the same, and when Michael put down the phone he was warmed, smiling. It was a few minutes before the memory flooded back of that frail pale figure on the great bed upstairs.

Chapter Three

The future member of the Almighty's Mafia had hardly an
auspicious beginning. No angels attended his birth, only a circle of
white-robed nurses and a drunken doctor; which presented something of a problem for Michael who arrived feet first, garroted by
his umbilicus. He would have been no more than a digit in the statistics on infant mortality had not the senior presiding nurse – a
formidable woman of chunky body and mannish demeanor – jammed an elbow into the doctor's solar plexus, seized the purple
infant in her glistening hands and wrested him from his convuls-
ing prison. The voice that would enthrall thousands from a hundred marble pulpits in years to come made as its first cry a howl of
outrage at nature's inhumanity to man.

His parents, the Reverend and Mrs. Duncan Athlone Maloney,
were Calvinists, specifically Northern Presbyterians who, only five
years out of Princeton Theological Seminary, were just getting
established in a church, their second charge, in a suburb of Philadelphia. The membership was small but the sanctuary was new
and attractive, and its postcard prettiness enchanted newcomers to
the area: suburban sprawlers, early beneficiaries of Henry Ford's
assembly-line techniques, part of a generation feeling a new
mobility and anxious to lose its roots. They wanted short sermons
and a sunny theology, and the Reverend Mr. Maloney – ambitious, enamored early of Freud and deep into Higher Criticism of
the Bible – was eager to oblige. He was a polished preacher despite
his relative youth, personable, gregarious and much in demand at

service clubs, and the congregation grew. It was inevitable that he be summoned to the pulpit of one of the great urban churches, and sure enough, one sunny spring Sunday morning an all-male delegation (the pulpit committee from Knox Presbyterian church in New York City) sidled unannounced but obvious into a pew. They liked what they heard and one month later returned to extend a formal call. The youthful minister – who knew they were coming and on what mission – said with the perfect mix of authority and humility that he would pray about it. Upstairs, on the bedroom phone, Katharine Maloney was telling her mother that they were moving to New York.

They moved into the new manse in October. Duncan's maiden sermon followed by three days the crash of the stock market. Straining, he took as his text: "Lay not up for yourselves treasures on earth . . . but in heaven." The debut was a debacle; as was the entire first week. He was required to conduct three funerals on the Monday: two men whose hearts had failed them for fear and a third who – in the dining room of his home for some obscure reason, while dinner was being laid – had quite messily blown off the back of his head after placing the barrel of a revolver between his teeth. On the Tuesday the choirmaster was charged with bigamy. On the Wednesday the chairman of the Board of Stewards reported that the annual fund-raising drive had come to a shuddering stop and recommended that it be postponed until the members could at least determine where their next dividend was coming from. The entire first six months were, as Duncan put it in retrospect, "a time of testing."

But they survived. No, they did much better than that. In comparison to most, they prospered. Duncan's salary (or "stipend" as he preferred it to be called) was cut by half after he'd been on the job three months, but was still for those times substantial. He was becoming renowned as a preacher, mixing as he did scripture truths with *Readers' Digest* facts and integrating them with snippets and patches of popular psychology in such a fashion as to bring "aware" New Yorkers and ambitious young theologs swarming to the sanctuary on Sundays – the former to quote him at cocktail parties and the latter to pilfer his illustrations without attribution for their own fledgling homiletic flights.

Michael went to church each Sunday morning without fail. Until he was twelve he sat up front in the minister's pew with his mother and his younger sister by two years, Eleanora, acutely aware of and relishing being pointed out as "the Reverend's son." After his twelfth birthday he was permitted to sit alone, and chose the back pew. Though he had attended Sunday school and the appropriate youth groups from childhood and had heard his father preach hundreds of sermons, Michael never gave serious thought to God until he was in his mid-teens. The first time he looked level-eyed at Jesus followed a night spent at the home of a class-mate, a Baptist, who, to Michael's acute embarrassment, pressed him to "get saved" and become a Christian (Christ almighty! – wasn't he *already* a Presbyterian!) and who, before retiring, had ostentatiously read a much-thumbed pocket New Testament and knelt by his bed to pray.

Michael would have none of that, it seemed vaguely obscene; but the following evening he went to Duncan's study, picked up Goodspeed's translation of the New Testament in modern English, took it with him to bed and read the four gospels straight through. It seemed almost a revelation and so excited him that he lay still in the bed, wide-eyed until dawn. The man in the text was unlike the Christ he'd heard declaimed about for as long as he could remember. This wasn't the effeminate, vacant-faced figure of stained glass windows nor the impeccably robed, perfectly coiffed refugee from a Cecil B. de Mille movie he'd seen reproduced in church school literature. And how different the familiar sayings seemed when they emerged from *his* lips. "Gentle Jesus, meek and mild" – nonsense! Nothing meek about him. This was a revolutionary of astounding commitment: strong, opinionated, contentious, impa-tient and often quick-tempered. He showed no slightest interest in turning away wrath with a soft answer; indeed, he frequently pro-voked his enemies. He challenged frontally the religious power structure of his time and confounded the authorities in every con-frontation. Nor was he aloof: he was gregarious, much given to dining out – whether in the homes of the riffraff or the respectable didn't seem to matter – but so indifferent to protocol that he was sometimes rebuked for not troubling to wash before meals. Yet there remained the paradox: for all his sociability he was a loner.

In subsequent weeks Michael had trouble with some of Jesus' teachings. He judged the miracles incredible, the inevitable embroidering of the facts by unimaginative men who didn't find his genius enough. Jesus' belief that he was equal with God the

Father Michael found puzzling and put aside for later consideration. He rejected all episodes that included intervention by angels: thus the virgin birth and the resurrection. They seemed unlike the rest of the text; more like legends or myths than actual events peopled with flesh and blood men and women. He felt no inclination to worship Jesus. He was enthralled by him, regarded him as a genius, a giant among his fellows, incredibly insightful – but hardly Almighty God.

Coming to maturity, he never prayed to Jesus but to the Father, and ceased to do even that as he entered his twenties. The next time he reached out to God he was twenty-three and pinned down by sniper and mortar fire behind a ridge on an island in the south Pacific, the only survivor of his company. Afterwards, he sought out and had the first of a series of conversations with the Roman Catholic chaplain.

Dr. Harris G. Gordon, Chairman of the Department of Oriental Studies (Emeritus) in the Faculty of Archaeology at Albright University, Philadelphia, Pennsylvania, was taking inventory. Shouldn't take but a few seconds, he thought with a wry grin. There on the glass stains on a grubby hotel room table were most of his worldly possessions: in cash, $442.78, two American Express travellers' checks for $100 each, and a one-way plane ticket Rome-JFK. In the closet, two suits, a pair of slacks and two sweaters. On the luggage-rack, two scruffy suitcases stuffed with a mix of mismatched and threadbare haberdashery and assorted toilet articles. Aboard a ship enroute to New York City, a steamer trunk filled with those oddments commonly described as "personal effects." As well, in the care of Manhattan Storage, perhaps two dozen cartons of books and papers, concerning which a professional bill-collecting agency had been hurling intemperate *Last Warning!* thunderbolts at him for months now. There were also – if one might list them in an inventory – three wives: one lost somehow, one divorced and one deserted. And seven children by wives Two and Three, although the children, he thought, had always been more of an expense than an asset. Granted a few inadvertent omissions, that was about everything he owned in the world.

What did he *not* own that most men of sixty did? He did not own any real estate, a car, any furniture, any stocks, bonds or securities, all or any part of any business firm, nor any insurance that hadn't lapsed. Hold on a moment, he thought: there was that pension fund at Albright (which would come to him at age sixty-five) and, of course, he would soon benefit from the largesse of his fellows by virtue of the United States Social Security scheme – but, again, not until age sixty-five. Ah, the magical age of sixty-five, he thought sourly, that anniversary of one's natal day on which legislative fiat decreed that one must step back from productivity to take a seat in nature's waiting-room to await the summons to shuffle off this mortal coil.

It was not that Harris Gordon was feeling sorry for himself. He had never been an accumulator of things and never thought of himself as rich or poor – they were categories into which it would never occur to him to place himself. What was important at the moment was the fact that his scarcity of tangible assets was damned inconvenient. The airline had charged him $46.75 to insure and ship home his precious box, and that, as the saying has it, had made a small dent in his bankroll. The box would by this time be safely ensconsed in the atmosphere-controlled storage room at the museum in New York and probably better housed than he would be. Which, he decided, was not inappropriate.

The immediate problem was: where was he to live when he'd finished his research and was back stateside? He grimaced; last thing in the world he'd do would be to go crawling to the university. "Bastards," he said aloud. How did the letter go? *I regret exceedingly, my dear Harris, having to inform you that it has become necessary to terminate your employment here at Albright. Your sabbatical has already been extended twice, and the Board of Trustees etc. etc. etc. . . . Permit me to say, Harris, that your obduracy in refusing to disclose the nature of your discovery or the location of the dig has left us with no option but to etc. etc. etc. You upbraid us, it seems to me, unfairly.*

So be it, but they would dance to another tune shortly. By God, wouldn't they though!

His thoughts returned to the telephone call. It had been good to talk to Mike. He'd sounded a bit stuffy, but only a bit, and that was to be expected. Perhaps he was the man to talk to about his find. He'd had the secret bottled up within him so long that it was becoming unhealthy. What he needed more than anything else at the moment, more even than money, was someone he could take into his confidence and from whom he could get counsel. Mike would, of course, be shocked when he broke his news – it would be fascinating to watch his reaction – but he was a sophisticated and worldly man and would soon adjust. And who better to tell? *Cardinal* Maloney, no less! He grinned: after all, if you can't trust a priest, who can you trust?

Chapter Four

Michael had on a previous trip to Rome discovered a restaurant in the Vitalle section of the city run by the Sisters of the Order of the Precious Blood and named L'Eau Vive, and despite Rinsonelli's protestations that members of the Curia seldom ate in popular public places, insisted that they go there to dinner that evening. The two men donned woolen scarves, gloves and overcoats and ventured into the raw weather that had thrust past the Alps overnight. A bumptious wind harassed them as they went bent over to the car and then fell to buffeting the rain, driving it horizontally across the twin cones of the headlights. The driver from the Vatican car-pool had no words for his passengers, but through the journey railed sotto voce at the condensation forming on his windshield, leaning forward to wipe it from the dappled glass with furious circlings of his palm, finally cranking down the window to drive with his head half out. Rinsonelli sat huddled and hugging himself in the rear seat, complaining of his arthritis and scolding the night and the neighborhood.

In a district of grubby shops, small factories and unlit alleys, they nosed through a nondescript square to penetrate a narrow and convoluted street. Finally, there was the unprepossessing facade of the restaurant. But the door opened on a room that was bright and spacious and redolent with the scents of spices and food, and the warmth of the smiling woman who greeted and seated them at a table sufficiently removed to make conversation private changed the mood. After wine had been uncorked and sampled, Rinsonelli allowed, albeit with some reluctance, that he was glad he'd come.

"The food will be slow in arriving," Michael warned, "but the wait is worth it."

So they talked: of Italian politics, of the American presidency, of Vatican bureaucracy, of electronic eavesdropping, and finally with the liqueur and coffee, of Gregory's illness and the need to find a successor.

"He would have to be an Italian, of course," Michael said. He had decided not to mention, even to Paolo, Gregory's words about his own candidacy.

"Not *this* time!" Rinsonelli said with sudden vehemence, striking a fist on the table, causing the silverware to chatter, diners at nearby tables to grow silent and a gout of wine to leap from a wineglass. Michael laid a hand on his arm and when he continued he was more contained.

"We must break with the tradition *now*," he said with passion. "It has been the blood and sinew of the church but its time has passed. Italy produced churchmen as Britain produced diplomats, but every strain in nature runs out, and we ran out after John XXIII."

"But surely Gregory—" Michael began.

"I will not speak ill of the man," Rinsonelli broke in. "He's my friend and my mentor, and he's dying. But this I will say: while the apostle Paul did name charity the greatest of the virtues he did not say it was the only one. It must have its roots in strength and resolution. The enemy today is not the kind to be loved into the kingdom."

"You want strength and resolution," Michael said, "but you were often critical of what you called Pope Paul's intransigence."

"That's precisely my point: in Gregory's case the sword is not drawn, in Paul's it was sometimes used as a bludgeon."

"I have my own views on the succession," Michael said, "but I want to hear yours. Why not an Italian? Why not Della Chiesa? Why not Benedetti?"

"I shall speak of the cipher first," said Rinsonelli, acid lacing his voice. "Della Chiesa you can dismiss. He is an old man – my age, but an old man. If he is elected it will only be because the church is unsure and wants a caretaker pope. His escutcheon should read: Don't rock the boat and let sleeping dogmas lie. Our jeopardy is

Benedetti. I have served four popes; he is like none of them. He has none of Gregory's love, or Paul's principles, or John's openness, or Pius' wisdom. There is no substance. He is all things to all men but nothing to any. Is strength needed? He will play the lion. Is vision required? He will counterfeit the eagle. Courage? He becomes the bull. Deviousness? Behold the serpent. It would not be so bad if he were any of these but he merely simulates them as the scenario demands, unfortunately with the credibility of a great thespian. But he is at heart a fox; knowing his limitations, he substitutes for mind and heart, craft and cunning."

He seemed depressed by his summary and sat silent for a moment. A sip of wine and he added: "The danger lies in the fact that the tradition of Italian popes is so ingrained that the College will not examine its options."

Michael knew that in theory any adult male Roman Catholic could be elected pope, but long practice had limited the choice to members of the College of Cardinals and to Italians. He was aware that the last non-Italian had been elected in 1522: Adrian VI, a Netherlander. The church had chosen Italian popes for understandable and pragmatic reasons. Italians formed by far the largest group in the College and they guarded their prerogatives with a passionate and prickly jealousy. Beyond that was the fact that the vast and complex apparatus of the Vatican is operated predominantly by Italians, and if to do no more than to communicate efficiently and protect himself against the intrigues of the bureaucratic hierarchy, a pope needed to be fluent in the language and insightful about the Roman character.

"If not Benedetti, then who?" Michael asked.

Rinsonelli held a square brown hand before him, the broad fingers spread, and seizing the tip of each in turn ticked off the names:

West Germany's Boehmer: fluent in nine languages, the greatest canonical scholar in decades, fashioner of the final draft of all of Gregory's declarations, but an abrasive man, intolerant of others' opinions.

Canada's Castonguay: unquestionably a genius and probably a saint, he had followed the example of one of his predecessors, Léger, and had lived in Africa among lepers, but there were questions about his administrative skills and about his health.

Africa's Kalumbulu: a giant in stature and intellect, conciliator of the third world and Nobel prizewinner. He would make a great pope, but were the world and the church ready for a black pontiff?

The Republic of Ireland's Meyer: the same questions had to be put. Renowned scholar that he was, brilliant and lyrical polemicist that he was, creative theologian that he was, he was a convert from Judaism.

"Which brings me to Maloney of the United States," Rinsonelli said, looking full into Michael's face. "Do I do a précis on his strengths and weaknesses?" When Michael made no response he continued. "His greatest weakness may be that he doesn't recognize his strength, or that he isn't – how do the sportswriters put it? – hungry enough."

Michael returned his friend's gaze for a moment and then looked down at his fingers as they twirled the stem of his wineglass. The stain on the linen beneath his hand looked like blood.

He said: "Should one lust for the papacy?"

Rinsonelli shook his great mane and let out a snort of impatience. "I have always cringed when I've heard it stated by others," he said tersely, "but it has been my observation nonetheless that God does *indeed* help those who help themselves. I do not believe that God seeks the man or that the man seeks God; there is a mutual attraction as between the lightning bolt and the charge that leaps from the ground to meet it. It is true that faith is the gift of God. One does not say, 'Go to now, I think I'll have faith'. But even so, God gives the gift only to the man who yearns for it. There may have been popes who didn't want the job (although I can't think of who they were), but I'll wager they were not the great ones. The great popes have been those men who saw the need and knew they'd been called by God to meet it."

"Perhaps that's how Benedetti sees it."

"Benedetti sees the opportunity, not the need."

Michael was not prepared to admit it, but he had imagined himself on Peter's throne. It would have been impossible not to contemplate the possibility: it had been speculated about by the press and broached by his fellow prelates – even that day by a man as distant from the church as Harris Gordon. Had not the Holy Father himself, balanced on the edge of darkness, said, "God may call you to succeed me, Michael" ?

He had not dwelt on it, had not let the aspiration lodge like leaven in his breast, but the imagination was not always subject to the will and on occasions when he made his way through the Basilica and stood before the heroic marble tributes to pontiffs long gone, when he descended to the crypt and viewed the sarcophagi in which lay the remains of men who had once been as he, his normal longing for immortality fashioned a similar place of honor for his own bones, perhaps even a mausoleum fresh with flowers and crowded always with worshipers as was John XXIII's. The first time he'd descended the ornamented spiral ramp at the Vatican Museum and seen the names of the popes unroll like an endless ecclesiastical rollcall on the metal ballustrade, he had involuntarily added his own name. Could one have the biretta placed on his head without the thought that the only higher office was the papacy? When he had spoken of the sin of pride to his confessors, it had had to do too many times with that particular conceit. Indeed, once, abed, he had chosen the name by which he would be proclaimed: Columbo I. Columbo for Italy and for his native land; Columbo for the man who in faith had set out across the sea not knowing the end of his venture; Columbo for the man of vision who had joined continents in the name of God.

Michael knew the measure of himself. Introspective, he had stood apart and judged himself: the manner in which he dealt with crises; his responses to the mighty and the weak; the imagination he brought to financial and administrative problems, and the empathy with which he identified with the spiritual aspirations of both the poor and illiterate and the cultivated and blasé.

And he had measured the needs of the church, a church reeling from a succession of blows from without and within. The confrontation in Italy was serious but things were little better elsewhere. The ancient claim to universality was now more tenuous than ever. In truth, the Roman church had never been dominant in Russia or Christianity in Asia, and such enclaves as had been obtained were disintegrating. England, having established her own church centuries earlier, was evincing no hint of a yearning to return to Mother Church. In Europe the long decline of the twentieth century had continued, even accelerated, the falling away having been exacerbated by the rebelliousness of some of the more radical theologians and priests and by an adverse reaction to the inflexibility of Paul VI in matters of sexual morality, birth control, abortion and divorce. Africa, despite the zeal and commitment of the faithful there, now seemed in jeopardy, convulsed as that continent was with birth pangs, and struggling awkwardly toward self-realization. Even in the western hemisphere there was little to give comfort. In Central and South America the church was facing a growing restiveness among the laity, and in some countries, confrontations with leftist governments. In the United States and Canada, faith was still vital and the numbers were impressive, but a pervasive secularism and a growing rejection of traditionalism and authority were creating problems.

But Italy, the heartland of the faith, posed the greatest difficulties. In the long battle with Communism, an intolerant and inflexible hierarchy had alienated the general population. Many devout Catholics had made it clear that they would no longer be instructed in political matters by the church at any level including the papacy, and thousands were voting for and working with the Communists for social and legislative reform. And now, securely in power, the Marxists had dropped their pretense of cooperation with the church. And if Lieberman's sources were right, the battle had only begun.

He was returned from his reverie by a falling off of the conversation in the restaurant and the emergence of the gentle voice of the woman who had greeted them when they entered. Standing at the center of the room, speaking in French and barely audible, she was asking the diners to join in a moment of devotion. Michael and Paolo picked up from the table pieces of paper on which were mimeographed the words: *Tous les soirs à 23 heures, ici à l'Eau Vive, le chant des "AVE de Lourdes."*

Standing on each side of the hostess were two younger women, sisters of the Order, waitresses, slender girls of no more than eighteen, their eyes betraying their nervousness, their wavering smiles their shyness. One was African, a saffron sash wrapped about a plain white gown, her hair drawn back and bound with a circle of tiny beads. The other was oriental, her dress a simple sheath of pale mauve brocade, the collar high on her slender neck. Now all three began to sing, their voices thin and wavering, their eyes on a tiny makeshift altar on which two candles guttered in amber glass receptacles, between which there was a small statue of the Virgin.

Un jour Bernadette
ramasse du bois
avec deux fillettes

qui pleurent de froid.
  Ave, Ave, Ave Maria . . .

The women's voices were weak, unsure, reedy, but now with the refrain, others began to join in.

Au pied de sa Mère
l'enfant qui la voit
apprend à bien faire
le signe de Croix.
  Ave, Ave, Ave Maria . . .

Michael looked about the room. A half-dozen girls in their teens and early twenties had come from the kitchen and were standing against the wall, singing. They were from as many countries, their skin ranging from black to fair, their eyes round or slanted, their hair close-cropped or coiled under tiny linen cook's hats. Many of the men and women at tables about the room had joined in, and with varying degrees of assurance, were singing the words. Other diners sat silently watching.

L'enfant la supplie
que dit votre coeur
"Je veux que l'on prie
pour tous les pécheurs."

Now the singers had gained assurance and the sound resonated and gathered texture as it lifted to the high ceiling. Michael looked about. The waitresses at the center of the room had forgotten their shyness and their eyes, glistening, were fixed on the tiny statue. The other girls were in full voice, too, their heads lifted, their sound carrying above the diners', the devotion in their faces unmistakable.

We've been speaking of our problems, Michael thought. Of power and ambition, of crowns and continents and worlds . . . and of defeat. But the victory is here, in the reality of God in the faces of the singers.

"Ave, Ave, Ave Maria," he sang.

Chapter Five

In London as the week ended, the chill mist hung hesitant or hastened off at the wind's bidding. Glass and stone and metal cold-sweated. The streets gleamed neon-garish, reflecting shops and streetlights. Normally at the dinner hour the sidewalks would be thronged, the talk festive, the laughter frequent; on this night the silence was funereal – even the taxis shushed softly by. Those on foot clutched at coat collars with one hand and with the other tilted umbrellas against the wind. To little effect: the damp sifted through fabrics, wilted linens, uncoiled curls and slipped chilly fingers beneath each skirt. Those in taxis cranked a slot in the window to get bearings, and disembarking, scurried to shelter, heads drawn in like turtles.

His Eminence, Michael Cardinal Maloney pulled down his hat, stepped from the opened door of the limousine that had met him at Heathrow and strode easily into the lobby of the Dorchester. He signed the register and stopped at the newsstand to purchase three Havana Primero cigars, a copy of *Harper's* and – great good luck! – the Sunday edition of the *New York Times*. As he walked to the elevator, a thin, stooped bellman fell in behind like an acolyte. In his suite he tipped the man, shook the beaded damp from his overcoat and hung it in the closet, sprang open two scuffed suitcases, placed them on the luggage rack to air and put the reading material on the night table by the bed. Then he washed his hands and rinsed his face and went down to dinner.

The maitre d' – immediately obsequious at the sight of the

small scarlet patch at the base of the Roman collar and the chain leading to the crucifix in the vest pocket – bowed, paced solemnly before him and seated him against the far wall removed from the flow of traffic and the orchestra. Michael wished now he had changed from clerical garb in his room. He'd had five days of sycophancy in Rome – quite enough, thank you.

His entrance did not go unremarked. It was difficult not to notice him; six feet two, two hundred pounds, and at sixty, flat-bellied and erect. The face strong and mobile; an Irish face with slightly close-set denim-blue eyes, a slightly long upper lip and slightly grayed black hair. Even here in the main dining room of the Dorchester, accustomed as it was to second-echelon royalty, senior government officials and sundry celebrities, eyes followed as he went to his table and a bejeweled and laquered woman of forty, having appraised him with jaded eyes, turned back to her dinner companion and murmured, "What a waste."

Would he have a drink while waiting? He would. The flutter of a fan of menus and a flagging down of the wine steward. Within minutes the bottle was offered for inspection, the cork popped and approved and the goblet baptized, swirled, sniffed and savored. Then a coiling of the golden liquid within the glass, the bottle shrouded and buried in the bucket and he was, at last, free of attention.

He spread a film of butter on a piece of melba toast, bit off a chunk and let it lie at the exact center of his tongue. Then a sip of wine and a commingling of flavors. When he crunched the toast and relished the separate tastes his mind involuntarily offered a morsel of praise to God whose goodness had created the fruits of the earth and the acuity of the senses.

He looked about. The dining room was not yet one-third filled and conversation was contained. The six members of the string orchestra were displaying little enthusiasm for the slight Mendels-sohn sextet with which they were occupied and the waiters and busboys, who at this hour outnumbered the diners, were mostly ranged along the walls at their various stations. One, seeing him looking about, started toward him. He waved him off with a gesture and took another swallow of wine. No need to hurry: Harris wasn't due for ten minutes and he was at ease in indolence.

Michael was in London in hope of getting some money: specifically, ten million dollars. Which was fine, fine indeed, except that he would have preferred a source other than Lady Sophie Hambleton, the widow of Rogers T. Hambleton, who had sent him word, relayed to him URGENT at the Vatican by the Chancery Office in New York City: "She now flatly refuses to speak to anyone but you in the matter of her proposed gift of a new children's wing at St. Clare's."

Sophie Hambleton had seemed an unlikely candidate for the peerage. As a girl of eighteen she had met her future husband in Toronto, Canada, where she was a minimally dressed waitress at a seedy cocktail joint and he was the operator of a bucket-shop out of a ten dollar a day room at the Ford Hotel. Rogers, who had once been a commercial radio announcer and possessed a voice that could speak with equal conviction of cathartics and concertos, sold worthless Canadian mining stocks by long distance telephone to gullible Americans during the forties and had escalated the profits of that operation by getting control of three depleted Ontario gold mines and floating a stock issue of two million shares. He drove the stock up through a series of camouflaged purchases, sold every share he owned, married Sophie, and decamped to Costa Rica.

Hambleton invested in legitimate enterprises the ten million dollars he had realized through his Canadian buccaneering and within a dozen years had multiplied it threefold. When he died – some thought appropriately of a massive heart attack in the street outside the London Stock Exchange – Sophie, fifty and fat and given to wearing dresses all flounces and furbelows and two sizes too small, suddenly found herself the sole owner of houses in Costa Rica and New York City plus thirty-seven million dollars in negotiable bonds and securities. Rogers had seldom given her much money for her personal use and she immediately went on a buying binge in hope of impressing her way into what she presumed was the international jet set. She bought a decaying castle in Warwickshire and sold it within six months ("The damn thing was so bloody cold!"), replaced it with a handsome country house outside London, paid close to a million dollars for a yacht once owned by Aristotle Onassis – with, it developed, patches of dry-rot – and bought enough diamonds and rubies to give her now formidable bosom the appearance of a Manhattan gem dealer's display window. She also managed to be bilked of a few hundred thousand dollars by a former Broadway actor with a magnificent voice (not unlike Rogers') who found visiting rich widows' beds more rewarding than touching bases at casting offices.

On her fifty-fifth birthday, Sophie had begun to feel intimations of mortality: an increasing number and variety of aches and pains in chest, arms and stomach. Contemplating the possibility that her tomorrows were limited, she began to dwell on a somewhat bowdlerized version of her girlish piety as a regular communicant at St. Joseph's Cathedral in Toronto. One day, after a bad night, Sophie decided to make a gift to God. Being a practical woman, she decided that the Archdiocese of New York rather than St. Joseph's would be the recipient of her largesse; in part because a return to Toronto to view any edifice she might endow could lead to conversations with the Ontario Securities Commission, and because she now concluded that she had once had a visitation from God on a steamy Sunday morning while on a vacation in New York City. In retrospect she saw the divine disposition as having taken place in St. Patrick's Cathedral as the result of a sermon by the great Cardinal Spellman (she had swooned in her seat in the middle of it and had been carried out) and having had no relationship to the fact that she was at the time hungover and squeezed in a pew against a rock-sinewed Joe DiMaggio.

Having given it thought, Sophie concluded that an even trade should do it: a hospital wing for a laundered soul. She had over the years observed her husband buy so many officials that it seemed not unreasonable to believe that a clergyman could be bought if saving children's lives was the coinage and the sum ten million dollars. There was, however, one complication. Sophie's bequest included a rider: that the new building be named the Rogers T. Hambleton Wing and include a bronze statue of Sophie herself; the sculptor, to judge by the sketch, improving not inconsiderably on nature, representing the widow as a sylphlike figure in flowing robes, arms outstretched presumably to embrace the children of the world – the effect being marred somewhat by the inclusion of the full galaxy of Sophie's necklaces and rings.

Michael had long cherished the dream of a children's wing for St. Clare's, a rundown hospital in Manhattan, but balked at the inclusion of a perpetual Sophie. He would permit a small bronze plaque naming the donor but no more. Sophie had countered by asking for a large bronze plaque in the foyer including a bas-relief of herself, but Michael had remained adamant. Through all these negotiations he had remained once removed, but now there was no avoiding a confrontation. Tomorrow morning he was to meet the lady at her country house in Covington. Sophie was threatening to renege and go over to the Episcopalians, and that prospect did not please.

The dining room was beginning to fill. The tempo of activity and sound had increased. The waiters were moving from table to kitchen with practiced efficiency and the orchestra was applying itself with zeal, striving to be heard above the clamor of conversation and the clink of cutlery and china. The wine steward turned aside in his passage to attend to Michael's glass and went on. As Michael raised the glass and let the ice-cold liquid glide down his throat he saw a man enter the dining room, speak to the maitre d' and fall in behind him as he crossed the room.

It couldn't possibly be Harris. Harris had been movie-star handsome at Princeton: tall and erect, with a shaped mound of thick wavy hair, ruddy cheeks and an insolent smile, his superb physical condition evident in the way he carried himself – almost as though he were bearing his shoulders to market, Michael had once mused. But the man approaching was cadaver-thin, stooped and nondescript. Even the clothing wasn't Harris; a too-large tweed jacket with a badly knotted wool tie against a tan shirt.

But it *was* Harris. As Michael rose, the maitre d' said, "Your guest, Your Eminence," and Michael shook hands with the stranger and asked him to sit.

A mahogany tan overlay the lower part of the archaeologist's face and made almost invisible the ten thousand miniscule wrinkles in the parchment skin. Above the eyes the color graduated to alabaster white. The pate was traversed by coarse strands of sandy-gray hair drawn from near the left ear. The mouth was a long lipless line which, when he smiled, turned down at the corners. The eyes redeemed the face, softened it: they were a washed-out blue flecked with amber motes: like opals, Michael thought. The man looking through them seemed friendly, but he bore not even a vestigial resemblance to Michael's onetime classmate.

He looked at Harris and thought how cruel time can be: the ultimate vandal, destroying beauty, mummifying skin, beclouding eyes, sapping vitality, bending and gnarling and debilitating, and the particular enemy of beautiful women. He suddenly wondered what Harris was seeing. The question was quickly answered: "My God, you look great," Harris said. "Maybe there's something to be said for chastity."

In the cynical jest Michael recognized his old friend and the intervening years evaporated. "I can recommend it," he said, adding a friendly riposte, "Even though you'd be coming to it a little late."

"I'd be coming, if I came," Harris said drily, "because there was no option."

"Well, that pretty well covers that subject," Michael said. "It's good to see you."

Harris swiveled his head around, scanning the room and the diners. "Very posh," he said.

"Where are you staying?"

"Five minutes away but miles removed. The Haverford Arms. Two pounds a night. In advance, please . . . the W.C.'s just down the hall." He settled in his chair. "Do you think we could signal somebody to get me some of whatever it is you've got in your glass? I've been at the British Museum all day and that, believe me, is guaranteed to stimulate a thirst."

That need supplied, they went on to ten minutes of jousting, with much warmth and great good humor. The meal ordered, they settled down to serious talk.

"You said something on the phone about being waylaid by history," Michael said, prompting.

"Did I say that?"

"Yes."

"A touch melodramatic," Harris said, "but accurate."

He attacked the sole amandine for a minute, washed it down with a great mouthful of wine and picked up the thread. "I told you I'd been in Israel?" he asked. Michael nodded. "A sabbatical," he said. "Then, just as I was getting ready to head back to the classroom, I got – how was that again? – waylaid, and stayed on." He forked some of the fish into his mouth and chewed on it reflectively. "They still list me in the catalogue as Emeritus but the bastards filled the chair and cut me off."

"That was how long ago?"

"Year and a half."

"What did you do for money?"

"Did without mostly. I wangled a small grant from the Ford

44

Foundation, but I wasn't prepared to file reports and they were, typically, reluctant to cast their bread on the waters without the requisite paperwork."

"You have me curious," Michael said. "What's this project that has you so engrossed?"

Harris didn't respond immediately, but sipped slowly at his wine, his mouth turned down in a half smile. It seemed to Michael that his eyes went off somewhere, far away. When the silence extended, Michael filled the dead air:

"You said something about wanting to talk about it."

"Yes, I did. God knows I need to. I've had the damn thing locked up inside me for so long I'm going squirrelly."

"Goodness!" Michael said lightly, "Such mystery. Such suspense. One would think you'd dug up Moses."

Harris's smile unaccountably broadened. "You're getting warm," he said.

"Well, if you think I'm going to play twenty questions," Michael said not unkindly.

"Maybe later," Harris said.

The talk diverted to Michael's career, Harris making much of the incongruity involved in the man he once knew entering the priesthood. "But maybe I shouldn't have been surprised," he said. "I twitted you on the phone about Mingles and you took the Fifth. Mingles was the tip-off you'd end up celibate."

Mingles had been the measure of the difference between the two men in their attitudes toward women. Michael had invariably been surprised at the type of women Harris was drawn to: "broads" he called them. It was not that they were unattractive. Michael had often been fascinated, sometimes stirred by their overt sexuality, but they were – there was only one word for it – cheap. For all their variety they had a number of things in common: their conversation was callow, their clothing advertised their bodies, they laughed a lot, frequently for no evident reason, and somehow managed to discover sexual connotations in the most casual of comments.

"Where do you find these . . . broads?" he had asked Harris as they lay abed one night after a double date during which his girl had suddenly decided she had a big day tomorrow and wanted to get home early, and Harris's broad – drunk and having displayed an awesome gift for obscenities throughout the evening – had suggested that the three of them go make daisy-chains at a motel. "It's called a menagerie," she added helpfully.

"You find what you want to," Harris had said. "Look, I've got years of study ahead. Last thing in the world I want is to get serious with a woman. When I take a girl out it's to get laid. You don't mean anything to her, she doesn't mean anything to you, and if you make out first time it's because you both wanted to. Nobody's kidding anybody."

"But what do you say to each other?" Michael remonstrated. "I'd be so bored I wouldn't want to get her to bed."

"What do you *say?*" Harris hooted. "Conversation you can get in the Common Room."

Michael, whose experiences with women were limited and as often as not platonic, pondered what Harris had said and a week later suggested, "What say we get ourselves a couple of your broads Friday night?"

So, that Friday, in Harris's car, they drove into Trenton and took up positions at the bar in a singles joint known as Mingles. Husbanding their second beers, they made contact with two girls from the Ewing area. Harris, who knew one of them in some connection, put an arm about her waist and drew her to the bar and Michael inherited Charlene, who was nineteen and worked as a key-punch operator.

At the best of times he was awkward at small talk and this time proved to be anything but the best. The table to which they removed adjoined a tiny raised bandstand on which a male singer was braying to be heard above the mounting surf of sound in the room. He was assisted in this unequal contest by a large amplifier so positioned as to be immediately behind Michael's head, the sound from it, like a gale wind, hurling Charlene's words back in her teeth.

A round of beers downed, Harris suggested that they "Get the hell out of here," but the girls had come to drink and preen and peer through the murk for familiar faces and had no intention of leaving until they'd tied on at least a small bun. Harris made no attempt to hide his intentions, and Susan, a kewpie-faced redhead, countered by remarking often that she "knew his kind." Every few minutes Harris would wink at Michael, lean close to Susan and whisper in her ear. She would listen, eyes dancing and a smile growing until it burst in laughter, and would affect to push Harris away, saying, "Oh, you're just awful!" She would then call Michael to witness: "Isn't he just awful?"

Michael set out to draw Charlene into conversation: He spoke of how hot it was: he was sodden with perspiration. Her response was, "You always stifle in this dump." He ventured that Princeton would lose to Yale in Saturday's game. Her response was, "I've only been once in my life; my steady took me. I never could tell who had the ball." Did she think Roosevelt would take the United States into the war? Her response: "Guys get a uniform and they think they're everything. Well, they're not . . . not with me they're not." She brightened when he asked if she liked to go to the movies. Her all time favorite picture was *Wuthering Heights* with Merle Oberon and Laurence Olivier. Her absolute favorite actor was Tyrone Power, with John Garfield second. Michael, who saw perhaps a dozen movies a year, soon ran out of questions and his input was further limited by the need to ask Charlene to repeat most of what she said. She soon tired of that and withdrew from the conversation except for frequent vague noddings and an occasional, "Yeah, me too."

Michael noticed that Harris's left hand had been beneath the table for the past five minutes and that there was a certain fixedness to Susan's eyes. When he looked at Harris he was given a wink and a slight inclination of the head toward Charlene. He finished off his beer and spent the next five minutes firming his resolve. As the waiter bumped down four more steins of draught and swivel-hipped away, he put a hand beneath the table and found Charlene's knee. It was surprisingly cool, damp with perspiration. He glanced at her, half seeking permission, but she seemed disengaged from what was happening, looking about, scanning the room, her head bobbing slightly to the rhythms of the organ. Slowly, he began to inch his fingers above her knee, but although he leaned forward as far as possible, he couldn't reach above mid-thigh, and the edge of the table leg was cutting cruelly into his forearm. Charlene, without a change of expression, shifted her chair closer and opened her legs, but this provided an advantage of only a few more inches. He saw the singer watching him, an amused smile on his face, and withdrew his hand.

Harris banged his empty stein down on the table and shouted above the cacophany of music, laughter, conversation and clinking glass, "Let's blow." The girls began to stow compacts, cigarets and lighters in their handbags and to apply vivid lipstick over stretched mouths. As they walked to the parking lot, the men fell behind and Harris whispered urgently, "They want to go to the dorm, but the hell with that; we mightn't be able to get rid of them after. We'll go to Lake Carnegie. I know a good place. You drive."

When the girls learned where they were off to there were protestations. Harris swiftly mollified Susan and there were the sounds of bodies moving about in the rear seat, with occasional giggles and silences. Charlene limited her displeasure to saying sullenly, "I don't suppose you've noticed I'm wearin' a white skirt. You better have a blanket, that's all."

Lake Carnegie is part of a manicured park area on the outskirts of Princeton, its trees skillfully positioned to simulate the random-ness of an idealized nature, the grass and clumps of bushes clip-ped, the trees tended and the water suitably blue. Michael parked the car under the concealing canopy of an enormous willow and Harris, a blanket under his arm, led the way up a mowed slope to a knoll surrounded by a variety of flowering bushes. He pushed aside some branches and restrained them until the others had passed through and found themselves in a cul de sac almost entirely hidden from passers-by. The air was still and warm and heavy with the scents of dogwood and lilac and freshly cut grass. The stars seemed attached to the branches of the encircling trees and a scimitar of blood-red moon hung suspended in the black sky.

Harris flapped the blanket expertly and floated it flat onto the grass. Michael was about to propose to Charlene that they move apart from the others and then remembered the white skirt. They lay on their sides and he put his arms around her. As her bare arms encircled his neck there was a slight muskiness from her armpits. He kissed her gently but she opened her lips and thrust her tongue into his mouth. There was a taste of spearmint and tobacco. He felt her arms tighten, her thighs against his and her body writhing. He simulated passion, breathing deeply, and fenced with her tongue. He ran a hand down the curve of her back, clutched one of her buttocks, then brought his hand around and tried to insinuate it between their bodies. She moved so that he could slip a palm onto one of her breasts and then pulled back, unbuttoned her blouse and jammed her mouth back on his.

In the near darkness, not two feet away, he heard Susan whisper urgently, "No, let me," and could just make out that Harris was lying on her. He felt a mounting dismay: his penis was acting independently and was coiled flaccid in the crotch of his jockey shorts. He kissed Charlene hard, pushed his hand inside her brassiere and tweaked a nipple with his fingertips. But he could not shut out the proximity of the others, the irregularity of their breathing and the tiny moans and catches of breath that were beginning to be emitted by Susan. He took his hand from Charlene's breast and slipped it down between their bodies. He felt the flatness of her belly and the warm puffiness of her pubic mound, and stroked and cupped it. But he could not concentrate and was close to panic in the knowledge that he was not going to have an erection.

He pulled his lips away and laid his head alongside hers. "Do you want me to make love to you?" he whispered.

"I don't mind," she said.

"Well you can go to hell," he said and got to his feet.

He thrust through the bushes and they clawed at him. He heard voices – Charlene's voice, raised, and Harris's – but couldn't make out what was being said. He walked back to the dorm, drenched in sweat, and pretended to be asleep when Harris returned an hour later. Neither mentioned the incident afterwards.

Chapter Six

Harris had come to dinner with the intention of sharing his discovery with Michael but once there his resolve lost its sinew. The place was inappropriate, the interruptions were too frequent. After dinner, in his suite for a nightcap, Michael could see that Harris was taut as a towline. As they sat talking, he shifted in his chair every few minutes and got out of it half a dozen times: to ice or to freshen his drink, to relieve himself in the bathroom or to go to the window to part the curtains to peer into the thickening fog. At times his eyes took on a distant, preoccupied look. At one point Michael put a question and Harris made no response. He asked the question again.

Harris started. "I'm sorry," he said. "You really must forgive me. My mind was off somewhere else."

"Do you want to talk about it?" Michael asked.

It wasn't that he wanted to know what was exercising Harris, but years in the confessional had taught him that the failure to ventilate a fermenting thought could oppress. "You know the saying," he added, as much to break the lengthening silence as anything else. "The reason secrets aren't kept is because some are too good to keep and the others aren't worth keeping."

"This one's been kept," Harris said with what seemed unnecessary assertiveness.

Harris was back in the chair now, studying Michael, appraising him, absently stroking with a flat palm the long sparse hair on the top of his head. Michael found his curiosity piqued. For all the fact that he had no desire to probe unbidden into the life of another and was often excruciatingly bored by the revelations unloaded on him because of his vocation, he was intrigued. This was no ordinary man sitting opposite, peering at him like a suspicious owl, restless as a man waiting for the jury to come in or for his wife to have the baby, and who now, unaccountably, broke into what was obviously an irrepressible grin. It widened.

"Well, if you're set on enjoying the joke by yourself . . . " Michael said. He glanced at his watch.

Harris put out a restraining hand. "No, wait. I'm sorry. I do want to talk to you." He was positively beaming. "As they say: if you can't trust a priest, who can you trust?"

"You wouldn't expect me to take issue with that," Michael said and sat back in his chair.

Harris took a turn about the room as though on a search for his opening words. "I'm not sure you're going to like what I've got to tell you," he said.

"Try me."

"Well, you'll know soon enough," Harris said, returning to sit down and look full into Michael's eyes. "I've discovered Jesus' grave," he said, his voice soft but electric with excitement.

Michael felt his heart bump and then beat at an accelerated rate. "Jesus' tomb!" he said. "Congratulations."

"Thank you," Harris said, suddenly bemused.

Jesus' tomb! How marvelous, Michael thought. He had often hoped it would be discovered. He had never been impressed by the claims made for the Garden tomb just outside the old city of Jerusalem. It was all too movie-set pat: the scrupulously tended garden, the picturesque stone slab rolled aside from the entrance to a cave carved in a cliff; and nearby, the so-called Gordon's Calvary – *Golgotha*, "the place of the skull" – the side of the hill stratified and pitted, revealing to a credulous eye the vaguest configuration of a human skull when the light was right. It was like so many of the "holy sites" in Israel: historically suspect or downright fraudulent, places exploited by sometimes competing religious orders, reeking of the souvenir industry and obviously having been designated "authentic" years ago by some unimaginative official anxious to pander to the expectations of pilgrims.

"Tell me about it," he said. "Where in Jerusalem?"

Harris hesitated, frowning, pursing his lips. "Maybe I'd better begin again. What I've discovered are two of the tombs in which Jesus was buried, and—"

"Hold on a second," Michael said, his face clouding. "Did you say *two* of the tombs?"

Harris smiled thinly: "Actually, there were three."

Michael searched Harris's eyes, looking for a glint of mischief (he wouldn't put it past him), but he looked, if anything, suddenly morose. "This isn't one of your jokes?"

"Believe me."

Michael shook his head as though to clear it. "Then you're going to have to bear with me. To this point I'm beautifully confused." Harris was about to speak but Michael pressed on, a small note of acerbity in his voice. "I take it that what you've discovered is Joseph of Arimathea's tomb?"

"Well, actually, no."

"But you said you'd discovered Jesus' grave."

Harris sighed heavily. "Look, it's complicated. Let me take another run at it."

"Please do."

Harris shot him a look. "This time without interruption?"

Michael raised his eyebrows and spread his hands as though to say, "But of course."

"What I've discovered," Harris said, speaking carefully, "are two of the three tombs in which Jesus was buried. You're quite right: after his body was taken from the cross – and I agree that the biblical record is trustworthy here – it was placed in Joseph of Arimathea's tomb. However, at dawn two days later, it wasn't there—"

"Precisely," said Michael, surprised at the resentful tone in his voice. "He'd risen."

"I'm afraid not," Harris said gently. "Actually, the body had been stolen and moved to another tomb, the family tomb of Simon the Zealot, which tomb I discovered in Jerusalem. Later, after a reburial ceremony, it was removed to a cave near Qumran."

"The Essene community?."

Harris nodded. "Yes. Where they discovered the Dead Sea Scrolls."

Michael felt a chill sweep through his body and following it, a flush of anger. What was Harris talking about – three tombs? And a reburial ceremony! He knew the Jewish customs of that time:

when a member of a family died, the body was anointed with herbs and spices and walled up in the wing of a tomb for a year to allow decomposition to take place. The bones were then gathered, and in a formal reburial ceremony, placed in a limestone container called an ossuary, granted the family could afford one. But what had all this to do with Jesus?

Harris rose from his chair and began to pace. "It's the first time I've told this and I'm afraid I'm telling it badly," he said. "As a matter of fact, I'm having second thoughts about telling it at all."

"Surely you don't intend to stop now?"

"It's a long story . . . "

"The essence of it, then."

Harris glanced at his watch. "I don't think the moment is right. And it's getting late . . . "

Michael leaned forward, hands planted on spread knees, jaw thrust out, eyes steely. He presented a formidable appearance. "Harris," he said, and his voice was commanding, "Seriously . . . ! You say you've discovered Jesus' tomb – *tombs*, you say – then you propose to drop the subject as casually as though you'd been talking about the death of a distant maiden aunt. I'll be blunt with you – and I mean no offence – were it not for the fact that you are who you are, I'd assume that this was an enormous put-on. But obviously you're serious. You're hardly a neophyte in your profession so I must take you seriously. But really, Harris, to judge by what you've said to this point, you're either misled or confused. I don't know what else to think."

"I know. I know. I'm not surprised at your reaction. It's an incredible story." He paused a moment and then shrugged. "What the hell; the fat's in the fire.

"There's a new housing project in the Mount Scopus area in Jerusalem. Two years ago, come April, a workman was clearing away some debris with a back-hoe, and picked up a large boulder. Beneath it was the opening to a tomb. It's not uncommon; happens often."

"Yes, I know."

"At any rate, the guy on the back-hoe called his foreman and he put in a call to the Department of Antiquities. There was nobody else around so I took the call. I'd done a six-month stint with the American College for Oriental Studies and had worked for the department. They know me, so off I went.

"When I got to the site, there were already a couple of orthodox Jews there. You know the type: the long black coat, the broad-brimmed hat, the beard, the pigtails. Discover a tomb and there's always at least one of them ready to give you a hard time about the bones . . . "

"It's a matter of their religion," Michael said huffily. "People don't take lightly to it being tampered with."

"Well, be that as it may, I slipped through the hole and found myself in a forecourt perhaps twenty by twenty with three loculi, burial chambers, leading off on each side. First thing I noticed was that there were five ossuaries right by the entrance, placed randomly. If I can jump forward: the conclusion reached later was that the family whose tomb it was had reason to believe that it was about to be desecrated, presumably by Roman soldiers, and were getting ready to remove the ossuaries.

"I checked them. Four of them contained bones; three a number of skeletons. Nothing extraordinary. The fifth ossuary had obviously been used, but it was empty, except for a fragment of a dried flower. In a corner was a tooth, a molar.

"I had no idea of the importance of what I'd found; I was simply curious. I crouched there looking about, and suddenly the whole thing became a puzzle. How come this single molar in the empty ossuary? One by one I examined the skulls and jawbones, and wherever a molar was missing, tried to fit the one I'd found into the socket. Didn't fit any of them. I put everything back as it had been and sat down, the tooth in my hand, running every possibility through my mind."

Michael broke in. "Are you saying that this was Joseph of Arimathea's tomb and that . . . ?"

"No, no, no," Harris said quickly. "We know it wasn't Joseph's tomb. It belonged to a family named Yehuda. That was established later."

"Go ahead."

"Anyway, there I was, sitting on the floor, trying in my imagination to go back to the first century, trying to reconstruct something that made sense. The most reasonable explanation for the tooth was that there'd been some bones in the now empty ossuary and that it had become necessary to move them in a hurry, and secretly. If not in a hurry, why had the tooth been overlooked? If not secretly, why was the ossuary itself not taken? Obviously because it would have been too bulky, too conspicuous. You can measure the urgency if you bear in mind how reluctant a good Jew would be to disturb the bones of a man properly buried."

He returned to sit opposite Michael, his face flushed in the refreshing of the memory. Michael's face was blank.

Harris drew a deep breath and continued. "I'd gotten stiff sitting in one position, so I shifted. The beam of my flashlight fell obliquely on one end of the ossuary and I noticed some scratches. Time had softened them but I could make them out."

Michael hardly dared the question: "Was it a name?"

"Often a name is carved on the end, but in this case, no. Just these scratches. I took a page from my notebook and made a rubbing. Didn't tell me much. Looked like someone had carved a series of crude inverted hemispheres, and beneath them, the Christian fish-symbol in a small declivity."

"The symbol used by the early Christians?"

"Yes. Slightly below was the Aramaic word for Essene."

He reached into a pocket and pulled out a bulging wallet, dug into it, withdrew a folded piece of paper and passed it to Michael. "This is the rubbing I made."

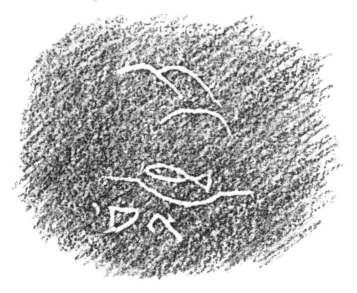

As Michael studied it, Harris continued. "I reported what I'd found to the department, although I didn't mention the tooth. News of the find was published in the *Israel Exploration Journal* but it didn't create anything by way of a stir. The four ossuaries, with their bones, were properly interred, and the fifth sits with some others in the courtyard at the Rockefeller in Jerusalem." He smiled. "They have no idea of its importance, but they will. They will."

Michael handed back the rubbing without comment. He was striving to maintain his composure. Outwardly calm, he was seething with conflicting emotions: a burgeoning excitement, a chill dread, an irrational anger.

"Were you able to decipher the scratchings?" he asked, his voice flat.

"Not for almost three months. I did a lot of reading on the discoveries at Qumran – I'd done a fair bit before, of course – and made half a dozen visits to the Shrine of the Book where they keep the Dead Sea Scrolls, half hoping to see similar scratchings. Talked to some of the men who'd worked on the scrolls. Drew a blank everywhere. Went to Qumran and did a careful examination, especially of the stones near the scriptorium. I guess I examined every faced stone in the area." He shook his head, remembering. "I really don't know why I went to such trouble. It was as though I was under a compulsion. Some 2,000-year-old bones had been removed under mysterious circumstances from the tomb of an undistinguished Jewish family living in Jerusalem. So what? Looking back, I can't understand what motivated me. If I were a religious man I'd think it was spooky. And I can't justify keeping the tooth. It's a crime in Israel to keep any antiquity without official permission." He smiled wryly. "I used to keep it in my pocket . . . a kind of feelie.

"It was in my pocket that day at Qumram. I was standing on the wooden staging over the original watchtower, just looking about. Suddenly it struck me that the mountains off to the west resembled the jagged, flattened M on the ossuary. I can't begin to describe to you what I was feeling. I was just beginning to be aware that I had a bum heart, and I remember being a bit worried because it was pounding so hard in my chest. I fumbled in my wallet for the rubbing and held it up in line with the mountains. Yes, there could be no doubt about it! There, in the proper relationship to the mountains and the place where I was standing, was an outcropping in the midst of the plain, a small mountain, actually. Obviously the inverted U in the scratchings."

Michael was about to ask a question but Harris held out a hand. It was trembling. His eyes were glowing and his skin was flushed. "I knew, knew beyond question," he said, his voice rising dramatically, "that somewhere on that mountain were the bones of the man who'd been buried in that empty ossuary in Jerusalem.

"I took a room at the Jordan Intercontinental Hotel in Amman and spent the next eight days climbing over that outcropping. Nothing. Not a cave, not a crevice, no place where anything could have been buried. The attendant, the guy who sells tickets there, began to kid me. He'd remind me, as if I didn't know, that the area had been gone over God knows how many times by teams of archaeologists, by units of the Israeli army, and by the *anz barri* – the word means mountain goats – the Bedouins.

"I divided the area into sections and instead of searching indiscriminately went over each segment carefully." He shot a glance at Michael. "Appropriately, it was a Sunday when I found the place. I'd pried a fair-sized rock out of a hollow, and there, underneath, was the opening to a cave. There was a second, smaller rock, and after a struggle I got it moved." His eyes were blinking rapidly now and a slight unsureness had entered his voice. "I can't tell you what I was feeling: it was as though I was going to disintegrate. I was quite literally faint from the excitement.

"I went into the hole feet first and found myself in a cave no bigger than ten feet in diameter, carved from the limestone. I fumbled in my pocket for my flashlight, dropped it, I was shaking so, found it again and turned it on. There, in the center of the cave, in a shallow basin carved in the floor, was a pile of bones; not just heaped up but carefully arranged: the long bones on the bottom, and on top, a skull.

"I sat for a minute, catching my breath. Then I picked up the skull and turned it over. Mike, maybe you can imagine what I felt when I saw an empty socket among the upper teeth! I reached into my pocket, took out the molar and pushed it into the socket. And Michael, *it fitted!*"

He subsided, his mouth open, breathing heavily, his face blotched with pink patches, his eyes glistening. He was not looking at Michael, but off, as though once again he was seeing the shining skull in his hand and once again feeling the sensation as the roots of the tooth slid into the bony cavities like a bolt into a lock. Michael became conscious that he, too, was trembling and that his scalp was drawn tight, as it had been since Harris had reached the climax of his story.

But hold on a minute – there was nothing in what Harris had said that would identify the bones as Jesus'.

"Harris," he said slowly, "what you've been telling me is fascinating. Utterly fascinating. But what does it have to do with Jesus? Surely you're not going to argue on the ground of a Christian symbol scratched on an empty ossuary and a skeleton in an ancient cave that—"

Harris held up a hand. "Mike, please," he said, "will you hold it just a minute?" Michael fell silent. Harris composed himself and resumed.

"There's more," he said.

He was subdued now, as though the remembering had siphoned off energy. "There was a manuscript. It was lying beside the declivity in which the bones were arranged. It was wrapped in what was left of a linen cloak. Much of the cloak had disintegrated and it was in an exceedingly fragile condition. I wanted very much to unroll it, of course, but that was impossible in the cave, so I left it there, climbed out, rolled the larger stone over the entrance and went into Amman. I bought a wooden box for half a dollar and picked up some absorbent cotton and a roll of pliofilm. I hired an Arab with a pickup truck, and the following afternoon went back to the cave. I had the Arab wait outside – told him nothing, of course – while I packed the manuscript and the bones. Then I nailed up the box and had him carry it to the truck.

"We had to wait until dark to go back to Amman. Qumran is in the occupied Left Bank and the Israelis have strung wire along the Jordan. You can cross the Allenby Bridge and take a chance on an inspection, sometimes they pass you right through, but I wasn't taking any chances. Skip the details; enough to say that my man got me through.

"Back at the hotel I locked the door, cleared a large table and very carefully tried to unroll the cloak. It practically disintegrated. However, the manuscript itself was in incredibly good condition. There was some damage from insects, some breaking along the edges and some discoloration, but it was really quite amazing. I tried to unroll it – you can imagine with what care – but it was too risky. I was able however to read the opening words. They were in Aramaic and poorly written; you could see they'd been inscribed in a hurry by someone who wasn't a scholar. I could make out the opening sentence. It read: *I, Shimon ben Yehuda, called to be an apostle by Yeshuah ben Yoseph, did on the eve of Shabat in the year . . .* " That was as much as I dared read. I was afraid the parchment would crumble or break if I stressed it further —"

Michael interrupted, frustration in his voice. "For heaven's sake, Harris! You're stretching it out like a cheap murder mystery!"

"Sorry, I thought you'd want all the details."

"Well, I do," Michael said, curbing himself. "But later. Right now I'd like you to get to the point."

"Fair enough," Harris said, his voice conciliatory. "I didn't get the manuscript unrolled for a full month. Stayed right there in Amman, rented a humidifier and worked at it, slowly, carefully—"

"Harris . . . " Michael prompted, his voice edgy.

"Sorry. The manuscript was written, as I say, by the apostle spoken of in the New Testament as Simon the Zealot. As you undoubtedly know, the Zealots were a group of radical Jews who wanted to precipitate a rebellion against the Romans. Pretty scary bunch, actually. Apparently Simon, who was a genuine follower of Jesus, believed that if Jesus *seemed* to be resurrected – he'd often said he would be – it would provide the spark needed to start a general uprising. He didn't believe that Jesus would be resurrected, of course; none of the disciples did, as you know. So, during the night, he and three other Zealots jumped the guard at the tomb, killed him, hid the corpse, rolled the stone away from the opening and carried off Jesus' body. They took it to Simon's family tomb, placed it in one of the loculi and sealed it up with rock and plaster.

"The uprising they'd hoped for never happened, of course. The story that the body had been stolen got out, and that was the end of the plan. About a year later, Simon had an ossuary made, took the now desiccated bones and went through a reburial ceremony."

"But surely members of his family would ask questions."

"They probably did. I don't know. I imagine he told them the dead man was one of the leaders of the Zealots, or something like that, and that they were to keep it quiet. I don't know. At any rate, in what I'm fairly certain was just before the first Jewish revolt, when the Romans were desecrating Jewish graves as punishment, Simon and his brothers planned to move all the bones in the family tomb to a safe place, and actually did move Jesus'. They were never able to get the others out. We can only presume they were killed before they could. It was a bad time in Jerusalem."

The two men sat in what became a long silence, looking into each other's eyes. Harris found himself utterly spent. Exhaustion lay heavily on his body and mind. Michael's passion had ebbed, and his thoughts were far away. He was seeing a tiny cave in the desert, undisturbed for nearly two thousand years, silent and cool and dry. And a small pile of bones lying at its center.

"Taxi, Guv'ner?"

Where was he? Suddenly aware, he looked about. Hard to tell in the fog. Ah, there was Black Lion gate; he was on the Bayswater Road. The drizzle had plastered his hair to his head, water was dripping from his nose and chin and running in icy rivulets down the back of his neck. His feet were sloshing within his shoes and the bottoms of his trousers were sodden and dragging on the pavement. He was suddenly marrow-cold and leaden tired and began to shiver, and having begun, was unable to stop.

"Taxi, Guv'ner?"

The voice was insistent: a taxi was traveling with him as he walked.

He climbed into the cab and said, "The Dorchester." The driver, glimpsing the roman collar, looked at him closely and then said, "The Dorchester it is."

Michael held up his wrist as they passed a street light: three o'clock. Harris had left at midnight, the sound of nearby church bells offering the opportunity to break off. He was sick from the conversation and wanted to hear no more. Nor had he the stomach for a debate. Nor did Harris delay leaving when he rose from his chair speaking of work needing to be done before bed. His secret vented, Harris had become dispirited, almost lethargic. As he paused to say goodbye, at the door he said with a half-smile, "Maybe I should have kept my big mouth shut."

"Nonsense," Michael said, a shade too heartily. "No problem. Really, no problem. You'll join me for breakfast?"

"Yes," Harris said. When he extended a hand it seemed an awkward thing. "Ah well . . . " he said.

Michael's original intention had been to have a relaxed dinner and then, warm with wine and satiety, to repair to his suite, read the much-trumpeted expose in *Harper's* about CIA infiltration of the Italian Communist party, section his way through the *Times* and seek sleep early. Instead, here he was many hours later, his clothing sodden heaps on the tile floor, immersed to his chin in the oversize bathtub. The chill had yielded to the water and he lay motionless, grateful for the warmth and for the clarity that had returned to his thinking.

He had gone over Harris's story half a dozen times, seeking holes, ferreting after inconsistencies on which he could hang the denials his inclination cast up. He had found none. If Harris had found only the bones the story would have little credibility; but there was the manuscript. In Aramaic, he'd said. It would be, of course; it was the common language of the time, the *lingua franca*, the language Jesus himself spoke.

There was a disturbing credibility to the entire account. The stories of the resurrection in the Gospels and in the Acts of the Apostles had long troubled scholars. There were contradictions in the texts, apparent interpolations, sections that seemed not to jibe, others that yielded evidence of having been added by other authors. Years earlier, in preparation for Easter, and in part as an exercise to maintain his facility with Greek, he had essayed to synthesize the five accounts, only to give up the task as almost hopeless. There was no entirely satisfactory way to reconcile the differences.

It was plausible that Simon could have decided to steal the body. It was clear in the texts that none of the apostles took seriously Jesus' prediction that he would rise from the grave; they doubted it as late as their final meal together on the night of his arrest. There was no hint in the record that any of them had ventured to visit the tomb after the burial. (It was hardly likely that they would have been deterred by the Sabbath: Jesus had surely said enough on those restrictions.) And if one were to take the New Testament reports as substantially true, it was evident that they discounted the various reports of the resurrection that did come to them. After Mary of Magdala told Peter and John that the tomb was empty, they had run to the site, gone in, looked about and returned to the city "puzzled." Mary herself, even after "the young men in radiant clothing" had told her that Jesus was not dead but risen, returned to the tomb, and seeing Jesus in the shadows (taking him to be the gardener) had asked what he had done with the body. Then there was that curious business about the Jewish elders and the guards entering into a conspiracy to assert that the body had been stolen by the disciples. The record in Matthew says: "And to this day that is the story among the Jews."

Early in his studies Michael had gone beyond the problems in the text. He had concluded that they reflected the inevitable confusion that would have arisen under the circumstances surrounding the arrest and the crucifixion, particularly with the disciples – terrified that they might come to the same end – hiding behind locked doors. The details, he decided, weren't that important. What was important was what had happened to Jesus' followers after his death. This tiny rag-tag-and-bobtail group of semi-literate nobodies – craven, dull-witted and self-seeking as they had shown themselves to be – had suddenly become men aflame with zeal and bold with courage. *That* was the proof of the resurrection. Whatever had actually happened, there remained the undeniable fact of their transformation, a mystery that would now never be resolved. And whether God had literally started Jesus' heart to pumping again, or whether the resurrected body was unlike the one he wore for some thirty-three years, or whether the resurrection was the perseverance of his spirit in some fashion beyond present understanding, was secondary. Ineffable mystery; Jesus was alive! And the disciples were so sure of it that they were ready to lay their lives on the line.

Then came the thought that made him shudder even in the water of the tub: Suppose Jesus' skeleton *had* been found, a heap of bare bones in a cave, a grinning skull – even so mundane a thing as a missing tooth! – all that remained after decay and desiccation had done their work. Michael knew he could cope with such reality, but could others?

Could the church?

It would be vain to argue that whether or not Jesus' body had been resurrected made no essential difference: it made all the difference in the world. The apostle Paul had put it succinctly: "If Christ be not risen, then is our faith vain." Even if one insisted that the resurrection was essentially a reviving of the *spirit* of Jesus, the argument grew gruel-thin when you could visit a museum and see the bones – the very *bones*! – and know that he had not triumphed over death; that, as happens to all men, his heart had stopped, the impulses in his brain and nervous system had faltered and ended, and for all the myrrh and aloes and spikenard, for all the wrapping in a shroud impregnated with spices, the corruption of his flesh had taken place and in the end there was nothing but the bones.

But surely the church could assert: Yes, there lie the bones, but here lives the body of his truth! Here, in ideas undiminished by time, here in a life unparalleled in history; here in the food of the saints in every century; here in the miracles his eternal spirit has wrought is the Christ. Surely the church could say *that*! Yes, but would it be believed, even by those disposed to believe? What thoughts would intrude upon the mass when the supplicant felt the wafer laid on his tongue and was told it was the very body of Christ? What dark and debilitating thoughts would arise each time the chalice was raised high in the drama of the Eucharist? Would not doubt stalk every service and lurk in every cathedral? Would it not make a mockery of Easter? Would it not make discordant every song of faith triumphant? Would it not brood about every crucifix on every wall of every home in every parish? Would it not poison every prayer, even sour the daily bread of communion with God? *Hail Mary, full of grace. . . .*

If the son is suspect, what of his mother? Had she, after all, been assumed into heaven, knowing not death, untouched by corruption? Will not someone soon uncover *her* bones in another ancient crypt? Would not the black garb of the priest and the somber habit of the sister soon come to symbolize a mourning for the dead God?

Michael could cope with it; could others?

Could even he in the face of the assault that would surely be mounted by the enemies of the church? Oh, the malicious, exultant joy that would spawn in their breasts, the cackling, demonic glee. Consider the scorn that will be vented, the lips that will be curled, the denunciations that will be sounded, the diatribes that will be loosed. Consider what letters to the editor will be penned, what vindication will be claimed, what treatises will be written, what books will be rushed to press. Ah yes, the press! Dorothy Parker had once participated in a competition among fellow writers to devise the most sensational possible newspaper headline. She had won with the words, POPE ELOPES! But even such a scandal would be relegated to the inside pages on the day Harris broke his news. No newspaper would have headline type bold enough. And television! Would any program be beyond preemption? Would anyone of eminence go unquoted; from pope to president, to politician, to professor, to pundit to panderer? Jesus had bidden his followers take the message of eternal life to the uttermost parts of the earth, and over the centuries they had. But the message of his death would encircle the globe in milliseconds, and men and women who had never heard that he had lived would learn that he had died.

"I think I may have a solution for you," Michael said.

He and Harris were at breakfast, Harris segmenting a kipper with evident relish, Michael toying with some scrambled eggs. He had recovered from the shock and depression of the night before. It was to have been expected, following on the bad news from Josh Lieberman, the seriousness of the Holy Father's illness and the realization that he might be called upon to succeed him. Little wonder his faith had momentarily faltered.

"A solution?" Harris asked.

Harris was not at ease. After the door had closed on Michael at midnight, he had walked to his hotel along the gleaming empty streets, feeling the betrayer, feeling that he had failed a friend, that he had committed a sordid act and was somehow soiled. He hadn't known beforehand what Michael's response would be, of course, and had in the first sharing of his secret been so caught up in recalling the thrill of the quest and the find that he had been unaware of the effect his words might be having. Last night, Michael had sought to cover his perturbation, but his face had been a trifle pale and his voice a trifle forced and his manner a trifle stiff. This morning, though, as they met in the lobby and went in to breakfast, he seemed serene.

"You were saying last night you didn't know where you were going to work when you got home," Michael said.

"Yes. Right."

"Why don't you stay with me? I live in a big barn of a place. Nobody there but my niece and a housekeeper and my two secretaries. Priests."

Harris levered apart a chunk of the white flesh of the fish and moved it about in the melted butter before responding. "That's very generous of you," he said noncommittally.

"There's a guest room. Self-contained. It's seldom used. And there's a separate area in the basement. Dry as a bone and ventilated. Lock on the door. . . .You said you were planning to do a paper?"

"A monograph."

"Lots of room to spread out. Absolute privacy."

A waiter came with a pot of coffee, another of hot milk and the marmalade Harris had ordered. When he had gone, Harris remained silent, chewing meditatively and seeming to find it important to spread the marmalade evenly on every part of the surface of the toast.

Michael said, "Don't misunderstand me. I'm not minding your business. It simply occurred to me that—"

Harris stopped him with a raised hand. He finished chewing the food in his mouth, swallowed hard and for the first time in a while looked at Michael.

"Don't misunderstand me either," he said, "I appreciate the offer. I really do. Sounds like an excellent solution. It's true, I don't have any place to go." He paused, probing to dislodge some food with the tip of his tongue. "It's just that . . . well, I wonder about the fitness of doing my work there. It's. . . . " He left the sentence unfinished and occupied himself again with the marmalade.

A smile began at the corners of Michael's mouth, broadened and ended in a burst of laughter. "Oh that," he said and chuckled. "Where better to learn you're wrong than in a house dedicated to God?" The smile waned. "My dear Harris," he said, and his voice was suddenly earnest, "I don't mean to reflect even for a moment on your professional competence, but I'm as certain as I am that the sun will rise tomorrow that when you've had a chance to examine all the evidence you'll come to other conclusions than you have to this point." He paused. "How much time have you actually spent on it?"

Harris was immediately defensive. "I'll grant you, not enough, but—"

"Exactly. So let's leave the question begging for the moment." Harris was about to offer a rejoinder but thought better of it. "I'm prepared to take the risk," Michael continued cheerfully, "and it would be good to have you around."

So it was arranged. Harris would stay on in London for a week to do some reading at the British Museum and would then fly to New York. There would be no need to do any preparation of the room; that could be handled after his arrival. He might want to make a few changes – supplement the lighting, perhaps, bring in a dehumidifier, things like that – but those decisions could be made after he saw the layout. He hazarded a guess that he'd need anywhere from three to five months to finish his writing.

"That quickly?" Michael said, surprised.

"It's not a work of art," Harris said. "Most of the research is done."

"Then we're agreed."

"I don't know how to thank you," Harris said. "I was worried about where I was going to go." He smiled his downturned smile. "I was pretty ungracious a minute ago."

"Nonsense," Michael boomed. "What about your things? Your clothes and so on?"

Harris's smile was touched with ruefulness. "There's not much."

"The manuscript? The bones?"

"They've been shipped to me care of the Museum of Natural History in New York. I'll have them sent around after I get there."

"You're not worried about customs?"

"No problem. The waybill has all the appropriate descriptions. I have my customs broker clearing it. There's never any trouble when you ship to a museum."

Later that morning as Michael maneuvered the hired car along the meandering country roads south of London on his way to Hambleton House, the morning sun had burned off the fog and chill of the night before. The sky was an almost radiant blue and the only clouds lay low and diffuse on the horizon. He cranked down the window and let the clean air blow on his face. For all his lack of sleep he felt refreshed.

Chapter Seven

Hambleton House was approached by way of a long avenue lined with precisely placed poplars. The slanting winter sunlight cast a barred pattern across the dun-colored driveway. It fluttered on the car's hood, and made driving difficult. The house was Tudor in style and at least two centuries old, but it had been so meticulously and so recently refurbished that it conveyed the impression of holding a pose for the photographer from *The Stately Homes of England*. The lawns would have been the pride of the greenskeeper at St. Andrew's, the hedges were so carefully contoured that they suggested plastic, and the clumps of trees, bushes and flower beds were reminiscent of architects' renderings.

Ten minutes late, Michael parked the car in the circular driveway behind the gleaming Rolls, smiled in amusement as he passed the sculpted dwarf cross-legged on a concrete toadstool, and pulled the bellcord. A man in a houseman's uniform swung open the enormous door, informed him that Lady Hambleton was expecting him and asked him please to have a seat in the library.

Sophie, who had been awaiting his arrival at a window in the sitting room off her bedroom, checked her wristwatch, and when she had kept him waiting exactly ten minutes, tap-tapped her heels down the great curved staircase and swept into the library, offering her hand as she crossed the room in a manner clearly influenced by Greer Garson. She gestured Michael to a chair, poured strong tea through a silver strainer into Belleek china, put two digestive biscuits on a matching tea plate and gave them to him. Then she poured herself some tea and seated herself opposite in a wingback chair where the light was flattering.

There was talk of the weather, of the drive from London and of the difficulty of getting good servants. Michael did little but concur, contributing slight bobs of his head while concentrating on rebuking the smile that threatened to surface at the eccentricities of Sophie's acquired English accent which, when it remained constant long enough to be analyzed, could be identified as two parts *My Fair Lady* and one part bastardized Australian. She was wearing a green, floor-length gown, slit on the side to above the knee. A ruby encircled with diamonds nestled in the crepey cleft of her decolettage. Earrings repeated the motif and drew the eye to a miniature coronet, also made of diamonds and perched in the blue-tinted hair.

Sophie soon had had enough of chit-chat. She put her tea aside and said straightforwardly, "I assume you coming here today means we've got a deal."

Michael liked directness but was taken aback by Sophie's frontal assault. He slipped the blow. "I've been looking forward to our conversation," he said.

He was not at all happy with Sophie's beginning. He'd been warned that she was difficult and decided to take the offensive. "I want you to know how much we appreciate your generosity," he said. "I've already asked Father Jamieson to work out the wording for the plaque."

Sophie turned pink and looked steadily at him for a moment. "You said a plaque," she said.

"Yes," Michael said, fashioning an ingenuous smile. "As I believe Father Jamieson told you; a bronze plaque suitably inscribed on the wall in the foyer."

Sophie was in the midst of revising her opinion of the man in the chair opposite. She had no illusions about priests: they were men of God and custodians of the grace of God but mortal men subject to the weaknesses of men. She'd had an affair with a "whiskey priest" in Belize, and earlier, having entered puberty at twelve, had been intrigued by a Father Jansen, an instructor at St. Agnes school in Toronto, who found frequent opportunity accidentally to touch or to brush the back of his hand against the swell of her young breasts. None of this disillusioned her or diminished her conviction that the clergy were the conduit through which

God's blessings came while being at the same time, men. But this cardinal. . . . Here quite obviously was a different breed, and as was becoming evident, no pushover. Fair enough.

"Haven't you talked to Father Jamieson in the past week?" she said.

"I'm afraid not," Michael said, taking a sip of his tea. He was more pleased now with the way things were going; Sophie was having to play catch-up. "I did have a cable from him earlier, confirming the time and place for our meeting." He nibbled at the biscuit.

Sophie let out a breath of exasperation. "Your Eminence," she said, "the last time I talked to Father Jamieson I made two things crystal clear: I told him to inform you that, in return for my donation, there had to be appropriate recognition of the donor, and that if you people weren't prepared to do that I'd have to reconsider the whole thing."

"And that appropriate recognition?" – making her say it.

Sophie was up to it: "That a statue I will provide be placed in the lobby."

"A statue of the Virgin?" Michael said, leaning ever so slightly on the last word.

Sophie was in no way intimidated. "A statue of me."

"I see," Michael said. He took another sip of his tea and put the cup and saucer down on the table by his chair. "Mrs. Hambleton . . . " he began.

"Lady Hambleton."

"I think I should in fairness give you a bit of background." He placed the tips of his fingers against each other and regarded them. "The Roman Catholic church is much given to the placing of statues in buildings – in my view, too much given; but that's another matter. These statues are depictions of Our Lord, his Holy Mother and various saints. They're placed there for purposes of veneration—"

"There's a statue of a Lillian P. Bailey in—"

Michael held up his hands. "I was about to say, there are exceptions: they aren't saints, in that they haven't been canonized, but they are men and women whose lives are an example to others." He opened his eyes widely and looked directly at Sophie. "I wouldn't want you to misunderstand my meaning," he said equably, "but this is hardly the case here."

Sophie saw that the sparring was over. "A children's wing at St. Clare's would do more good than a dozen of your examples," she said coolly.

"Indeed it would. But we're not discussing the relative merit of good works." He evaluated his next words and then released them. "Madam," he said simply, "you aren't even a Christian."

Sophie, stung, said, "Then why'd you come all the way here to see me?"

Michael followed on his advantage. "Let me be candid with you, Mrs. Hambleton—"

"Lady Hambleton," Sophie snapped.

"I had two reasons, both equally important. One was to help you make a contribution to the work of the church; the other was to try to persuade you to commit your life to God."

The son of a bitch, Sophie thought. The double-dyed son of a bitch! Not only is he telling me no, he's trying to rub my nose in it.

But Sophie was vulnerable. She very much wanted the matter consummated. The ten million dollars was of no moment – small change; she couldn't possibly spend the money Rogers had left her – and this was the one thing she really wanted. She'd become a hypochondriac. Devils spawned in her childhood psyche had emerged to torment her, manifesting themselves in a variety of disguises. These, combined with menopausal aberrations and frequent hangovers, had made her acutely conscious of her mortality, the while enriching three Harley Street doctors who had departed the national health service for such as Sophie.

The children's wing was Sophie's way of preparing to meet her maker. She was not hypocrite enough – nor was she disposed to – to launch on a life of piety to achieve that end. And God was not a fool to be bamboozled by the jiggery-pokery of a feigned holiness. But He was obviously a pragmatist – as witness His commendation of the proper use of money in Jesus' parable of the talents – and would recognize in Sophie's gift her particular brand of commitment.

But barring her way was this damn priest. He seemed determined to keep her from warming her soul at the flame of her particular righteousness. All right, she'd cool it and wait him out. He wanted the money as much as she wanted to give it. And, by God, it *was* ten million dollars!

For his part, Michael, having established the ascendancy, was upbraiding himself for his attitude. He'd been jabbing at Sophie, not simply because she needed humbling, but because he resented her: her money, her way of life, and most of all the assumption he could read in her eyes that he would eventually capitulate. Who did this incarnation of bad taste think herself to be? Who was she to judge *him*? He didn't like Sophie, but that didn't excuse what he was feeling nor the cruelty of his attack, hidden though it may have been beneath his skill with words. He was further irritated that, at this time of crisis, he had been detoured to London and dragged into the country because this graduate strumpet was heir to a fortune and wanted to use some of it to buy immortality.

He glanced at his watch. "Lady Hambleton . . . "

"That's better."

" . . . I must get back to London. I'd like you to give the matter more thought. You should know, however, that there are certain pre-conditions: I would want you to begin a course of instruction with your local parish priest, make your confession and become a practicing Christian again. As to your wish to make a contribution to St. Clare's, I'll be grateful if you choose to do so but, as I've explained, I could only accept the gift under certain conditions."

Sophie blew. "You priests!" she fumed, her carefully cultivated accent coming off like a mask at midnight. "You'd think you were doing me a favor taking my money!"

"Madam," Michael said, his own temper fraying, "neither I nor any other priest, as you put it, takes your money. None of it ends in my pocket. What the church does is provide the instrument by which you can help others in the name of God." He reached down, picked up his attaché case and rose to his feet.

"So you're turning down the money?"

"By no means." He was suddenly out of patience and his voice took on an edge. "What you don't seem to comprehend . . . "

"Lady Hambleton."

"*Lady* Hambleton," he said, imitating exactly her emphasis. "What you don't seem to comprehend is the fact that while your husband's benificences may have bought him a peerage, the Roman Catholic church does not barter its honors."

"Hah!" hooted Sophie, casting about for a weapon with which to wound. "The church hasn't always been so picky. It's made plenty of deals in its time, some of them pretty sleazy, and you damn well know it."

"I won't deny that," Michael said, pausing at the entrance to the hallway, "but this is another time and another place. Perhaps your misfortune is to be born in this century."

As he turned to the door she shouted after him, "I'll give my money to the Episcopalians!"

"The choice is yours to make," Michael said, opening the front door and pulling it closed behind him.

Later, in the long solitudes, in the vocation of silence, Michael would remember often the moment when the thought first insinuated itself into his mind.

The sun was high, and after the pervasive cold of the great stone house, warm on his bare head. He stowed the top in the boot and, gearing up and down, nosed his way along the meandering narrow road leading to the high road to London. As he went he reviewed the week that now seemed a lifetime long: the summons in the night to Rome, the troubling news from Lieberman, the skeletal form of the Holy Father in the great bed, the labored voice, the whispered words, "Michael, Our Lord may call you to succeed me," and in contrast, the flat unemotional statement by Harris, "I've discovered Jesus' grave."

In his preoccupation, he rounded a curve and was suddenly among a flock of sheep. They scattered before him with quavering cries. He followed as they went before their shepherd down the road and then sat idling until the last recalcitrant was herded through a farm gate. In the sylvan silence the soft bleating of the flock as it flowed and eddied into the field made his memories seem far removed and unreal. But were they? Driving through Covington, the only church he'd seen was St. Anne's. So the death of the pope when it came would reach into even this country enclave. Harris's bones would raise a specter here, too.

It was all too much! Poor Mother Church, where was there not a hand raised against her? Wounded daily by her enemies, smitten within the house of her friends – even by her children. How many more blows must she suffer? He must protect her where he could. Which was why, in part, he'd invited Harris to stay with him: out of friendship, of course, but also to learn just how serious the threat was and to prepare to counter it. Perhaps he could dissuade him by argument, disarm him by challenge, force him back to his data until the error of his conclusions was revealed. It could not possibly be Jesus' grave: the centuries of witness were not a lie. God is not mocked. Christianity is no tenuous myth to be shattered by a boxful of bones. Harris had erred; but what hurt that error might wreak!

The thought occurred: Harris might never complete his work. In the early part of last evening he'd said something about wanting to get the work finished soon because of his heart. Yes, and he'd mentioned it again in describing the state of his excitement at Qumran. What if his heart were to falter and fail? What if he should die before he could publish . . . ?

He thrust the thought away. How unfeeling of him. How ignoble to measure your own inconvenience against the span of a man's life. But it wasn't simply his convenience that was at stake, it was the welfare of the Christian church; not just the Roman Catholic church but every denomination, every sect, every congregation from Eastern Orthodox to Plymouth Brethren. All would be bruised, wounded, perhaps maimed.

What if Harris were to die?

He shook his head to dislodge the thought but it returned. He turned on the radio and traversed the dial until he found the diversion of a news broadcast.

Part Two

Chapter One

The Cardinal Archbishop of the Archdiocese of New York resides in a substantial, four-story gray stone house on the corner of Madison Avenue and Fiftieth Street, backing on and connected to St. Patrick's cathedral and facing the dark bulk of the old Villard Mansion, a block of six townhouses built in 1885, in later years serving as the archdiocesan administrative offices but now deserted and soon to be converted into the foyer to a hotel. The only external evidence that this is the house in which the spiritual leaders of the two million Roman Catholics in the archdiocese have lived and worked for the past three-quarters of a century is an inconspicuous bronze plaque affixed to the stone and reading: *Pope Paul VI, on the occasion of his historic visit to the United Nations Assembly, was a revered guest in this home of the Archbishops of New York, October 4, 1965.*

The house rises straight from the sidewalk, unrelieved by ornamentation save for a series of free-standing gable facings, its general appearance being marred on the second, third and attic floors by air-conditioning units set in the windows. The front door is reached by ascending ten wide stone steps. A gleaming brass bell-button is set in the stone to the right, the area around it stained by frequent polishings. Heavy wrought-iron bars behind the glass of the door protect the entrance. All street-level windows are also barred against intruders, and the interior from the view of passers-by by curtains of delicate Belgian lace.

Cardinal Maloney did not occupy the great house alone. Living there also were his niece, a housekeeper and three priests – his two secretaries and the Chancellor of the Archdiocese. On the street level, the area is divided into two large reception rooms, the cardinal's study, a formal dining room, a serving kitchen and two bathrooms. On the second level there are secretarial offices, a so-called Consulters Room, the guest room and the cardinal's living quarters. A further flight up are a private chapel, the living quarters of the cardinal's niece and the chancellor – he being in hospital suffering a terminal illness. The two priest-secretaries occupy small gabled rooms on the top floor, the housekeeper two semi-basement rooms, partially below ground level. There had been mutterings in the archdiocese about the propriety of the cardinal's niece living at the residence, but they had quickly subsided when the circumstances became known and when Cardinal Maloney had made it clear that the matter was not subject to discussion.

When Michael moved in as cardinal he was no stranger to the residence. He had lived there for ten years as secretary and Chancellor, having been plucked from his post as Procurator at St. Clare's hospital where his administrative skills had brought him to the attention of Cardinal Murtaugh. So began a rise almost unprecedented in the hierarchy of the Roman Catholic church in the United States. Within the brief span of ten years he had been made a Papal Chamberlain, appointed Vice Chancellor of the archdiocese, raised to the rank of Domestic Prelate by Pope Paul, appointed Chancellor and honored again by the pope who elevated him to Protonotary Apostolic. That same year, Cardinal Murtaugh named him Vicar General (his deputy) and six months later, in St. Patrick's cathedral, ordained him Auxiliary Bishop. Within a year he had been designated Archbishop to succeed Cardinal Murtaugh, and so became the eleventh Bishop and the eighth Archbishop of New York, the most prestigious Roman Catholic see in the United States. Two years later to the day, on his fiftieth birthday, in the presence of three hundred American and other friends, he was created a cardinal in a Consistory convened at the Apostolic Palace in Vatican City and received from the hands of the pope the red biretta which now reposed in a glass case in the entrance hallway and would, on his death, be suspended with his predecessors' high above the altar in St. Patrick's.

Ten thousand New Yorkers – the crowd swelled by hundreds from nearby cities and states and distant countries – welcomed him home. A police escort led his open car to the steps of the cathedral where the clergy and various dignitaries were assembled. The governor of the State of New York and the mayor tendered formal greetings. The Vice President brought a message of congratulations from the President and then attended a Mass of Thanksgiving at which the new cardinal was the principal celebrant. Afterwards, in full regalia, he returned to the cathedral steps and blessed the crowd jamming Fifth Avenue, staying for an hour, walking among the people, shaking hands and chatting.

Then in a gesture that electrified the crowd and was an augury of the ecumenical spirit that was to characterize his leadership, he made his way north to St. Thomas Episcopal church, and standing on the top stair in full view of the crowd, embraced the rector who had come out to meet him. The cheering rose to a sustained roar when the senior minister of the nearby Fifth Avenue Presbyterian church climbed the stairs to join them.

The new cardinal now assumed responsibility for the Vicariate areas of Manhattan, Staten Island, the Bronx and the seven counties to the north of the city, taking under his supervision 408 parishes, 1,004 priests, 397 elementary and high schools with an enrollment of 175,000 students, seven institutions of higher learning and nine hospitals. He became a member of two hundred ecclesiastical boards and three New York state and two federal commissions. As Military Vicar of the Armed Forces he assumed the pastoral care of more than a million servicemen and the supervision of more than nine hundred chaplains. Additionally, he became a member of the Synod of Rome, of the Congregation of Bishops and of three pontifical commissions.

In the tradition of his predecessors, he normally worked twelve-hour days. Rising at six, he would read his breviary and then shower and shave while listening to the news on radio. At seven he celebrated mass with the members of his staff and breakfasted alone, reading the New York, Washington and Rome newspapers. At nine he repaired to his study to clear his desk and answer mail. Then to the Consulters Room where he, his private secretaries and, usually, the vicar general discussed the business of the archdiocese. Lunch would be used to meet with individuals and groups, ranging from foreign ambassadors to visiting clergy to politicians. After lunch he might perform some ecclesiatical duty such as the granting of medals and honors, doing so in the appropriate setting of one of the reception rooms with the portraits of Cardinals McCloskey, Corrigan, Farley, Hayes, Spellman, Cooke and Murtaugh looking on. Afterwards, on three or four days of the week, he would be driven – or on good days would walk – the ten blocks to his office at the Chancery building on First Avenue.

Days and evenings there were public functions where his presence was mandatory, as well as optional occasions such as the funerals of priests in the archdiocese and the significant anniversaries of churches. Three or four times a year he journeyed to Rome and would usually, en route, pay a visit to an American Armed Forces base. On a dozen or more occasions each year he went to Washington for conferences with government officials.

His only recreation came when, after dinner, he would retire to his study to read or to watch television programs of which his staff thought he should be aware, viewing them on cassettes. Friday evenings, when he could, he would take two briefcases stuffed with papers, and driving himself, would escape to The Cottage on Round Lake in the Poconos where he would read and study reports, breaking to cut firewood or perhaps go fishing in a small lapstrake runabout powered by a 25-horsepower outboard engine.

His life was spartan and his tastes were simple except in food and the arts. His private living quarters consisted of a sitting room, a bedroom and a bath, the sitting room being furnished in what one of his staff described as "early neo-mediocre." The only change he made after moving in was to remove to storage the pictures Cardinal Murtaugh had left and to substitute his own. His bedroom was almost austere: uncarpeted and furnished with a metal double bed, a large mahogany wardrobe, two end tables and two straight-back chairs. At the head of the bed hung the only picture in the room, a gilt-framed portrait photograph of Pope Gregory inscribed in Latin, "To my brother in Christ's love." In a corner, on a small table faced by a prie-dieu, stood an exquisite reproduction of the statue of the Virgin by Moldarelli in the purest white Carrara marble.

It was into this house that Harris Gordon moved on a tempestuous mid-January morning. He brought little with him: two scruffy suitcases, one with a broken hasp and bound with sashcord, and a

BOAC handbag. Two days later a steamer trunk, a dozen corrugated boxes marked BOOKS and a wooden box bearing a warning, FRAGILE: SCIENTIFIC INSTRUMENTS, were delivered unannounced by a truck from Manhattan Storage. Michael had had Harris picked up at the airport by Father Carroll, and with Miss Pritchard, the housekeeper, took him on a tour of the residence. He scarcely glanced at the guest room, which had been brightened by new curtains and warmed with two vases of cut flowers. "What do you think?" Michael asked. "Will this do?" Harris shrugged and gave an indifferent nod, and Miss Pritchard made a small sniff.

But the room in the basement excited him. He padded about, muttering to himself, checking for electrical outlets, operating the ventilating fan, placing a hand on the concrete floor to test for dampness, examining the lock on the door and asking if there would be any objection to his adding another. There being none, he closed and locked the door and tested it with a vigorous shaking. He would need some tables; perhaps three. Nothing fancy, but large. Michael looked at Miss Pritchard and said, "We'll call the parish office and get them to send over three of the folding tables they use for banquets." Miss Pritchard ventured to inquire as to whether tablecloths were wanted and Harris snapped, "No."

Later, over her afternoon cup of tea with Mrs. O'Donahue in the kitchen, she said: "Now don't be gettin' me wrong; it's not that I mind him comin' – though faith knows the extra work it'll be; him bein' diabetic and all – it's just that he acts like your Lord High Muckety-Muck. Never so much as a by-your-leave or thank you Mum. Shakes hands like you wasn't there."

Samantha Pritchard was a plumpish maiden lady of indeterminate age and fixed opinions. She had emigrated at seventeen from Portadown, Ireland, where her father was a stone mason who spent his days cutting grave markers and his nights drinking Guinness and cuffing about his wife and eleven children. After forty years in New York City, Miss Pritchard's brogue remained thick as peat. The day after she walked down the gangplank at Ellis Island she sought out one of the priests at St. Patrick's, handed over a letter from her priest, made her confession and became a member of the parish. Three months later she was hired as a kitchen maid at the residence and remained there through the tenures of Cardinals Spellman, Cooke and Murtaugh, eventually reaching the exalted position of housekeeper-cook, living in.

Her skin was white as milk and without a wrinkle. It blushed pink when she was in any way discomfited and flushed red when she was angry. Her hair had been drawn back into a bun since she was a child and the only change that had come with the years was that the color had graduated to gray and the bun was worn higher to cover a thinning at the crown. She had developed a proprietory attitude about the residence ("After all, there was none of them here when I first come"), and was fussbudgety about changes made by any of the residents, with the exception of the cardinal and his niece. Her devotion to Michael, who sometimes called her Sam and teased her by imitating her brogue, was total. When he joked with her she never responded in kind – "I know my place," she used to say – and only occasionally permitted herself a slight smile. With Mrs. O'Donahue she referred to Michael as "Himself," but with all others he was "His Eminence," and she had a way of saying it with a tilting back of the head and a looking down the nose that was intimidating. She spent her off-work hours in a sitting room with an adjoining bathroom, both all antimacassars and handmade silk lampshades and crocheted rugs. She seldom went out, except to church or to visit a sister in Hoboken, and usually only if Michael was away.

The other occupant of the residence was Michael's niece, Jennifer O'Neill. On the morning that Harris came to inspect his future quarters, she – much to the displeasure of Miss Pritchard who held higher aspirations for her – was taking an hour from work to have her hair washed and cut in preparation for a dinner date with Detective Copeland Arthur Jackson of the New York County District Attorney's office.

The meal was finished. The tiered cart, laden with deserts that looked more like ceramics than sustenance, had been waved off and they were sipping coffee and cognac in a rosy haze of content. In the wavering candle's light, Copeland was studying Jennifer's face, its color heightened by the wine and by the moment. She glanced up, and in a thin thread of silence that each was reluctant to break, they looked steadily into each other's eyes, holding nothing back.

After a moment she said, "Do you realize that I know almost nothing about you? It's the first time we've really been alone."

"And do you realize that you intimidate me?" he said, smiling.

"I do?" she said, eyebrows arched. "Or is it that Uncle Michael's who he is?"

"I'm not sure I can separate the two."

"He's bigger."

"No, I mean, I'm not sure that if I laid a hand on you there wouldn't be voices from heaven."

"So that's out."

"I didn't say that. I was hoping you'd reassure me."

"Voices from heaven aren't my department. So far, not even a whisper. But then, as I say, I know almost nothing about you. Mind if I – do you call it an interrogation?"

"No . . . I mean, yes. Yes we do call it that, and no I don't mind."

"I'll begin with what I know: age forty."

"Thirty-nine."

"Not a Jack Benny thirty-nine?"

"No."

"Not a New Yorker."

"No. Born in Canada. Toronto. Does it show?"

"Just when you say 'owt' and 'abowt'."

"I don't say 'owt' and 'abowt'. Do I really?"

"You just did."

"Oh well, everybody talks funny in this town."

"Vocation, policeman."

"Unfair. Haven't walked a beat in years. Detective Jackson, if you don't mind."

"Your ambition was to be a hockey player but it was too violent so you became a policeman – a detective."

"Closer to the truth than you know."

"Let's see now; policemen run in families. Your father was with the Royal Canadian Mounted Police."

"Sorry. Nothing so glamorous. He was a compositor on the *Toronto Star*. Still is."

"You haven't said whether you're married."

"You haven't asked."

"I'm asking."

"No, I'm not."

"Ever been?"

"No."

She put a finger tip against his lips and he kissed it. There was a slight smile as she said, "Sweet thirty-nine and never been wed. None of my business, but why?"

His answer came slowly. He took her hand and kissed each of the fingertips lightly. He was asking himself whether, having pulled back from the brink perhaps half a dozen times in the past twenty years, he should now take that step of commitment. "I don't know how to answer that without sounding incredibly corny," he said.

"Why not try?"

He paused and then answered. "I suppose mostly because I've never met anybody like you."

A reflex quip almost got past her lips but she caught it. She was suddenly short of breath and aware that her face and neck were flushed. She couldn't think of what to say and so said nothing, but studied his face. His eyes were on the glinting liquid in the bowl of his brandy snifter.

Almost forty years and never once fully ready to commit himself to any woman. He had often wondered why; as had others. He certainly didn't fit the easy generalizations of the amateur psychoanalysts: heaven knew he hadn't been an unhappy child, hadn't come from an unhappy home. He had been raised in the pleasant, leafy section of Parkdale in the west end of Toronto, a child there in the postwar years when Europeans and Maritimers had moved in in such number that their weight had thrust highrise out of the ground. His father was a big, stooped chunk of a man with abnormally long arms ending in oversize hands. He worked on the stone in the *Star* composing-room making up advertising layouts to be thrown into the hell-box when completed – a typographer's make-work device – and it was a small marvel how such ungainly fingers could so nimbly insert or flip out slugs of type. He bore the mark of his trade, printer's-ink-stained fingers, and so long had he worn a freshly folded newspaper hat on his balding head that the rub-off had left a gray band across his forehead.

Copeland's mother was a cheery butterball with red hair and a round and rosy face on which china-blue eyes surmounted a disproportionately small nose and a very red mouth. She spoke a language of laughter, each sentence it sometimes seemed ending in freshets of chuckling. Her thoughts bounded about like a football, leaping tangentially in unpredictable directions, giving others, and herself, endless amusement. She was Mother Eve, enfolding husband and children and friends and puppies and cats and gerbils and anything else animate in her warmth. And the heart of the house was her kitchen.

Copeland inherited his mother's hair and his father's body. Big and strong, he was uncoordinated until late in his teens, by which point he had become indifferent to sports and had begun to write. He hunt-and-pecked out intricate detective mysteries, dangling misleading clues on convoluted plots like ornaments on a tree. His father wangled him a job in the *Star* newsroom, and after an apprenticeship covering the courts, he was moved to the police beat where he spent his days writing about the prosaic activities of real criminals and his nights the flamboyant escapades of fictional ones. As the result of a series he did on an extradition fight to return a Canadian hoodlum to prison, he was offered a job on the *Brooklyn Eagle*, and because it would take him closer to the potential market for his writing, he took it.

In two years he sold one piece of fiction, and it was so edited as to be unrecognizable. In the meantime, he had so bedeviled the sergeant in Homicide at the 14th Precinct for details of police procedures with which to authenticate his stories, that the officer asked to read one of his manuscripts. He suggested a night course in modern criminology at John Jay university. After three years, a degree won, Copeland became a policeman.

For all his size, perhaps because of it, he was a gentle man, shy, and attractive to women, many of whom, incongruously, felt a constraint to mother him. He accepted their attentions and returned them, for he was a sensual man, but when "his lady," as he liked to call them, began maneuvering "to put a ring on her finger and another in my nose," he quickly slipped the noose. He was not promiscuous and had been enamored of at most a dozen of his "ladies" when he met Jennifer at a dance at the parish house.

She was fifteen years younger than he. He knew she was the cardinal's niece, so when a Paul Jones dance ended with them partnered by proximity, he was so intimidated by who she was and by her beauty that he danced like a spastic and conversed like an oaf. The band took a break and they were carried by the crowd to the punch bowl and thence to the buffet. By then Copeland had recaptured his composure and she had begun to be intrigued by something indefinable about this big man. The evening ended with his walking her the long way home through a warm and windless snowfall, with the flakes fat and lazy and the muffled city mounded with beauty. Now, ten days and three dates later, they were at a corner table in a pseudo-French restaurant trading half-serious banter in a cozy camaraderie.

"But surely in thirty-nine years there must have been lots of girls," she said, not pressing.

"Some. Not all that many."

"Not that it matters. I wasn't prying."

"And you?"

"I don't know what average is but I would think, average. A few wild oats in my teens." When he made no response, she added, "Are you one of those men who want their women virginal?"

He hesitated. "I was going to say no, but in your case, . . . "

"My, so serious."

Again he was silent, pursuing a breadcrumb with a fingertip, almost brooding. She said, "Mind a personal question?"

"No."

"Are you in love with me?"

He took a breath but didn't look up. "I think I am," he said. After a moment he looked at her. "Yes, I am."

"I think I am, too," she said. She sat silent, blinking, thinking, and then said, "You have no idea how unlikely this all is; you being a policeman."

"We're not all bad."

"I didn't mean that," she said quickly. She was about to go on but decided not to. "I'll explain it to you sometime."

At the residence, in the entrance hallway, Copeland kissed her. Her mouth was open on his and the moistness was sweet on his tongue. He felt her breasts soft and her body hard against his. His heartbeat was pulsing in his neck and pounding in his groin and he had to pull his lips away to regain his breath and open his eyes to counter a dizziness.

"Where can we go?" he whispered.

She stood in indecision. "Not here . . . "

"Your room?"

"No . . . Uncle Michael might be back."

"You said he was in Albany."

"Yes. I know. But . . . "

He put an arm about her waist and opened the front door. They buttoned against the cold and went silently to his car. As Copeland inserted the car into the flow of traffic he wondered whether by not somehow seizing the moment they might have lost it. As he turned down Second Avenue, Jennifer realized they were going to his apartment; he'd said he lived near Stuyvesant Town. She reached out and put a hand on his forearm but it was dislodged when he took evasive action against a taxi and she didn't replace it. He parked in a rubbish-cluttered slot beneath the dirty underbelly of East River Drive and they walked toward a sagging link fence and through a broken gate leading onto a dingy street. The river followed them, stinking of oil and rot, and the wind whipped Jennifer's hair above her head and forward like the scarf of snow off the crest of a mountain. She linked her fingers in his, squeezing hard.

"It's just up the street," he said.

The street was a repetition of tenements, many with graffiti on the eroded red brick, some of it as graceful as Arabic. He turned in at an entrance undistinguished from the others, and leading her by a stride, half ran up the stairs to the porch. In the lobby there was a baby carriage chained to a hot-water radiator, and a smell of boiled cabbage. He turned a key and opened the inner door.

"Third floor," he said. "Hope you're in shape."

The cabbage-eaters lived on the second floor as did the baby, who was being screamed at and was screaming, and as did some older children. Copeland led her through a confusion of tricycles and pedal-cars and galoshes. Jennifer had felt a dark of disappointment as they had entered upon the street and it deepened as they mounted the steep stairway to the third floor. He was awkward with the key in the gloom. Then he got it and swung wide the door and moved aside so she could step into the doorframe.

Fairyland! Midtown Manhattan agleam and framed behind glass. An entire wall dappled with thousands of random patches of amber and white, glowing spires and shadowy rectangles on a field of deepest blue; even the winking red and green running-lights of a jet traversing. Jennifer caught her breath and looked about. The room suggested the set of a Broadway play. A dozen pendulous plants hung at different levels, softening the frame of the window.

A sprawling corduroy sofa slumped on deep shag broadloom. A palette of pillows was strewn in a heap. A chess table crouched between twin camel saddles. A sheepskin was thrown over a love-seat, and a Himalayan cat, his face like an owl's, rose from it, stretched, and bearing his tail like a banner sauntered toward them. When Copeland flipped a switch, Jennifer saw a run of thea-ter spotlights hanging from a track mounted on the ceiling, emphasizing areas of the room and picking out two huge can-vasses on the end walls.

"A seduction center," she gasped, and then added with a short laugh, "This is a side of Copeland Jackson I hadn't imagined."

"Not guilty," he said. "Belongs to a friend of mine . . . "

"Joe Namath?"

" . . . who was moved to Los Angeles."

"What's his line of work — white slavery?"

His voice cooled. "He's a writer. I rent from him."

The moment that had been on them had gone. Jennifer was feeling buffeted and oddly aggrieved by the swift changes her emotions had undergone in the past half hour and was irritated at herself for the jealousy she was feeling over the other women who might have been – *must* have been – here before her. Copeland was mantled with a desolation that had settled on him when Jennifer reacted to the room. He cursed himself, certain he had aborted the perfection of the evening. In the car he had envisioned Jennifer in his arms before the door of the apartment closed behind them, but now they were alien and moving apart. Jennifer took off her coat, flung it onto the floor as a matador might discard his cape and sank deep in the sofa, looking about. Copeland hung her coat and his on an antique clothestree by the door and went to a small bar.

"A brandy?"

"Okay," she said indifferently.

As he busied himself, she rose and went to the window to stand, legs apart, looking at the city. "Tell me about your friend the writer," she said, putting an unnecessary emphasis on the word.

Damn his friend and damn his apartment and damn her mood – and his own! But there was a gulf to be crossed and he started across it tentatively, making his voice easy, casual.

"He writes advertising copy. Very good at it, I'm told. He found this place, tore out the wall and brought in a designer, a boyfriend, and . . . " He encompassed the room with a sweep of his hand. "This is the result."

She turned from the window but remained where she was. "It's hardly your typical cold-water walkup."

"I'm sorry," he said, concentrating on pouring the brandy. He felt depressed: perhaps there was no grace left for them tonight. He carried the glass to her and she took it without looking at him.

"I'm sorry I brought you here," he said. "I thought it would be good, but it isn't."

"No, I'm sorry," she said with a wan smile. "I don't know why I got so bitchy . . . . Yes I do; my mind was picturing other women here. It's not like me to be possessive. I'm sorry."

He would be oblique no longer. He leaned forward above her glass and put his mouth on hers. She had sipped the brandy and the raw taste on her lips and their responsiveness stirred him. "Will you make love to me?" he asked simply.

She put down her glass and put her arms about him and held him tightly, her cheek pressed hard against his chest. "Oh, Copeland, I want to. I want to," she said, but there was a tentativeness in her voice.

He tilted her chin and looked full into her eyes. "Make love to me, Jennifer," he said.

She hesitated only a moment. She unhooked a string of pearls and put them beside the drink, found the zipper on the back of her dress and with no coquettishness pulled it down. A small shrug and the dress cascaded about her feet. She was wearing a half-slip but no bra and in a moment was naked before him. He reached out and brushed his fingers over the tip of a breast. She watched him, a soft smile on her lips. He sat on the arm of the sofa. She walked between his knees and cradled his head as he buried it between her breasts.

In the bed, warm and langorous after an hour of holding and touching and exploring and loving, they lay close, Copeland on his back and Jennifer resting on an elbow, her hair forming a canopy about her face as she looked down at him.

"I *am* in love with you," he said quietly. "That's the first time I've ever said that."

She was silent, lightly brushing the palm of a hand over the hair on his chest, a slight frown on her brow.

"What's the matter?" he said.

"It's nothing," she said, and bent down to trail her lips softly across his brow. "It's just that I'm so happy."

"Don't be afraid," he said.

She lay back beside him and put a hand lightly on his thigh. They both stared at the ceiling, watching the sweep of light and shadow as cars passed in the street.

"I wonder what Uncle Michael will say when I tell him I'm in love," she said. "He's only met you, what – once?"

Rinsonelli's voice sounded as though it were coming from a stair-well, each word echoing a split second later and sometimes almost inaudible against a shifting background of contending electronic squeals.

"The negotiations are not going as well as we'd hoped," he said, speaking Italian and using the subterfuge they'd agreed upon to ensure secrecy.

Michael was alarmed at the unemotional quality of Paolo's voice. Even shouting, as he always did on long distance telephone, he sounded dispirited.

"Is there any possibility we might lose the deal?" he asked anxiously.

"Not at the moment, although yesterday it was – how do you say it? – touch and go."

"Your partners; has their diagnosis changed?"

"They're not much help. We're thinking about adding another man to the board. He's supposed to have had more experience in this kind of problem."

"I'm pleased to hear that."

There was a click and the line cleared. He could hear Rinsonelli's heavy breathing. "There's a real problem of security," he shouted. "Any premature announcement could adversely affect the shares."

"I can understand that."

"But how long can we keep it to ourselves? It's now almost three weeks and the President hasn't made any public statement. That in itself is extraordinary. It's creating speculation."

"I think you'll have to make an announcement. There'll be less conjecture if you do. I'd admit to some minor difficulty."

"I suppose . . . "

"And the sooner the better."

"Yes. Well, I'm meeting the directors later on. I'll pass on your counsel."

Chapter Two

Events were soon routine at the residence. Jennifer told Michael she was going to be married ("On June the first, the traditional blushing June bride"), and announced it that night at dinner to the congratulations of everyone present. Father Jamieson proposed a toast "To beauty and love, God's ultimate gifts"; Miss Pritchard, on being informed, sniffed and said, "I suppose it was bound to happen," but didn't stiffen or draw away when Jennifer laughed and hugged her; Harris went out the following morning and returned with a single red rose in a slender vase, placing it before Jennifer's plate at dinner that night – whereupon Jennifer kissed him on the top of his balding head and Harris colored. It was agreed that Copeland should come to dinner Sunday night and pass muster.

"In which case, we'll have the law and the prophets," Harris said dryly, to the groans of the others.

Harris had quickly settled into his own routine. He rose early to shower and shave, and while the others were at mass, ate breakfast. He was at work in the room in the basement by eight and seldom emerged, except for lunch, until it was time to wash up for dinner. Irregularly, he would appear at the top of the stairs leading to the kitchen, sometimes startling Hulda and Jeannie, the maids who came in daily – he padded about silently in bedroom slippers – to go to the refrigerator for some fruit or juice with which to maintain his blood sugar level. He never spoke except to complain if the fruit was pulpy or the skin blemished, and having prepared it at the table would untidily leave the peelings and the knife there. Miss Pritchard resented his daily excursions through her kitchen and each day would recite a litany of new complaints to Mrs. O'Donahue, with particular emphasis on the trouble she was put to to prepare Harris's special meals and his lack of gratitude for such.

Michael was busier than normal, conferring daily with selected groups, preparing the annual archdiocesan financial appeal. A custom soon established itself: nightly, in the late evening, Harris would go to the study where Michael would be finishing his day's work and they would have a nightcap and talk. It was a pleasant time and Michael looked forward to it. It was an opportunity to put away that day's particular problems and to bring himself abreast of the progress Harris was making. The work was going slowly; it had taken a week to establish a constant temperature and an ideal humidity, but now with those problems solved, Harris was buoyant.

Patrolman Arnie Knudsen, badge No. 13-725, twenty-two years old and only eighteen months a member of New York's Finest, was nervous and perspiring. As he had told his mates the night before, "I'd rather do a week on single-patrol in Harlem than go to this thing. Christ almighty, he's next to the pope!" Arnie was one of five policemen of various ranks who, with three firemen, had been invited to the cardinal's residence to be honored by His Eminence Michael Cardinal Maloney and His Honor the Mayor, Moses H. Deegan, having been cited "for conspicuous and extraordinary bravery in the performance of his duty."

Somehow Arnie seemed not to fit the role. It may have been that at the moment his fair skin was paler than usual or that the sharp angular face, emphasized by ears that were abnormally large and jutted at right angles from his crewcut head, was beardless. It may have been the bleached blue eyes fringed with spikey white lashes, or the way the narrow shoulders seemed to slope directly from the head. Whatever, in uniform Arnie looked like an imposter: like an actor in a rented costume in a church basement play. Certainly he didn't look the hero.

Yet here he was in the main reception room at the cardinals' residence about to receive his third decoration in less than a year, this one for venturing four times into a blazing apartment building to bring out in sequence two children, a baby and a ninety-year-old woman; she in a nightdress, slung over his shoulder in much the way he used to tote hundred-pound sacks of seed grain on his father's farm outside Charlotte. Here he was, front page hero of the *Daily News*, nominee for Policeman of the Year, trembling in the legs and stammering in conversation with Cardinal Maloney.

In truth, he didn't have Michael's undivided attention. Beyond Arnie, through the lace curtains, Michael had seen a white panel truck draw to a stop on Fiftieth Street at the rear entrance to the residence. The truck bore on its side the inscription, THE 7 SANTINI BROTHERS and he knew they were specialists in transporting objects of art. He had also seen Harris, who must have been waiting, suddenly appear and approach the truck as it was being jockeyed to the curb.

"They tell me, Officer Knudsen," Michael was saying, "this is the third time you've been cited for heroism."

"Yes, Your Eminence."

Harris and the driver had now moved to the back of the truck. The driver swung open both rear doors and latched them. Harris stood watching, hands on hips. He must be cold, Michael thought; in shirtsleeves and without a jacket.

"I'm told you're a Catholic?"

"Yes, Father."

"Which parish?

"Precious Blood, Father."

"I'm correct in my understanding, am I not, that you helped some people from a burning building!"

"Yes, Father."

A police officer had come by and was standing twirling his nightstick. Harris was talking animatedly and pointing toward the back entrance to the residence. The driver was standing with a hand on one of the open doors of the truck as though to convey his willingness to close it and move off.

"The other decorations: were they for the same kind of rescue operations?"

"No, sir. Each was different, sir. I mean, Your Eminence."

The officer said something to Harris who nodded his head perhaps a dozen times; then he pointed with his nightstick at the truck and at the driver and sauntered off. Harris went to the back of the truck and leaned in.

"Tell me about them."

"It was really nothin', Your Eminence."

"Why don't you tell me anyway?"

Harris stepped back, pointing. The driver reached in and slid a wooden box to the edge of the truck floor. It was clear that Harris was offering to help carry the box and that the driver was refusing. He picked it up easily, crossed the sidewalk and placed it on the three foot high flagstone wall that retained the ground-cover and shrubbery surrounding the residence and cathedral, and then returned to the truck to close the rear doors. Harris went to the box and placed a hand on it.

"Well, Your Eminence, there was this time on the east side. There was this guy, this suspect, who had flipped out and was on top of a roof firin' a rifle, and I proceeded to apprehend him. The other time was, like, there was this junkie . . . excuse me, Father – I mean, Your Eminence – this narcotics suspect. On the IRT it was. Anyways, he was brandishin' a knife in a threatenin' manner and I—"

"Excuse me," Michael said and went to the window. He stood so he could see past the edge of the curtain but not be seen. The box was smaller than he'd imagined. He studied it: a very ordinary unpainted wood box with metal strapping around it, resting there in the brilliant sunlight. When the driver returned to pick it up, carrying it against his chest, it didn't seem heavy. Michael watched him as long as he was in view and then returned to Officer Knudsen.

"I must apologize," he said, "but there was a matter of importance. Now if you'll come with me I'll introduce you to his Honor the Mayor. I believe he has a presentation to make . . . "

"That's a particular conceit of Christians," Harris said, jetting a stream of cigar smoke at the chandelier. "Crucifixion wasn't invented by the Romans for Jesus; they crucified thousands of Jews before and after him. Any crime against the state. There were mass crucifixions during the revolt against the census and again during the Jewish revolt in 70 A.D."

He was in an expansive mood and had become the pedant at ease in his specialty, enjoying being the focus of attention. "As a matter of fact," he continued, "the Romans didn't even originate crucifixion. They probably borrowed it from the Phoenicians; it was part of their law—"

Copeland interrrupted: "Their capital punishment?"

Harris looked at him from the corners of narrowed eyes. "The voice of the lawman," he said. "No, I don't think you can compare their way and ours. We try to be reasonably humane when we do official murder but they were as brutal as possible short of individual torture. We're undecided as to whether capital punishment is a deterrent but the Romans had no doubts on that score. Crucifixion was their way of saying as graphically as possible, 'Crime doesn't pay.' They flogged the poor beggar first, then they tied or nailed him to a cross and set it up beside the busiest thoroughfare. It was an exceedingly cruel death, took hours, even days, and every moment of it, including breaking the victim's legs so he couldn't support his weight, was designed to say in unmistakable terms, 'Have a care, troublemaker, this could be you!' "

"Some were tied to the cross?" Copeland asked.

"Some of the ancient sources suggest that," Harris said. "We also know they used three types of cross: one in the shape of a T, the so-called *tau* cross, another in the form of an X, what we now call the St. Andrew's cross, and the Latin cross, the type on which Jesus was crucified."

"How do you know it was a Latin cross?" Michael asked.

Harris shrugged. "It's the only reasonable conclusion. The New Testament says a superscription was posted above his head; that wouldn't be possible on either the *tau* cross or the St. Andrew's."

Jennifer broke in. "A few minutes ago you said they'd found the bones of a man who actually was crucified. Can you tell us more about him?"

Harris smiled at her. "What do you want to know?"

"Well, for instance, where did they dig him up?"

"In Jerusalem."

"When?"

"The spring of 1972."

"Do they know when he lived?"

"Yes. The time has been pretty reliably fixed as between the beginning of the first century and approximately 30 A.D."

"That's almost exactly when Jesus was here on earth."

"Yes."

There was wonder in Jennifer's voice. "Is it possible he was one of the disciples?"

Harris smiled. "That requires too great a leap of faith for me," he said amiably. "Let's say it's not impossible, but it's highly unlikely."

Copeland interjected. "I remember reading something about it."

"Yes. A *Time* reporter based in Jerusalem, name of Levine, heard about the find and talked to the people at the Rockefeller Museum who had examined the bones. Wrote a piece on it. There was some pretty wild-eyed speculation at the time that it might be Jesus."

"There isn't any possibility he could be?" Jennifer asked, her voice very small.

"None whatsoever," Harris said flatly.

"Because Jesus rose from the grave," Michael said as flatly.

"No, *not* for that reason," Harris said, turning to look at Michael, "but because there is evidence to the contrary . . . which we won't go into at the moment." He returned to Jennifer. "Beyond that, are you prepared to think of your Lord or any of his apostles as being deformed and having a cleft palate? This man had both."

There was silence. Harris sipped his drink. Jennifer said with great seriousness, "Tell us the rest. There *is* more?"

"A great deal more," Harris said. "But it's a pretty grisly business. Hardly the subject for a dinner table at which we're celebrating such a happy event. Afterwards, if you wish."

The four of them were lingering at the table after a late dinner in celebration of Copeland's and Jennifer's engagement. Copeland had come to the table tense. It was the first time he'd been in Michael's presence for an extended period of time and it was his first meeting with Harris. Jennifer had stimulated his curiosity by telling him about the coming of the archaeologist to the residence and he'd been looking forward to meeting him. To his precise investigator's mind the arrangement seemed odd. Why was a man of Dr. Gordon's eminence working in the basement of the residence where conditions would be anything but ideal? Why the secrecy surrounding the project? And why, in a house occupied only by clergymen, Jennifer and Miss Pritchard, had he taken the precaution of installing a second lock on the door to his workroom?

Jennifer had regaled him with stories of how Miss Pritchard's nose had been out of joint since Harris had moved in: how she resented the fact that the basement room ("my root-cellar") was now barred to her and how, when she had gone to Harris with an offer to clean the room once a week, she had been dismissed with a curt no. All of this had not only infuriated her but had served to goad her curiosity. Jennifer merrily depicted the housekeeper doggedly trying to learn what was going on in the room.

"I can just see her," she laughed, "waiting like a cat at a mouse hole until she's sure he'd gone out and then putting her eye to the keyhole only to find it's been covered." The picture amused her greatly. "She thinks she owns the place, you know," she said with affection in her voice. "She regards the rest of us as transients; you can imagine how she sees him."

"But haven't you ever wondered what he does in there?" Copeland asked.

She shook her head. "I gather he's writing a book."

Copeland's curiosity had been sufficiently stimulated to send him to the pages of *Who's Who*. He found nothing unexpected. The condensed data delineated a man whose brilliance as an archaeologist had brought him eminence in the academic world, memberships in learned societies, two honorary doctorates and numerous honors. He was the author of two books and a contributor to various journals. He had been married three times and the issue of those marriages were seven. The final notation showed him Chairman of the Department of Oriental Studies (Emeritus) in the Faculty of Archaeology at Albright University in Philadelphia. Strange, Copeland thought. Why, if he was doing a book, hadn't he returned to Albright? Or to his home? Why had he chosen to toil in a dismal basement with no immediate access to reference materials? And why had Michael invited him – for all the fact they had once been classmates? The whole thing didn't add up.

Puzzling about it while shaving in preparation for the dinner, Copeland had looked in the mirror, smiled at his reflection and said aloud, "Always the gumshoe."

But those questions were far from the forefront of his mind at the moment. Harris was an engaging dinner companion: a sophisticated man of eclectic interests, an engrossing conversationalist, the possessor of a dry wit and given to teasing. As the meal began he had been quiet and withdrawn, but the glass of wine he'd sipped at had relaxed him and loosed his inhibitions and his tongue. As a bottle of champagne was opened, he rose to propose a toast and went on for five minutes, telling two hilarious stories, both bordering on the risque, and ending by saying, "For all the fact that I hold not the slightest hope for the institution of marriage, perhaps these we toast tonight will change my mind." He raised his glass. "This is my wish for both of you: May your days be long and your troubles short. May none of your children be either clerics or academics. May the groom keep his waistline, his hair and his virtue – the last being an unlikely possibility, working as he does for our present District Attorney." He addressed himself to Jennifer and his face softened. "And may the bride remain the incarnation of ineffable loveliness and charm she is this night."

Copeland was about to rise in response but Jennifer touched his arm and said quickly, "No, let me," and with affection in her voice said felicitous words about how pleased they all were that Harris had come "to join our family."

Copeland was interested to observe the relationship between the two men. In his contacts with Michael he had seen him treated with a deference that was more often than not obsequiousness, and had not yet himself learned to be at ease in the churchman's presence. But Harris was anything but intimidated. As the meal progressed he twitted Michael at every opportunity, made small jokes at his expense, and over coffee recounted a hilarious story about an escapade in which he and Michael had been involved during their undergraduate years. Michael obviously enjoyed the telling. He chuckled at the memory of the prank and listened with his face animated, interjecting chidingly from time to time, "Now that part I *don't* remember," or calling out in feigned rebuke, "Harris . . . *really!*" But at the climax of the story he threw his head back and loosed a great bellow of laughter, and for the next few minutes shook with intermittent inner chuckling.

After dinner, in the sitting room, with a fire licking lazily at some logs, it was Michael who returned the conversation to the man who had been crucified.

"It's a sad story," Harris said after a long pause. "The poor wretch was cursed before he was born, cursed in his lifetime, and cursed again at his death."

He was obviously feeling his liquor but it was not affecting his mind and only occasionally his articulation. It did evidence itself in a courtliness of manner when he spoke to Jennifer and in an occasional waspishness when interrupted by others. He made a small ritual of the lighting of a cigar. Then, floating a nimbus, he began:

"In the spring of 1968 the Israel Ministry of Housing was doing some excavating in Jerusalem and chanced on a number of Jewish tombs in the *Giv'at ha-Mitvar* section. There were nine in all, family tombs mostly, and pretty well typical of others found in the area; small caves cut in the soft limestone common to the district." He drew deeply on the cigar. "Perhaps I'd better explain something of the burial habits of the Jews of that period. When a member of a family died, the body was anointed with herbs and spices – not least to cover the smell – wrapped in a shroud and placed in a tomb for about a year, by which time the flesh would be pretty well decomposed and the bones clean. The tombs were essentially caves. They tended to have an entrance that was little more than a hole. The entrance led to a burial chamber, which was a roughly rectangular room with a trench or pit in the center. The function of the pit was to let you stand upright. Leading from the central chamber were loculi, short tunnels, in which bodies or ossuaries were stored . . . "

He held up a hand to forestall a question from Jennifer. "I'll explain," he said, smiling. "I wish all my students were as zealous." As he continued, it was clear that at times he was back in the classroom: his gaze would rise to the ceiling, his eyes would glaze as though he were reading notes off the back of them, and his voice would take on the formal tone of the lecturer.

"To elucidate," he continued. "An ossuary is a small, rectangular box carved from limestone or, occasionally, formed from clay. In some, the workmanship is very fine – it was a genuine craft; they have a polished finish and elaborate decorations ranging from rosettes inscribed within circles to stylized palm trees, and so on. The designs undoubtedly had something to do with their beliefs about the afterlife.

"These ossuaries were used as receptacles for the bones of the dead. They would take the denuded bones and place them carefully in the box, sometimes one skeleton to an ossuary, sometimes many, and then go through a reburial ceremony. Not all Jewish families could afford them, of course, in which case the bones were gathered in a common pit . . . sometimes pretty indiscriminately.

"These tiny caskets are very important. It's generally agreed that they weren't in use before 50 B.C. and we know they weren't used after the burning of Jerusalem in 70 A.D., so you can see how they help us date what we find."

He puffed on the cigar a moment. "You may think I'm going into too much detail, but there's a reason." He turned to Jennifer. "To speak to the question you asked earlier: It's because of the data I've just mentioned, in part, that we're able to say with reasonable certainty, Yes, our man lived at the same time Jesus did, and living in Jerusalem may very well have seen him and heard him preach."

Copeland broke in: "But how do you know he was crucified?"

Harris arched an eyebrow and peered at Copeland. "I'll get to that shortly," he said, "and perhaps you'll learn that we archaeologists are up to the best of your boys in the forensic labs."

He fixed his eyes on the ceiling again and Copeland decided that it was an *aide memoire*. "There were thirty-five skeletons in all, some of whom had died violently. One had been burned to death. Another bore wounds inflicted by a mace. Another had been wounded by an arrow. Three had died of starvation. In one case, a woman had died in childbirth; the head of the foetus was already engaged. It's evident that she died for want of a midwife because the pelvic passage was adequate." Jennifer shivered involuntarily. "It was a cruel time," Harris said, "and life was cheap."

"The crucified man," Michael prompted.

"Ah yes, Michael, you would want to know about the crucified man. His bones were in an ossuary with the bones of a child of three or four of undetermined sex. He was between twenty-four and twenty-eight years old and was 167 centimeters tall; that's about five feet seven, average for Mediterranean people at that time. He had a slender body and his bones reveal that he'd never done heavy physical work. He'd been healthy; there were no signs of nutritional deficiency or disease. He had no dental caries and had all his teeth except for the upper right canine which was missing congenitally. The vertebrae were well developed and showed no deformation. The bones were straight and firmly built. Professor Haas, of the Department of Anatomy at the Hebrew University, summed up his physique succinctly. He said, 'The young man, whoever he was, especially in motion, would have had a graceful, almost feminine allure.' Dr. Haas said he was reminded of the Hellenistic ideal, *ephebe*."

He paused to sip at his drink. The room was silent, the others seeing in their imaginations this graceful young man striding the streets of the ancient city, perhaps joining the crowd pressing about Jesus.

"So much for his body," Harris said, putting aside his drink. "His head was another matter. As I mentioned earlier, he had a cleft palate. He also had a misshapen head as a result of serious difficulties at parturation—"

"Birth?" asked Jennifer.

"Birth. Now, as I understand it, a palatal cleft is not the result of genetic factors but of environmental ones: namely, some dramatic and critical circumstance in the life of the mother during the first two or three weeks of pregnancy. It can result from many things: a sudden deterioration in the mother's diet, or severe mental distress, for instance. You find palatal cleft more frequently among the underprivileged where there's a greater likelihood of serious undernourishment. But that wouldn't be the case here because, as I said, there was no evidence that his diet was inadequate nor any indication that he had to work as a laborer. It's not unreasonable to conclude that he was the child of a relatively well-to-do family whose mother suffered some – how shall I put it? – traumatic event in her life immediately after becoming pregnant. I leave it to you to imagine what that event might have been."

"Fascinating," breathed Jennifer.

"Yes, isn't it," Harris said in an almost proprietory manner. "As for our man's head," he continued, "I'm afraid it was not prepossessing. It was asymmetrical, as though it had been pushed to the left and upward. The forehead was slightly flattened on the right side. The overall shape of the skull was pentagonoidal – five-faceted – with the back of the skull somewhat triangular. The entire jawbone was drifted slightly to the right." He breathed deeply. "Decidedly, not an attractive face."

"The crucifixion?" Michael said. "What's the proof he was crucified?"

Harris turned to look at him. "Patience, Mike," he chided. "Believe it or not, I've come to that part of the story.

"It was the last thing the investigators were expecting. They'd come to the calcanean bones, the heel bones, which were at the bottom of the ossuary. At first they mistook them for a single bone – they were entirely covered with a thick calcareous crust – but then they saw something that quite literally startled them: a nail, an iron nail with a bent tip! Despite the crust you could make it out quite clearly. It had been driven right through the two heel bones and out the other side. You can imagine their reaction."

He paused for a sip of his drink. No one had a mind to interrupt; each waited for him to continue.

"They faced a problem, however. Before they could investigate further it was imperative that they dehydrate and clean and impregnate the entire mass in order to preserve it, it was in that precarious a condition. Also, they had to get special permission from the government to extend the time before reburial. When finally they were able to do a thorough examination, they discovered a most extraordinary thing. They'd presumed – once they knew they had before them a case of death by crucifixion – that the feet would have been nailed to the cross in what might be described as an open position. Like this . . . " He placed his feet on the floor, the heels overlapping and the toes pointing outward. "It was a natural assumption, many artists have depicted it that way. But it soon became clear that this wasn't what had happened. There was a small piece of acacia wood between the head of the nail and the heel bones. The astonishing thing they discovered was that the heel bones had been nailed together with their medial surfaces laid adjacent . . . Let me explain: nailed together as they would be if the feet were side by side. Like this." He demonstrated. "It was obvious that what the Romans had done to the poor fellow was to place him on his right side on the upright member of the cross, probably while it was still on the ground, get a nail started through the piece of wood, hold his feet together and drive the nail through his heels into the wood of the upright. Unfortunately, after the nail entered the upright, which was made of olive wood, it struck a knot and the tip was bent back. Nevertheless, it was in sufficiently to hold.

"There was another surprise. It has always been presumed that in crucifixion the nails are driven through the hands. That assumption derived undoubtedly from the New Testament accounts of Jesus' crucifixion in which the nails were indeed driven through the palms of the hands." He glanced at Michael and their eyes held for a moment. "However, in the case of the poor wretch we're discussing such was not the case. With his legs bent to the side, they twisted his body around and drove the nails into the crosspiece through his forearms, between the radial bones, just above the wrists. There was the mark of the nail on the right radius.

"It's generally agreed that the Romans used a *sedecula* – the word means, literally, a cliff edge – a crude seat fastened to the upright in advance. It was no more than a perch for the buttocks, but it gave the victim some support. It prevented his collapse and therefore prolonged the agony. In the case of our man, it seems evident, his feet being attached insecurely with the bent nail and his legs turned to the side, that they would have had to improvise a special kind of *sedecula* if he were to rest anything but one buttock on it. An exceedingly uncomfortable position, as you can imagine."

"The poor man," Jennifer said, her eyes wet.

"The rest is pretty grim," Harris said. "Are you sure you want to hear it?" The others looked at Jennifer. She nodded, blinking back the tears.

"As was the custom, the victim's legs were broken between the knee and the ankle. Our man's left leg was brutally fractured into large sharp slivers as a result of a blow with some kind of club. The right tibia and fibula, however, were snapped on a single oblique line. What happened, obviously, is that someone struck a single, strong blow. The blow shattered the bones of the left leg, the one actually struck, and the other snapped cleanly against the edge of the upright beam of the cross. Among other things, this confirms that his knees were flexed and turned to the side.

"When the man was dead and they began to remove the body, the bent nail I mentioned earlier presented problems. They would have had no difficulty tearing the arms loose, but the tip of the nail driven through the heels was hooked into the wood of the upright and they couldn't free the feet. What they did, I'm afraid, was to chop off his feet with an ax and remove them separately. There's an almost horizontal sectional cut on the left talus."

"The poor, poor man," Jennifer said, her eyes brimming. Copeland placed an arm about her shoulder. Michael produced a handkerchief and blew his nose noisily.

"I'm sorry," Harris said. "But do remember that this happened some two thousand years ago and that thousands were killed the same way."

Jennifer dabbed at her nose with a piece of lace. "It's just that I can see him: all alone, with his pathetic, twisted face, cursed, as you said, from before he was born."

Michael cleared his throat and said softly. "I was thinking of Our Lord. I've meditated on and preached about his sufferings so many times, but what you've been telling us about this man has made it all the more clear."

"At least they both had friends who loved them," Harris said.

"How do you know that?" Jennifer asked.

"Well, we know about Jesus' friends, of course, and the man we've been talking about must have been loved, too. Remember that his bones were buried in an ossuary. There were dried flowers in that ossuary and dark brown stains at all the points where the bones were broken. We're reasonably sure that such stains are the result of a ritual anointing of bones before they're reburied. Obviously, somebody cared for him."

Chapter Three

Michael was at his desk. There was a peremptory knock on the door. Before he could respond, it opened and a pale and agitated Miss Pritchard said, "I think you'd better come quickly. Dr. Gordon isn't himself."

"Where is he?"

"In the kitchen."

As they went, Miss Pritchard trotted behind, words tumbling out. "I'm just startin' dinner and I hear him comin' up from the basement. Like always, I say, 'Good afternoon, Dr. Gordon.' You know, not lookin' round. He don't answer, but then I'm used to that. Then Jeannie lets out a kind of gasp and I turn round and there he is . . . . Just standin' there white as a sheet, leanin' against the wall and actin' kind of . . . like he's drunk or somethin' . . . "

They entered the kitchen. Harris was seated at the table, slumped forward, head on his forearms, one leg at an awkward angle. Jeannie and Hulda were standing against the wall, obviously frightened. On the floor was a small white cardboard box. Michael went to Harris and bent over him. His breathing was fast and shallow and had an odd odor.

"Harris!" he said, "Harris! Are you all right?"

There was no response. He lifted Harris's head and pulled him upright in the chair. His brow was wet with perspiration and was cold. He loosened the collar of his shirt and as he did, Harris's head fell forward and lolled to the center of gravity. He raised the head again, and the eyes slowly opened, the lids seeming reluctant to lift. Then they closed again and the body slumped.

Michael struck him sharply on the cheek. "Harris, what's the matter?" The eyes fluttered. He slapped him again. "Harris. . . . Wake up! Wake up!"

Harris's eyes came open and managed a degree of focus. He tried to speak but the words were blurred. He seemed drunk. Michael sniffed at his breath; there was no scent of alcohol, only the odor he'd noticed before.

Harris's words were almost inaudible. "Glucagon . . . "

Of course! He was a diabetic. His blood sugar was in imbalance; he was going into shock.

He lowered Harris's head to the table, picked up the carton from the floor and passed it to Miss Pritchard. "Get the needle ready," he said quietly.

He bent over, picked up Harris bodily and heaved him on his back onto the kitchen table. In swift movements he loosened Harris's belt, unzipped his fly, lifted the body at the waist and with one tug pulled trousers and shorts half way down the thighs. Miss Pritchard let out the smallest squeak of dismay at the sight of Harris's crotch, the penis brown and wrinkled, nesting in the coarse graying hair above naked testicles. But she had the hypodermic prepared and when she held it out to Michael her hand was steady.

The thighs were spindly, china-white and covered with sparse dark hair. On the outsides of the thighs were the marks Michael was looking for; an area large as a spread hand, blotched with red and blue spots.

"Did you check the dosage?" he asked Miss Pritchard, elevating the needle between his eyes and the kitchen light and pressing the piston until a small jet leaped from the tip.

"Yes," she said, her voice strong.

He bent over, found a spot on the thigh free of discoloration and shoved the needle into the muscle. He pressed the piston, withdrew the needle and massaged the area with the heel of his hand. Miss Pritchard went to a cupboard over the sink and returned with a small bottle and a tuft of absorbent cotton. She doused it with the disinfectant and swabbed the area where the injection had been made.

"Give me a hand, please," he said.

He put his arms about Harris's waist and raised him. Miss Pritchard tugged at the shorts and trousers and worked them to the waist. She pulled the zipper and buckled the belt and then reached for a towel which she folded and placed beneath Harris's head.

Within a minute Harris stirred. Color began to suffuse the gray skin of his face and after a moment his eyes slowly opened. He looked dully into Michael's face.

"You were in shock," Michael said. "We gave you a shot of glucagon. You'll be all right now."

Harris didn't respond for a minute, then he licked his dry lips with a raspy tongue. "May I have some water?" he said, his voice hoarse.

Miss Pritchard gave a quick nod of her head to a pale and frightened Jeannie and she brought a glass of water, her hand trembling violently. While Michael raised his head, Harris sipped at the water. His eyes were brighter now and the drowsiness was retreating.

"How do you feel?" Michael asked.

Harris looked at him vaguely for a moment and then said, "What a pity. I was having such a nice sleep."

Michael had not been back at his desk half an hour before there was a tap at the door and Harris entered. "This is your day for interruptions," he said, a sheepish grin playing at the corners of his mouth. "I'm not in the mood to work. How's about I bother you?"

"Why not?" Michael said. "My concentration's not all that good either. How are you feeling?"

"Fine," Harris said, "Fine. I'm a tough little bastard. Probably outlive the bunch of you."

He went to sit down. "Just before you get settled there," Michael said, "how'd you like to come with me over to the cathedral? I've got to have a word with the rector. Have you ever been?"

"Wouldn't want the roof to fall in."

"I'll chance that," Michael said.

While Michael discussed some arrangements for Jennifer's wedding, Harris wandered about. Michael found him standing in an aisle looking up at the great marble pulpit. As he joined him Harris said, "I was just imagining you up there in all your glory."

"Doesn't happen very often. I don't preach here more than three or four times a year, if that."

"It would intimidate me," Harris said, looking back at the nave. "This place filled with people. Me telling them how they should live . . ."

"It intimidates me," Michael said.

On their way toward the passageway joining the cathedral and the residence, Harris noticed a broad marble staircase leading to below the chapel, and opposite it another to beneath the altar. "What's down there?" he asked.

"The crypt on the left and the sacristy on the right– where we put on our vestments."

"Who's buried in the crypt?"

"My predecessors."

"That's where they'll stash you?"

Michael smiled. "That's where they'll stash me."

Harris was bending, craning. "Would you like to have a look?" Michael asked.

"Yes," Harris said, "I would."

The custodian had been hovering nearby. When Michael nodded to him he came, removed a brocaded rope barring access to the altar, and at the head of the stairs, unlocked the heavily barred gate. The cathedral had been cool; the crypt was cold and Harris shivered. Their footsteps resonated and echoed against the marble floors and walls. Ranged against the walls were marble sarcophagi, each different, each with candles flickering before it.

Harris walked slowly, reading the inscriptions. He returned to Michael who had remained at the foot of the stairs. "Do you come here often?" he asked.

Michael shook his head. "No."

"You should. It'd remind you that you're mortal."

"My vocation never let's me forget that."

"Where will they put you?"

Michael pointed. "Over there, I presume."

"Doesn't it give you a funny feeling to know where you're going to be for the next few hundred years?"

"It did the first time I came here." He paused. "You must remember that only my body will be here. I won't."

"Here cometh the sermon," Harris said.

"No, don't worry. But I wouldn't be faithful either to my calling or to you if I didn't remind you that you were pretty close to the edge this afternoon."

"Not to the edge," Harris said. "To the end."

When they returned to the residence Harris followed Michael to the study and, uninvited, sat down. He seemed in need of conversation. Michael rang Miss Pritchard for coffee and they talked.

Harris, smiling tightly, said, "I took a look at your crypt; how'd you like to take a look at mine?"

"I don't understand."

"In the basement."

Michael said, "Oh," and then added, "No, I don't think so."

Harris studied him, still smiling his tight smile. "You surprise me," he said. "I'd have thought you'd be dying to have a look."

"Why?"

"If for no other reason, curiosity."

"Well, perhaps one of these days."

Harris was silent for a moment. "You really don't believe they're Jesus' bones, do you?"

"To be blunt – no."

Harris's voice was quiet, reasonable. "But Mike, they *are*."

There was some impatience in Michael's response. "Harris, you'll forgive me, but you don't know that for sure. The bones you found depend for their authentication on the manuscript you found, and I know enough about antiquities of that sort to know how often they are forged. Around the end of the last century the British Museum paid a man by the name of Shapiro a very large sum of money for a scroll purporting to be the Old Testament book, Deuteronomy, and supposedly more than two thousand years old. Shapiro thought it was. So did a lot of the experts who examined it. It was later shown to be a forgery. You know how many forgeries are sold to dealers in antiquities. You know how many scrolls were trotted out by the Bedouins after the discoveries at Qumran."

"But I didn't get my manuscript from a dealer or from some Bedouin out for a fast buck. I found it myself."

"You found it, yes. The question is; who put it there?"

"The man whose signature it bears; Shimon ben Yehuda."

"His name may be there, I won't debate that, but is it his signature?"

"There's no reason to doubt it."

"But why have you taken no steps to authenticate the dating?"

"Michael," Harris said patiently, "you must realize what would happen if word got out of what I've discovered. We'd be besieged."

"I realize that. But you wouldn't have to specify precisely what it is you're seeking to authenticate. Why, for instance, haven't you submitted the material to the carbon-14 dating process?"

"Because it's impractical and because it's unnecessary."

"Why is it impractical?"

"Because the process requires a substantial amount of material and the material is destroyed in the testing. Would you want me to destroy part of the manuscript? If so, which part? Most of the bottom edge is gone, as is some of the upper. What was originally the end of the scroll is badly deteriorated and the inner edge has scarcely any margin. I daren't destroy part of the text." He looked at Michael, challenge in his eyes. "And surely, on the presumption, even the possibility that they are Jesus' bones, you wouldn't want to see part of the skeleton destroyed. What did the Psalmist say? 'Not a bone of his will be broken . . . ' " He quoted the prophecy in a thin, slightly mocking voice.

"Then you'll never know for sure."

"I know for sure now. Face it: what was unearthed in Jerusalem was unquestionably a first-century Jewish tomb. The Israel Department of Antiquities has established that beyond question. The carbon-14 system would merely confirm what we know."

"But that empty ossuary – the one you say contained Jesus' bones before they were transferred to Qumran – it could have been placed in the tomb at a later date."

Harris shook his head slowly and exaggeratedly. "Afraid not. It was made of the same type of limestone as the others. Same craftsman, same rosette design on the face. And in it, remember, I found the molar that fitted the skull at Qumran."

Michael sat, slumped, interlacing his fingers, regarding them gravely. "I can't argue it with you, Harris. I get out of my depth. But the whole thing taxes credulity. Thousands of people were crucified back there – I checked into it yesterday: fifty thousand Palestinians alone – yet in all history the bones of only two men bearing evidence of having been crucified have been discovered. Only two. And you claim that one of them, the one you have downstairs, is Jesus of Nazareth. It argues a coincidence that's simply incredible."

"Not really. People have been finding artifacts in the Holy Land for centuries, but scientific archaeology has been going on there for only the past three-quarters of a century. There are new finds all the time. Who knows what will be unearthed tomorrow?"

Harris had been rubbing a palm against his chest as he talked, massaging it. Now he grimaced. His skin was gray and he suddenly looked very old.

"You may never get to publish your findings," Michael said.

"Why not?"

"That heart of yours."

Harris smiled thinly. "Are you suggesting God may strike me dead?"

"Have you seen a doctor?"

"Your doctor. Dr. Raymond."

"And?"

"Says it's angina. Gave me some pills." He reached into his shirt pocket and took out a tiny silver pill box. "Glycerine, I think."

He popped open the pill box and placed a tiny round pill under his tongue. In the quiet of the room Michael could hear a rumbling from his stomach.

"There's a question I should ask you," he said.

"Yes?"

"You're a realist: in the unlikely event that your heart should, uh . . ."

"Stop."

"In that event, what do I do with the manuscript, your notes and the skeleton?"

"I've decided to leave it all to the Rockefeller Museum in Jerusalem. It'll end up there anyway."

"Have you notified them?"

Harris gave a short laugh. "And have the law on me? Mike, old boy, I've told no one in the world but you. One whisper about what's downstairs and they'd be buzzing around here like flies: the press, the police . . . you name it. What was it Jesus said? – 'Where the carcass is, there will the vultures be also.' No, everything's to go to the Rockefeller except for my monograph and the pictures

I've taken. They go to Harper and Row; they published my other stuff." He glanced quickly at Michael. "You don't mind me leaving it with you?"

"No."

"Thanks."

"How do you know you can trust me?"

"I'm not worried."

Both retreated into their thoughts. A dying ember in the fire gave a sudden pop, flared a brief bright flame and died. "Perhaps you should be," Michael said. "Have you thought about the harm that will be done if you publish that book of yours?

"To the Roman Catholic church?"

"To the church and to people. Little people. Simple people. Defenseless people. Vulnerable people . . ."

"I've thought about it. But what would you have me do? You're committed to God and truth – right? Well, I have my own kind of commitment. Would you want me to betray my truth?"

To his surprise Michael heard himself saying, "What is truth ?" He added quickly, "It's doing the will of God."

That night, abed, Michael threshed about far from sleep. What would he do – what *should* he do – with the skeleton and the scroll if by chance Harris died before his work was finished? With their potential to damage the church and maim the faith of so many, should he be the instrument to place them in the hands of those who might exploit them? But dare he take it on himself to withhold the discovery from the world? Did he have any option but to do what he had been asked to do, and leave the judgment to responsible people? Surely then the truth would come out. To fail to do so – would that not be a betrayal of a trust?

But what assurance was there that those involved would act responsibly? He had no illusions about the objectivity or the infallibility of scientists. He remembered the sharp divisions among men of equal eminence over the Dead Sea Scrolls when they were first discovered. Was there a hypothesis that someone of prominence didn't advance and argue? Could he in good conscience put such a volatile issue in the hands of men who too often were motivated by intellectual pride or by a thirst for notoriety or by a love of controversy – even by the desire to buttress a pet theory?

What if Harris had died this afternoon, his work hardly begun? What if he had not been in his study at the time, or had not known what to do in the emergency? What would have happened then? The matter would have passed from his hands. The bones and the scroll and Harris's notes would have become part of his estate, and fall, after the law's delays, into the hands of his wife – whoever and wherever she was.

He slipped from his bed and knelt at the prie-dieu. "Holy Mother of God . . . "

They had been at Copeland's apartment where they had played house. She had made a salad while he broiled steaks and steamed some vegetables. They had finished a bottle of wine together and had laughed a lot and had made love on the sofa and on the mound of cushions and now, closing on midnight, were in his car returning her home. The night was rude and filled with February bluster, howling and hurling hail about in fitful tantrums. Jennifer had been chilled after the walk to his parking slot beneath the East River Drive, but now the heater had routed the cold and he touched a switch to diminish its roar. Neither had said anything for a dozen blocks.

Jennifer bunted a shoulder into his and wedged it there. There was a pervasive glow of happiness on her. "Mr. Jackson, sir," she said dreamily, "you are a beautiful lover."

He twisted sideways and kissed the crown of her head. They went on in silence for a few blocks and stopped for a light. "How's Dr. Gordon's work going?" he asked.

Jennifer was back at the apartment and answered vaguely, "Fine."

"Has he said what he's working on?" he asked, not quite casually.

Her mind was still away. "Hasn't said a word."

"Doesn't it seem strange to you that he doesn't talk about what he's up to in that basement room of his?"

Jennifer realized that he wasn't just making conversation so she gave attention. She'd learned that he was given to mulling silently over problems, and afterwards often made notes in a tight, precise script. She sometimes called him, "Mr. Meticulous."

"Doesn't seem strange to me," she said. "He's a scholar. They usually don't talk about their work except with people in their field."

There was a bite in his tone. "It's been my observation that they're about the same as everybody else. Maybe a bit more neurotic."

No, he *wasn't* just making conversation. She turned her head so she could see his face. It was in profile and light was fluctuating on it from shops and streetlights and oncoming cars. He was chewing at his lower lip. "You don't like him, do you?" she said matter-of-factly.

He dismissed that with a small shake of his head. "It's not a matter of liking or not liking," he said. "Although if you want the truth, no, I don't."

"But darling, why?"

"It isn't personal, if that's what you mean."

"But it is. It really is, and it puzzles me. I watched you the other night when he was telling that story about the man who was crucified." She snuggled again into his shoulder. "You're some detective – your expression's a dead giveaway." She sat musing for a moment. "I wonder if Uncle Michael can tell by your expression when we've been making love."

"You get a nose for these things," he persevered. "You sense it when things don't add up."

She reached up and tapped the tip of a finger on the tip of his nose. "If it takes a nose to be a good detective," she said, "you'll make chief by the weekend."

But he wasn't going to be diverted. "Seriously, Jen. If, as your uncle says, he's writing a book, why of all places in a basement?"

"I'm sure there are good reasons."

"And why two locks on the door?"

Her eyebrows arched. "How did you know there were two?"

"I just know."

She swung around and looked at him, her voice lightly chiding: "Copeland Jackson! You checked."

"Of course not."

"Uncle Michael told you?"

A trifle lamely: "I was talking to Miss Pritchard and she happened to mention it."

She let out a peal of laughter. "Oh, darling! Dear Sam's been in a snit ever since he moved in. Maybe if he'd flirt with her . . . " She glanced at him archly. "Maybe you think he flirts with me."

"Maybe I do," he said. "I'd still like to know why two locks."

She made her voice portentous. "He's a modern-day Bluebeard and the basement is littered with the bodies of ravished women." She encircled his upper arm with hers and hugged it and put her cheek against his shoulder. "Darling, what does it matter?"

"Maybe it doesn't," he said stubbornly, "but when the facts are untidy my mind starts asking questions."

His Eminence,   *February 25*
Michael Cardinal Maloney,
The Archdiocese of New York,
452 Madison Avenue,
New York City, N.Y. 10022
USA

My dear Michael:
You will undoubtedly be surprised to receive this since, as is well known, I am not much given to the writing of letters. However, of late I have little confidence in the security of the telephone system here, within and without the Vatican, and thought it the better part of wisdom to write inasmuch as I have two matters of grave import to discuss with you, matters requiring the utmost secrecy.

I shall refrain from any comment on either the weather or my health other than to state that both are execrable.

As to the health of our mutual friend, however, more needs to be said. It would be difficult to conceive of a more undesirable situation. There are days when I am buoyed with hope; there are others when I am cast down in despair. It is now ten days since last he spoke. He is no longer comatose but, it would seem, has suffered a further embolism and is bereft of speech. He now lies by the hour wide-eyed but silent and unmoving, looking – I weep as I write it – like those waxen images in museums of the famous and the infamous. It will touch you to know that among the last things he spoke was an inquiry after you. You have his heart, Michael. And, blessed be God, from somewhere, somehow, he brought us a smile.

Who can know what comes before his eyes? The doctors say he sees nothing but this does not impress me — my regard for their profession decreases in a direct relationship with the increase in my years. I believe that when he is away from us he may well be regarding the face of Almighty God. Sometimes as he lies there, a beatific expression transforms his poor wasted face — I have myself observed it on three occasions — and dare anyone deny the possibility that our Blessed Lord is in the room along with the respirators, oxygen tanks, intravenous tubing and other paraphernalia that have replaced, with dubious advantage, the leeches, plasters, purges and herbs of an earlier time.

As for the official prognosis: the only men who exceed physicians in ambiguity are ambassadors. I should like to see an escutcheon devised for medical men on which is represented an ostrich with two heads, each looking in an opposite direction, and bearing the inscription Sed in mane alia, which as you know, being translated, means, "But, on the other hand." There is no comfort in them. Their prognosis is today as it was when you were here last: "We hope for the best but are prepared for the worst."

Now to the other matter. I presume you are acquainted with a woman of the British peerage, one Lady Hambleton. She represents herself as having had an extended correspondence with your office and one meeting with you. You should be aware that she has taken the somewhat extraordinary step of addressing a letter to His Holiness in which she states that she is desirous of contributing the sum of ten million dollars toward the provision of a new children's wing at St. Clare's hospital in your archdiocese, and represents you as having rejected her offer for reasons she does not specify but does manage to suggest are trivial. A response has gone forward to her over the signature of the Papal Secretary pointing out that this is not a matter properly to be drawn to the attention of His Holiness and suggesting that she discuss it further with you. You will receive in due course a copy of her letter and of Renaldo's response.

It is not for me to comment on this rather extraordinary circumstance (it caused quite a flutter here, I might say); but I nonetheless will. I will even be so presumptuous as to suggest that if, after further discussion with the lady, you still feel constrained to reject her offer, I would be more than pleased to have you refer her to me. It is now so long since such a glittering opportunity has presented itself that I salivate at the possibility.

But to be serious. The matter poses a problem of no small consequence. Benedetti, whose lust for the Papal Throne is now such that he studies the physicians' daily bulletin with the avidity of a beggar reading the lottery numbers, is using the incident to militate against you. Not, of course, frontally — we speak of the fox, remember — but in such a way as to cast doubt on your capacity to deal skillfully with what he describes as "matters requiring a certain touch of delicacy." I overheard him yesterday in conversation with Renaldo — I am not at this stage in life above eavesdropping — clucking his tongue like a drake in heat at the possibility that such a bequest be lost to the church through inflexibility. He followed this, as one knew he would, by expatiating on the virtues of flexibility in the papacy, mentioning favorably, of course, both our ailing friend and John XXIII. He cannot do too much harm at this juncture, for the question of succession is not yet moot, but when it is before the membership of the College (as I fear it soon may be, God forbid) your Lady Hambleton may become a point of vulnerability in my quest to see you elected. It will be a particularly sensitive issue in this locus of austerity. Resolve it soon if you can, is this old man's counsel.

There are other matters but my arthritic knuckles command them to wait. I salute you across the miles in the love of Christ.

Paolo Rinsonelli

116

Chapter Four

A tap on the study door and Miss Pritchard standing there drawn up, her mouth drawn down.

"A woman to see you, Your Eminence" – her voice prim as a maiden aunt's.

He felt a quiver of impatience at being interrupted and at Miss Pritchard's demeanor. She was signaling her disapproval of something by undercommunicating and overarticulating. At such times she irritated him.

"Can't Father Jamieson or Father Carroll see her? I'm busy. What does she want?"

"She says she's Mrs. Gordon. Mrs. Harris Gordon."

"Dr. Gordon's wife?"

"So she says, Your Eminence."

"Have you told Dr. Gordon she's here?"

"He's not in. She's been here . . . " A heavy put-upon sigh. "She's been here I don't know how many times. He won't see her."

"And she wants to see me?"

"She *insists* on seeing you."

"Well then, Miss Pritchard, I suggest you bring her in."

Harris's wife . . . ! He'd never mentioned a wife in the two months since moving in and had conveyed the impression that he was a widower. Michael had a vague memory of a wife – someone he'd married soon after graduation. Yes, it was coming back now . . . an Egyptian woman. There'd been an invitation to a wedding in Cairo and a snapshot of the two of them: she dark and strikingly handsome.

But the woman at the door of the study obviously wasn't the woman of the photograph. She was in her thirties and fair-skinned. Her honey-blonde hair had been teased into an afro, her blue eyes were surrounded with blue makeup and she was wearing a tight wraparound black dress.

The announcement befitted an ambassador: "Your Eminence . . . Mrs. Dr. Harris Gordon!" (Sam, you are *such* a pain at times!)

"Will you come in?" he said cordially, moving from behind his desk to greet her.

Mrs. Gordon didn't reply but, head up, crossed the study and sat in the chair he indicated. Miss Pritchard slowly swung the door to, her eyes visible at the opening as it narrowed and closed.

Michael had a moment to study his visitor as she placed her purse on the floor beside the chair and tugged at her skirt to bring it closer to her knees. She was a pretty woman: a trifle shopworn under the makeup, self-consciously voluptuous, and as was evident in the uptilting of her chin when she first looked directly at him, feeling somewhat righteous at the moment. As their eyes met, hers shifted and seemed to focus on a spot a few inches above his head.

"You're Dr. Gordon's wife," he said tentatively.

"I certainly am," she said, as though it had just been denied.

"It's a pleasure to meet you," he said, making his voice friendly. "I'm an admirer of your husband."

There was a slight further tilting of the chin. "I'm glad you think so," she said ambiguously. "I wish I could say the same."

So that's the way it is, Michael thought, feeling awkward. "I'm sorry he's not in."

She sniffed. "He never is to me."

"Is there something I can do for you?" he said, deciding to bring her to the point of the visit.

She was looking about the study now, missing little. "There certainly is," she said, "You can tell him to look after his wife and children like he should."

Michael took the opportunity to study her as her eyes foraged about. He had no intention of getting involved in Harris's domestic affairs, but that might not be easy to avoid. The woman before him obviously had a sense of mission and was not going to be easily put off.

For want of something better to say he said, "You live here in New York?"

"I certainly do. In Queens. The five of us in two rooms you wouldn't believe. Two rooms." She then added as an exclamation point, "On the third floor." She had now taken in the subdued elegance of the study. "While he's here, free as a bird and living like a king."

Michael cleared his throat. "I hope you'll understand, Mrs. Gordon, that I really can't discuss your, uh . . . relationship with Dr. Gordon . . ."

"Why not? He lives here, doesn't he? And you're his priest."

Michael decided there was no option but to be firm. "He is indeed living here," he said, "but he hasn't spoken to me about his relationship with you and the children and consequently I'm not free to discuss the matter."

"But you're his priest."

"Madam, I am *not* his priest. Dr. Gordon is an old friend. I invited him to live here until he makes a permanent arrangement, but that gives me no right to interfere in or to discuss his private life. I'm sure you can understand that."

Indignation having failed, Mrs. Gordon's demeanor altered. Her eyes were suddenly glittering with tears. "All I want you to do is get him to send us something to live on," she said, beginning to weep.

Michael, to whom women's tears were a commonplace, rose to indicate that the interview was over, but she was undeterred and continued to rummage through her purse for a handkerchief, sniffing frequently as an interim measure.

"For three years not a letter, not even a phone call. And not a dollar. With Billy not old enough for school I couldn't go out to work so we had to go on welfare . . . " The recounting of her woes stimulated her self-pity and freshened the flow of tears. "I've talked to the family court but they won't do anything." She gave up the search in her purse. "Do you have a kleenex, or something?" Michael passed her his pocket handkerchief and she blew her nose with a surprisingly loud honking. "I haven't got the money for a lawyer. Harris won't come to the phone or answer when I write." Her sentences were now punctuated with sobs. "I'm not asking for charity . . . I just want somebody to talk to him . . . "

It was ten minutes before Michael could get her sufficiently composed to lead her to the door. She did seem to make a rapid recovery once he promised to "have a word" with her husband. But for all the fact that she might have been simulating more grief than she was feeling, Michael was convinced that she was genuinely distressed, and with four children dependent on her, was desperate.

He mentioned his visitor to Harris that evening as they sat alone after dinner, lingering over coffee. Harris lowered his brows as he listened and when Michael was finished, let out a harsh laugh.

"So Dodi was here crying poor?"

Michael found himself resenting Harris's cavalier reaction. "Perhaps I didn't make it clear," he said stiffly. "She didn't ask for charity."

"But she did touch your heart with her sad tale of being abandoned by a faithless husband," Harris said, grinning humorlessly, a ragged cigar clamped between his teeth.

"Something like that," Michael said, wishing he'd never made the promise, or having made it hadn't kept it.

Harris tilted back his head and expertly popped soft rolling smoke rings toward the chandelier. "Used to blow them for the kids," he said for no apparent reason. He suddenly reached forward to tip the ash from the cigar and to look up at Michael from beneath his brows. "Did you want an answer for the lady?" he said, his eyes hard.

"Not particularly," Michael said. "It's none of my business. I'm simply a messenger."

But Harris wasn't ready to drop it now that Michael had lost whatever zeal he'd had. "I'll give you a message," he said, butting the cigar almost viciously, and his hand trembling, pouring himself another coffee, overflowing the cup. "Tell her I said to go get herself manipulated." He laughed coarsely and drank some of the coffee, dripping it on his tie.

"I have no doubt she told you, complete with histrionics and half a litre of tears – a great weeper, Dodi – how I just up and walked out on her and the kids. But I'll wager that what she *didn't* tell you is that for at least two years she was shacked up with some chiropractor in the Bronx. And all the time dunning me for money."

Michael couldn't resist it: "But did you send her any?" he asked. He immediately retrenched. "Sorry," he added, swallowing a smile, "that was presumptuous."

"Yes," Harris said, "it was."

He was in a surly mood and it showed in his voice and manner. He looked at Michael for a long moment and then took a great gulp of coffee, grimacing as it scalded his throat. "Mike," he said, apparently expansively but with a clink of ice in his tone, "permit me to do what nobody else in the world would dare to do: instruct you on the institution of marriage."

"Oh, no!" said Michael in mock dismay.

"Which institution, let it be said, you clergy stoutly defend while personally wanting no part of it."

He replaced the cup on the saucer with a clang and lit another cigar. Then he leaned back in his chair, observing the rope of smoke ascending from the tip. "Marriage," he began, "is beyond question the worst of all the arrangements imposed by man on his society; a wholly unnatural arrangement superimposed on the normal male-female attraction. It's man's second worst inhumanity to man (war being the worst, although many a man has gone to war to escape a marriage) and has obviously been devised as a means of punishing man for his failure to love God by destroying normal affection through an arrangement which demeans the participants and transforms what should be joy into duty."

"Are you extrapolating from personal experience?" Michael interjected.

"At least, one of us has *had* some experience," Harris shot back.

He's in a strange mood, Michael thought. He's feigning jocularity but there's a snarling underneath. Of all things! He's feeling guilty about the way he's treated his family and is trying to expiate it by railing at it.

"We begin at the beginning," Harris said, his voice pontifical, "with two people in love: immature and usually uninstructed on the subject of love and marriage and knowing nothing more about it than what they've observed – heaven help them! – in their own homes or learned from their grubby peers or heard howled about by some bearded crazy twanging an amplified guitar. They know little about each other except that they can kiss without bumping noses and that each creates pleasant sensations in the other's groin.

"Society now conspires to put these children under pressure to marry, and sooner or later they enter upon a tribal ritual as kooky as any practiced by the most benighted of aboriginals. She and he and all their friends play dress-up, and the entire ridiculously costumed group ends up in a church." He shot a sly glance at Michael. "There's always at least one of your chaps on hand, and he mumbles some ancient words to which nobody pays the slightest attention. Impossible vows are taken, various lies are sworn to, metal rings are traded, and in tones that might better be reserved for the announcement of the end of time, our two unfortunates are informed that they're husband and wife.

"Afterwards there's a party where everybody drinks too much and the bride's mother ritually cries. All this mandatory nonsense out of the way, the hapless children get into a car with lewd witticisms painted on it and drive off to a motel bedroom smelling of stale tabacco smoke and boasting of VD-free toilet seats. There, despite the fact they're utterly exhausted and a bit drunk, and would be better off if they went to sleep, they feel duty-bound to copulate."

He reached out and tapped the ash from his cigar. "And so they live unhappily ever after."

Michael looked at him in bemused disbelief, slowly shaking his head. "Cynicism," he said, "thy name is Harris Gordon."

Harris was unabashed. He tilted the coffee pot but only a trickle emerged. Michael reached for the button on the table before him to ring for Miss Pritchard, but Harris said, "No, I'll have a spot of this." He picked up a decanter, splashed a small amount of the tawny liquid into a goblet and looked inquiringly at Michael.

Michael covered his glass with a hand. "I'm drunk on your oratory."

Harris cupped the bowl of the goblet in his hand and swirled the brandy. "The fatal flaw in all this is, of course, that it disregards the single most important fact of life: the fact of change. Wasn't it Plato who said something like, the one unchanging fact is the fact of change? But marriage is based on the idea that the partners will remain as they are. In truth, however, they'll change so much over the next few decades that, were they to meet then for the first time, neither would give the other a second look. So, as surely as night follows day, time passes, ardor cools and one or the other wants out.

"Now, there was a time when that wasn't so likely to happen. Divorce? – no way! The edict was, 'till death do you part,' an arrangement set up centuries ago through the collusion of the church and the state – don't glare at me, Michael, it's true – as a means to keep the power structure intact and to control the transfer of property from one generation to another. If you want an ordered society you need to know who's married to whom, and even more important, who are the parents of whom."

Michael, who had at first been amused, had now grown nettled. His face colored. Harris peered at him over his spectacles. "Do I offend you?"

Michael was about to set upon the arguments but thought better of it. "Go on," he said. "You're much more entertaining than the lies on television."

Harris drew a deep breath. "I've spoken about how things were, but ah – how times have changed. The old families and the church don't run things any more, so most of the rules have been scrapped. People are doing what comes naturally and the women are into it as much as the men. As the song says, 'Anything Goes.' Our entire culture has become sex-oriented: literature, art, music and the popular entertainments, television and movies, are designed to do one thing; to encourage man's proclivity to polygamy, and monogamy is a tattered flag on a tottering staff."

He had been rattling along, running with his thesis, entranced by the sound of his arguments. "Mike," he said passionately, "it's true. The institution of marriage is simply unworkable today. We fill the air with the musk of sexuality and then say, 'No fornicating before marriage and no playing around after.' We make it easy to marry and hard to divorce when we should be doing the opposite. Marriage turns men into hypocrites and women into parasites. Better than one in three ends in divorce and the number is growing. And who do we have to thank for this impossible state of affairs? – mostly the Christian church."

Michael had resisted the urge to interrupt. Now Harris looked at him in anticipation of a rebuttal. After a moment he said, "Well . . . ?"

Michael's expression betrayed nothing of his thoughts. He looked at Harris and said quietly, "Methinks the gentleman doth protest too much. All I said was that Mrs. Gordon had dropped in to see me this afternoon."

Harris glared at him. Then a smile formed and broke in laughter. "You really are something," he said. "If they don't make you pope they're sure missing a bet."

Michael smiled thinly, but his eyes were grim.

Chapter Five

Winter began to yield. Winds that had careered chill through the city's canyons, now bore intimations of spring. The last sodden heaps of filthy snow trickled to death, coats came unbuttoned, car windows were cranked down, bedding went out on windowsills and clotheslines, lunches were eaten out of doors with faces upturned to the sun, shop windows tempted to shorts and swimsuits, children skipped, basketballs swished through hoops, and the *Daily News* heralded in headline and photograph the first brave shoots of spring.

The weeks had gone swiftly, too swiftly for Jennifer, who had occasionally to stop to catch her breath and get her bearings in the maelstrom of arrangements and shoppings and errands and showers that circled her days like bees a hive. Copeland was more hindrance than help. In his meticulous way, he made checklists for himself and reminder-notes for her. He pored over styles of invitations, checked in person three possible locales for the reception, liking none of them, compared the components and prices of menus and even suggested revisions in the ceremony itself. He was obdurate at only one point: he would not be married in black tie; he was too large to be fitted by any of the suit rental shops and objected to wasting the money on a tailor-made suit he might never wear again. "But," rebutted Jennifer, "I'll never wear my wedding dress again." Whereupon Copeland responded in mock seriousness, "You may, if you don't treat me better after we're married than you've done lately," and ran chortling for cover.

Harris had lately imposed a more rigorous discipline on himself and its effects were beginning to be apparent. He began his days earlier, was now taking a lunch with him when he went to the basement mornings, and frequently labored on after dinner. His face had grown gray and his eyes dark-encircled and deep-set. Michael, at Jennifer's instigation, had spoken to him about the demands he was making on himself, but Harris had responded with a flow of asperity and Michael had backed off. Their easy camaraderie was now only occasionally there. Harris had become increasingly short-tempered and was sometimes barely civil; except with Jennifer with whom he was almost courtly. He had begun going out evenings, perhaps twice a week, and the following day often revealed evidence of it.

Michael's schedule had reached its seasonal peak. The annual fundraising drive in the archdiocese was in its final stages of planning. He had been to Washington twice in the past month to confer with the Secretary of State and to Los Angeles for the Conference of Bishops. It seemed that each week a church or a priest or a parish house was celebrating a significant anniversary and he was absent from the dinner table as often as he was present. Even his jealously guarded weekend retreats to The Cottage were frequently foregone.

For weeks he had spoken about wanting to get together with Copeland "for a fatherly chat," but each appointment had yielded to other priorities. Copeland contemplated the appointment with some apprehension, mentioning it to Jennifer. She laughed it off with the warning that Michael's intention was undoubtedly to wrest from him the vow that all their sons be priests. But now that the time had come – the evening being warm and Michael having suggested that they stroll out of doors back of the cathedral – there was no strain between them.

"I suppose I should have asked you for Jennifer's hand," Copeland said, making conversation.

"Too bad that's not done any more," Michael said. He placed a hand on Copeland's shoulder. "I'd have been pleased to say yes."

"Thank you."

"The reason I wanted this few minutes with you is because I don't know what you know about Jennifer's background."

"We've talked about it, but not much. I gather her parents were Protestants."

"Presbyterians. So was I until I was in my twenties. They say nobody's as zealous as a convert and that's probably true of both of us. It certainly was of me." He smiled at the memory "Partly, I was in reaction to my father, but even more important was a chaplain I met in the south Pacific. The other chaplains I'd met didn't seem to understand who they were. They were like Rotary Club greeters, God's glad-handers, company nose-wipers, letter-writers. They had this compulsion to be thought of as one of the boys. Father Souchak was the opposite. He had none of the so-called social graces. Spoke dreadful English. Incredibly bad preacher, and he never tried to pressure you." He laughed. "I almost had to force him to baptize me." He walked on a few strides, remembering. "You could almost smell God on him."

He returned from his reverie. "Sorry. We were talking about Jennifer. Has she talked about her parents?"

"No."

"Too painful, I suppose. Even now. Her mother – my sister, Eleanora – and I were both, as the phrase has it, children of the manse. Our father was a preacher, a very prominent one, actually. He took it as something of a reproach when I converted to Catholicism. We never had been close and my going into the priesthood made things worse. Jennifer was raised a Presbyterian – she was an only child – and when Eleanora and Tim were killed she was all alone. She's told you about that?"

"She mentioned an accident. No more than that."

"I'm not sure she'll ever get over it. One of the reasons I've been so happy about you two is that she seems to have conquered the depression that used to overtake her. She has trouble accepting happiness, you know."

"Yes, I know."

"She's never talked about the accident? Or about afterwards?"

"Not really."

"Or how she came to live here?"

"No."

They walked on a few yards in silence and then Michael said, "Perhaps I'd better tell you about it."

On the afternoon of Jennifer's seventeenth birthday, her parents, festive in anticipation of a dinnertime celebration, had driven to a nearby shopping plaza to pick up a decorated cake and the Siamese kitten she had been coveting. At the same hour a classmate and a friend had "borrowed" his father's new Olds Toronado. Travelling too fast, he saw the police cruiser parked in the lee of a Kentucky Fried Chicken drive-in, panicked, and with a shriek of rubber, sped off. The cruiser whooped in pursuit like a crazed Indian. A chase ensued, lasting no more than five minutes but reaching speeds of up to a hundred miles an hour. At the plaza, Jennifer's father, with the cake on his wife's lap for safekeeping and the kitten protesting hoarsely in a carton on the seat between them, saw too late the car bearing down on them and instead of continuing on, braked. The Toronado screamed, spun, rolled and then leaped through the air, exploding at the end of the arc as it rammed the O'Neill car.

At the funeral the matching caskets sat head to head, closed. The electric organ vibrattoed thinly through "Rock of Ages" and "Jesus, Lover of My Soul," and by reason of the limited repertoire of the funeral parlor organist, "For Those in Peril on the Sea." The Moderator of the Synod, in black gown and Doctor of Divinity hood, maundered on oleaginously and interminably, but did manage to induce some reaching for handkerchiefs with a concluding illustration. The performance was flawed further by the fact that he got the name of the "dearly beloved Eleanora" wrong, referring to her a half dozen times as Lenore. At the cemetery it rained, which did have the advantage of abbreviating the reverend doctor's remarks.

Jennifer fulfilled what was required of her without once raising her eyes or dropping a tear or saying a word. She sat or stood or walked or rode, and accepted condolences and pats and embraces and kisses with her body rigid and her hands fists. A conference of distant relatives decided that "she must never go back to that house again; the memories would be too much," so she was taken in temporarily by a great-uncle and aunt who lived nearby. For three weeks she stayed in her room, coming out only for meals and to go to school. One afternoon she didn't return. The police were called and after forty-eight hours a missing-persons bulletin was issued. She was found two weeks later when a neighbor saw someone entering the O'Neill home by a rear window in the darkness. Police found two empty gin bottles, some bread and milk and canned meat and a scattering of candy wrappers in the kitchen, and Jennifer in a closet. It was evident that she hadn't bathed or changed her clothes and had slept the while in her parents' bed.

She was diagnosed as suffering from severe depression and committed to the Trenton Psychiatric Hospital where she was roused daily from a valium-induced vacuity to respond vaguely to questions from a young psychiatrist whose luxuriant black beard had two carefully sculpted white tips. She was rescued from this abyss by Michael, who had been presumed to be too busy and had not been informed of her condition, and taken to live with him. The first weeks were difficult, but Michael and Miss Pritchard simply rejected her rejection of them, and cheered and cajoled and fussed and loved her back to normalcy. At one point she determined to become a nursing sister but was dissuaded. Instead, at nineteen, she enrolled at Columbia, graduated *magna cum laude* with a bachelor's degree in business administration, and after two years with the Rand Corporation, went to work at the Chancery office as a secretary in the office of the Society for the Propagation of the Faith.

"I worried about you and Jennifer at first," Michael said. "The difference in your ages, the speed with which you fell in love and decided to get married . . . " He laughed. "You mustn't take that personally; I've worried about every man she's ever gone out with. I'm worse than the stereotype father."

"She loves you very much."

"It pleases me to hear that."

"If you'll forgive my familiarity, she worships you."

"That doesn't please me. Matter of fact, it worries me. I don't think we ought to put too much faith in any other person; we're all so fallible. We all let each other down at times."

"It's hardly surprising, though. The way she sees it, you saved her life."

"No, when she needed someone I happened to be there. We were talking about the zeal of the convert a moment ago: at first, she was all for going to the mission field; the upper Amazon region, the most dangerous place she could think of. I had to talk her out of that."

"Why? Not that I'm not glad you did."

"She's not very strong. And I wasn't sure she'd be able to handle it off by herself. I think she needs people, needs to be able to love them and to draw strength from them." They went on a bit, silent. "A few minutes ago I said that she was afraid of happiness, and you agreed. Have you seen that in her?"

"I think so – the first time we both realized that we loved each other. And sometimes also when we talk about the future – you know, our own home, children, that kind of thing – she'll be laughing and excited, and then her mood will change."

"Yes."

"But not for long."

"As I said, that's what pleases me. She used to get so very low. Sometimes for days."

"I'll be good to her. I will."

"I'm sure you will," Michael said. "I'm sure you will."

"The trouble with Christians — "

"Now just wait a minute! What do you mean, the trouble with Christians? You can hardly make us all one; even God hasn't been able to accomplish that."

The voices were raised and heated. Michael and Harris were in the study late in the evening in what had become in recent weeks a running debate. They seldom saw each other until the day was well spent and then only two or three times a week. Each night, one or the other would arrive first at the study, check to see that the elaborately chased sterling silver ice-bucket, presented to Michael by the Knights of Columbus (Harris called it the Ark of the Convenant) was filled, and get into a book while waiting for the other. Of late, their discussions had become debates and acrimony often crept in. On this night, fuses were short.

"But you can be lumped together," Harris persisted. "You are all, all of you, Catholic, Protestant and the other 57 varieties obsessed with this notion of sin. You spend half your time fretting about, confessing to, doing penance for or generally carrying on about sin. Think of the guilt such a preoccupation must induce."

"Think of the guilt the church removes," Michael said. "I'd hazard a guess, more than all the psychiatrists from Mesmer to Menninger."

"Perhaps, but guilt you induced in the first place," Harris shot back. "Sex, for instance – why is it so great a sin? The church is forever having at it from the pulpit, warning against it in the confessional or uttering papal pronouncements on it. Paul VI was really quite incredible on the subject. Seems to me, so long as nobody's hurt and the people involved aren't unduly promiscuous it's probably the least of sins. God himself put the appetite there so where's the harm? Surely it's good for people who like each other to be close. Why should they have to be married, for goodness sake?"

"You're saying in effect that fornication is merely the logical extension of a kiss on the cheek?"

"No, I'm not saying that. All right, I *will* say that; if there isn't going to be a pregnancy, how is anybody injured by sexual intimacy?"

"Among other things," Michael said crisply, "fidelity makes for mental health. Promiscuity destroys marriage and injures the children of that marriage. There are also some practical problems . . . the spread of venereal disease being only one."

Harris shook his head: "You *do* see the seamy side."

"Perhaps," Michael said coolly, "but the fabric of life does have a seamy side." He pulled at his lower lip for a moment. "But that aside: you said a moment ago that there's no harm in sexual activity so long as the people involved aren't promiscuous. Why except the promiscuous? If, as you say, being close is good, why not be as close to as many as you can?"

Harris looked out from beneath his eyebrows, smiling for some inner reason. "Mike, I excepted the promiscuous because they're the enemies of loving. They don't want to be close to the other person as a person, they're interested in using the other person's body as a means for masturbation."

"Would you not call *that* sin?"

"Sin? No." There was a gleam in Harris's eye. "Promiscuous people are simply . . . crass. Gross. They have no taste. It would be my uneducated guess that they dislike the opposite sex in something of the same way a whore dislikes men."

Michael loosed a short incredulous laugh. "Am I hearing rightly? Is this Harris Gordon, the man whose ambition in his senior year was, to descend to the colloquial for a moment, to get laid every week?"

Harris gave him a roguish grin. "We've changed, haven't we?" he said archly.

"I think you're trying to put me on," Michael said, "but, regardless, I'd like to take you up on this business of being close. If all that's needed is to feel affection for your partner, might you not feel affection for two at a given time? And if two why not three? And if three why not a dozen? When does being close begin to be being promiscuous?"

"It has to do with the people involved."

"You're evading the point," Michael said, and there was tartness in his voice. "How does one differentiate between the person who is promiscuous and the person who is merely very affectionate?"

There was a bite in Harris's tone, too. "Perhaps one doesn't try. He leaves the judging to God."

Both realized they had grown ill-tempered and neither said anything for a moment. Michael rose, went to the sideboard and dropped a cube of ice into his glass. "What are you drinking?" he asked.

Harris grinned slyly. "A whiskey sour. Couldn't you tell?"

Michael laughed heartily and the air cleared. "Shall we drop the subject?" he asked.

"Not unless you want to. I've been telling you more or less what I think. It's your turn." He held out his glass. "Just ice, thank you."

Michael dropped two cubes into Harris's drink, tipped a splash of scotch into his own and went back to his chair. He took a moment to gather his thoughts.

"We see sex as a gift from God, a precious gift. So, because it's a gift of value and given by someone you love, we treat it with reverence. God gave it for procreation and love and companionship. Man's spiritual nature is created in God's image and is eternal, and sexuality may or may not have a part in it, but physical man is mortal and must reproduce, as all of God's creatures must or the world becomes barren. So, in part, to perpetuate creation, God created sexuality—"

Harris broke in. "Am I permitted to interrupt?"

"Be my guest."

"I had to stop you there," Harris said, "because it seems to me that the church is, if not hypocritical, inconsistent. If God gave sexual desire to perpetuate the species, why doesn't he remove the desire from a pregnant woman? An impregnated animal will reject a male; a pregnant woman doesn't."

"But, Harris, I just said that sexuality is given for love and companionship *as well as* for procreation."

"Okay. But here's where your logic completely escapes me: You say that sexuality is given for two essential reasons, yet at certain times in the woman's cycle, unless the goal is procreation, you forbid sex as love and companionship."

"We don't forbid it; discretion dictates it."

"But if sex is for love and companionship, why is it wrong to enjoy it simply because some kind of device is used to avoid pregnancy?"

"Because the device, as you call it, has one purpose: to frustrate the will of God. Your hypothetical couple is perfectly free to enjoy God's gift of sexuality any time they please. They do so, however, in the knowledge that God may use their act of love as the means by which he perpetuates the species."

"The simple fact is, you approve a birth-control device, too – only it's a calendar instead of a condom." A grin spread slowly across his face. "In other words, don't shoot if you're going to score."

Michael didn't smile with him. "There's no need to be vulgar," he said indifferently.

"Sorry, I sometimes forget who you are."

"I'm exactly what you are," Michael said with some spirit, "a human being. With one difference – I'm a priest. Being a priest makes me different; not better, mind you, but different. It's something like being married; you're the same person but you're different because of a relationship."

Harris looked at Michael appraisingly, absently smoothing the hair on the crown of his head. "Okay," he said slowly. "If you're who you've always been, and if I'm not cutting too close to the bone, let me take you back to our undergraduate days, specifically to Margaret Robertson. Remember her?"

Michael gave no visible hint of the impact the sudden introduction of the name had had on him. "Of course I do," he said.

"You were going steady, as the expression had it. You were in love with her, or so you said, and while you never talked about it I assumed you were being intimate." He glanced across at Michael. "Am I getting out of line?"

Michael shook his head and made a small shrug. "No plaster saint, I," he said. "What's your point?" But it *was* cutting close to the bone.

He sometimes remembered Margaret. Not often of late, but even now. Suddenly, unbidden, usually unexpectedly, her memory would resurrect and there she would be before him with the vividness of yesterday. As on that exquisite summer's day when they'd packed a hamper and gone to the mountains, and she, in a coltish exuberance, had run ahead, her long hair bouncing behind; had gathered her skirts and in a flash of long lithe legs had leaped ankle deep in a stream to stand there, legs apart, eyes wide and mouth drawn into a surprised circle at the bite of the icy water. He'd thought suddenly of the singer in the Song of Solomon: *Your hair is like a flock of goats frisking down the slopes of Gilead.*

And in the sun, nested in the tall fragrant grass, her lips: soft beyond imagining, trailing excitement on his cheek, soft beyond imagining on his mouth, sweetly painful in their reckless urgency. And the darting probe of the tip of her tongue . . . *Your lips, my promised one, distill wild honey. Honey and milk are under your tongue, and the scent of your garments is as the scent of Lebanon.*

In the sun, her body; the skin shining, pale. The slender neck, the square, spare shoulders, the blue-veined whiteness of her breasts, the nipple probing at his palm or forming between his fingertips. *Your two breasts are as two fawns, twins of a gazelle . . . .*

He felt again on his fingertips the faint undulations of her ribs, the heartbeat beneath his palm, the taut slope of her belly and the breadth of her hips, and the down that softened the softness of the skin and made a trail for his lips to the fleece between her thighs. *Your navel is a bowl, well rounded with no lack of wine . . . . The curve of your thighs is like the curve of a necklace.*

Their loving was infinite in its variety: sometimes filled with languor, sometimes rough to the point of pain, welcomed pain. Sometimes there was a snatching at loving, as though it would not always be there and they knew. And sometimes there were hours of loving: gentle, exploratory, inventive, unrestrained, and they were sure, as lovers are, that none before them had so explored each other, ever so utterly opened themselves the one to the other, ever so zealously sought to pleasure the other. And then, afterwards: lying with thighs and shoulders hot against each other, fingers entwined, in the center of the scent of their loving, with the mind and every nerve-end luxuriant with the softness of a candle's glow.

At times her ghost would insinuate itself past the carefully buttressed defenses to materialize in his mind. Sometimes in the night, when continence was burden rather than strength, she wrested from him the tribute of a groan. Thirty-five years earlier, prostrate on the cold polished marble before the altar at St. Patrick's, making his final vows; even then as he marshalled all his senses to focus them on God – his eyes to glimpse the glory, his lips to utter praise, his ears to await command, his hands ready for service, his nostrils flared to draw the *pneuma* deep within his spirit – even then the memory had come near, and he had bumped his forehead on the marble to drive it away. Once, years ago, he had seen her as he was preaching, far back in the cathedral at the center of one of the pools of light spilled on the congregation from the vaulted ceiling, her face apart from those about her. And the sentence on his lips had faltered. But he had looked away and not looked again, and afterwards had gone directly to the sacristy and remained there until the congregation had gone.

Margaret!

You ravish my heart my promised bride. You ravish my heart with a single one of your glances, with one single pearl of your necklace. What spells lie in your love . . .

Once he had inquired about her. She hadn't married until she was thirty and had divorced five years later. She was a fashion buyer for Sak's and lived in an apartment not a dozen blocks from the cathedral. Though he vowed not to – there was no avoiding it – he looked for her face in the congregation when he was the preacher, but saw her only once (or thought he did) in the rear of the cathedral standing half behind one of the pillars. He had prayed that she would not come again.

You are beautiful, as Tirzah, my love; fair as Jerusalem. Turn your eyes away, for they hold me captive . . .

Harris's voice shattered the moment: "Well, *was* what was between you and Marg, sin?"

He was remembering the agony in the writing of that letter from the south Pacific to tell her he was going to become a priest. He had no heart now for the discussion but could hardly break it off. "Yes," he said, "I now believe it was."

"Did you back then?"

"No."

"So what's changed is not the act (God! – to call what was between them an act!) but your view of it."

"It's not my view or anyone else's that matters. It is God who defines sin."

"So, because it was outside marriage, it was sin?"

He'd had enough of this prolonging of the discussion of his personal attitudes. "Yes," he said shortly.

Harris caught the impatience and was curious about it, but decided to leave Margaret in the past. "What I'm getting at," he said, "and maybe I got too personal, is that the church tends to think of sex as evil. The priest demonstrates his commitment by renouncing it. Abstinence is glorified by the vow of chastity. But it's not surprising, really; the apostle Paul was hung-up on sex, so it's inevitable that his followers will be."

That was a little too much! "Paul? Hung-up?"

"He forbids sex outside marriage, right?"

"That's being hung-up?"

"Wait. First, he forbids sex outside marriage. Then he goes on to say, Look, you're better not to get married, but if you can't hack it without a woman go ahead and get married because – and this I find incredible – because, he says, it's better to marry than burn. Wow!"

"Oh, come now, Harris," Michael flared. "Be fair. Remember the context. Paul didn't believe there was going to *be* a tomorrow; he thought the end of the world was imminent. It was in that light he urged celibacy. His objective was that the Christians of that time be free and unencumbered so that in the brief time that remained they could give themselves fully to the task."

"Is that why the clergy are forbidden to marry?"

"Not because we believe the world is going to end, of course not, but so that a priest is free to do God's work. You surely wouldn't argue that a married man isn't encumbered by family obligations? Then, too, it's in imitation of our Lord."

"But the apostles were married. At least some of them were."

"Oh? And where did you dig up that information?"

"There's a reference to Peter's mother-in-law in one of the Gospels . . ."

"Yes. Jesus healed her."

"Right. So if he had a mother-in-law he had a wife. But the fact he was married didn't stop Jesus from chosing him as one of the apostles nor you Catholics from appointing him your first pope."

Michael looked across at Harris who was sipping his drink and peering over the rim of his glass. The tolerant amusement he'd felt when the discussion had begun had been replaced by hot anger. When he responded, there was a tight smile on his lips but his eyes were flinty.

"Harris, old friend," he said, "you really are given to leaps of presumption: a veritable rhetorical mountain goat. One hopes the evidence on which you base your conclusions as an archaeologist is less tenuous than that from which you've just proceeded. First, the church doesn't teach that the apostles were all unmarried. Second, the gospel writer does indeed say that Peter had a mother-in-law. He does not say, however, that he had a living wife. In fact, the account specifically states that after Jesus healed Peter's mother-in-law she got out of bed and prepared a meal for them all. Why she, if Peter had a wife? Not that it matters."

Harris caught the umbrage in Michael's voice and was tempted to drop the subject, but he too had grown testy. "Why, Mike," he said, taunting, "you're angry. Have I been presumptuous, daring to voice an opinion on a religious matter?"

"No one begrudges an opinion. One merely hopes it's based on some knowlege of the subject."

Harris flared: "Oh, so religion is sacrosanct. Off limits. Thou shalt not poach on our preserve!"

"Nonsense. But I put this to you: is there any other area of expertise (and I'm not directing this at you necessarily; it happens to be a pet peeve of mine) is there any other area of expertise where the rank amateur feels so justified in attacking or dismissing the conclusions of those qualified to know what they're talking about? Theology had been called the Queen of the Sciences, but any fool, any village atheist, takes it as his right to dismiss out of hand the conclusions of scholars and saints as if they were no more than casually arrived at opinions. If he were to challenge the conclusions of, say, archaeology, or anthropology, or physics with the same temerity, he'd be dismissed as a presumptuous idiot."

"Oh, come off it, Mike!" Harris snapped. "Theology isn't the sole province of the clergy. The church doesn't *own* God. I'm a scientist and you're a religious; that doesn't mean I'm crippled when it comes to thinking about the nature of the universe – because that's what you're talking about when you talk about God. We come at things differently. Religion's based on a set of fixed beliefs, many of them centuries old, and the church's duty is to keep them from being sullied and to hand them on intact from one generation to another. New ideas are heresies, and they're to be rejected and opposed. We don't see things that way. Science is based on the thesis that our beliefs are theory and that our task is systematically to try to eliminate the false theories. We believe that every theory should be challenged, every idea subjected to critical examination. Not to do so is to perpetuate ignorance."

"If that isn't the most simplistic nonsense I've ever heard," Michael said hotly, "it's certainly a candidate for the award! Science the Savior! Religion the last bastion of ignorance and reaction! Harris, you're right out of the nineteenth century. So what happens when you, to use your words, eliminate the false theories and get to the facts? Surely one of those facts would be that to kill a man is wrong – 'Thou shalt not kill.' Would you be kind enough, though, to tell me how knowing that fact changes anything? We've known *that* fact for centuries: I wish you'd tell me one war or one murder that this knowledge has stopped."

"But 'Thou shalt not kill' isn't a fact, it's a moral maxim. It's a general rule of behavior, and as with all rules, subject to exceptions. Surely you're not going to tell me that it's *always* wrong to kill. I don't think you'd argue that for a moment."

Before Michael could respond, he held up a hand. "Look, let's leave that and go on. In the meantime, I'll give you that bit of trivia about Peter's mother-in-law although I must say it reminds me of the nit-picking arguments of the Scholastics in the Middle Ages about how many angels could dance on the head of a pin."

"Oh?" Michael said, his voice all innocence. "I thought it was you who raised the question."

Sheepishly: "Maybe I did at that. But to hell with it, I want to get back to this business of sin."

"Then let me put the question again: What would you call what we call sin? If a man is unloving to his neighbor, lies about him, steals from him, even kills him, what would you call that?"

"Certainly anything but sin."

"What, then?"

"Crime . . . Anti-social behavior . . . impropriety, perhaps."

"Murder's an *impropriety?*"

"Your question isn't pertinent. It's not what an action's called, it's the emphasis put upon it."

"If it's not what it's called, why do you object to the church calling it sin?"

"Because calling it sin muddies the waters. When a man beats up or steals from or kills his neighbor, it's a criminal act and the law gets into it. The community has agreed that certain acts are anti-social, and punishment for committing them is meted out by the society here and now, not by some God somewhere in some distant tomorrow. My quarrel with the church isn't over what I think we'd both call crimes, but over what you call sins. You make it a sin, not merely to harm your neighbor or society as a whole, but to disobey the church: not to go to confession, not to attend mass, not to carry out a penance." He chuckled. "It used to be not to eat meat on Fridays but you had second thoughts on that. What the church has done is to invent an entire hierarchy of duties, obligations and observances, and if people don't do as they're told you tell them that they're sinning against almighty God. And if they persist you bar them from access to God and damn them to hell." He made a futile fluttering with his hands. "It's all so . . . so damned presumptuous."

Harris had grown exercised as he talked and finished leaning forward in his chair. Now, his face flushed, he slumped back and took a sip of his drink. An ambulance whooped by on Madison Avenue.

Michael's eyes were narrowed. "Harris," he said equably, "are you a member of any archaeological societies?"

"Of course."

"Are there standards for admission?"

Warily: "Certainly."

"And rules to be obeyed if you wish to remain a member in good standing?"

"Yes, but hold on a minute — "

"No. Let me finish. Can you be ousted if you flagrantly break the rules, rules to which you assented when you joined?"

"Yes."

"Well, we in the church are an association, too. An association of men and women who hold certain things in common. We joined our association knowing the rules, rules laid down by our founder. To break those rules, he said, is sin. It is not we who say that; it is Our Lord."

"But your analogy won't wash. My society can't and doesn't try to punish me beyond barring me from membership. You not only do that, you presume to bar people from the presence of God now and forever."

"Which is precisely what Jesus said would be God's judgment on sin. And we don't bar them from God; they can come to him any time they choose."

"So long as they do what you say." Michael was about to break in but he held up a hand. "This time, let *me* finish. The presumptuousness lies in the fact that you not only bar your own people: I'm not a member of your association and you damn me."

"But you are a member of our group in that we're all, willy-nilly, children of the Creator. If you rebel against the rules he's laid down – sin, if you will – you bar yourself. It's not we who do it; it's you yourself."

Harris sputtered with indignation. "But the whole damn thing is based on the *a priori* assumption that you are right and the rest of the world is wrong. I find that intolerable."

"Why? Columbus was right and the rest of the world wrong. Would you have found him intolerable?"

"Oh for God's sake, Mike! Apples and oranges! He'd reached certain conclusions about the earth that were demonstrable. But you don't do that. You base your claim to truth on the teachings of an obscure young Jew with messianic pretensions who, let's face it, didn't make much of an impression in his lifetime. There isn't a single word about him in secular history. Not a word. No mention of him by the Romans, not so much as a reference by Josephus, who damn well mentioned everything else. Not a word."

"But why do you specify secular history? What about the Gospels and the rest of the New Testament? Surely as an archaeologist you know their validity as historical documents is beyond question. We know more about Jesus than we do about Plato. You say Jesus made no impression on the world? He changed the course of history. Radically."

"No, no, no! Paul and Constantine changed the course of history. What Jesus said would probably have been forgotten, but Paul took it and formed it into a set of structured theological propositions, borrowing from half a dozen sources. Later, Constantine urged or imposed those ideas on the masses."

Their voices had raised to shouting and at first neither heard the tapping on the door.

"Come," Michael called out.

It was Miss Pritchard in a heavy tartan bathrobe, a nightcap on her head and her face fretful. "Were you callin' me?" she asked, her eyes darting from one face to the other.

"Did we disturb you?" Michael said.

"No," she said, her voice conveying yes. "I heard you callin' and thought maybe you wanted somethin'."

"No. Nothing, thank you."

"I'll be away to me bed then," she said. "It's almost one o'clock," she added pointedly. She pulled the door closed.

Michael smiled at Harris. "Conduct unbecoming, she's thinking."

Harris swirled the ice in his empty glass. "I don't think your Miss Pritchard approves of me." He sucked one of the chunks of ice into his mouth and chewed on it. "I don't get you mad, do I?"

Michael pursed his lips. "At times."

There was a puckish look on Harris's face. "Wouldn't want you to fall into sin."

"Wouldn't be the first time."

Michael rose and stretched and walked to stand with his back to the spent fire. After a moment he said, "You realize that I have no option but to see you as the enemy."

"A tool of the devil?"

"Perhaps," Michael said thoughtfully. "You haven't yet become disabused of your theory?" he asked.

"About the bones?"

"Yes."

"No."

"How far are you along with your writing?"

"Perhaps another month to go."

"Really? That soon?"

Harris stood. "There's something I've been wondering about."

"Uh huh?"

"Have you thought about what you're going to say when the press comes around to ask about my working here at the residence?"

"No, I haven't."

"Hadn't you better? It's going to seem very odd."

"I'll think about it when the time comes," Michael said, heading for the door. "I'm going to bed."

140

His Eminence
Michael Cardinal Maloney,
The Archdiocese of New York,
452 Madison Avenue,
New York City, N.Y. 10022
USA

March 18

My dear Michael:
A note in haste. I have just come from a meeting with the doctors. Belatedly, something by way of a firm conclusion from them. It is not good news, however. There is consensus on the ground of a series of tests just completed – infinite in their variety, it would seem – that there is no reasonable hope the Holy Father will survive. Indeed, I gather we should pray that God in his mercy will take him, and soon. Apparently there has been considerable brain damage and any recovery, short of the miraculous, would simply be an extension and an amplification of a tragedy. I marvel at the tenacity with which his frail body clings to life.

I regret to be the bearer of such tidings but thought you should be informed. I shall write at greater length soon.

Affectionately
Paolo Rinsonelli

"Any new business?"

The chairman of the Board of Directors of St. Clare's Hospital looked about the long mahogany table not all that happily, for if unexpected problems were to arise this was the time at which they would surface, and being a man of precise habits he preferred things tidy. On this occasion his hope that nothing irregular occur was almost fervent, for present at the meeting – he attended at most twice a year – and seated at the opposite end of the table, was the cardinal of the archdiocese. He had compressed his lips as Michael had slipped into the room, unexpected and fifteen minutes late, but it was a cross he bore and he had moved through the agenda regardless, with no recognition of Michael's presence other than to say, "We are honored this evening to have His Eminence Cardinal Maloney join us." For his part, Michael had not spoken.

"There being no new business, the chair would ask the secretary to introduce a matter that has come to his attention and which requires the consideration of this board."

The secretary, a man of astounding corpulence who spoke in short phrases, each separated by a wheezing intake of breath, was more than normally wet with perspiration. "I am in receipt of a letter," he began, "from a Lady Hambleton, which the chairman has asked me to read." With fingers like croissants he removed from its matching envelope a letter on mauve stationery and cleared his throat.

The resonant voice of Cardinal Maloney: "Mr. Chairman . . . "

"Your Eminence?"

"I didn't quite catch the name."

The secretary read: "Lady Sophie Spinks Hambleton, Hambleton House, Covington, near Godalming, Surrey, England."

"Thank you. The letter is addressed to the board?"

"No, Eminence," the chairman said, "it's addressed to the secretary personally. He has shared its contents with me and it seemed appropriate to . . . "

"Thank you," Michael said, his voice flat. "I'm acquainted with the lady, Mr. Chairman, and I'm curious as to why she is, in effect, addressing herself to this board."

The chairman's hands had begun to tremble. "With respect, Eminence, that will become apparent as the letter is read."

He resented Michael's presence. It was commonly known in the archdiocese that St. Clare's was Michael's "pet" among the various institutions in his charge and that he took more than a normal interest in its welfare. He had been Procurator at St. Clare's before being summoned to serve his predecessor, and since then the fortunes of the hospital had declined. The chairman held the opinion – voiced frequently to his wife, and not entirely without justification – that, inevitably, the achievements of the hospital were attributed to Cardinal Maloney while its problems were seen as his. Beyond this, he chafed at the fact that with Michael present the discussions tended to be directed to his end of the table.

"Mr. Secretary," he said, prompting him with a nod, "will you proceed, please."

The secretary took an audible breath. "Dear sir—"

"Mr. Chairman . . . "

"Your Eminence?"

"If I might add one more word?"

"Of course, Eminence."

"My office has had a considerable correspondence with Lady Hambleton. Father Jamieson has spoken to her a number of times and I met with her personally on my recent visit to England. Those conversations relate to a proposal she has made, a proposal I find unsuitable. I am somewhat troubled if she is now circumventing my office and addressing herself to this board."

The chairman looked intently at the pencil he was twirling furiously between his fingers. "You'll forgive me, Your Eminence, but I am confused. Are you asking that the letter *not* be read?"

Michael's mounting anger edged his tone. He was furious at Sophie's presumption and swiftly losing patience with the chairman whose resentment he had long sensed and which with the passage of time was less carefully covered. But he would tread softly.

"I think it better that the matter be left where it has rested for some months now," he said amiably.

"You'll excuse me, Eminence, but the letter is a long and detailed one, and it may be that it contains facts of which your office is not aware."

The silly man is like a bulldog; he doesn't know when to let go. "The more reason for forwarding it immediately to Father Jamieson for his perusal," Michael snapped, his affability gone.

The chairman had grown pale and his brow glinted with perspiration. He suddenly put down the pencil, realizing that it accentuated the shaking of his hands.

"I shall be happy to do so, if that's your wish, Eminence. I merely intended — "

Michael now wanted to have done with it. "Good," he said curtly. "Please do."

"—intended to bring it before this board," the chairman persisted, his voice trembling, "because of the extraordinary generosity expressed in it. Ten million dollars is a lot of money . . . "

"Ten million dollars!" The words were repeated sotto voce and with varying degrees of incredulity by half a dozen voices around the table.

"Yes," the chairman said. "Lady Hambleton has offered St. Clare's ten million dollars toward the building of a new children's wing. Her offer, she says, has been refused – for what I'm sure are valid reasons – so she's come directly to us. In light of what our esteemed Cardinal Archbishop has said, however, I shall be pleased to refer the letter to his office."

No one spoke for a moment. The chairman managed to extend the silence by suddenly involving himself in an industrious search through a batch of papers on the table before him. Michael remained silent, nothing but a slight narrowing of his eyes betraying his rage. The chairman, having run out the silence to where it was beginning to unravel, looked up. "If there is no further business then, the chair will entertain a motion to adjourn."

"One moment, Mr. Chairman."

The speaker was Cliff Orpen, an impressive man of about fifty, lean, with a rugged face dominated by jutting black eyebrows and straight black hair. "I don't want to speak out of turn here," he said tentatively, "but I can't help sayin' I'm a bit reluctant to adjourn without . . . " He looked at Michael. "I wonder if His Eminence would care to give us a bit more information?" He laughed uneasily. "It's a little like droppin' one shoe . . . know what I mean? I mean, ten million dollars! Is the lady some kind of nut?"

Michael had resolved to say nothing further but he could not but respond to Orpen's question. Orpen was a wealthy contractor and one of the leading laymen in the archdiocese. Only six months earlier the pope had made him a papal chamberlain in a ceremony in Rome.

"It's a rather complicated thing, Cliff," Michael said, speaking directly to the contractor and in so doing removing the chairman from the conversation. "No, the lady's not a nut, as you so succinctly put it, she is however something of a problem. In addition to writing this board and badgering my office, she has written a letter – a somewhat similar one, I take it – to His Holiness." He rubbed the tips of his fingers on his temples. "She is, as I say, something of a problem."

"Could I ask just one more question?"

"Of course."

"Is she an actual Lady?" He laughed. "I mean, is she really a member of the British nobility?"

"She was a Canadian citizen who lived here in Manhattan for some years. But, yes, she's titled."

"And she *has* the money?"

"Oh yes."

Orpen scratched his head and drew a deep breath. "I don't know . . . " he said. He looked at Michael in the manner of a boy hesitant to broach the borrowing of the family car from his father. "I said that was my last question . . . . If I'm not out of line, Your Eminence, might I ask – I'm sure on behalf of all of us – " There were small murmurs of assent. "What's wrong with her money? She didn't steal it, did she?"

"No," Michael said, "she didn't steal it." He realized now he had no option but to proceed. "I would have preferred not to get into an extended discussion of the matter," he said, "but your chairman has seen fit to decide otherwise—"

"Your Eminence, I'm sorry if I've seemed to—"

Michael rode right over him. "That, however, is of no moment now." He looked at Orpen. "To be responsive to your question, Cliff, the gift is conditional upon St. Clare's granting her certain recognition, recognition that is, in my judgment, inappropriate."

The chairman's pallor was almost alarming and a tic was tugging at a corner of his mouth. "Perhaps His Eminence will tell us what it is the lady wants that is sufficient to deny St. Clare's a children's wing – an addition, as we are all aware, we have needed for many years and have been unable to afford."

God's truth! Michael thought, we'll have a new chairman next year if it's the last thing I do.

Orpen realized that there was a small shooting-war going on and felt some responsibility for it. He was about to move adjournment when Michael, aware that he was warping the facts but determined to end the discussion before matters deteriorated further, responded.

"Before her late husband was granted a peerage, Lady Hambleton was a topless waitress in a bar. She is not a practicing Roman Catholic. Despite that she insists on placing a statue of herself in the foyer of the new wing. I have told her unequivocally that I will not permit it. Now, if you will be kind enough, gentlemen, to leave the matter with me, I hope to change her mind. I'll keep you informed."

He looked at the chairman, his eyes hard. "I think, Mr. Chairman, we are now ready for a motion to adjourn."

"So move," said Cliff Orpen.

Chapter Six

It was Harris on the phone to say he wouldn't be home until after midnight and not to wait up. His consonants slurring, he was shouting into the phone over the sounds of partying in the background. As Michael put down the receiver he wondered who Harris's friends were and why he never mentioned them. He glanced at his watch: five to eleven. Miss Pritchard had come by the study an hour earlier to ask whether there was anything she could get him; a wee snack, perhaps? Thank you, no. She thought, then, she'd be off to bed, but just in case, there was some ham left over from dinner and some strawberries ("nice big fresh ones") in the refrigerator.

Now, hungry, he put aside his book and made his way to the kitchen where he found a chunk of cheddar cheese, a lettuce leaf and a slice of whole wheat bread. He folded the lettuce about the cheese and the bread about them both, poured a glass of milk into a tumbler and pulled up a chair to the large porcelain-topped table at the center of the room. The refrigerator motor clicked off and the silence suddenly seemed palpable. He could hear the crunch of the food between his teeth and that familiar creaking in his jaw. Outside the window the gusting wind let out a howl and cast rain like a handful of gravel against the glass.

He munched on the sandwich, letting his gaze drift about the kitchen. She was a tidy one, Miss Pritchard; everything wore a sheen of cleanliness. His eyes traversed to the door leading to the basement and his thoughts returned to Harris. He pictured him, preoccupied, head thrust forward as he walked, not troubling to so much as nod to Miss Pritchard or to respond to her greeting as each morning he headed for the basement. He smiled remembering her face the day he told her Harris would be using the basement as a place to work, recalling how she'd managed to convey her displeasure without being impertinent by drawing down the corners of her mouth and emitting a small huff of exasperation. She didn't much like the prospect of Harris "traipsin' through" her kitchen every morning and night and was certain the day staff wouldn't like it either. Michael realized he had handled it badly in not breaking the news to her earlier – postponing it until the morning of Harris's arrival – and had aggravated her disgruntlement by borrowing her key to the basement room and not returning it. He'd had Father Jamieson have it duplicated, had given the copy to Harris and had added the original to the cumbersome collection fanning out from his own key chain. When Harris insisted that a second lock be added, he had ordered it done, had given Harris one of the keys and had kept the other.

Now he was considering whether to go down and have a look at the room. A part of his mind immediately forbade it but there was the unacknowledged awareness that, with Harris delayed, Miss Pritchard abed, Jennifer with Copeland at the theater and his secretaries at a meeting upstate, the house was empty. Why should he not take a look? Early on Harris had invited him to have a look around but, perhaps significantly, had only once renewed the invitation since the day the museum had delivered the wooden box. Even though he'd been made privy to what was in the box and to what Harris was about in the workroom, there was a certain impropriety in entering it without Harris's knowledge. And clearly, the door had been doubly secured to one end: to ensure privacy.

Over the past three months Michael's conviction that the bones downstairs were not Jesus' had only occasionally wavered. It was, of course, possible that they were, but he had concluded that that eventuality was highly unlikely. This conviction had deepened as time passed and a theory had germinated and grown in his mind. His early affection and respect for Harris had cooled. There were aspects of his character that Michael found reprehensible, even unsavory. The man had few principles. He scorned everything Christian, disdained tradition, was cynical, expedient, and as he had confessed late one evening while despondent, deeply resentful that he had been bypassed by time and neglected by his peers. He had been enraged when Albright had refused to extend his sabbatical and that umbrage had been inflamed when, as time passed, no other university pursued him. It became clear in the recounting that these slights had been nurtured and were roiling in his gut. Consequently – so Michael reasoned – might he not be hungering to retaliate? Might he not be planning the ultimate rejoinder: a coup unparalleled in history, a triumph ranking with Leakey's African fossils and surpassing even the discovery of the Dead Sea Scrolls? If his hope for immortality had now receded beyond reach – the years lying heavy and even his heart threatening to betray him – might he not be preparing to seize center-stage with the most monumental of all frauds, the more to be relished because it would be undetectable?

Michael's suspicion had slowly hardened into a conviction. As he saw it, there were only three possibilities: first, that the bones were Jesus' remains, which Michael rejected as inconceivable; second, that, beguiled by his ambition, Harris had lost his objectivity and was making an honest mistake, a mistake that would be rectified when other archaeologists had access to his finds, but only after immeasurable damage had been done; and third, that Harris was deliberately and meticulously fabricating a hoax stunning in its effrontery.

It was all so possible. Harris could have come upon a first-century tomb; perhaps precisely under the circumstances he had described that night in London. How simple to remove the skeleton and an ossuary. How easy for a man with Harris's experience to add the cryptic scratches and to "age" them by rubbing the limestone with silica. The story about discovering the molar apart from the skull and finding that they matched could be invention – who was to say him nay? – and the discovery of an appropriate cave in the neighborhood of Qumran, although admittedly difficult after the many organized searches of the late forties and fifties, would be by no means impossible. And what an ideal site at which to locate his "find." Qumran! The very word was magic and oozed authenticity. It was perfect: the place to which a Zealot, inevitably, would spirit the body – far enough from Jerusalem, isolated from Roman patrols, a community of dedicated Jews, long argued to be Jesus' own community. After the discovery of the Dead Sea Scrolls dozens of articles in academic journals and in the popular press had put Jesus in Qumran during his so-called "silent years," the eighteen years between his appearance in the Temple and the beginning of his ministry at the age of thirty. It was at first commonly believed that he had spent those years among the Essenes. There were undeniable parallels in his and the community's teachings and there was the curious fact that, although the sect was as well known in Jesus' time as were the Pharisees, the Saducees and the Herodians, no mention is made of it in the New Testament. How appropriate it would seem that Jesus' body had been returned to the community of which he had once been a part.

But the bones and the tomb were not enough to make Harris's case. They were not in themselves conclusive, certainly not sufficiently to validate beyond question a claim by anyone, no matter how reputable, that they were Jesus' remains. More specific proof would be needed; thus, the manuscript. It was clear to Michael, however, that even as the manuscript would be the linch-pin, the forging of it would pose almost insoluble problems. Not the composing of the text or the inscribing of the Aramaic script – Harris could readily manage that – but how to duplicate the ancient carbon ink? How to age the chemicals of which it was composed? How to obtain a piece of parchment appropriately stained by the centuries, dehydrated by two millennia in the desert and deteriorated by air and insect? Once the manuscript was made available to scholars, it would be scrutinized by paleographers, epigraphists, chemists, and others in related fields, each of whom would approach it with both awe and skepticism. Most would have spent much of their lives poring over antiquities and would be immediately alerted by any incongruity, by any of the miniscule flaws that betray a forgery. But Harris knew the criteria they would be applying, knew them as well as any man, and if he was in fact concocting a fraud, would he have begun were he not confident he could carry it off?

But was Harris capable of perpetrating such a hoax? It would require an enormous ego, but he had that. Michael smiled tightly recalling the aphorism: "Man has created God in his own image and worships his creator" – it was certainly true of Harris. He saw himself as above the strictures applied to ordinary mortals; how otherwise could he have smuggled the bones and the manuscript out of Israel without a qualm and have confessed it to Michael with a shrug of indifference? He scorned others' ideas, spurned the possibility of a power higher than human reason and suffered dissent badly. Yes, Michael decided, he did have the ego for it. But did he harbor sufficient malice? From the day he'd loosed that diatribe against his wife and against the very institution of marriage, sneering at love itself, Michael found it easy to believe that he did. Had he the arrogance to believe he could gull the entire scientific community? Of course he had; wasn't he prepared cavalierly to lob a bombshell into the heart of Christendom?

Michael was not unaware that he might himself be fashioning an elaborate rationale to avoid facing the unpalatable thesis Harris had posited. He'd examined that possibility carefully and rejected it. If Harris's claims were true they made a mockery of the presence of God in the world. It would mean that he had permitted the church to mature as it had over two thousand years only to bring its central message into disrepute in the end. It would mean that Jesus was wrong about God and about the nature of the universe – for had he not predicted, not once but many times, that he would rise from the grave? He had also said he would build his church on Peter, "the rock," and Peter's first message to the world after the crucifixion was, " . . . You killed the prince of life. God, however, raised him from the dead, and to that fact we are the witnesses." The chief among apostles, Paul, had predicated everything on the resurrection: "If Christ has not been raised then our preaching it is useless and your believing it is useless." And the popes, without exception, had reaffirmed that belief. It did not matter whether the resurrection was physical, it was real. *However* he had been raised from the dead, he had been raised from the dead, and that was why Easter was the great festival of the church; it celebrated an empty tomb. If now Jesus' bones were to be brandished before the world it would make difficult, almost impossible, belief in this central doctrine of the church and make every claim of the church suspect. Michael found it impossible to believe that God would so mock the men and women and the institution that had served him so faithfully across the centuries.

But always, no sooner did he shore up his convictions and reinforce his faith, than he was confronted by Harris. Damn Harris! Harris with his quiet confidence, Harris with his imperturbable certainty: not the excessive assertiveness of the man who compensates for his insecurity with adamancy, but the uncontentious assurance that is the more unnerving for its absence of stridency.

But enough of speculating; it was imperative that he know what was to be known. He rose, walked to the door, turned on the light and went swiftly down the stairs.

The basement was lit with three naked bulbs but was dark at the perimeter. The locked room was at the far end. As he went, he reached into his pocket for his keys. Shuffling through them at the door he suddenly felt chilled. His hands had begun to tremble and he had difficulty inserting the keys. The bolts withdrawn, the door swung toward him. He pushed it wide, and fumbled on either side of the doorframe and then remembered that the light switch was mounted on the far wall. To his right he saw a table on which there were a three-turret microscope, a Polaroid camera, an assortment of bottles, some flat pans, a bunsen burner, a variety of sculptor's tools, some camel's hair brushes and a pad of notepaper covered with neat jottings. Beyond, in the near darkness, he could just make out two longer tables, three dish-shaped floodlights on stands, and a chair. An acrid smell flared his nostrils.

He walked to the far wall, stepping carefully over the electric cables that snaked across the floor to an outlet, and flipped the light switch. One of the floodlights was directed into his face and he was momentarily blinded. He put up an arm to block the light, closed his eyes and turned away, remaining where he was until his pupils had adjusted. The only sound was the sustained whirr of the dehumidifier.

On the near table, pressed flat between two sheets of plate glass, was a manuscript perhaps two feet long and ten inches deep. The bottom edge had disintegrated in an irregular fashion, in places intruding into the text, and was dark brown, almost as though it had been burned. The upper edge had also suffered deterioration but was not seriously eaten away. On the left hand edge scraps had flaked off and had been placed in position under the glass, some as perfectly matched as pieces of a jigsaw puzzle, others so placed as to line up with the margin of the text. Despite the fact that the entire manuscript was dun-colored, with areas shading into deeper browns, the script was clearly legible. Michael recognized the language as Aramaic.

The far table was covered with green baize. On it was a human skeleton. Michael approached it slowly. As he went he turned the stand on which one of the floodlights was mounted, focusing it on the table. The wheels screeched on the concrete floor.

There before him lay the skeleton of a man long dead, the bones varying in color from off-white to a burnished mahogany brown and so arranged that the skeleton seemed to be lying on its back, legs slightly spread, arms by the sides. Alongside was a wooden yardstick. The jawbone had been wired in position beneath the skull. Beside it lay a single molar. Astride the bones on a tripod was a still camera, the lens directed downward.

Michael stood by the table, breathing rapidly, the tips of the fingers of both hands resting on the baize covering. His eyes traveled slowly down the skeleton beginning with the skull, following the vertebrae, tracing the concentric lines of the ribcage, passing the pelvis and moving down the legs to the splayed feet. His entire body was trembling now and he felt faint. He looked at the hand nearest him; leaning forward, searching among the tiny bones for a mark, an abrasion. None. He stared fixedly at the skull, unblinking, and lost all consciousness of time and place. His imagination clothed the shining bone with flesh, covered the grimacing teeth, filled the empty eye sockets and created skin and hair and beard until a face was there, a face with the sheen of health and a gleam of life in dark solemn eyes . . .

He had been trembling and now began to shake. His skull constricted and his brain dissolved behind his eyes. He was smothering but couldn't draw a breath and was certain he was dying. He grasped the table with both hands, striving to stay erect. The muscles of his legs went slack and he pitched forward and slumped to the floor, unaware of the crash of the table, and of the bones and the camera clattering to the concrete about him as he clutched the green baize covering:

Before him . . . the whole of creation, weeping. The trees bowed down and weeping. Each petal of every flower, weeping. Every blade of grass, weeping. The clouds and the skies and the very heavens, weeping. All of time and space; all that is and has been and ever will be, weeping. And above and around and through it all, God, weeping. Weeping for man: for his pride, his obduracy, his waywardness, his thousand cruelties, his multitudinous hatreds. And at the heart of the eternal sorrow, the shadow of a cross and a silhouetted figure, and the face he had just seen . . . weeping.

When consciousness returned – after how long he couldn't tell – he found himself crouched on the floor on his knees and forearms, his forehead against the cold concrete, his body heaving with great spasmodic gasps. Slowly the shuddering subsided and he pushed himself up and sat back on his heels. In the silence he became aware again of the hum of the dehumidifier, and after a moment, of another sound behind him . . .

There in the doorway, eyes wide, mouth agape and her face dead white, was Miss Pritchard.

In the kitchen, seated by the table, Michael standing with a hand comfortingly on her shoulder, Miss Pritchard was becoming herself again.

"I didn't know what to think," she was saying, a tremor in her voice, each hand massaging the other, pressing at arthritic knuckles. "I'm in me bed and I hear somebody go down the stairs. There's nobody home but you and it don't seem likely you'll be goin' to the basement. But then I says to myself, it *has* to be himself, and I'm just droppin' off when I hear this crash – you know, like somethin' fell over. So I get out of me bed and I'm on the basement stairs, and there's the door to the root-cellar open and light pourin' out. It did give me a turn . . . "

She hesitated and Michael was about to stop her but then thought it better that she say it all: he had no idea how long she'd been standing in the doorway. And she'd be better for saying it.

"For a minute I don't know what to do," she continued. "I just stand there on the stairs gettin' me bearin's. I don't want to be stickin' me nose in, but there *had* been this crash and now there's not a sound except like somebody's hurt, so I figure maybe I'd better have a look-see. Not to be stickin' me nose in, you understand?"

"I understand."

"Well, anyways," she continued, the interruption shifting her into the past tense, "when I got to the door and looked in, there you was, down on your knees gettin' ready to clean up the mess. And then you looked around at me . . . " she looked up at him, "and you looked like death itself. I thought maybe you'd had a spell or an attack or somethin'."

"I'm afraid I stumbled and knocked over the table." he said. "But," he added lightly, "no harm done."

It suddenly broke on Miss Pritchard that she was seated in Michael's presence and that he was attending to her. Flustered, she stood up quickly, slipping Michael's hand from her shoulder by dipping away as she rose. "Oh my goodness!" she said. "You'll have to excuse me, Your Eminence, but you did give me a turn. Oh, my . . . !" she said unhappily, realizing that her hair was unbound and on her shoulders, and gathering it back with two hands. "Oh my . . . !" she said in fresh dismay, drawing the bathrobe tightly about her and knotting the belt.

"I appreciate your concern," Michael said. "Thank you very much."

Miss Pritchard now wanted to make her exit as soon as was feasible and started for the door, gathering her hair and pushing it back as she went. She paused at the door. "Do you want me to clean up downstairs?" she asked distractedly.

"No, I'll take care of it."

"You're sure?"

"Yes, I'm sure. Away you go to your bed now," he said, affecting a small smile and simulating her brogue. "Sure and you'll be needin' your sleep now."

"Well, if you're sure," she said doubtfully. She held at the door for a moment and her frown deepened. "If I'm not askin' questions out of school," she said, "what's all them bones?"

Michael might have been remarking about the weather so offhanded was his tone. "Archaeologists . . . you know. They work with bones. It's probably a thousand-year-old ape. Something like that."

Miss Pritchard managed an appropriate shudder. "Ugh," she said, without much heart. "Good night, Your Eminence," she added and went off, drawing her hair to the front as she turned her back.

Michael decided to wait up for Harris. He had considered righting things downstairs but realized that was impossible, and although he was reluctant to admit it, didn't want to go to the basement again. He went to the study, set the door ajar and seated himself in the wingback chair so he could see the front door.

What had so affected him downstairs? In retrospect it was puzzling, disturbing. It was unlike him. Typically, he decided to review all that had transpired from the moment he opened the door to the basement room. There was his mood: the dead silence of the empty house with the rain rattling erratically at the windows had created a sense of eeriness. There was the knowledge that he was trespassing: he remembered a touch of guilt as he turned the keys in the locks. And he was nervous, of course. That was inevitable. Although he'd become convinced that the bones weren't Jesus' he couldn't dismiss the possibility, and when he swung the door wide and peered into the darkness of the room, he recalled feeling something of the same mixture of awe and apprehension he'd experienced the first time he'd visited the crypt where St. Peter was entombed. He recalled also being offended by the smell of acid and by the tabletop covered with tools, offended oddly enough in the way he often was in Israel by the tawdriness of the souvenir stands at the holy sites. He remembered his taking care not to look directly at the table on which the bones lay, but seeing them in his peripheral vision as he peered at the manuscript. And then there was the despair that had settled on him as he recognized the apparent authenticity of the scroll.

And, of course, the bones . . . .

How willful the mind, he thought. How futile to command it. You can't say, "Go to now; I will not permit myself, even for a moment, to believe that these are the bones of my Lord." No, the mind is unruly as a globule of mercury: elusive, running where it will, contrary. For all his disbelief he had found himself seeking the mark of a nail on the bones of the hand. He thought of Thomas – "Doubting Thomas" as he'd since been called – Thomas, who had been afraid to believe and afraid not to, being bidden by his Lord to look and to touch. Even as had Thomas, he too had looked for the nailprint. And he had studied the skull. How fearful man's visage with the flesh gone; the eye sockets empty, the ragged triangle of the nasal cavity, the insane grimace of the teeth . . . .

But what lurking primeval memory of the mystery of death, what vestigial horror had stormed and overwhelmed his mind? He got out of his chair and pulled down Von Hugel's *Philosophy of Religion*. He hadn't opened it since seminary days. Perhaps the experience of others could illuminate his own strange flight from reality.

The clock on the mantle startled him by its chiming. One o'clock! He'd been reading for more than an hour. Where the devil was Harris?

He put aside the book, got out of the chair, walked to the window, pulled aside the curtain and looked out on Fiftieth Street. The street was deserted. A young woman was dressing a window at Sak's. When he'd first come to New York the streets were peopled until two or three in the morning; now few went walking late and even the taxis were scarce. Where the devil *was* Harris?

He'd better plan what he would say to account for the chaos downstairs. No, none of that; no elaborate explanations. He would have to account for knocking over the table. He'd already misled Miss Pritchard on that; he'd repeat the story to Harris. It was an innocent enough lie.

Sounds from the front entrance. He went into the hall. It took two keys to get into the house; one to enter a small foyer and another to open the door to the hall. Through the fluted sheers covering the glass of the door he could discern two figures, one recognizably Harris, the other smaller, and to judge by the laughter, a woman. Harris was talking in loud whispers consisting mostly of entreaties to "Shh. Be quiet for Christ sake," and fumbling at the lock. Michael was about to go to the door and open it when it suddenly swung inward with Harris stumbling after it, grasping the edge to keep from falling. This struck him as exceedingly funny and he began to laugh, pausing to shush the woman who, seeing Michael standing by the doorway to the study, said "Hi." She was perhaps forty, with auburn-dyed hair loosened by the evening, some of the tight curls dangling. Italian, Michael decided; something about her coloring and her eyes. She was wearing a powder-blue simulated leather coat, open, revealing deep cleavage and the inverted curves of slack breasts lifted and compressed.

Harris, clinging precariously to the edge of the door, which was making fitful attempts to get away from him, turned with elaborate care and looked at Michael out of solemn eyes, blinking. He turned back to the woman and said, "See. What'd I tell you? That you'd wake ev'rybody up – right?" The door almost got away from him but he brought it back. "Be seein' ya," he said to the woman, closing the door, standing with his back to it, both hands behind him on the knob, looking at Michael with a fuzzy smile.

"I thought I tol' you not to wait up," he said.

Michael was at a loss. What to do? Harris was hopelessly drunk; how could he possibly explain to him what had happened?

156

He'd wait until morning. No, he couldn't do that; he had an early appointment and Harris would probably sleep late and rise hungover. Damn! – there was no option.

"Come in a minute," he said, turning to the study.

He heard Harris following but didn't look back. He went to his chair and sat down. Harris slumped in the wingback chair across from him and began a disorganized search of his pockets for a cigaret. Michael took a deep breath, composing himself.

"Harris," he said tentatively. Harris was occupied going through his pockets. "Harris," Michael said more strongly, "will you give me your attention, please?"

Harris looked at him, blinking heavy-lidded eyes. "There isn' a cigaret aroun' here anywhere, is there?" he asked.

"Harris . . ." Michael began.

Harris had slid forward in the chair and was now reaching into his back pockets, his head lolling. "Thass a helluva note," he said, "I had a whole pack in the taxi . . ."

Michael got out of his chair, went across the hall to the reception room, took a cigaret and a book of matches from a silver humidor and returned to the study. Harris was in the midst of lighting a bent cigaret. He held it aloft triumphantly. "Tol' you I had some – right?"

Michael sat down, "Harris," he said, "there's something I must talk to you about."

"How 'bout a nightcap?" Harris said, pushing to his feet.

"Harris, will you *sit down!*" Michael shouted.

The sharpness of the command cut through the fog in Harris's brain and he lowered himself into the chair, summoning some concentration and looking questioningly at Michael. "Somethin' the matter?" he asked.

Michael spoke slowly and deliberately, his voice strong. "I went into your workroom tonight and I'm afraid I had an accident. I . . ."

Harris's head was unsteady but his eyes had lost their blankness. "You went into . . . into my workroom?" he said.

"Yes, And I had an accident. I knocked over the table on which you're assembling—"

Harris pushed to his feet and walked to the door, turning toward the kitchen. Michael followed, sick with despair, wondering if he should reach out and take Harris's arm – he was lurching as he went – but knowing that if he did he'd be thrust away. As Harris started down the stairs, he stumbled and Michael caught his breath, but he seized the bannister and was swung into the wall and then went on. He half ran across the basement and stopped, both hands on the doorframe, looking into the room. After a moment he turned. Michael remained at the foot of the stairs. They were separated by some forty feet. Harris's face, the brilliant light of the room behind him, was in shadow.

"I'm sorry," Michael offered.

It was a moment before Harris responded. He was breathing heavily but his articulation was precise. "What the hell do you mean," he hissed, "going into my room?"

Michael considered saying: It's my room, you know; or, You've invited me, remember? or, Why shouldn't I? Instead he said, "I *am* sorry, Harris. I hope I haven't done any damage."

Harris stood in the doorway, swaying. He went off balance for a moment and put a hand on the lintel. When he spoke his voice was cold and controlled. "Would you please give me the keys?"

Michael reached into a pocket, brought out his key chain and removed two keys. As he walked toward him, Harris stretched out a hand. Michael dropped the keys on his palm. Harris looked at them for a moment, closed his fingers over them and put them in his pocket. He turned and entered the room, slamming the door behind him, leaving Michael standing alone in the darkened basement.

Chapter Seven

The joyous spring air was filled with the sound of mourning. In Michael's ears, as he stepped from the limousine before the tiny imitation brick bungalow, the sound was like the wail of the March wind at The Cottage when nature bustled through the forest, spring housecleaning. Drawn by the incongruity of the gleaming black Cadillac in their street, children came running and others followed on. Someone within the house must have noticed Michael's arrival, for there was a brief silence and then an intensification of the volume of the mourning. The front door to the house opened and a man in white shirt and black trousers, squat and bowed in the legs, stood in the doorway, squinting in the sunlight, framed against the darkness of the interior.

"That's her brother Emilio," Father Colombo whispered as they walked toward the house.

Father Colombo was a priest in Our Lady of Sorrows parish. It was he who had called Monsignor Jamieson to suggest that His Eminence might like to know about Francesca Andreotti. Michael had read her story in the *Times* but the report had been restrained and the details underplayed. He had invited Father Colombo to join him at breakfast, and the young priest, lean and darkly handsome and nervous in the presence of his cardinal, had related the details. Mrs. Andreotti and her husband had been boiling maple syrup in a large cast-iron cauldron on a propane stove in a shed at the rear of their house. They had tapped the trees in a sugarbush on her brother Emilio's farm in New Hampshire, and were reducing the sap to syrup. The stove, installed only the week before, had exploded.

"All the details aren't clear," the young priest said, "but it seems the cauldron struck her husband and killed him instantly. The boiling sap scalded the children and they were dead on arrival at hospital. They were twins, a sort of second family that had come along late." His voice thickened and he had to clear his throat. "Today would have been their sixth birthday."

"How dreadful," Michael said.

"The shed was set on fire by the explosion. After getting the children out, Francesca tried to go in after her husband . . . but it was hopeless."

"Was she badly burned?"

"Miraculously, hardly at all. A few blisters on her legs from the syrup, but nothing really."

"How is she?"

The young priest shook his head slowly. "Your Eminence, I really don't know. She's in some kind of shock. They released her from hospital last night. I took her home and stayed with her a while. She didn't seem to know me. She didn't recognize her brother or her other children."

"How many children does she have?"

"Five, now. All grown. Her eldest son's studying for the priesthood." He shifted restlessly. "I think I should go, Your Eminence. The funeral's this morning."

"Leave the address with Father Carroll. I'll go by this afternoon."

As Michael reached the front porch, Emilio dropped to one knee and kissed his ring. The wailing fell off and ceased except for a wizened old woman keening in a corner, fingers gnarled as the roots of a vine, fondling a rosary. There were a dozen women in the small living room, all in black and all wearing veils.

"Where is your sister?" Michael asked.

Emilio, who was trembling, didn't speak but pointed to a door. Michael went to the door and pushed through. There in her kitchen in a wooden rocking-chair beside a wood stove sat the widow. She was a tiny woman, not five feet tall and weighing perhaps ninety pounds. She had a peasant's body; bony and humped at the shoulders, the head thrust forward on a sinewed neck. Her face was a relief map of the toil and sorrows of her forebears, the skin brown and leathery and marked with liver spots. Small black eyes recessed in dark cavities looked out blankly. A full mug of tea was cupped in two hands on her lap.

Seated at the kitchen table or standing against the walls were her three sons and two daughters. As Michael and Father Colombo entered, they turned, their faces mirroring surprise and then confusion. One and then the others genuflected awkwardly and went quickly and silently from the room pulling the door closed behind.

Michael picked up a chair, placed it directly in front of the woman and sat in it. Gently, he unwrapped her fingers from about the mug and placed it on the table. Then he leaned forward, took her hands in his and began to speak Italian in a voice so soft that Father Colombo could barely make out the words.

"Hail Mary, full of grace," he said, his brow almost touching hers, "the Lord is with Thee. Blessed art thou among women and blessed is the fruit of thy womb, Jesus."

As he prayed, the rhythmic emphasis of the vowels making his speech like a whispered chant, his voice gradually grew louder and the words took on an assurance and an authority that started tears to Father Colombo's eyes. The woman did not move and her eyes were opaque and fixed, as though on some distant object.

"Blessed Father, look in mercy upon thy handmaiden, Francesca. Draw near, gracious Lord, and comfort this thy child in her time of sorrow. Thou, Father, thou dost understand our sorrow; the sadness and the heartbreak when we are separated from those we love, for thou didst send thy son to die for our sins.

"Blessed Lord Jesus, draw near. Thou knowest the agony we feel. In thine own agony in Gethsemane thou didst sweat great drops of blood and on the cross suffered as never man has suffered. Grant thy peace to thy servant, Francesca.

"Blessed Virgin, holy Mother of God, thou dost know how it is to lose a son, for thou didst watch his enemies nail thine own son to the tree and thrust the spear into his side and leave him there to die. Thou dost understand our pain. Grant the gift of faith to thy servant, Francesca. Draw near, blessed Mother of God. Speak to her. Touch her. Comfort her in this her hour of sorrow."

As he prayed, his head inches above the woman's, her body began to lean toward him and her head slowly bent forward. She made no sound, but tears began to fall on Michael's hands as they grasped hers, holding them so tightly that his knuckles were white. A great shudder went through her, a sound like a rush of wind issued from her mouth, and she began to tremble and then to shake. Finally the pain gushed out in hoarse, anguished sobs. Michael put his brow against hers. After a while she grew silent and they remained motionless for a time. Father Colombo had walked to a window and was staring unseeing at the cloudless sky, tears falling from his face.

The woman drew a great breath, withdrew a hand from Michael's, found a large handkerchief in the pocket of her dress and wiped the tears from his hands. Then she wiped her face and blew her nose and raised her head, and Michael sat back in his chair. She looked at him, her eyes still awash with tears, and her English thickly accented, said in a strong voice, "Thank you, Father."

From the living room, the wailing that had abated as Michael's voice had risen, mounted again. Francesca lapsed back into Italian. "I must speak to my children and my friends," she said. Michael rose and replaced the chair at the table. Francesca walked to the door and passed through it.

"Can we slip out the back way?" Michael asked.

"I think so," Father Colombo said, and together they went into the sunny afternoon. There was the black skeleton of the shack.

"Have it cleared away and a new one built," Michael said. Father Colombo made a quick nod.

As they came around the side of the house they saw that perhaps a hundred people had gathered and were standing in silence in the street in a semicircle beyond the limousine. As Michael came down the path, three news photographers ran forward and then scuttled before him, clicking their shutters. A television cameraman, standing in a plot of flowers, panned with him as, face grim, he walked swiftly to the car.

Within, as the limousine pulled slowly through the lane that opened in the crowd, he turned to Father Carroll, his face black with rage. "Who told the press I would be here?" he demanded.

The priest flinched before his anger. "I'm afraid I did. I thought it would be all right."

Michael's voice was controlled but steel-hard. "You will never do that again," he said. "Do you understand?"

"Yes, Eminence. I'm sorry."

162

Nothing was said as the car swept through the Midtown tunnel and south to Gracie Mansion. Glancing at his watch, Michael saw that he was already ten minutes late for the reception for the newly elected mayor of New York.

The following evening Michael was in the study going over reports on the annual Archdiocesan Appeal for Catholic Charities and Education Services. The drive was not going well and there was doubt that the goal of four million dollars would be met. Harris joined him later than usual, the flesh of his face vertical with fatigue. He poured himself a small brandy and went wearily to his usual chair. Michael said, "Hello," and returned to his work. Harris sipped his drink, watching, and then said, "Aren't you going to congratulate me?"

Michael looked up: "Sorry, I missed that."

"I said, aren't you going to congratulate me?"

"Should I?"

"I've finished the first draft of my book."

"That's very fast. It's taken you what? – not quite three months."

"It's not *Gone With the Wind*."

"How much more have you to do?"

"Maybe a month. Some revision and then I'll show it to my publisher."

"I hope you won't think me uncivil," Michael said, "but I must finish these reports. Got a meeting early tomorrow."

He went back to work and a silence settled on the room, broken only by the shuffling of paper and the faint sound of traffic sifting through from the street. Harris, a sardonic smile playing at the corners of his mouth, watched Michael, whose concentration was total. After perhaps ten minutes he sighed heavily, scribbled some notes, gathered the papers and put them in a manilla folder. His brow was furrowed and it was obvious that he was still occupied with the material he'd been studying.

"What engrosses you so?" Harris asked.

"Nothing that would interest you."

"No. Tell me."

"Reports on our fundraising campaign."

"You're right. It doesn't interest me."

"To each his own," Michael said, putting the folder in the OUT basket.

Harris said: "I see you've been going about doing good."

"I don't follow."

"On the television tonight and in the papers." He spread his arms as though displaying a newspaper headline. "Cardinal Visits Bereaved Widow."

"Oh, that."

"Are you in the mood to be twitted by a congenitally irreverent old agnostic?"

"To tell you the truth, I don't think I am tonight."

"It's been that kind of a day?"

"It's been that kind of a day."

"All I was going to ask was: Wasn't it the Pharisees Jesus chewed out for doing their good works in public?"

"It was."

There was a humorless smile on Harris's lips. "But then how could even he have known what it would be like in the twentieth century where the PR man is king."

Michael made no response but began putting his desk in order, picking up paper clips and putting pencils and a tiny calculator in a drawer.

"Was she a good Catholic?"

"As good as we come."

"Doesn't that kind of thing make you wonder?"

"Why should it?"

"Here's this poor woman. Good Catholic. Loves God. Loves her family. Never had much in life, but tries to do the right thing. Then – Zap! – her husband's killed, her kids are scalded to death, she's burned. That kind of thing never makes you wonder?"

"Lots of things do, but they don't alter my faith, if that's what you mean. There are a hundred things to make you question God but a thousand to strengthen your faith."

Harris wanted to worry it some more. "There she is, a saint, and all her life she gets the dirty end of the stick. And here's this old sinner, me. Always done what I want, gone where I want, taken what I want. Doesn't seem just; wouldn't you agree?"

Michael said, "God doesn't mete out justice with a balance-scale in this world. If he did, who would stand?"

"And here I am," Harris persisted, "about to tell your saint that her God's a man."

"Yes," Michael said. "I know."

Michael was seated on the side of his bed, head in hands. He had gone from the study directly to his room in hope of falling immediately to sleep, but in the darkness his mind was like a screen on which a kaleidescopic series of images were being cast. He saw again the columns of figures on the reports sheets and read their meaning. In swift review, all the institutions for which he was responsible came before him: he saw the untenanted faces of the retarded, the handicapped struggling with recalcitrant limbs, the blind with their opaque eyes, the husks of the aged in their beds, the adult foetuses fleeing sensation in catatonia, the poor with their animal wariness, the rickety infants, the pregnant children. And he saw the schools and hospitals in the archdiocese; saw their doors closed against those seeking to enter.

Then all of that dissolved and was replaced with the face of Francesca Andreotti. He saw her, borne up by her faith, walking from the kitchen to comfort her friends. And he saw Harris's face and heard his words: "And here I am, about to tell your saint that her God's a man."

He could not permit it. He could not allow Harris to loose his lie in the world!

He had leaped from his bed to pace the floor. The possibility that he might not achieve his financial goal was disturbing, but it was as nothing compared to the threat to all of the faithful in every parish of every country of the world that lay potential in Harris's fraud. He had been right that night in London when his emotion had conjured up the hurt that Harris could wreak. He could deal a mortal wound to the church. It would matter little that he was perpetrating a lie; if it couldn't be demonstrated to be a lie it would be as though it were true. And the blow would fall when the church was least ready to bear it: beleaguered in Rome, divided in her own ranks, her leader empty-eyed and impotent.

The lurking thought surfaced: that night, after having retrieved Harris from diabetic shock, he had contemplated him dead. Now it entered his mind that, in God's name, he might have to kill him. Unthinkable as that might be, evil as the taking of life undoubtedly was, was it not a greater evil to stand by silent and passive while the greatest wickedness in history was visited on the defenseless? Indeed, was that not the great new sin of modern times; the unwillingness to get involved; turning away while the girl was raped, while the old man was robbed, while the victim was mugged? The blind eye and the deaf ear. The sin of omission. *If a man know to do right and doeth it not, to him it is sin.* That was Jesus' criticism of the Pharisees; that they had left undone what they should have done.

But *was* the refusal to get involved a new sin? Was it not the sin of the priest and the Levite who, seeing the traveler in the ditch, beaten, bloodied and robbed, had crossed to the other side of the road and gone on their way? Jesus had used the man who had intervened, the Samaritan who had taken the wounded man to where help could be given, as his example of loving one's neighbor. It wasn't a new sin at all. It was the sin of Chamberlain and Daladier when they sacrificed Czechoslovakia in an attempt to avoid getting involved. It was the sin of those who could have stopped Hitler but who backed away when the task required that they bloody their hands.

When Jesus went to the Temple in Jerusalem and saw the money-changers desecrating the holy place he didn't draw back from the confrontation, dangerous though it might be. Rather, the Prince of Peace had embraced violence. He had fashioned a whip from cords and had moved among the merchants, upturning their tables and driving them out of the Temple by the fury of his indignation. Some of the popes had raised armies to withstand those who would have destroyed the church. The Inquisition had gone to extremes and had done great evil but its goal had been right; to cut out as a cancer the error that could damn men's souls.

But with the years the church had grown soft. Its voice had lost its thunder. Its sinews had gone slack. That was why he had supported Pope Paul in his anguished outcry against the tide of immorality rising across the world. It had been an unpopular stand to take, but surely some voice needed to be raised, and if the church was silent who would speak? Wasn't the unfettered eroticism now infecting the world the direct result of inaction, of silence, of the fear of being scorned as reactionary, of wanting to be hailed as liberal and broadminded?

And now here he was, Michael Maloney, servant of God, knowing that an evil was about to be loosed on the world, that a

166

lie that could warp men's lives and vitiate their hopes and steal from them their faith was about to be uttered. It was not enough to argue that God's truth would triumph over this lie as it had triumphed over others. God triumphed through men. He effected his will through men. He routed falsehood through men. And he, Michael, was the one man in the world who knew what Harris was planning: could he do other than stop him?

But how?

It would be useless to importune him. He'd tried that and been rebuffed. Harris, as the Devil was wont to do, had quoted scripture to him: "The truth shall make you free," he'd said. The truth, yes, but not the lie that lay spreadeagled on a table in the basement below. The incredible effrontery of the man! Seeking to ascend to immortality on the bones of an unknown Jew centuries dead. And, ultimate sacrilege, to give that unknown the most sacred name in human history!

If only there was someone with whom he could discuss the problem. He had considered broaching it to one of his confessors but had rejected the idea. Jimmy Kelley was now old and "weary in welldoing," and there were signs of senility in him. He dare not entrust this of all secrets to a mind not entirely within its owner's control. He had contemplated flying to Rome to lay the dilemma before Paolo Rinsonelli. It would be safe with him – the well-being of the church was his life – but Paolo still saw him sometimes in a teacher-student relationship and might decide arbitrarily to take an action he would not concur in. If only Gregory were well . . . .

There was no option: he would act alone – he and God.

He donned a bathrobe over his pajamas and went quietly up the stairs to the chapel. He was there, prostrate on the floor before the altar, when at six o'clock Monsignor Carroll came to make preparation for the morning mass.

The decision made, the means had to be found, and the problem nagged at him like an unsound tooth, intruding into his days, going with him to bed at night.

How . . . ?

However done, it would have to be instantaneous and painless. He recoiled from the possibility of inflicting pain or causing Harris even a moment of apprehension or fear. Whatever the method, it must permit no possibility of bungling. He winced, seeing in his imagination the deed done but botched, and the necessity to administer the *coup de grace*. God! For all the rightness of his cause, for all the strength of his resolve, would he have the stomach for it? That exigency must never be permitted to occur.

However done, it would have to appear to be death from natural causes. There must not remain the remotest possibility that Harris's death come to the attention of the police. But, even best-laid plans go awry, and if for reasons beyond reckoning a flaw did appear, there must be no way by which an investigator could follow the spoor to him.

Michael had no doubt that he could achieve his objective. He had few illusions about crime and criminals. The commonly held belief that there was no such thing as a perfect crime was, he knew, nonsense. A cursory examination of police statistics would reveal that. Thousands of crimes are committed and never solved. Those in which the perpetrators are apprehended are usually crimes of passion committed without planning, or are such that the motive is obvious and culpability easily determined. He knew that most criminals are men or women of little intelligence lacking the wit to plan and mount a criminal act of any complexity. When a person of above average intellect did undertake to break the law, more often than not he succeeded. When he failed it was usually for predictable reasons: an associate blundered or betrayed; an examination of motives led inevitably to him; the crime completed, the perpetrator acted foolishly or – and this was the aspect that gave Michael concern – was ensnared by some unforeseen event.

He was aware that the police always sought to establish two things, probable cause and opportunity: in layman's language, who had a motive and could have been there when the crime was committed. In this instance, while he might have no option but to be at the scene of the crime, what possible motive could he be seen to have? None but he knew the nature of Harris's discovery. He was certain of that, not simply because Harris had stated it but because he knew the zeal with which the archaeologist had guarded this, the most important secret of his life. And once the bones, the scroll and Harris's manuscript had been hidden or disposed of, the motive would have been removed. And would anyone entertain even for a moment the thought that a cardinal of the Holy Roman Catholic church would commit murder? Posit even that something did go awry and that suspicions were kindled, would he not be the least likely of suspects? He and Harris were lifelong friends; their friendship having begun forty years earlier and having been reaffirmed when he offered the archaeologist a place to live and work.

There was a problem there: there would be the need to account for what Harris had been working on over the past few months. That he was involved in a project of significance was known to a number of people: Miss Pritchard, for instance, and the maids. One or all of them must have seen the driver for the museum deliver the box and take it to the basement. He would have to ascertain with discreet questions just what they did know. And he must not forget that Miss Pritchard *had* seen the bones.

His secretaries, too, knew that Harris went daily to the basement and labored long. Early on, at dinner, Father Jamieson had asked Harris what he was working on. Michael remembered the reply: "I'm doing a monograph on a find we made at a dig in the Middle East." That had been the end of it; the subject had never been raised again.

Someone at the museum would know about the box. It had been shipped there from Amman and stored for a time. But whoever knew that would not know what the box contained. Harris had told him the waybill was misleading and Michael himself had observed when the delivery was made that the box was still secured with metal strapping.

Jennifer knew, too, and that posed another kind of problem. She would be hurt by Harris's death. She had become attached to him, had taken to calling him "Uncle Harris" and to putting her cheek to his when leaving for work in the morning or returning at night. It was easy to understand her affection; she had been an only child and when her parents died there remained no blood relatives save Michael and a few distant great-uncles and aunts. But all that aside, Jennifer knew that Harris was working on something of importance and had wondered aloud a number of times, "What in the world is he doing down there in that gloomy old place?"

One other disturbing thought: Copeland knew. There was irony in the fact that Jennifer's fiancé was a detective attached to the New York County District Attorney's Office. When it first became apparent that Jennifer had fallen in love with him, Michael had appraised him carefully and had concluded that he was a decent man, a devout Catholic and that he had a first-rate mind. He realized now that it was the kind of mind that would inevitably pose questions unless, after Harris's death, some reasonable explanation accounted for the archaeologist's long and solitary hours downstairs. It was a problem that would demand serious thought.

The fundamental question returned: how to accomplish Harris's death? It was possible that, with his angina exacerbated by diabetes and overwork, he might expire from natural causes before he could publish. But that was hardly a dependable circumstance. No, he would have to take whatever steps were required.

For a time he despaired of finding an acceptable means. As his mind, touched with horror, ranged over the ways by which humans take other humans' lives, each was rejected out of hand. To begin, he was simply incapable of committing an act of violence. Could events then be so arranged that Harris seemed a suicide? Not a fruitful ground for speculation, he realized. In the company of others the archaeologist was normally in good spirits – although recently he had become churlish – and was a most unlikely nominee for death by his own hand. So far as Michael knew, he was the only person to whom Harris had confessed his despondency at not attaining his professional goals and at not receiving the recognition he felt he merited. Beyond that, suicide had the disadvantage that it would automatically be investigated by the coroner's office.

Death by poison? Virtually impossible. He would first have to determine what to use, arrange to get it and then administer it. And if by chance Harris's death were to be investigated, such were the skills of the forensic scientists that, whatever the potion, it would surely be detected. He had read somewhere of a poison (a snake venom? an extract from a plant or berry?) that left no residue in the body. But even if he could discover what it was, how could he obtain and administer it?

Death by apparent accident? There were possibilities there: a traffic accident . . . the car that plunged over a cliff . . . the fall from a height . . . drowning . . . perhaps a defective electrical appliance?

In his imagination he saw Harris enter the basement workshop, saw him reach out to determine why one of his floodlights was inoperative, saw him touch the stand, saw the searing flash of flame, saw Harris's body on the concrete floor, rigid, shuddering, the mouth gasping for breath, the eyes wide with the knowledge of death . . . .

He was overtaken by nausea and in the bathroom kneeled by the toilet bowl, retching.

Chapter Eight

Blessed Lord, loving Father, I come to you in the name of your holy Son, our Lord, Jesus, and in the love of the Blessed Virgin. Look in mercy on me, Father. Help me to lay bare my heart before you. It is heavy almost beyond endurance.

"Father, you know how I've struggled beneath the burden you have laid on me and how often I've echoed the prayer of our Blessed Lord in his agony in Gethsemane: 'If you are willing, take this cup away from me.' But you have not seen fit to remove it so I come now seeking the courage to drink it.

"I have asked for a sign whereby I may know the truth, but there has been no sign. Instead you have brought to my mind our blessed Lord's words, 'It is an evil and unfaithful generation that looks for a sign. The only sign it will be given is the sign of the prophet Jonah. For as Jonah was in the belly of the sea monster for three days and three nights, so will the Son of Man be in the heart of the earth for three days and three nights.' I have taken that as your word to me, Father – He *is* risen!

"Loving Father, across the centuries you've raised up defenders of the faith. Now I, who am the least of the least of these, have been called to follow in their train. But my heart fails me. Give me the courage to do what I must. Give me the wisdom to find a way. In the past your servants did what seemed evil to do what was good; even so must I. In your name the saints have persecuted those who have defamed you; so must I. For your glory the church has put down your enemies; so must I. That the faith might be known and honored your servants have defied the laws of men; so must I.

"You know, blessed Father, why I do this thing. It is solely to do your will, solely to serve your church, solely to preserve the faith. The times are evil. The ungodly surround and oppress. The glory of this world obscures the glory of the world to come and many of your children are apostate; some even rail against the faith. Surely their number will grow if the dread word is spoken, 'He is not risen.' I put myself in your hands. Your will be done on earth as it is in heaven.

. . .

"Father, I thank you. My heart is lighter. My faith seems stronger. I will do you will. Blessed Lord go with me."

"Dr. Raymond's office. Miss Hughes speaking."

"Dr. Raymond, please."

"May I say who's calling?"

"Cardinal Maloney."

"Oh, my goodness! Yes, of course . . . Cardinal Maloney!"

"Is the doctor busy?"

"No. I mean, yes, he's with a patient. But I'm sure he'll speak to you. Will you hold a minute, please."

. . .

"Your Eminence, what a pleasant surprise. I trust you're well."

"I'm fine, thank you."

"I'm pleased to hear that."

"I hope I'm not disturbing you. You're with a patient?"

"No, I came to the other office."

"I'll get right to it. I wanted to have a word with you about Dr. Gordon."

"He's not ill?"

"No, he seems to be fine, but he worries me."

"Uh huh?"

"He's working too hard. He won't look after himself, and nothing I say has the slightest effect."

"He's not an easy man to help."

"Just how serious is his condition?"

"He worries me."

"What is there I can do to help? That's the reason for this call."

"Your Eminence, you pose a problem for me."

"I do?"

"I make it a practice not to discuss a patient's condition with anyone other than his family. You do understand?"

"Of course, of course – doctors, lawyers and priests. I understand. I wouldn't want you to do anything untoward but, quite simply, I need your counsel. You knew he went into shock a few weeks ago?"

"No, I didn't know that."

"He didn't mention it?"

"Not a word."

"About a month ago. Late afternoon. He became drowsy, almost as though he were drunk and passing out."

"Uh huh."

"He was too far gone to take any juice or anything like that. Actually, he was unconscious. I gave him an injection."

"Glucagon?"

"In the muscle of the thigh."

"How quickly did he respond?"

"He began to come out of it within minutes."

"I must commend you."

"No problem; I worked as a paramedic in the war. That's why I called; I don't want to meddle, but I do want to help if I can."

"Yes, of course."

"He tells me he has a heart condition, too. Angina."

"It's not uncommon in older diabetics. There's an interrelatedness.

"My concern is simply to know what to do if there's another emergency. He's a very old friend, you know."

"Well . . . I suppose for all practical purposes you're family. The fact is, Eminence, he's not at all well. There is, as you say, the problem with his heart and that's exacerbated by the malfunction of the pancreas. Diabetics can lead virtually normal lives, thousands do, but only if they observe the rules. The body's a magnificent mechanism and will put up with quite incredible abuse, but it can be unforgiving of certain mistakes, and that's especially true of the diabetic. Unfortunately, Dr. Gordon's not very cooperative. He's careless about his diet. He drinks too much. He works too hard, takes too little exercise – all the wrong things. It would be my guess, the day he went into shock he'd simply been careless."

"Could insulin shock be fatal?"

"Yes, indeed."

"What brings it on?"

"Any number of things, usually in combination. As I say, carelessness. Working too hard. An overdosage. Then such things as delaying a meal, exercising unduly before eating . . . "

"Are there danger signals?"

"Yes, although they vary with the individual. The patient may seem drunk. Irritability is common. There may be some sweating, fatigue. He may seem to . . . ."

A note from Father Jamieson that Sophie Hambleton was in the city and that she had telephoned to say she had decided not to make a contribution to St. Clare's. Michael rang him on the intercom.

"Where is the lady staying?"

"At the Waldorf Tower."

"Did she mention that?"

"Yes."

"I'd like to invite her here. Please arrange for a messenger."

"I don't know, Eminence. She was quite adamant."

"Then why did she call? And why did she manage to let you know where she could be reached?"

Michael wrote the note by hand and suggested ten o'clock the following morning. At five minutes past ten Sophie, who had been driven the intervening four blocks in the limousine she maintained for her use in Manhattan, climbed the steps at 452 Madison Avenue and pressed the bell-button. Michael, who had been pacing the floor and looking occasionally into the street, went to his desk and seated himself. Miss Pritchard, who had been told that Lady Hambleton was coming, brought her to the open door of the study and went off. Sophie was dressed in a Harris tweed suit a shade too small and was a harmony of browns, from the identical leather of her shoes, purse and gloves to the beige silk blouse and ascot.

"Good of you to come, Lady Hambleton," he said, rising to shake hands.

"How often do you get invited to visit a cardinal?" Sophie said matter-of-factly. "Where would you like me to sit?"

Michael indicated a chair near the desk, seating himself as she did.

He had planned how he would begin and went immediately to the point. "I presume you know why I invited you here," he said briskly.

Sophie took the time necessary to remove her gloves, place her purse on the carpet beside the chair, and make herself comfortable. "No, I don't," she said, "unless it's to tell me you've decided to go ahead with the children's wing."

"No, it's not," Michael said, matching her directness. "It's to make it unmistakably clear to you that the tactics you've been employing since last we met are a waste of your time, and to ask you, please, to stop."

If Sophie was surprised that the battle had been joined so quickly it was not evident. She looked down, unbuttoned the jacket of her suit, puffed the ascot at the open neck of her blouse and said, "But, Your Eminence, you didn't need to bring me here to tell me that. It could have been done in a letter. Didn't Father Jamieson tell you I'd withdrawn my offer?"

"I thought it better to tell you face to face," Michael said somewhat lamely.

There was a silence. "Is that all?" Sophie said, some incredulity in her voice.

"Unless there's something on your mind."

Sophie compressed her lips and drew an extended breath. "Well then," she said, reaching down to pick up her purse, retrieve her gloves and begin to put them on, "I'll be going." She rose from her chair.

Michael was caught out by her reaction. He'd expected anger, argument, perhaps a move to shift the direction of the conversation, possibly acquiescence. But no, quite clearly Sophie was preparing to leave. He'd have to yield for the moment.

"Sit down, Lady Hambleton," he said sharply. "There is something more, something you don't seem to understand, and it would save a great deal of trouble if you did."

Sophie sat, but only just, keeping her feet under her, her purse on her lap and her gloves on.

"Quite clearly you don't understand the structure of the Roman Catholic church. You have tried to go over my head by appealing to the Board of Directors at St. Clare's and to—"

"I've appealed to nobody," Sophie interjected. "All I've done is make them the same offer I made you."

"But that's precisely the point. St. Clare's can't accept a contribution of the amount you propose without the approval of the head of the archdiocese—"

"Namely, you."

"At the moment, yes. Nor may any organization in Rome, nor – and I say it with respect – nor can the Holy Father himself accept a gift on behalf of an institution within the jurisdiction of an archdiocese. The decision in such matters rests solely within the purview of the resident bishop."

"I know that."

"And yet you've persisted. Why?"

Sophie bent over and placed her purse on the floor. A flush had begun to suffuse her cheeks. "Because this thing's become important to me. I want that wing built."

"Then it's very simple; make your gift unconditional. Leave the manner of recognition to St. Clare's."

"Which means you."

"I would want to approve it, yes. But if you're sincere about wanting the wing built, why not do as I suggest?"

Sophie's exasperation showed itself in the set of her jaw. "Because I don't think you've got the right to decide what's right and what's wrong. You act like you think you're Almighty God."

Michael blinked. "Then you don't really want it all that much," he said.

Sophie had come prepared for combat and wasn't about to back off now. "Your Eminence," she said, "you told me in England that *you* wanted the wing built – for the children of the area, you said. Do you really want it that much? If you did, would you turn it down simply because of a statue in the foyer?"

"There's a principle involved."

Sophie broke in. "Not any more. I'm a Catholic now."

"You are?"

"St. Anne's parish, Covington. Made my confession three weeks ago."

"I'm pleased to hear that."

"Doesn't that change the picture?"

Michael was seeking to regain his footing. "Let's say it's a step in the right direction."

Sophie was pressing. "That takes care of the matter of principle, right?"

"No, Lady Hambleton, it doesn't." He had his balance again. "Let me remind you that my objection was to the *nature* of the recognition you want. It still stands."

Sophie was ready: "In the instruction I took at St. Anne's, Father Samuel said that when God forgives sin it's forgiven. Gone. Forgotten. Never to be held against you here on earth or in the world to come. Right? He used the example of Mary Magdalene who, it says, had seven devils cast out of her." She picked up her purse and dug into it, extracting a small New Testament and beginning to riffle its pages. "According to St. Luke – it's in the seventh chapter – Mary and some other women traveled with Jesus and the apostles and . . . " a note of triumph entered her voice as she found the place " . . . and met his needs *out of their means*." She looked up, excited. "So God's work was done with contributions even from Mary Magdalene!"

Michael smiled paternally. "Just before I speak to that," he said, "if you've decided to become a student of the Bible, let me warn you against trying to prove things by the use of isolated portions of the text. It can cut both ways. Now, as to the point you're making: of course they helped take care of Jesus' financial needs, he had no income. But surely the relevant point here is that, granted Mary of Magdala did make contributions, there's nothing to suggest that he erected a memorial to her for doing so."

Sophie's face reflected dismay. She had thought her argument unanswerable. It was as though her assurance flowed down a drain. Michael permitted her no respite. "That *was* the parallel you were making?"

Sophie put the New Testament in her purse and snapped it closed. When Michael continued, his voice was kindly and his manner open.

"Lady Hambleton, let me be absolutely candid with you. I do want a children's wing at St. Clare's. I want it very much. But not at any price. It may seem a small thing to you: a statue in the foyer in exchange for an invaluable service to the children of Manhattan – and I'm sure you see me as infuriatingly stubborn in the matter – but there's more to it than that. Much more. If I were to agree to your conditions, three results would flow from that act, all of them harmful.

"First, a relatively minor point. When we do build the new wing I don't want a statue of *any* kind in it, even the Blessed Virgin. As I told you at Covington, the church has been too much given to the use of statues. It's argued by some that they are aids to the unimaginative, but they forget that they also circumscribe the imaginative. Show a child a statue and that limited three-dimensional object largely determines his or her view of the saint represented. I'd much prefer that the child be free to conceive in his mind the person he venerates. If there were no statues or pictures of Jesus, for instance, how would we see him? Very differently than we do, I'll venture.

"Second, and please forgive my bluntness, your conversations have made it obvious that you believe that, if the price is right, anything can be bought. Were I to say to you, 'Yes, Lady Hambleton, we accept your gift and your conditions,' you'd be gratified but you'd also be disappointed—" Sophie was about to interrupt but he pressed on. "You'd be disappointed because, in effect, I'd be saying, 'Yes, everything *does* have its price; even the church,' and while that may sometimes be true it certainly is not a fact.

"The third and most important point is this: I'm interested, Lady Hambleton, in you. Here you are, a wealthy woman. You have more money than you can spend and no close relatives to leave it to. You've decided to give some of it to God. Fine, but don't allow yourself to be cheated. Why not get something worthwhile in return for your gift, not just a statue in a foyer which nobody will notice six months after it's installed? You quoted the scriptures to me a few minutes ago; let me quote a verse or two to you, bad practice though it may be." He picked up a Bible and flipped through the pages. "Let me read you something that Jesus said: 'Be careful not to parade your good deeds before men to attract their notice; by doing this you will lose all reward from your Father in heaven. So when you give alms, do not have it trumpeted before you; this is what the hypocrites do in the synagogues and in the streets to win men's admiration. I tell you solemnly, they have had their reward. But when you give alms, your left hand must not know what your right is doing; your almsgiving must be secret, and your Father who sees all that is done in secret will reward you.' "

He leaned forward, his hands clasped before him on the desk, and looked full into Sophie's eyes. "Lady Hambleton, I have a suggestion for you. I've agreed to a plaque. My suggestion is that you forego even that. Give your gift anonymously. You have no idea how much pleasure it will give you and how much good it will do your soul." He smiled at her, an almost affectionate smile. "And if you'll join me in a covenant, I'll make a solemn promise never to tell anyone where the money came from."

Sophie had been listening intently, revealing none of her thoughts. It was a full minute before she responded.

"You know something, Father," she said slowly, "You are a son of a bitch. You really are."

"Thank you," Michael said.

"I came here this morning with my mind absolutely made up. I've been threatening to give my money to the Episcopalians but I never really intended to. Today, however, I was going to do exactly that if we didn't get things threshed out." The smallest smile began to form. "And now here I am, not only taking no for an answer but not even getting a compromise, and ready to make a deal to keep the whole thing secret."

She continued to look at Michael who was suppressing a smile. Her own smile grew. She stood up and put out a hand. "Okay, Father, you've got a deal."

Michael stood and took her hand but didn't release it. "Welcome to the kingdom, Sophie," he said.

Chapter Nine

So it would have to be done tonight. Very well, tonight.

He had returned from preaching in the cathedral to find the house empty. He did not frequently occupy the pulpit at St. Patrick's; certainly not on Easter Sunday mornings (normally he used preaching occasions there as opportunities for public statements of importance, usually inviting the press), but he had felt the need to make a public affirmation and had notified the pastor only late Saturday.

Jennifer had gone with Copeland to Toronto on Good Friday to meet his family, Fathers Jamieson and Carroll were in their home parishes for the holidays, and Miss Pritchard, having left supper in the refrigerator, had gone early in the morning to visit her sister in Hoboken. ("Me brother's here from the Old Country and it might be me last chance to see him in this world.") He called out for Harris and heard only the echo of his own voice.

He went to his quarters and changed to a shortsleeved shirt and slacks and went down the stairs grateful for the solitude. He was seldom alone and needed to be; that was the reason he guarded so jealously his weekends at The Cottage. He opened the door to the study and there was Harris: small in the wingback chair with his legs on a hassock stretched straight before him, a book open in his hands.

"Good morning," Michael said, hiding his disappointment.

"I thought I heard you come in," Harris said affably. "I was downstairs." He turned the book over and laid it like a tent on his thigh. "On what mission of mercy were you this morning?"

"I preached at the cathedral."

"Ah," said Harris, "they brought in the big artillery. What was the occasion?"

"It's Easter," Michael said dryly.

"I thought it was a week away. So *that's* why nobody's home."

Harris's manner jangled Michael's nerves like the strumming of a slack-stringed guitar. The glory of the service was still on him: the sunlight slanting through the stained glass to lay down fields of color on the Easter finery in the crowded pews, the voices of organ and choir soaring to the vaulted ceilings; the triumphant hallelujahs echoing and reverberating and lingering and seeming to descend from heaven. And then his sermon: the unequivocal certitude of the text, "He is not here; he is risen!" The ancient words had fired his own words, and his passion had risen and borne him on a crest, setting him to soaring beyond the mundane, lifting him to that holy moment when the spirit of God came upon him and the words he spoke were not his own. The moment had remained with him until now.

"And what did you tell the faithful?" Harris asked, that note of banter in his voice.

"I preached on the resurrection."

Harris swiped at a fly that was encircling his head. "Of course. What else?"

Michael remained in the doorway, indecisive. He had intended to sit in the study with his breviary and to remain there in contemplation until it was time for lunch. But that plan had now aborted and he was debating whether to join Harris or to go to his sitting room. Harris settled the matter for him.

"Sit down a minute," he said. "I've got some news."

Unreasonably irritated – he would have preferred to make so simple a decision himself – Michael lowered himself into the chair opposite Harris and perversely, because he didn't want one, took a cigar from the humidor, bit off the end, spat it off the tip of his tongue onto the hearth and flared a match and lit it. Harris waited in silence, his face composed and oddly contented.

"You have some news," Michael said.

"I've finished the book. I have an appointment tomorrow with my publisher."

Michael masked his reaction by drawing deeply on the cigar. *Holy Mother of God! – tomorrow!*

"Tomorrow?"

"Tomorrow morning."

Perhaps it was already too late. Perhaps he'd already revealed his subject. "What kind of reaction did you get when you told him what the book was about?"

"Oh, I haven't told him yet." (*Thanks be to God!*) "My old editor, the man I used to deal with, died. There's a new man." He gave a short laugh. "I haven't kept it to myself this long to broach it on the phone to a stranger."

"What difference would it make? Your secret will be out the minute you commit the book."

"No. I'll impress on him the need to keep the subject matter under wraps until the revisions are done and it's on the presses."

"You're kidding yourself, Harris. Secrets don't keep; certainly not one like yours. Too many people will know."

"So, okay, it'll get out. I'll have the Israelis and the press on my tail but I can stall. Our own government will probably get into it but it'll be months before anything's settled and I'll be published by then."

A silence fell between them. Each was off in his own imagining. Michael's face was impassive but his brain was throwing off thoughts like a child's sparkler. Harris was watching him, feeling something like compassion. The news must have been a shock but give him credit; he showed no evidence of it. Nevertheless, for all his pretense at disbelief, Michael must know that the bones are Jesus'. Even if he had been able to reject the possibility and had managed to construct a rationale, he was man of the world enough to know the impact the announcement would have. He decided to be kind.

"I'm in a mood to celebrate," he said. "I don't suppose you'd care to . . . ?"

Michael put a smile on his lips and then added it to his eyes. "Why not?" he said heartily. "Today we celebrate the greatest of the Christian festivals. Why not, indeed?"

"I meant—"

"Harris, I *know* what you meant." He made his voice convey a friendly tolerance. "You misjudge me. You think I can't possibly celebrate with you. But why not? It is error, but it's also an achievement. I can separate the two."

"You really *don't* believe what I've told you."

"Let's say that, however suspect your reasons, you believe it, and leave it at that."

Harris felt patronized, was nettled and wanted to retaliate: "Others will, too, Mike."

"I think we'll weather the storm," Michael said lightly. "As we have others."

"Then you'll join me?"

"What do you have in mind?"

"Nothing much, actually. I have a bottle of Château Lafitte de Rothschild stashed away. We might open it for dinner."

"You won't expect a toast to your book?"

Harris laughed: "Friendship does have its limits."

"It'll have to be a cold supper. Miss P.'s away."

"What time?"

"Shall we say six?"

"Six it is."

"Good," Michael said, and rose to his feet. "Now, if you'll excuse me, there are things I must do."

In the chapel he could not concentrate.

"Loving Father, you know my heart. You know my purpose is only to do your will . . . " *Had he overlooked anything? – the needle for the injection, the CO_2, the pliofilm, the absorbent cotton, the moisture absorbents . . .* "Father, grant me the assurance that what I must do is being done in defense of your children, in defense of those who . . . " *Was there any chance that Miss Pritchard might return early? He'd call her at her sister's on some pretext and reassure himself.* "Father, I . . . " *Would anyone be likely to drop by? Not on Easter.* "Father . . . " *He must see if there is a bottle of Château Lafitte in the wine cellar.* "Loving Father, my heart fails me . . . " *He must remember to call the garage and arrange to have the car sent around.*

Michael went to the refrigerator. Everything was Miss Pritchard neat. There, wrapped in pliofilm or sealed in plastic containers, was supper. Even a note:

Your Eminence, I reely feel gilty for not being here but it's my only chance to see my brother. Here's what I've left for you and Dr. Gordon. Some nice fresh made consomay (excuse my spelling!) It'll be nice cold — the radio says it's going to be a hot day. P.S. There's some chives to sprinkle on. There's baked ham (Easter, you know) and I made a tomatoe aspick with fresh veg in it for a salad. There's peach tarts for desert, two regular and two with sackarin in for your diet. They're on the left. There's a choice if you'd rather have diet jello, depending on what Dr. Gordon wants. There's hard rolls in the bread box. Nice and fresh. Don't forget I bought some of that granulated sackarin for your diet. Don't get it mixed up with the real sugar that's in the silver dish. I'll be back tomorrow by dinner time. Respectfully, Miss P.

He went swiftly to the basement. He hadn't been there since that night and he paused at the bottom of the stairs. There was the door behind which the bones lay; an unexceptional slab door stained dark brown. He grimaced in the realization that his heightened imagination seemed to endow it with menace. In the wine cellar he found a bottle of Château Lafitte. He took it to the kitchen, wiped away the dust with a tea towel and placed it high and out of sight in the cupboard.

Michael, thy name is Dissembler.

The supper was almost over and he had deceived by word or silence a dozen times. Yet his voice had not betrayed it, his hand had not trembled and his manner had seemed normal.

But then, did not his vocation almost demand that one dissemble? To know the good was to be sensitive to one's own wickedness. What a burden to wear the mantle of God and to be judged by your fellows, godly. How often his viscera had squirmed when he had been unduly praised by a parishioner or lauded by an effusive spokesman at a public function. He knew better. The apostle Paul had said of himself, "Christ Jesus came into the world to save sinners, of which I am chief." Not I *was*, but I *am*. Only he who would be pure can grasp the breadth and depth of his own sinfulness. Only the saint knows how unworthy he is. The gross criminal counts as sin only misdeeds such as theft or violence; the saint knows that, "Sin is transgression of the law of God " – and who has not been disobedient? that, "All that is not of faith is sin" – who has not failed to trust? and that "He that knoweth to do good and doeth it not, to him it is sin" – the sin of omission: not merely doing wrong, but failing to do right. If the greatest commandment is, in part, to "love the Lord thy God with all thy heart . . . and thy neighbor as thyself," the greatest sin must be the breaking of that commandment, and thus be the failure to love. Little wonder the saints seem obsessed with the grace of God; they know the magnitude of their sin and the miracle of forgiveness. Little wonder the pastor is reverenced by his flock: the humblest priest holds in his hands the greatest gift, absolution, and gives it in the confessional, a vertical coffin in which the past is interred.

But who could measure *his*, Michael's, sin this night? Here he was, a priest of God, a prince of the Holy Roman Catholic church, a man who might soon ascend to the papal throne, taking a friend to the grave before his time, and doing so with a smile on his lips and bonhomie on his tongue.

At ten to six he'd gone to the bottom of the stairs and called up to Harris that dinner would be delayed but not long, and would he bring down the wine so he could decant it and give it time to breathe. When Harris had returned to his room, Michael poured the wine into a decanter, opened the second bottle, added half of it and put the remainder back in the cupboard. What now appeared to be a bottle of wine was actually a bottle and a half. He put away the sugar, took the dish of saccharin to the table which Miss Pritchard had laid for two and put it by Harris's place. He then went to the basement, took six cartons of books from the storage shelves, set them on the floor by the stairs and carried another to the study. At six-thirty he called Harris to come to dinner and went immediately to the basement. When he heard footsteps in the kitchen, he shouted, "Be there in a minute."

Harris came to the top of the stairs. "What in the world are you doing down there?" he said.

"Won't be a minute. Some books I want to take to the study."

"Let me give you a hand."

"Won't take me long," Michael said, starting up the stairs with a carton in his arms, "and you shouldn't be climbing stairs."

"Nonsense."

In three trips they carried the books to the study. Both were breathing heavily when they returned to the kitchen. "Now for dinner," Michael said heartily. "Goodness, look at the time!"

Harris was sniffing at the wine. "Any good reason we shouldn't whet the appetite?"

"Can't think of any."

"If you'll get the glasses, I'll pour."

He splashed the brick-red liquid into the bowls of the goblets. They held them up to the light and admired them.

"Seems almost sinful to drink two hundred dollars' worth of *any* liquid," Michael said.

"It would be sinful not to."

"Such a wine really demands a toast."

"Why not to the wine itself?"

"Why not, indeed," Michael said, lifting his glass. "To the God of excellence."

"To excellence."

They touched glasses and made much of sniffing and sipping and savoring and swallowing. Afterwards, Michael took another swallow and said, "Why don't you just work on yours while I set out supper."

"I'll help."

"Okay. Peach tarts or jello for dessert?"

"The tarts. I could use the sugar."

"They're in the refrigerator. Yours are the ones on the left."

Now, with supper almost over, the telltale indications had begun. Harris had grown irritable. As he held out his glass for more wine, Michael said, "Don't you think you'd better ease off?"

Harris extended his arm further. "Mike, old boy" – his voice was waspish, impatient – "for once in your life resist the temptation to tell others how to live. The thing I detest most about the church is that you usurp everybody's conscience. You want to tell us all what to do. You say, 'Don't eat meat on Friday,' and then you say, 'Oh, sorry, you can eat meat on Friday.' Do this, don't do that. Right now I want some of my wine; what I don't want is a sermon."

Michael emptied the decanter. The goblet was trembling in Harris's fingers. There was a sheen of perspiration on his brow.

The skin was white as the tablecloth. He half emptied the glass in a series of gulps and placed it on the table with a bump that sent wine over the rim and onto his hand. Idly, he licked the liquid from his hand, let it fall heavily to the table, and then sat motionless, his mouth slack, the eyes heavy-lidded, blinking slowly.

"Sugar," he mumbled, and reached forward, dipping out a spoonful of saccharin. Spilling half of it he put the remainder in his mouth.

"Are you all right?" Michael asked.

It was a moment before Harris responded. He was concentrating on swallowing. "I'm fine," he said. Then he added, "I'm going to throw up."

He pushed back his chair, put his hands on the table and thrust himself erect. As he did, he went off balance, staggered and bumped the table. There was a crash of glassware and the candelabra toppled. His wine glass put a spreading blood-red stain on the linen between them. He put a hand on the back of his chair, swaying and breathing rapidly, mumbled, "Glucagon . . . in my room," and sat heavily in the chair.

Michael went swiftly up the stairs and paused at the landing. Could he go through with it? Harris was dying. There, before his eyes, his old friend was losing consciousness from insulin shock, slipping into an insensibility from which he wouldn't return unless the sugar level of his blood was increased immediately. He couldn't refuse him.

But he *must*. There could be no drawing back now. He must bring all his resolve to focus. The discipline that had fashioned his life and directed his days must prevail. He had settled the question on his knees weeks ago: too many men had died that the faith might be preserved; the death of one more was not too great a price to pay.

He went to his bedroom, unlocked the bureau drawer and found the hypodermic syringe. He fumbled for the vial he'd filled with CO_2 and, his hand trembling, thrust the needle through the stopper and drew back the piston. In a vein, the bubble would move swiftly to the heart. Death would be instantaneous, and with Harris unconscious, painless. Afterwards, unlike air, the gas would be absorbed by the tissues and be beyond detection.

Descending the stairs he saw that Harris had slumped forward on the table. He had vomited and one side of his face was resting in it. His breathing was rapid and there was a bubbling in his throat. Fighting nausea, Michael placed the syringe on the table, grasped Harris beneath the armpits and hauled him to the floor. As he did, the chair tipped and struck Harris on the brow. Blood oozed from a broad gash. He struggled but couldn't free Harris's arms from his jacket and had finally to tug it off over his head. The button at the shirt cuff was stubborn but he got it undone and with one jerk ripped the sleeve to the shoulder. Reaching for the syringe, he turned to Harris and seized the upper arm, encircling it tightly with his fingers, pressing with his thumb on the vein at the inside of the elbow joint. It bulged blue against the pale skin. He brought the needle to it.

Harris stirred. Slowly he turned his head toward Michael. The eyelids fluttered and partially opened and dull dead eyes looked through. The lips, slack and flecked with vomit, quivered and strove to form a word. Then the eyes lost focus, the head fell back and the only movement was a rapid rising and falling of the chest.

He could not do it!

He ran for the stairs, mounted them two at a time and went to Harris's room. The glucagon – where would it be? He looked about the untidy room and went to the bureau. He jerked open the top drawers, pawing aside handkerchiefs, socks, shaving materials and bits of paper. Nothing. He went through the lower drawers, dumping clothing onto the floor. Nothing. He stood for a moment in the center of the room. Think! Where would he be liable to keep it? Of course – in a drawer in the night table by the bed where it could be found in the dark. Yes, there it was. He seized the syringe and picked up a bottle. Insulin. He threw it into the drawer and found another. Glucagon. Swiftly, he thrust the needle through the stopper and withdrew the liquid. The syringe was calibrated. How much should he inject? Too little and Harris would expire; too much and it might kill him. But there was no time to read the label and without his glasses he couldn't.

He ran down the stairs. Harris had moved; he had twisted about and his head was beneath the table, hidden by the tablecloth. Michael encircled the thin arm with his fingers, brought the needle to it and paused. The rapid, labored breathing had stopped. The heaving chest was still. He thrust his head beneath the tablecloth and put an ear to Harris's mouth. No breath. He poked a forefinger into the side of his neck, seeking the carotid artery. No pulse. He put an arm behind Harris's neck, raised the shoulders and pushed back the head. Pulling the jaw down he put his mouth against Harris's and breathed out, and so continued for a few minutes.

Afterwards, he took the keys to the basement room from Harris's pocket, rose to his feet and walked wearily to the telephone.

It was ten minutes before the ambulance whooped to the door. In that ten minutes Michael had rearranged the dishes, put the second bottle of wine with other bottles in the garbage-masher, and had broken the vial in which the CO_2 had been stored, flushing the pieces down the toilet. He moved slowly, his body weighted with fatigue and his mind numb. Raising an arm exhausted, climbing the stairs required an act of will, a pulling of himself upward with the bannister. After he opened the door to the white-garbed medics, he had gone wearily to the study and slumped in a chair, his eyes unfocused, his brain numb, wondering vaguely and without alarm whether he was dying.

In a few minutes there was a tap on the door and a voice called out respectfully, "Father . . . "

He roused himself to say, "Come in."

"I'm sorry, Father, but I'm afraid he's dead," the man said. He was in his thirties, dark of hair and eye and jaw, and ill at ease. There was a stain on the knees of his uniform.

"Yes, I know," Michael said.

"I'm sorry."

"He was a diabetic."

"Yeah, I seen the needle marks. My guess is it was a coronary, though."

Michael thrust through the murk. "A coronary?"

"Anyways, I notified the coroner's office. They'll be along to get him pretty soon they said."

His mind was clearing. Every muscle howled with pain. "You're not taking him?"

"No, Father. Like . . . he's dead. Nothin' they could do for him at hospital. Like I said, I called the coroner's office. They won't be long." He took out a small notebook and a ballpoint pen and licked the tip. "Could you give me his name, Father?"

190

"Gordon, Dr. Harris Gordon."

"Middle initial?"

"G."

"Would you happen to know his age?"

"Sixty."

"Address?"

"Here. He was living here."

There was a thin, high-pitched squeal. The man put a hand in a pocket and the sound ceased. "Well, that'll be all I guess, Father. Would it be okay if I used the phone in the hall?" He smiled apologetically and patted his pocket. "They're tryin' to reach me. Prob'ly another one."

"No, go ahead," Michael said.

The man bobbed his torso in an afterthought genuflection and left, pulling the door to, gently. Immediately it reopened and he said, "Sorry, Father, but if you haven't called the deceased's doctor, maybe you should."

It was almost nine-thirty before they were all gone: the men from the coroner's office, carting off the slight mound beneath the strapped down blanket as though it had never been a man; the chief coroner himself, an oily sychophant who recounted in detail how he'd just been sitting down to dinner but felt, it being at the residence, he ought to come himself "to see that everything was handled satisfactory"; Dr. Raymond, who had asked few questions but had insisted that he take a sedative. The telephone rang. It was the city desk at the *Daily News*. He hung up. It continued to ring until he lifted the receiver from the cradle. The unlisted telephone in the study rang. The *Times*. He pulled the jack. In the meantime the door chime had begun to sound and continued to sound its Avon-lady notes over persistent knocking. When he went with the chief coroner and Dr. Raymond to the door, there was a gabble of reporters on the steps. They loosed a sheet-lightning storm of flash bulbs and questions.

"I'm sorry, gentlemen," he said firmly, "I will be making no statement of any kind tonight so you might just as well go away." As he closed the door against their clamor he noticed that it was raining and heard the chief coroner beginning an interview. After a few minutes the door chime resumed, and the knocking.

His exhaustion had eased now and his senses were acute. He looked into the dining room and saw that someone had tidied up. He climbed the stairs (how many times had it been tonight?) and changed to an old pair of slacks and a heavy cardigan. From the bureau he took a pair of scuffed pigskin gloves and stuffed them into a hip pocket. Descending the two flights of stairs to the basement he noticed that the tumult at the front door had fallen off. Standing before the door to the workroom, feeling for the keys, he became aware that his entire body was thrumming like a bowstring and that his heart was a hammer in his chest. He couldn't get enough air and his mouth was open, gasping. A shudder swept like a wave down his body and he was suddenly cold.

He turned the keys in the locks and the door swung open. In the darkness he crossed to the far wall and found the light switch. He rotated one of the floodlights on its casters, directing it toward the table on which the bones lay, but did not look at them. He went to the wine cellar and took the roll of pliofilm and the boxes of absorbent cotton from where he'd stored them. Back in the workroom, he placed them on the table on which the scroll was spread. The wooden box was in a corner. He brought it to the table and removed the top. Then he put on the gloves and turned toward the table on which the bones lay.

He spoke aloud: "Father forgive me. I know not what I do."

Part Three

Chapter One

Yes, sir. Got it. Just let me double check to be sure: Dr. Harris Gordon. Sixty years old. Archaeologist. Last known address, Albright University. Check. Leave it with me, sir, I'll get right on it. Fine, sir. Thank you, sir. Nice talkin' to you, sir. I'll get back to you. Goodby."

Copeland, passing Captain Schultz's office, heard the name through the partly open door. He paused, pondered, and then tapped lightly on the frosted pane.

"Come in," a voice rasped.

Schultz's office was a cluttered cubicle ("My lousy hole in the wall") fitted out with nondescript government-issue furniture, all of it scuffed and in need of washing: a gray steel desk and matching four-drawer filing cabinets, two chrome chairs with padded vinyl seats, an off-perpendicular clothestree and a long rectangular desk against a wall. Heaped on it were yellowed and dog-eared report forms bundled with broad elastic bands and more or less arranged alphabetically. Behind Schultz's chair was a dusty, slightly concave map of New York City and environs. On another wall was a cork notice board, a vertical litter of outdated memoranda and curling photographs of "wanted" criminals.

Captain Schultz was ugly as his office. He was about forty-five and gone to paunch and jowls in the ten years since coming off cruiser duty. His face suggested a mistake on an assembly line: the upper half being balding and unseamed and baby pink and innocent, the lower half grim and gray and coarse, the jaw stippled with black and appearing forever unshaved. His body was covered with a curly fur which tufted at the vee of the open shirt collar and matted on his simian forearms. As a nineteen-year-old rookie with a foul mouth and a sinewed mind he had been nicknamed Grizzly, and the diminutive, Grizz, had stayed with him, no one save Schultz remembering its origin.

He kept his head down as Copeland entered, printing laboriously with a ballpoint pen on a quintuple report form. Finished, he added his signature with a flourish that was almost a seizure and raised his baby-blue eyes.

"You're in Albany on that immigration thing," he said.

"All wrapped up," Copeland said. He pointed at the IN basket "You've got my report there."

"Payoffs?"

"Yes."

"Figures. Anybody in the legislature?"

"Assemblyman Palik."

"That figures, too."

Schultz leaned back in his protesting chair and put his feet on the desk and his hands behind his head. "Isn't *that* the shits," he sighed. "The goddam papers and TV will be buggin' the ass offa me."

"No. The FBI's in. So's the Department of Immigration. We're through . . . except when it comes to trial, of course."

"We do the work and the Bureau takes the bows," Schultz said sourly. He shifted, raised one buttock and farted resoundingly. "What's on your mind?"

"I couldn't help hearing you mention Dr. Harris Gordon."

"So?"

"I know him. At least I did. He died about a month ago."

"How come?"

"You mean, how come he died?"

"No, for Christ sake, I mean how come you know him? He's a big archaeologist. Was."

"I met him at Cardinal Maloney's."

"Right. I keep forgettin' you're in there like Flynn with the dogans."

"He was living there."

"What'd he die from?"

"Heart. It was in the papers."

"So, lots of things are in the papers." He reached forward, grunting with the effort, and picked up the report he'd just completed. "Well," he said, "that's different, maybe." He looked up at Copeland. "Did you know your dogan friend was a thief?"

"A thief?"

"That's what I said. That phone call was the D.A. Him himself. He's got a complaint, a goddam official communication from the state of Israel and he wants me to look into it. Your fancy dogan friend smuggled some archaeological stuff out of Israel, and that's a no-no." Copeland was remembering the basement room, remembering the sense of something odd. But after Harris had died he'd been so concerned about Jennifer's reaction – a month later she wasn't entirely recovered from it – that it had slipped from his mind. Now, with Schultz's words, all the questions revived.

"I'd be glad to check it out for you, Grizz."

"It's not a homicide, for Christ sake," Schultz growled. "You buckin' for a transfer?"

"I could save you a lot of time."

Suddenly he wanted very much to be assigned to it. He didn't want other officers sniffing about the residence, asking questions, rekindling memories, perhaps even nudging Jennifer into the pit of depression from which she's only just climbed. And he was curious. So Harris *had* been up to something. How satisfying to have your suspicions confirmed.

Schultz had sprung his chair forward and was musing, tapping drumrolls on the desk top with the ball point pen. "Maybe you could at that," he said absently. He pondered for another few seconds and then skidded the report across the desk.

"Okay," he said. "But clear it with Murray. It's really his baby."

Copeland went by Lieutenant Murray Kornblom's desk, showed him the report, and a touch of apology in his voice, explained why he'd been assigned to the inquiry. Kornblom, in his normally doleful way, seemed almost pleased.

"Jesus, Cope, you're welcome to it. I got crapped on from on high last time we had one of these. Schoolteacher on his honeymoon picked up a chunk of clay and the Israelis screamed bloody murder. You should've seen the damn thing." He held out a thumb and forefinger three inches apart. "Nothing! Four thousand years old, they said. Believe me . . . nothing! I didn't want to lay a charge; he was a nice guy; like I say, a schoolteacher. Didn't know it was against the law – took it as a souvenir. So I worked out a deal: he gives it back and I don't press the charge and no names mentioned. The A.G. thought I should have prosecuted so he looks good to the Israelis. Like I say, I got shat on – I mean from a great height. So, you're welcome. In spades you're welcome."

Copeland said, "Thanks," and turned to leave. Kornblom stopped him at the door with, "The file's in Records under ISRAEL – *Customs*. Ask Jill. She'll dig it out."

Sergeant Jill Thurston turned up the file within seconds. It was a thin one: a photocopy of correspondence on the letterhead of the Israel Department of Antiquities citing the accord between the United States and Israel re the illegal exporting of stolen property from one nation to the other, quoting chapter and verse on the Israeli statute prohibiting private ownership of any ancient object or artifact without a permit and requesting the District Attorney of the County of New York to be so kind as to investigate one Joseph Harmon, United States citizen, schoolteacher ... etc. There was an inter-office report signed by Lieutenant Kornblom detailing the actions taken by his department and specifying that the artifact – a fragment of a 3,900-year-old Babylonian cuneiform tablet found at Hazor, Israel – had been formally turned over to the acting Consul General of the State of Israel in New York City. There was a polaroid picture of the fragment, an acidulous exchange of letters with the Attorney General's office and a few other bits and pieces. Copeland made notes, made a call to the Attorney General's office, spoke at length to his executive assistant, read up the law on smuggling and international theft and then called Jennifer.

At lunch he told her the story, carefully, easing into it. She listened in silence – her eyes like purple pansies, he thought, adoring her – until he was finished. He was relieved that there were no tears.

But there was incredulity. "I don't believe it," she said. "I simply do not believe it. Not Uncle Harris. What's he supposed to have stolen?"

"They don't know for sure. He dug up something near Qumran and took it away in a box. Shipped it here. They don't know what it was but they damn well want to. The Dead Sea Scrolls came from Qumran, you know, and if he found another one it could be worth ... " He shrugged.

"I still don't believe it. Why would he steal something like that? He's an archaeologist."

"I'm not saying it was a scroll. That's just a presumption because it was in the Qumran area. It could have been gold. Serving plates, maybe. Goblets. Jewelry."

"What happens now?"

"I thought I'd come by your place tonight and have a word with your uncle if he's going to be in."

Jennifer had heard Michael telling Miss Pritchard to have dinner at seven, so it was arranged that Copeland would arrive about eight. Copeland, whom Jennifer had been twitting about developing a "pontifical paunch," had an early dinner, walked from the restaurant to the residence, carrying his topcoat in order not to perspire unduly, and pushed the doorbell just before eight. He heard Jennifer call out, "I'll get it," and the sound of her heels. The door had only just closed behind him when they kissed in a long embrace, he releasing her only when he heard Michael's footsteps approaching from the dining room.

Michael smiled at them, said "Good evening, Copeland," and began ascending the stairs. He was dressed in clericals. Not looking back he said, "If you two lovebirds can endure an old man's company, Miss P. is serving coffee and liqueurs in the study in about five minutes. I'll be down as soon as I change."

Copeland hung up his topcoat and they went hand in hand to the study. The floors creaked as they walked. Faintly, they heard the bells in the cathedral tolling eight. A mood was on them and they settled in its contentment on the sofa facing the fireplace in which a young fire was cavorting. After a while, Jennifer took and held his hands. "You're warm," she said. "Did you walk?"

"Got to watch my weight," he said, teasing.

"You're such a goose," she laughed. "I'd love you if you had a belly like a Buddha."

There was an air of preoccupation on him and she sensed it. "You're worried?" she asked.

"No, I was just thinking . . . "

"About?"

"About your uncle. About him seeing us in the hall."

"Darling, you're not serious? He's happy for us."

"I don't mean that," he said, and hesitated. "I was simply wondering what it would be like to be a priest; to see other people in love and know it can never be for yourself."

"But it's been like that all his life, at least since he took his vows. He . . . " She wanted to summarize it. "He gives his love to God, and to people."

"It never dawned on me before how lonely he must get."

There was a small frown at the center of her brow. "I suppose he must sometimes," she said, dismissing it.

But Copeland, still in the aftermath of the embrace and contemplating a Michael he had only just now glimpsed, hadn't done with the subject. "A priest's a man," he said.

A note of irritation entered Jennifer's voice. "Darling," she said, "you talk as though we're the first people in love that Uncle Michael's seen." Then she added, her voice dropping off, "Anyway, I'm sure he doesn't think that way."

"But some priests *do*," he said earnestly. "That's why so many are getting out or are fighting for the right to get married."

"Maybe there's something lacking in their dedication," she said, her voice cool.

He was now aware of her change of mood. "What's the matter, darling?"

"Nothing."

"Did what I said bother you?"

She looked at the floor. "It's not that it bothers me, it's just that it reminds me of . . . of what we do, and I don't like to think of Uncle Michael in that way."

"But sex is a normal thing – for anybody."

"I know, I know, I know. It's just that *he's* not anybody." She turned and looked directly at him. "I know he's not perfect – he doesn't pretend to be – but . . . " She couldn't find the words and so finished lamely. "You have to be around him to know just how good a human being *can* be, that's all."

He studied her face as she watched the play of flame in the fireplace. The flickering light edged her profile and shone on her hair and he was moved by her beauty and her seriousness. "Our making love worries you, doesn't it?" he said gently.

She didn't answer immediately. "It isn't that it worries me. I've never known anything so beautiful. It couldn't be more perfect, but . . . " She broke off, not wanting to complete the thought.

"But it's a mortal sin."

She turned to face him. "It is, you know."

"Do you feel guilty about it?"

She drew a deep breath and expelled it in an exasperated sigh. "I'm not sure what I feel; I'm feeling so many things." She looked at him steadily. "Do you confess it?"

"No, I don't."

"Why not?"

"It's very simple, actually: I don't think of it as a sin. We're going to be married in a few weeks. And then, the priests at the cathedral know me. They know I'm engaged to you and . . . well, I don't think I should tell them. That's all."

She was gazing into the fire again. "Do you?" he asked.

"Do I what? Confess it?"

"Yes."

"Yes, I do."

"Doesn't it bother you that the priest knows who you are and that you might be reflecting on your uncle?"

"I slip into All Saints on my lunch hour," she said quietly.

The fire popped a shower of embers onto the hearth. Copeland took the broom and shovel from their hooks on the face of the fireplace and returned the smoking char to the grate. As he did, Michael entered dressed in slacks and an open-neck shirt. On his heels came Miss Pritchard, who set down a heavily laden silver tray and left. Michael went to the liquor cabinet.

"I'm taking orders," he said. "Copeland?"

"Grand Marnier, if you have it."

"Can do." He filled a tiny crystal stemglass and passed it to Copeland. "Jennifer?"

She rose from the sofa. "Nothing for me," she said. "I'm going to leave you two alone."

"Oh," said Michael, "it's going to be *that* kind of a talk?"

She laughed merrily. "Nothing like that." She put a kiss on the top of Copeland's head and left, closing the door behind her.

Michael poured himself some of the liqueur and then two cups of coffee. "Would you like to stay where you are?" he asked.

Copeland got up, taking the coffee from Michael's hand. "As a matter of fact it is a bit warm," he said.

"Why don't you try there," Michael said, indicating the wingback chair in which Harris had so often sat, and seating himself opposite. Both sipped their drinks in silence. The fire had lost its early vigor and was at ease with the logs. They heard a door shut off in the house somewhere.

"My pipe won't bother you?" Michael asked, and when Copeland shook his head, went about the business of getting it packed and lit and drawing well. Copeland was finding it difficult to shake off clinging bits of the conversation with Jennifer and, as though removed from himself, observed his failure to focus his mind even while impotent to do so.

Michael loosed a turmoil of smoke toward the ceiling, and smiled.

"Have you ever realized how fortunate I am?" he said. "It isn't given to many of my vocation to have a daughter."

Copeland brightened. "I hadn't thought of that. That makes me feel much better." Realizing he had made a *non sequitur*, he added, "Sorry, I was thinking of something we were talking about eariler."

Michael took another draw on the pipe. "I don't want to hurry you," he said, "but I have a delegation coming by. Perhaps we should begin."

"Of course," Copeland said, feeling delinquent. "Sorry." He put his coffee on a table beside his chair. "Did Jennifer tell you what I wanted to see you about?"

Michael shook his head. "No."

"It's an official call, in a way."

"Oh?"

"We've had an inquiry from the Israeli government; an official inquiry about Dr. Gordon, about the alleged theft of some archaeological artifacts."

Dear God, no! Michael thought. He said, "You can't be serious?"

"I'm afraid so," Copeland said, and quickly sketched the events of the afternoon. Michael's eyes never left his during the recounting, although a frown slowly lowered his eyebrows until he was looking out from beneath them with an intensity that caused Copeland to falter toward the end.

"So," he concluded, "if you don't mind, I'd like to ask you a few questions about the project Dr. Gordon was working on."

Michael decided that his pipe was not drawing well. He took a minute to tamp it with a forefinger and get it lit again. His mind was ricocheting about among a dozen thoughts. He must keep the conversation suspended, gain time, get his bearings.

"I must say, I'm at a loss," he began. "What you've just told me comes as a shock. I simply can't credit it. Why in the world would Dr. Gordon do such a thing – if indeed he did?"

"I was hoping you could help me answer that."

Michael took a few quick puffs, "I *do* wish I'd known what we were going to talk about. It will require some time." He glanced at Copeland for confirmation. "I think, perhaps . . . " He rose to go behind his desk and flip a page on a calendar pad. "Perhaps we ought to postpone until, say, tomorrow at four. I have this delegation coming – plans for a new elementary school in Staten Island – and I wouldn't want to just get started with you and have to break off."

"I understand," Copeland said, "but could we—"

"If I may make a suggestion?"

"Of course."

"Suppose we use the few minutes we have. I can fill you in on Harris's background . . . "

"But—"

"And you might like to take a look at the room downstairs."

"Yes, I would."

"We can fill in any gaps tomorrow."

Before Copeland could further remonstrate, Michael sat behind the desk and began a review of his friendship with Harris at Princeton. He went on to sketch the years between and the reunion in London.

"Poor Harris, he was in a dilemma. He'd lost tenure at the university and hadn't been able to make an arrangement elsewhere – truth to tell, I don't think he'd been asked – and he'd run out of money. I don't mean that he was penniless, but things were a bit straightened."

"He was married. Couldn't he have gone home?"

Michael raised an eyebrow. "Less said about that . . . "

"Have you met Mrs. Gordon?"

"She's his third wife, you know."

"Would she have any idea — "

"At any rate," Michael broke in, "not to jump around; we have a guest room here. So, for auld lang syne."

"Did he ever discuss with you what he was working on?"

Michael glanced at the mantel clock. "I'm afraid the rest will have to wait until tomorrow," he said, rising. "I believe you said you'd like to see the room in the basement."

Michael, by rising, had levered Copeland to his feet. He now followed along as Michael went to the hall and called out,

"Jennifer." When she appeared at the top of the stairs he said, "Copeland would like to see the room downstairs. Will you show it to him?" When Jennifer, affecting a courtly manner, curtsied and said, "My pleasure, sir," he took Copeland's hand, shook it and said, "Sorry we didn't have longer. See you tomorrow at four," and returned to the study. Copeland stood in the hall feeling somehow unbuttoned.

Michael, having closed the study door, went to his desk and put his head in his hands. "Oh, God!" he groaned. "No!"

Precisely what he had feared, the unpredictable, had happened. Not one month after that so-well-remembered night – the memory of that dead face only beginning to fade, time having made the burden of guilt only just tolerable, Jennifer again herself after weeks of depression – and now this numbing news: Harris's theft had not gone undetected after all. What irony, he thought, if Harris were to escape the consequences of his crime and he, Michael, were to trip on it. But more fearsome than the visage of the guilt risen from the grave was the possibility that Harris's dread secret might also be resurrected, and all that had been done to lay it to rest would come to naught.

Indistinctly he heard Jennifer's and Copeland's feet on the stairs to the basement and their muffled voices. There was nothing to fear there; he'd made certain of that. But had he been too peremptory with Copeland, too obvious in his controlling of the conversation, too brusque in terminating it? Perhaps, but there had been no option. He'd been struggling to maintain his composure after the impact of Copeland's announcement. Thank God for years before the public, and for the ability perfected to mask his emotions!

He'd told Copeland tomorrow at four, but that couldn't be allowed to stand. He'd specified that time because he knew it was the first free period he had. But that was precisely the difficulty: he'd be so occupied between now and then that he'd be unable to do the extended thinking necessary. He needed time: time to appraise the altered situation and to plot a new course, time to dissect the story he had so painstakingly fabricated before Harris's death and to determine wherein it was still valid. But to postpone the appointment might arouse suspicion. As it was, he'd risked kindling Copeland's curiosity with the subterfuge of breaking off the conversation in order to meet with the delegation from Good Samaritan. The delegation wasn't due for another twenty minutes and if Copeland was still about when they arrived, his hurried terminating of their conversation would be seen as contrived.

If he was going to break tomorrow's appointment there would have to be some compelling reason. Might he manage to be ill? No, that would necessitate the cancellation of the entire day's appointments and force him to simulate sickness. If he feigned mere indisposition, Copeland might argue the urgency of his mission and press to see him, and it would be difficult to refuse. If he affected an illness grievous enough to confine him to bed, the doctor would have to be called and he wanted no part of so elaborate a charade.

He must take care to fabricate no more lies than were necessary. He knew that lies about matters of consequence were immoral, but to tamper with the truth to a good purpose – choosing the lesser of two evils in a given situation; as when someone was dying and could not bear to know, or when the declaration of the whole truth would cause pointless pain, or damage a reputation, or put in jeopardy some worthwhile endeavour– was wrong but could be justified. But to lie casually and for one's convenience was repugnant to him and a venial sin. He knew, too, that lies spawned lies and that each lie required others to support it.

But conversely, deception was sometimes mandatory – as now. Perhaps he would arrange to be called out of town on urgent business. But on what business, and to where? Rome, perhaps. He could spend time with Paolo, and while there see the Holy Father. Would he dare broach the secret to Paolo? Perhaps he could be his confessor for this sin he'd dared confess to no one.

He shook his head, rose from behind the desk and began to pace, reproaching himself as he walked; his thinking was as erratic as a child's discovered in a secret wickedness. The situation was not nearly so bad as had first appeared. All that was new was that some official in Israel had become aware that Harris had smuggled something out of the country, and had caused inquiries to be made. From what Copeland had said, no one knew precisely what had been stolen. Who could the informant be? Why, of course! – the ticket-seller at Qumran or the Arab Harris had hired. If indeed one of them was the source (and who else *could* it be?) that was heartening. Harris had recounted how he'd left the Arab outside the cave while he packed the bones and the scroll and sealed the box. All the attendant could know was that something had been found: he'd seen a box carried away. So it was a blind inquiry, a fishing expedition.

Calm down; the problem was not all that intimidating. Hadn't he already devised a credible explanation for Harris's presence at the residence and for the secrecy of his labors there? As for such other potentially hazardous questions, he would simply identify them and prepare his response. He'd posit the worst and be ready for it. But he'd have to be careful not to leave the slightest crevice in which the smallest seed of doubt could lodge and germinate.

The greatest difficulty would be to devise a satisfactory accounting for the box and its contents. It could readily be traced to the residence: what had happened to it afterwards? He couldn't assert that he knew nothing of what Harris was working on; it would not be credible. And his reasons for removing the materials from the basement after Harris's death would have to seem reasonable. The trouble was, there was not only Copeland to satisfy. It was now known that Harris had committed a crime. Copeland's superiors would require an accounting, officials in Israel would be awaiting explanations, and there would be reports and files to be completed before the case was closed. Bureaucracy would demand its pound of paper.

Washington! The thought broke upon him; he would go to see Lieberman. The perfect excuse: Copeland would understand that one didn't say no to a summons from the State Department. There were matters needing discussion with the secretary, and afterwards, he would stay on a day or two in Washington, away from telephones and interruptions to work out the resolution of the problems that had so suddenly been revived.

He pushed a button on the intercom: "Father Jamieson, see if you can reach Mr. Lieberman at the State Department."

With Jennifer, Copeland had made his way to the basement, and in the poor light, to the room at the far end. The door to the workroom hung open. Jennifer went ahead and threw the switch. He could see that the room was empty except for a long unpainted worktable against the far wall on which there were two baskets of tomatoes, a sack of onions, a bushel basket of potatoes and some neatly stacked bundles of newspapers. He smiled: Miss P. had her "root cellar" back.

He ranged his eyes about the room. It was a dark, uninviting place. The whitewashed rough stone of the building's foundation formed two walls and exposed studding the others. Three naked bulbs screwed into porcelain sockets attached to joists provided gloomy light. The floor was concrete and painted gray. There was a pungent scent of earth and onions.

"No ventilation?" he asked.

Jennifer pointed. "There's an exhaust fan. The switch is over there." He crossed to the wall and touched a switch mounted on one of the vertical studs. There was a sudden small hum from a fan close to the ceiling. He turned it off.

"I believe Uncle Harris had a dehumidifier," she offered.

Copeland slowly circled the room, pausing briefly to examine some marks on the floor. He stood at the center, tilted back his head and scrutinized the ceiling, pivoting on a heel. Then he walked to the door and tested the locks. One was old, the other shiny-new.

"Seen enough?"

"There's little enough to see."

As they headed for the stairs, he turned aside to put his head into the wine cellar. When they entered the kitchen, Miss Pritchard was pouring steaming water into a large coffee urn.

"Give me a start when I heard you on the stairs," she said. "What in the world were you doin' down there, girl?"

"I was showing Copeland your root cellar."

"Don't tell me *he's* goin' to work down there," she said acidly. She reached into the refrigerator, removed a platter of petits fours and placed them on the table.

"What was Dr. Gordon working on?" Copeland asked.

Miss Pritchard didn't look up. "Don't ask me," she said sourly. "I'd be the last to know."

"You must have *some* idea?"

"He wasn't tellin' so I wasn't askin'."

"But surely the room had to be cleaned." His antennae were quivering at Miss Pritchard's reticence.

"Not by me, it wasn't."

"Then by Dr. Gordon. There must have been some refuse, some papers, something . . . "

Miss Pritchard looked at him crossly, but her umbrage was forced. "Mr. Copeland, are you thinkin' I'd go pokin' 'round in somebody's garbage, stickin' me nose in where it don't belong?"

She busied herself placing the petits fours on two silver cake plates. After a moment, head down, she added, "The poor soul's gone now anyways."

Copeland realized he hadn't been fair to her so he took a minute to explain the reasons for his questions. When he said he was on official police business she showed distress.

"There's nothin' I can tell you. You should be talkin' to Father Jamieson or to himself."

"I will be tomorrow," Copeland said, modulating his voice to calm her, "but help me a bit if you can." Miss Pritchard went to a cupboard, took down some cups and saucers and arranged them on the tray. "Did Dr. Gordon ever say anything at all about what he was working on? Think a minute."

She didn't need a second. "Never a word," she said flatly. She turned to him, pique showing. "Mr. Copeland, he never talked to me about nothin'. It was like you was dirt. He'd pass through every mornin' after breakfast like you wasn't here – or the day maids neither, far as that goes. You'd say, 'Good mornin', Dr. Gordon,' but you might as well of saved your breath. Off he'd go, down them stairs there, and that'd be the last you'd see or hear from him till lunch. He had his diabetes, of course, so sometimes you'd turn around and there he'd be in your fridge for some orange juice or in your breadbox there without so much as a by-your-leave or thank you, ma'am." She turned back to the tray, subdued. "I'm not one for speakin' ill of the dead, but he wasn't a friendly man, Dr. Gordon, although he could laugh and joke with the best when the mood took him."

Copeland picked up again. "There are two locks on the door downstairs. Do you have the keys?"

"I do now."

"Now?"

"Until Dr. Gordon died, he had a set and His Eminence had the spares. His Eminence borrowed mine to get it copied for Dr. Gordon."

"So, after Dr. Gordon moved in, you never got a look inside the room?"

Miss Pritchard's back had been to Copeland as she prepared the tray. She turned. "Will there be many more questions?" she asked, a small importunity in her voice. "You're gettin' me all fidgetty."

Copeland's voice was soothing. "Just a few more. When Dr. Gordon moved in, what did he bring with him?"

Miss Pritchard looked off and, stroking the dewlap beneath her chin, ticked off the items as though reciting a laundry list. "Precious little," she said. "Some things in a suitcase, a steamer trunk, some cartons of books — "

"No, I mean what went into the room downstairs?"

"Oh, there. Three tables from the parish hall, another table, a chair – two chairs, actually – three lights on music stands (looked like big mixin' bowls, the lights) and a whole lot of things I can't remember now. I saw him carryin' some sheets of glass one day. Oh yes, there was the dehumidifier. And that wood box."

"Tell me about the box."

Miss Pritchard shrugged. "What's to tell? It was a box. About so big."

"Any idea what was in it?"

Miss Pritchard shook her head. "You said only a question or two—"

"I'm almost finished. What happened to the box?"

"I haven't the slightest idea."

"Was it put out with the garbage?"

"No."

"You're sure?"

"If he'd put it with the garbage I'd of seen it."

"Did you clean out the room after he died?"

"Yes. Well, I didn't actually, Hulda did, but I told her what to do."

"Was the box there?"

"No."

"What do you think could have happened to it?"

"Mr. Copeland, you keep goin' on about the box—"

"Could it have been taken out without you knowing?"

"Yes. On a Sunday when I'm off, or if I was out of the kitchen at the time. And now, Mr. Copeland," she said firmly, "I really *must*—"

"Was there a manuscript?"

"No."

She picked up the tray, and bearing it before her, back arched, walked to the door, bumped it open with a practiced hip and went though.

Jennifer looked at him with a slight smile. "My! You *are* a persistent one," she said. "The old darling was just dying to get away."

He was making notes in his precise script. "The old darling wasn't telling me everything she knows," he said crisply.

"How do you know?"

He shrugged. "You just know."

She smiled at him fondly and went on tiptoe to kiss him. "I shall have to be careful after we're married."

He didn't respond, but said, "May I have a look at his room?"

"No reason why not, although I doubt it'll help much. It's back to being a guest room."

He spent only a minute, not venturing beyond the threshold. "What happened to his papers, his mail, his personal things?"

"Father Carroll gathered everything together and had them delivered to Mrs. Gordon. She was on the phone half a dozen times, bugging him. There was no will so there was no reason to hold things up."

"I'll have a word with her."

As they descended the stairs, Miss Pritchard emerged from the reception room. "Is the delegation here yet?" Jennifer whispered.

"Not yet," Miss Pritchard said, glancing at her watch. "Not for another ten minutes."

Copeland arched his eyebrows. As Miss Pritchard continued on toward the kitchen, he asked, "Is His Eminence in the study?"

"No," she said over her shoulder. "He's in the chapel. I'm to call him when they get here."

"Mr. Norris on the line, Your Eminence."

"Thank you, Father Carroll. Hello. This is Cardinal Maloney."

"Yes, Your Eminence. It's Gerry Norris at the *Times*. Thank you for returning my call."

"Not at all."

"I'm sorry to bother you, Eminence, but the city desk has been trying to reach you and they thought that, because of our past association, perhaps I . . . "

"What can I do for you, Mr. Norris?"

"I really must apologize for bothering you, but . . . "

"That's perfectly all right."

"I'm reluctant to trouble you with a speculative story, but there's a Reuters dispatch just in, quoting what seems to be a reliable source to the effect that the successor to Pope Gregory will be either Cardinal Benedetti or you. I wonder, would you care to comment?"

"I see. And what is this reliable source?"

"A minister in the Italian government, Giuseppe Ruffolo."

"Well now, you would hardly expect Signor Ruffolo to have the interest of the church at heart."

"I agree, Your Eminence, but would the story be substantially true?"

"I'm sure I don't know. And, Mr. Norris, beyond the question of the dubious taste of speculating on the successor to the Holy Father while he is alive, I make it a practice never to comment on rumor. The very comment, even no-comment, gives it a kind of credibility."

"But, Your Eminence—"

"Good afternoon, Mr. Norris."

Chapter Two

Harris's widow was a surprise. Copeland had envisioned a husk of a woman, sixtyish perhaps, sucked dry in the vacuum created by a husband off junketing about the world. He wasn't prepared for 1427 Lindbergh Drive and Dodi Gordon.

The neighborhood had once been middle-income suburbia but had long since lost whatever innocence it might have had. The street was littered, the lawns had gone to weeds, and the carcasses of two cars – glass pulverized, wheels gone and the roofs stomped – squatted by the crumbling curb. The trees, their tresses stained, seemed forlorn jades betrayed by a neighboring battery plant. Number 1427 was the right half of a three-story duplex, each half having been painted a different color even to the line bisecting a shared chimney.

Even though there was no name beside it, he pressed the topmost of three bell buttons. A skinny, string-haired girl with nubbin breasts under a T-shirt suddenly appeared in the open doorway to regard him from an expressionless face. She responded to his inquiry by bawling over her shoulder in an unexpectedly loud voice, "Dodi, it's for you," and went off to join two girls watching from the street.

He waited, expecting someone to make an appearance, or a summons to enter. Nothing. He leaned forward, craning his neck. A narrow staircase led his eye to a second floor but there was only darkness beyond the top stair. He called out a tentative, "Hello." Nothing. He turned to appeal to the girl but she and her friends had gone off down the street. No option but to press the bell again, which he did, and then did so insistently. A far-off voice: "I'm coming. I'm coming."

And she was indeed. Dodi Gordon descending: mules tapping an introduction to each step, a housecoat loosely gathered about the waist granting a generous view of generous and unconfined breasts, and parting as she walked alternately to expose a tanned thigh. So the hair was too blonde and too fussed-with and the face too made-up, the word that leaped into Copeland's mind was voluptuous. Tells me something about Harris, he thought.

As she reached the bottom stair she pulled at the material of the housecoat, closing slightly the vee at the neck, said, "Sorry. I was on the phone," and put out a hand. Copeland shook it and was surprised to find it wet: not damp but wet, as though it had just been washed and too hastily dried. She hadn't been on the phone, he decided, but on the john.

"I'm Detective Jackson of the District Attorney's office," he said. "May I come in?"

She looked at him appraisingly. "And after we get upstairs you turn into a bill-collector or you're selling encyclopedias."

"Sorry," he said, and displayed his badge.

"I'll take a look at that," she said, and took it and examined it and returned it. "What are we going to talk about?"

"Your late husband."

"That," she said, "would be a pleasure."

Turning, she gathered her bathrobe free of her feet and preceded him up the stairs. It was two flights, and with Dodi Harris trailing perfume and semaphoring sexuality directly in front of his face each step of the way, he didn't begrudge the climb. Tells me something about myself, he thought ruefully.

The bed-sittingroom smelled of ancient dust and recent food. The furniture, wallpaper and linoleum announced that they should have been replaced years ago. An exception was a brand-new television set on which Archie Bunker was fulminating only inches below a plate on which were the curling crusts of three wedges of pizza. Dodi turned down the sound, sat across from the sagging sofa on which he was seated, crossed her legs and gave him her attention.

As they talked, it developed that she and Harris had met at Albright at a faculty reception. He'd given her the flowers-and-dinner-at-the-best-places routine and they'd married in four months. The babies started coming: even more quickly, so did the problems. She didn't like his "artsy-fartsy friends," nor he hers, and soon they were living separate lives in the one house. He liked to rise early and she late. He needed silence in which to work and she couldn't keep the kids quiet, so he began to spend most of his hours at home in the bedroom with the door closed, emerging from time to time like a hibernating bear to growl at anything in sight. After a while she began to believe that her best years were being stolen ("Living with an old geezer who liked a book better'n a movie"), announced that she wasn't going to waste away on the vine and began to go out evenings, leaving the children with a baby-sitter, one of his graduate students. One evening, Dodi came upon him getting more than his money's worth from the baby-sitter and he without demur shortly afterward took off for parts unknown, which parts when they became known proved to be various archaeological excavation sites in Israel.

Two boys of about eight years, identical twins, interrupted her recital by galloping up the stairs, contending with piping cries all the way to the top. Upon achieving it and espying Copeland, they stopped as though ossified and studied him gravely.

"What is it now?" said Dodi, with a mother's passive impatience. Receiving neither a glance nor a response, she stated, "You want something to eat." To Copeland she volunteered, "You can't fill 'em up. Hollow legs." Then back to the boys: "There's peanut butter and jam." They went immediately to the kitchen, and the remainder of the interview was conducted fortissimo over the sounds of a flourishing sibling rivalry.

"The one you haven't met is Jimmy," Dodi resumed. "He's the five-year-old. He's out playing. God, will I be glad when he's in school! Five of us in two rooms. Five!"

She took a packet of filter-tip cigarets from a pocket of her housecoat, held it out toward Copeland, and when he shook his head, wedged one into a tar-remover cigaret-holder and lit it, drawing the smoke deep into her lungs. "He was a really cheap bugger," she said, expelling the smoke in a thin, swift stream. "Didn't leave a dime."

"There wasn't a will?"

"No will. Three hundred bucks in the bank – that's where that came from," she said, jabbing the cigaret in the direction of the television set. "A bunch of books, some assorted junk, and that's it."

"Insurance?"

"Lapsed about a year ago."

"His personal effects – would it be possible for me to see them?"

"What's to see? After he walked out on me he never settled anywhere. There was no furniture. When he died he was living with Cardinal Maloney. They sent around his stuff. There was a camera and some lights: two cameras, actually. I loaned one to a friend. I mean, what do I want with two cameras? I've never taken a picture in my life. Did I mention the books? There were a dozen or more cartons of them. They've gone to Albright. Would you believe they didn't even want to pay shipping charges?" She looked across at Copeland, waving her cigaret hand. "Let me tell you something if you don't know. University types . . . Cheap. Chee-*eep*!" Unburdened of that, she continued. "There was a microscope, which I pawned, and some junk. I gave his clothes to the Salvation Army. He never was much of a dresser, anyway." She gestured with palms up, "That's it."

"You said two cameras?"

"Right."

"There might be film in them that would help me."

Dodi looked at him, level-eyed, smiling cozily. "What's he done?"

"What do you mean?"

"I mean, he's done something. All these questions."

Copeland shook his head. "Just cleaning up some odds and ends. Nothing important. You mentioned two cameras?"

"I loaned one to a friend of mine. I kept the Polaroid. There's no film in it; I looked. The other . . . ? I could ask if you like."

"Could you ask now?"

She shrugged. "Why not?"

The conversation on the telephone was brief. No, there was no film in the camera.

"Damn," Copeland said.

"Sorry."

"That's okay. You mentioned some junk: was there, among that junk, anything that might be – you know, ancient. Anything that might look like junk but be . . . "

"You mean artifacts?"

"Exactly."

She shook her head.

"Was there a manuscript of any kind? You know what I mean."

"Of course I know what you mean," she said, with a small show of indignation. "I *was* married to an archaeologist, remember. The answer is, no."

"In with the books, maybe?"

"Nothing but a couple of notebooks."

"Do you have them?"

"They went to Dean Hudson at Albright with the books."

Dean Hudson had himself examined the notebooks. "They were merely jottings, notes, sketches from the dig at Hazor: all research for the book he did on the excavation there. Nothing extraordinary." He paused. "I'm sorry, but I'm afraid your name has escaped me . . . "

"Jackson."

"Ah yes, Mr. Jackson." He removed his glasses (he'd put them on and taken them off a dozen times during their ten minutes together) and looked at Copeland with wide ingenuous eyes. "I wonder, would it be inappropriate for me to inquire as the reason for your questioning? Dr. Gordon was, as you know, chairman of the department here for some years and . . . "

"Has there been any correspondence with him in the past three years?"

Dean Hudson shrugged deprecatingly. "There's a small file. It deals mostly with the proposed extension of his sabbatical." He shook his head slowly. "You can take a look at it if you wish, but . . . "

"So where are we at?" Schultz asked, his kewpie-blue eyes blank, his mouth grim.

"That's pretty well it. I see Cardinal Maloney at four. I'm hoping it'll be productive."

"You're hopin'! *I'm* hopin,' believe me! So far it's Nowheresville. I should never of let you talk me into puttin' you on it."

Copeland bridled. "I've only been on the case for twenty-four hours."

"So you've only been on it twenty-four hours – Christ, it's not the Brinks' robbery! Some old guy swipes a scroll or a gold vase or somethin' and in twenty-four hours you haven't turned up a single hard lead." He slapped the palm of a hand down on the phone. "I been sittin' here waitin' for this goddam phone to ring with the D.A. wantin' to see me. What am I goin' to tell him?" He leaned forward. "Maybe what I ought to do is toss it back into Murray's lap. It's his department anyways."

Copeland felt anger surge in his neck but contained it. He wanted very much to stay with the case. "Look," he said, his voice all sweet reasonableness, "my appointment's for four and I'm staying to dinner. Nobody's going to get more than I will. For Christ sake, Grizz," he appealed, "I'm marrying his niece."

Schultz rubbed a palm over his bald head and wiped it on his shirt front. "Maybe that's the trouble, he's got you scared shitless like he was her old man."

"I'll tell you one thing," Copeland said, putting the worst possible face on it, "he won't agree to see anybody else for weeks. He's a very busy man."

"Okay," Schultz said, a great sigh underlining his forbearance in the face of the ineptitude of subordinates. "What choice have I got? I'm here without a paddle anyways."

It happened that Copeland did not see Michael for three days. As he left Schultz's office he was paged on the intercom. "A Father Jamieson on the phone."

"Cardinal Maloney asked me to get in touch with you, Copeland. He's dreadfully sorry but he's been called to Washington. He asked me to apologize on his behalf."

"Damn!"

Father Jamieson hadn't expected so explosive a reaction and sought to palliate Copeland's disappointment. "I'm sorry," he said. "Off the record, he's with the Secretary of State. You'll understand, he simply had to go."

"Well," Copeland said, "if he's in Washington he's in Washington." He added. "Do this for me: have him get in touch as soon as he's back. It's very important."

"I'll certainly give him the message."

His immediate reaction was to report the delay to Schultz but he realized that to do so would be to blow the whole thing over to Kornblom's department. No, he'd tell him tomorrow and hope to turn up something concrete in the meantime.

He went to a cubicle in the lavatory to think. What avenue would most likely be productive? No question: that mysterious wooden box. It was the key. Whatever Harris had stolen had been in that box. Trace it and he was halfway home. It had been shipped from Israel so the airline involved would have records. It would have been cleared through customs so permits would have been required and be on file. It had been delivered to the museum and then trans-shipped to the residence, so perhaps a clue was to be garnered there.

The shipping clerk at the museum was a cadaverous man with rimless spectacles and a thin moustache darkened (inconspicuously, he believed) with eyebrow pencil. He nattered nasally about the problem of going back months in his files and when Copeland said icily, "Sorry to put you to so much trouble," said immediately, "Oh, I didn't mean that."

He went to a bank of filing cabinets and muttering to himself found the right one. He pulled open a drawer and fingered through it, murmuring, "Gordon . . . Dr. Harris Gordon." In a moment he said, "Ah, here we are," removed a pale pink piece of paper, and returning to his desk, peered over the top of his glasses at Copeland to say, "We keep very careful records here." Back to the paper: "Now let's see what we've got here. . . . Shipper, Dr. Harris Gordon, Care of Dr. Herman Unger, Curator, Department of Anthropology. Date received, January 7, Time . . . ?" He tilted his head back to see through the lower lens of his bifocals. "Time, 2:45 P.M. Yes, 2:45. Hold for shipment to Dr. Gordon. Special instructions: avoid extreme cold, heat or humidity — "

"Just a minute," Copeland said. He was making notes.

"Avoid extreme cold, heat or humidity . . . "

"Go ahead."

"Shipped to 452 Madison Avenue. Date of shipment, January 19."

"Anything on the contents?"

A peering at the paper. "Archaelogical artifacts, it says."

"Nothing else?"

"That's all."

"Nothing on the weight of the box?"

"We wouldn't be interested in that. We were just holding it for shipment. Beyond the basic information all we'd want to know would be, are there special instructions re conditions of storage. You have to be very careful about that sometimes. Some of the things we handle are extremely perishable. We have a humidity-controlled storage room for that very purpose."

"What kind of artifacts would be harmed by extremes of heat, cold or humidity?"

The shipping clerk shrugged. "Scrolls, leather, mummified bodies, certain kinds of fibres . . . "

"Do you get this kind of shipment often?"

"Perishable things?"

"No. Where something is to be held for forwarding."

"As a matter of fact, no. Most deliveries are for exhibits or displays. We ship them back after. If they're a gift or a purchase, we store them or display them. Depends."

"So something to be held for forwarding would be unusual?"

"Well, let's say it's not normal procedure. But there's this request from Dr. Unger." He tapped the piece of paper with a knuckle. "And then, of course, Dr. Gordon's known to us."

"But it *is* unusual?"

"Yes," he conceded. "You could say that."

Copeland flipped closed his notebook and put it in his shirt pocket. "Could you put me in touch with the man who made the delivery to Dr. Gordon?"

The shipping clerk looked over his glasses. "Oh, we wouldn't ship it ourselves. That was handled by the 7 Santini Brothers. They specialize in things like that." He squinted at the paper. "Signature looks like H. Melnyk. That's M-e-l-n-y-k."

"Sure I remember the shipment. I mean, I'm a Catholic and all these years I never knew Cardinal Maloney lived there back of St. Pat's. Driven by a hundred times."

Herman Melnyk was a jovial barrel of a man whose measurements, Copeland estimated, would be about 46-56-46. He was entirely bald; not clean-shaven after the fashion but without apparent follicles. Odd, Copeland thought, because he had bushy steel-gray eyebrows and a dark shadow of beard.

"The box," Copeland said. "Anything you can remember will help."

"What's the problem – somebody steal her?"

"No. Nothing like that. Can you remember anything specific about it?"

Melnyk closed his eyes and screwed his face into a mass of radiating lines. "The box . . . ? The box . . . ?" In a moment he brightened, ironing out his face. "I remember the guy it was shipped to."

"Man about sixty? Thin? Bald?"

Melnyk's lips formed a half-smile and his eyes twinkled. He ran a hand over his head, cupping it almost affectionately. "*Him* bald? Compared to me he's a hippie." Having made his joke he went on. "Yeah, that's him. Funny old guy."

"Funny?"

"I mean, a real character. Outside, waiting in his shirt sleeves. And this is January, remember. Wanted to carry the shipment in himself. You'd of thought it was full of diamonds."

"The box?" Copeland prompted.

"Like, what do you want to know?"

"Size? Shape? Weight? – anything you can remember."

Again a screwing up of the face. "The box . . . ? The box . . . ? Let me see. . . .Wood. Unfinished lumber. I'd say maybe two to three feet long, a foot high."

"Any—"

"Metal strapping around her."

"Any indication what was in it?"

Melnyk shook his head. "I don't remember. I just delivered her."

"Any idea what she weighed?" Copeland said, falling into Melnyk's jargon.

There went the face again. "That's a tough one. . . .I mean, it was months ago. I remember carrying her down to the basement. Wasn't all that heavy. I'd say maybe fifteen pounds. Twenty tops."

"You took her to the basement?"

"The old guy wanted to, but no way."

"Why not?"

"My job's to make a delivery and get a signature. Right? Somebody damages a shipment, who gets the shit?"

"So you took her to the basement?"

"Tell you the truth, one of the reasons I wanted to, was I wanted to get a look inside. Maybe see Cardinal Maloney. No luck."

"Did he open the box in your presence?"

Melnyk shook his head. "He give me my signature and offered me a tip – a lousy half a buck. But we ain't allowed to accept gratuities anyways. Company policy."

"Anything else?"

Melnyk did his concentration bit for a full twenty seconds and then said cheerfully. "Nope. That's it."

The agent at the Pan Am cargo terminal at JFK laughed humorlessly when Copeland asked him if he could recall the shipment. "You got to be kidding." he said. "Do you have any idea how many shipments go though here on a given day? Like, would you believe hundreds? Some days . . . " The shrug suggested infinity.

"Shall we give her a try?" Copeland said.

The man sighed in resignation and picked up a typewritten list of inbound flights, the paper laminated between soiled sheets of clear plastic. "Date of arrival and point of origin?" he asked wearily.

"Sometime during the week of January two. From Israel."

He flipped the sheet onto the desk. "We don't fly Israel. You sure it was Pan Am?"

"Yes."

"Another sigh. "It'd have to be a connecting flight then. Jesus – could be Athens, Rome, London . . . " He looked at Copeland gloomily. "It's not much to go on. You got the waybill number?"

"Sorry."

The agent scratched industriously under an arm. "Look, we're computerized. Gimme the date or the flight or the waybill number and I can get it for you in seconds." He patted a keyboard by his desk almost affectionately. "Suzy here's fast, but you got to feed her *something*." He looked at Copeland appraisingly. "You really need this information?"

Copeland leaned forward, lowered his voice and let his tone connote matters of the greatest urgency. "I'm sorry for the trouble but . . . " He leaned closer. "If I were free to discuss it, you'd understand." He jerked a thumb over his shoulder as though to indicate someone or something of enormous importance.

The agent's demeanor visibly altered. "Well, if that's what we're into," he said. "I'll tell you what." He glanced at his wristwatch. "It's coming up on noon and this isn't going to be easy. Hows about you come back around, say, two?"

A solemn pondering. "You couldn't possibly make it by one?"

An unequivocal shaking of the head. "No."

"One-thirty?"

A contemplative sucking at teeth and a reluctant, "Okay. We'll give it our best shot."

Copeland smiled appreciatively, gave the man a slight significant wink and said, "I won't forget it. Believe me."

In the terminal coffee shop he ordered a small steak with french fries. Too late he tried to call back the waitress to change the order to a salad. When it came, he set aside a third of the steak and ate only four of the french fries. Afterwards, he finished the steak and picked at the french fries while trying to flag down the waitress. "Lime jello," he told her, and added, "No whipped cream." Ten minutes later she brought raspberry jello with whipped cream. He put part of the whipped cream on the side of the plate and ate the jello. No point in worrying about the whipped cream: it was ersatz anyway and probably not fattening.

With time to kill, he ordered a second coffee and set himself to reviewing what progress he had made. What exactly did he have to this point? Beyond anything else he had that familiar feeling in his left kidney. Copeland's left kidney had achieved a degree of notoriety at the District Attorney's office. From time to time when an extraordinarily puzzling case had reached a dead end, Copeland would sense some nebulous something and announce that he was getting a message from his left kidney. It had nothing to do with his left kidney, of course, and might better have been described as a hunch or intuition. However, at such times he became indefatiguable in his commitment, and as a consequence, his left kidney seemed to be vindicated more often than not and he and his mates had developed an almost mystical confidence in it, tending to dismiss out of hand or to rationalize away those occasions when his urological forecasts weren't borne out. Right now the signals were loud and clear; the problem was: how to convince Schultz, (who put his confidence in tangible evidence), that his left kidney could be trusted.

What hard facts did he have? He'd established that Harris had shipped from Israel to himself, care of the Museum of Natural History, a sealed wooden box containing, so it would seem, certain archaeological artifacts. The box had been forwarded by the museum to the residence and had then disappeared. Granted the not unlikely possibility that it might have been disposed of unobserved, there remained the question, what had happened to the contents? Whatever they may have been, having been taken to the basement workroom, they had never been seen again. Even more extraordinary; when Harris had died, unexpectedly, the room when examined had yielded neither the box nor anything that might have been in it.

Back to his conversation with Mrs. Gordon. She'd been told – and no one at the residence would be likely to lie about such a matter – that everything Harris possessed at death had been forwarded to her. Yet nothing she'd received seemed related to whatever Harris had been working on. The notebooks were at least three years old. There was no manuscript, yet Jennifer had been told Harris was working on a book. If so, why was there no evidence of that project? Why were there no research materials related to it? There were cameras and lighting equipment, but no photographs nor anything worth photographing. There was a microscope, but nothing that had been forwarded to Mrs. Gordon would have been a likely subject for such scrutiny. It was as though Harris had been working with material that had self-destructed upon his death.

Back to the box and its contents. There was the curious fact that Harris had shipped the box to himself, care of the museum. Why? There was, of course, an entirely reasonable answer: he didn't know at the time where he would be living in the United States, and where better to have the box held than in a museum? But there were two other hypothetical explanations: One, it may have been a scheme designed to circumvent customs. Had he shipped the box to a private address, it would have been examined at the point of entry; shipping it to the museum enabled him to get it into the country without disclosing the contents. Two, by addressing the box to the museum, he'd provided himself with justification if it was discovered in Israel that he had made an undeclared find. He could argue that he'd attempted no secrecy, but had sent the artifacts to a great museum, intending to work on them there prior to declaring his find. The argument would be a bit thin but, depending on the nature of his discovery, plausible.

The waitress arrived with a second cup of coffee and it broke his sequence of thoughts. Hold on! He was going off half-cocked. It was possible that every conclusion he'd reached was subject to reasonable explanation. Michael might be able to give him answers to all of his questions. Until he'd seen him he had almost nothing to go on, and Schultz could shoot him down without even drawing a bead.

"Yes, sir, we were able to turn up the waybill and the papers."

"Great."

"Your information was wrong, though. The shipment didn't originate in Israel. It was cleared in Amman, Jordan."

Of course! He should have known. So punctilious is the security-check in Israel, there would have been no possibility of smuggling contraband out.

"May I have a look at it?" Copeland asked.

"No problem."

He turned to the keyboard and tapped out a sequence. The machine immediately chattered, ricochetted and thrust up a sheet of paper. The agent tore it free and passed it across the desk to Copeland.

He took out his notebook and sat down with the printout: From Dr. Harris Gordon to Dr. Harris Gordon – check. *Contents fragile. Handle with extreme care.* That would suggest that what he had found was exceedingly old or breakable: possibly the kind of jars in which the Dead Sea Scrolls had been found. *Archaeological artifacts.* Whatever the contents actually were, listing them as artifacts would justify their being shipped to the museum. *Not to be opened except in presence of addressee.* That would guarantee that no nosy official would go prying around. It would also give him room to maneuver if his customs broker had trouble clearing the shipment. He could argue the jeopardy of opening the box except in a proper environment. And the further instructions, *Avoid extreme cold, heat or humidity,* would bear that out, would even enable him if all else failed, to have the box returned unopened to Amman.

He flipped the notebook closed and slipped it into a pocket. "You've been very helpful," he said.

"No problem."

"Can I keep this printout?"

"No problem."

"I have a general question."

"Shoot."

"What would be normal practice with a shipment like this? Would it be passed without inspection?"

"Well, being addressed to the museum, and his customs broker coming in with a power of attorney, and ancient artifacts not being dutiable . . . yeah. I mean, nobody at the museum's liable to be into contraband."

"Let's say it was simply addressed to Dr. Harris Gordon, 452 Madison Avenue?"

"He'd have to come in to clear it. Or his broker."

"Would it be opened?"

"Depends. If there was some reason to be suspicious. If this guy Gordon was nervous, if he was evasive, if maybe the stuff was dutiable. There are a whole flock of ifs. One thing for damn sure: customs'd want to know what a private citizen was shipping to himself, and why, before they'd clear it."

"Thank you," Copeland said with a small fillip of finality, feeling like a prosecuting attorney on television who has just completed a successful cross-examination.

Chapter Three

Despite careful preparation Copeland approached the appointment with Michael with trepidation. After five months, he was still intimidated in his presence and hesitant to enter fully into the often animated and usually opinionated conversation common at dinner. Jennifer frequently pressed him to, and sometimes with little subtlety turned the talk in his direction. ("I want him to see you as I do," she would say afterwards. "I want him to know how lucky I am.") But, dammit, Michael was such a *presence* presiding at his own table, with the two priests and Dr. Gordon each holding forth in turn. His English was so precise, his voice was such an instrument, his mind was so acute and he was so aware – and so damned pontifical at times! – that when he was expounding his views on anything from American economic policy to Oscar Peterson's jazz it was almost a performance.

It was because Michael was so aware and his mind so acute that Copeland found it difficult to accept the idea that he'd been ignorant of the project Harris had been working on, particularly when they were such old friends and spoke so openly to each other. Surely Harris must have told him what he wanted the room for. Surely Michael must have pointed out its unsuitability – the poor lighting, the less than adequate ventilation – and surely in brushing these aside Harris must have stipulated his intentions. It could hardly have been otherwise.

Well, he would soon find out.

In Washington, preparing for the confrontation with Copeland,

Michael had decided to take full advantage of the prestige and trappings of his office. He scheduled the meeting to follow immediately upon a formal reception for Bishop Tuttle, who had only recently been elevated to the office, at which he would be required to wear his full cardinal's regalia. In it he was imposing. Over black trousers and a white neckband shirt he would don what was referred to as his "house cassock," black with cardinal-red piping and buttons. About his shoulders would be a silver chain from which would hang a jeweled metal cross, the chain hooked to one of the buttons at the center of his chest. About his waist would be a broad red sash, falling to the floor on the right side. On his head would be a cardinal-red *zuchetto*, a skull cap, and in his hands, the biretta, square in form with three standing tabs and evolved from an ancient academic mortarboard. Since the reception would end with photographs in the garden, he would be wearing over his cassock an ankle-length scarlet cape, open.

As had been arranged with Father Jamieson, Copeland had been ushered to the study on his arrival, and left there. At the conclusion of the reception, Michael told Bishop Tuttle to "Come meet Jennifer's fiancé," and ten minutes late, swept into the study to greet Copeland affectionately, taking his outstretched hand in his two and introducing him to the bishop. There followed five minutes of somewhat hyper conversation, with Michael dominant and charming, Bishop Tuttle striving to keep afloat and Copeland feeling doltish. Michael then walked the bishop to the door, bade him farewell and returned to sit behind his desk, placing the biretta before him and, as he commonly did, swinging the cross like a pendulum beneath his fingers.

"You'll have to overlook the working clothes," he said, spreading his arms deprecatingly but suggesting a great bird landing, "but it was come as I am or be delayed. Then, too, I thought you'd like to meet the bishop. Extraordinary fellow: used to be a newspaper editor but decided one day that he wanted instead to publish the Good News." He glanced at the mantel clock. "Sorry I'm late," he said, and then before Copeland could respond, added, "I trust Father Jamieson explained that I have to be out of here by four."

Copeland nodded. "Yes, he did, Your Eminence."

"I'm sorry about Tuesday, but there was no avoiding it. You do understand?"

"No, that's fine. I mean, yes, I understand."

"At any rate, here we are now and we should use the time to the best advantage." He leaned forward to convey a willingness to be helpful.

Copeland was not yet at ease. "Before we begin, Your Eminence, perhaps I should explain something."

"By all means."

"This is not the easiest assignment I've ever had; I mean, you being who you are, and knowing you in the connection in which I do . . . You see, I'm here officially, on police business, and that makes things a bit awkward."

"No need for that. Just proceed as you normally would."

Copeland bobbed his head to get the sentence started. "So you'll understand if I seem to press you with my questions."

Michael was displeased with the way things had begun. It removed immediately the advantage he'd counted on. It gave Copeland a freedom of interrogation that he would have preferred to and had intended to limit. He said: "Copeland, my boy, you have a job to do."

"Thank you, Your Eminence." He shifted in his chair. "One other thing; would you mind if I recorded our conversation?" He removed a small rectangular tape recorder from his shirt pocket. "It'll allow me to make notes later and save a lot of time now."

Michael hesitated. "I'm not sure about that," he said, not troubling to hide his displeasure. "I have no objection to your taping what we say, as far as you are concerned, that is, but I must say I am loath to have a private conversation floating about, to be heard by anyone. We may get into things about Dr. Gordon that I wouldn't want common knowledge."

"No, no," Copeland said quickly. "This wouldn't be for the department's records; just for me. It's simply to save time."

"Well," Michael said grudgingly, "if I have your assurance of that."

"Thank you," Copeland said and placed the recorder on top of the desk. "Now to begin—"

Michael broke in. "Would you like some coffee?"

"No, thanks."

"I may need one," Michael said. "I've been talking since morning. I told Miss Pritchard to serve us some. I could cancel it."

"No. Please don't."

"Very well," Michael said, turning up his presence to full candlepower, "let's get on with it."

Copeland drew a long breath. He could feel the perspiration trickling on his scalp and his hands were damp as he flipped the pages of his notebook.

"To begin, then: You told me last time about your friendship with Dr. Gordon and about meeting him again in London . . . "

"After almost forty years."

"It was at that time you invited him to stay here?"

"Yes. It became pretty obvious he'd fallen on . . . let's just say he was at loose ends."

"Can you remember the exact date?"

"Yes, of course. It would be the morning of the day I returned home from my last trip to Rome. Let me see, that would be January seventh." As Copeland checked his notebook, he asked, "May I ask why the date is important?"

Normally Copeland would have disregarded or skated around such questions, but he hadn't the temerity to do so with Michael. "Dr. Gordon shipped a box to himself from Amman, Jordan, care of the Museum of Natural History, and I was curious to know whether he shipped it before or after he learned he'd be living here."

"What difference would that make?"

"It might have been an attempt to avoid a customs inspection."

"Ah yes, I see," Michael said.

"The box was delivered here?"

"So I understand."

"Did Dr. Gordon tell you what was in it?"

"I gather there were some artifacts."

"He was no more specific than that?" The question was blunt but Copeland's tone wasn't.

"Indeed he was," Michael said without hesitation. "He said something about a scroll and some fossil remains. My impression was that he wasn't quite sure at that point exactly what he'd discovered."

"Do you know what happened to them?"

Michael shrugged. "I presume they were removed elsewhere for safekeeping."

Copeland checked his notes. "I believe you were the first person to go into his workroom afterwards?"

"Yes."

"There was no sign of the box or the artifacts?"

"I didn't take a careful look, but . . . " he shook his head.

Copeland cleared his throat. "Your Eminence, may I ask why you went to the workroom after Dr. Gordon died?"

There was no slightest hesitation. "He'd asked me to."

Copeland paused, expecting him to continue. When he didn't, he asked, "Why?"

Michael leaned forward and put his elbows on the desk, hands fingertip to fingertip. "Permit me a suggestion," he said, flexing the fingers against each other and regarding them as he did. "Leave that until later. I have some things to tell you, but I think it wiser that we get your questions out of the way first."

Copeland was about to press for a response and then reconsidered. "Fine," he said, returning to his notebook. "Now, as I understand it, there were two locks on the workroom door?"

"As you understand it?" Michael said, smiling. "I'd have thought you'd have *seen* them when you looked at the room with Jennifer on Monday."

Copeland flushed, "Sorry. Of course I did. I presume you had the spare keys."

Michael arched his eyebrows. "But surely, Copeland, you know that. Miss Pritchard told me you asked about it. I don't understand."

The perspiration was beaded on Copeland's brow. "Right. Sorry. Wrong place in my notes here." He flipped a page.

Michael continued. "Dr. Gordon was concerned about privacy so I had an extra set made and gave them to him."

"His concern about privacy: didn't that strike you as abnormal?"

"Abnormal?"

"I mean, what could be so secret he had to guard it against the people living here."

"I'm sure he felt he had good reasons. I never questioned it."

Copeland studied his notes. "Let's go back to the fact that, after his death, there was no indication of what he'd been working on. Do you have any idea what could have happened to the artifacts?"

Michael raised he eyebrows and spread his hands as though in recognition of the obvious. "I would imagine that, having finished his work, he'd removed them elsewhere."

"Did he say he'd finished his work?"

"The morning of the day he died."

"May I pursue that a moment: That would be Easter Sunday morning?"

"Yes. I'd preached at the cathedral and we had a brief chat after I returned."

"Did he mention moving his things out?"

"No."

Copeland mused a moment. "But you'd think he'd have asked for help. My information is that the box was a fair size and weighed over twenty pounds. And he had a bad heart."

Michael made a small deprecatory shrug. "Harris would think of that as admitting to weakness. In all the time he was here I never once saw him make a concession to his angina. Did you ever see him go easy on himself?" Copeland assented. "A pretty crusty character."

"To try to pin down the time: could he have removed the box that Sunday?"

"No reason why not. He was at home all day."

As Copeland looked at his notes Michael said, "Perhaps this might help. He asked if he could borrow my car that day. Perhaps it was to move his things."

Damn! Copeland thought. How in heaven's name do I trace the box now? He could have taken it around the corner or into the next state. It's a needle in a haystack now. Schultz will have my ass. Damn, damn, damn, *damn*!

He flipped through his notebook looking for something, anything that might freshen the trail. Baffled, he closed it and looked at Michael. "That's all I have for the moment. You said earlier there were some things you wanted to tell me."

"That's correct," Michael said, sitting back in his chair and drumming with the fingers of one hand on the desk. "During the approximately three months Dr. Gordon was living here, he was working on a book. He was aware, of course – because of his heart condition, and it exacerbated by diabetes – that he might never get to finish. Consequently he asked me, in the event of his death, to be responsible for it. The night he died, I went to the basement, found the manuscript and removed it."

Copeland brightened. All was not lost. "Do you still have it?"

"Yes, I do."

"That's marvelous. It will tell us what he was working on."

Michael shook his head slowly. "I'm afraid not."

"Oh . . . ?"

"I'm not at liberty to let you see it. Dr. Gordon entrusted it to me with the express understanding that it not be published until ten years after his death."

"You *do* have it in your possession?"

"It's safely put away."

Copeland's voice was touched with incredulity. "But surely, Your Eminence, you're not bound by his request. I mean, under the circumstances. A crime has been committed and the manuscript would undoubtedly shed light on it."

Michael put the question slowly, sure of his ground: "But Copeland, *has* a crime been committed? What, precisely, was stolen, and from where?"

Copeland's voice lost some of its assurance. "That's what we're trying to establish. The Israeli government has reason to believe that Dr. Gordon exported certain artifacts without a permit. Under Israeli law that's a crime. They have officially requested the District Attorney of the County of New York to assist in the inquiry and to take whatever action is necessary to return the stolen articles."

Michael leaned forward. His voice was controlled and reasonable. "Copeland, you'll forgive me: I don't want to seem argumentative, but I fail to see how a theft can have been perpetrated when it is not known what if anything was stolen. And, in candor, I must say that the actions of the Israeli government are high-handed and improper. They are in effect accusing a dead man of a criminal act without knowing whether or not that act was committed."

"But the box . . . " Copeland expostulated. "The secrecy . . . "

"What about the box? It was shipped, you say, not from Israel but from Jordan. How do we know it came from Israel? Do we know that the contents were stolen? I think not."

Copeland was about to respond and then retrenched. There were great holes in his information. Finally he said, "Do you feel free to tell me the subject matter of the manuscript?"

"I'm afraid not. I have not read it nor do I intend to."

He was desperate: "Did he discuss it with you?"

"Yes."

"But surely if he discussed it with you there'd be nothing improper in telling me."

"I'm afraid so. When the book is published it will be very controversial, and it would do a great deal of harm to a great many people if it were to be released prematurely. You must know,

Copeland, that it's not uncommon for a man to write his memoirs and place an embargo on their publication until a specified time in the future."

"Is it his memoirs?"

Michael smiled. "You must not try to read meanings into what I say. I'm simply saying that I'm not at liberty to tell you anything about the book, its title or its subject matter."

Copeland was at a dead end. He sat chewing on his lower lip, his brow furrowed, staring at the grain of the wood of Michael's desk. He leaned forward, switched off the tape recorder and put it in his shirt pocket.

"I really am sorry, Copeland," Michael said. "I can see what a disappointment it is to you. But surely you of all people can understand. Dr. Gordon told me things which I consider to be of the nature of a confession. They touch on his book. You must realize that as a priest I'm bound not to divulge anything of what he told me. Even if he were involved in a crime – and I'm by no means sure he was – I still wouldn't be able to reveal it. It's privileged information." He paused, "As you know, that's recognized in law."

There was a knock at the door. "That'll be Miss P. with the coffee," Michael said brightly. "Come!"

As Miss Pritchard entered, bearing a tray with the makings, Copeland rose. He was shaken. "If you don't mind, Your Eminence, I think I'll pass."

"Don't hurry off on my account," Michael said. "We still have a good twenty minutes."

"Thank you, but I've already taken up a lot of your time," Copeland said and headed for the door. "Thank you very much." He nodded at Miss Pritchard and was gone. She looked inquiringly at Michael.

"Yes, Miss P.," he said. "I think before I change I will have a cup."

She poured it and left. Michael sat quietly in the silence of the room, sipping the coffee meditatively.

"My God, why have you deserted me?"

At three in the morning Michael was kneeling at the prie-dieu in his bedroom, half-praying, half-puzzling.

"Loving Father, why do you hide your face from me? Surely you know that, though you slay me yet will I trust you. And surely you see that I'm confused. Why have you removed yourself from me? Why do you remain aloof? Father, I've rejoiced in the assurance of your presence in other days; why can't I find it now? You've always warmed me by your grace but now my heart is cold. I plead but you don't come. I cry out and there is nothing but silence. Why? Why? Why do you treat your servant so?

"You called your servant, Moses. 'Follow me,' you said, and the path led to a wilderness and to an unknown grave. You said to your servant Job, 'Follow me,' and he did, and found himself seated on the ashes of his success, loathsome and miserable. 'Follow me, Baptizer,' you said, and there was his head on a platter at the whim of a dancing girl. 'Follow me, Simon, and I will build my church'; but at the end of the road there was an inverted cross and an agony akin to yours. 'Follow me, Saul,' and he won persecution and shipwreck and snakebite and prison. 'Follow me, Joan,' and there were faggots at her feet and flame in her nostrils.

"How well, Lord, you knew the way: 'If any man would follow me,' you said, 'let him take up his cross.' 'Take nothing with you,' you said, 'save the clothes on your back and the sandals on your feet.' 'Take what you have and sell it and give it to the poor, and come and follow me.'

"That's how you called me, Lord. 'Follow me,' you said, and I did. On tablets of stone you had inscribed the words, 'Thou shalt not murder,' but on the tables of my heart I found a different commandment. And I was obedient . . . even unto the death. I've done your bidding, Father, but the days pass and the guilt doesn't; it lies like gray death within me. You've borne me up only to cast me down. With the Psalmist "I have eaten ashes like bread and have mingled my drink with weeping," and still there is no peace. And now the hounds of hell pursue again. The dread secret stirs. The grave cries out, and Harris would be avenged . . . Oh God, why have you deserted me?"

In the quiet a gentle tapping, and at the door:

"Jennifer!"

"I'm sorry, Uncle Michael."

In the dark hallway she looked very small in a capacious flannel nightgown, her hair down, her eyes swollen.

"What is it, Jennifer?" He put an arm about her shoulders. "Come in. Come in."

"I'm sorry. Did I waken you?"

"No. I wasn't sleeping."

"I thought I heard you talking to somebody."

"To myself mostly. But you're trembling."

"I'll be all right."

He wouldn't be content until he'd fetched an afghan and draped it about her shoulders as she sat opposite him at the center of the sofa with her hands in her lap. Little girl lost.

"I had a bad dream," she said.

"One of your old nightmares?"

She smiled wanly. "No, no clinging to the edge of a precipice. It was about Copeland and me." Her eyes glistened.

Michael was silent, not wanting to interrupt. She'd come to talk and he didn't want to set words in her way.

She swallowed and blinked and the tears were retrieved. "I'm so afraid," she said.

"Afraid?"

The tears welled again. "I love him so much, and it makes me afraid . . . " She reached for a handkerchief but of course there was no pocket in the nightgown. Michael went to the bathroom and returned with a box of tissue. She dabbed at her eyes and blew her nose.

"Have you had a quarrel?"

"No, no. Nothing like that. It's just that I'm so happy I'm afraid. I know that sounds crazy."

"You're afraid he doesn't love you?"

"Oh no, I know he loves me."

Now he understood: "You're so happy you're frightened that something will snatch it away, that some malevolent something will destroy this beautiful thing."

She bobbed her head vigorously, not trusting her voice. Neither spoke for a minute and then Michael said gently, "I think it would be good if you told me about it. If you want to, that is."

That gave her the control she needed. She blotted her tears and blew her nose again and gathered the afghan about her. She had to clear her throat to begin, but then her voice was sure.

"It sounds so trite, but I love him so much. I know now I never was in love before. He's everything I ever wanted in a man. We have fun together – we laugh at the silliest things – but we can be serious. Very serious. I can talk to him about things I've never been able to discuss with anybody . . . " She smiled and, her face brightening, looked up. "Isn't that just awful? I sound exactly like every schoolgirl who ever fell in love."

Michael smiled, too. "Go on. It makes me happy to hear you."

She grew solemn again and drew a great breath that ended in a shudder.

"Are you still cold?"

"No." Abruptly she was very intense. "What's the matter with me, Uncle Michael? Here I am, happier than I've ever been. There isn't a thing in my life I'd change. I have you, I have my work, I have Copeland, and we're going to be married. I should be the happiest person in the world. And I *am*," she expostulated. "It's just that when I'm feeling my happiest, suddenly there's this terrible dread and a voice inside seems to say, 'Yes, you're happy now, but for how long? Something's bound to happen.' It's as though I have no right to be happy and that to be happy is to risk disaster, actually to invite it." Her intensity had burned out and she lapsed into silence, drawing the wrap more closely about her.

"I understand," he said, waiting for her to go on.

She looked directly at him, perplexity furrowing the corners of her eyebrows. "The strangest part of it is, I think it's God I'm afraid of."

"Would you like some coffee?" he asked.

She was startled at the abrupt change of subject. "As a matter of fact I would," she said.

The electric kettle came swiftly to a boil, and by the time he'd set out two mugs and put a spoonful of granules in each, the water was ready. Neither said anything while he was preparing the coffee. Jennifer had taken the opportunity generally to pat her emotions back in place. Michael said, "It'll have to be black," and she nodded and took the cup and sipped the steaming liquid. He seated himself, and when they were both ready, said, "Have you figured out *why* you're afraid?"

A forefinger was tracing the pattern of the afghan. "I used to think it had something to do with unresolved guilt. That's the explanation a friend gave me – he's a psychiatrist – but somehow that doesn't seem right."

"You said that perhaps it's God you're afraid of. What makes you think that?"

"I don't know. I say to myself, that's crazy. God loves you; you know that. You love him." She paused. "But then all kinds of thoughts crowd in and I hear my mind saying, 'But wasn't it God who let Joan drown, and who let Mom and Dad die?' Then Uncle Harris is taken. These things happen in life, I know that, but it seems there's always disappointment at the end of hope. It even seems dangerous to hope, and that's why I'm frightened about Copeland and me."

Michael was remembering those moments when he'd had similar feelings: the sense of being alone and inconsequential in an indifferent, even hostile, universe; the not daring to hope for something with too great a longing lest the very intensity create the denial; the fear that something at the heart of existence thwarts joy and beauty and happiness. But when he spoke his voice was firm with reassurance.

"It's a difficult question; I suppose everybody's wondered about it at one time or another. Perhaps, Jennifer, it *does* have something to do with guilt. Not the guilt you take into the confessional and leave there, but the guilt the psychiatrists talk about. Psychiatry says a lot of silly things but there's some wisdom in it, too. I believe that, fixed within the mind, there are memories of things that happened when we were very young and very impressionable, with a mind like a blotter ready to absorb. As children we're taught that things fall generally into two categories, good and bad, and that bad actions are punished. We're told, 'Don't touch the stove,' or 'Don't pull the dog's tail,' or 'Don't put that in your mouth.' We disobey and get burned or bitten or get a bad taste. We observe that disobedience brings pain or unhappiness.

"But very soon we learn something else: that there are do's and don'ts which, disobeyed, *don't* necessarily bring pain. Things like, 'Don't lie,' or 'Don't talk back to your father,' or 'Don't forget to say your prayers.' We observe that when we disobey these prohibitions, it may mean pain or unhappiness – perhaps a spanking, or worse, the disapproval of the loving person we want to be close to – or it may not. We notice that if the loving person isn't aware of our disobedience we escape the punishment. The trouble is, however, that with our simple cause-and-effect sense of values we expect disobedience to be followed by punishment, and we figure that, if and when the loving person finds out about it, the punishment will yet come. Then, when the loving person is kind to us and we're happy, we suddenly remember that unpunished deed and we feel guilt."

He took a sip of coffee. "I don't know whether all this is true or not, but it seems reasonable to believe that early in life we may have done relatively innocent wrongs, suffered disproportionate feelings of guilt, and still have that guilt buried complete with the conviction that the punishment may yet come. Then, when we feel extraordinarily happy, that forgotten guilt is activated, and it warns, 'Have a care: that unpaid debt may soon be called.'

Jennifer had been listening intently but with a small frown of disbelief.

Michael continued: "There's another factor, of course. As Christians we're taught still another set of do's and don'ts, and we frequently disobey. Fortunately, we can get rid of most of that guilt by confessing it. I sometimes wonder, Jennifer, if we don't often confuse the different kinds of guilt and the different loving persons." He smiled at her. "Maybe that's why you're afraid of God."

Jennifer didn't respond for a moment. "It's possible, I suppose," she said slowly. The frown was still troubling her brow. "But somehow it doesn't seem true in my case."

"Why?"

"Because, three times in my life I've been very, very happy; more often than that, of course, but three times in particular. With Joan, for instance: we were fourteen; she was my best friend and I loved her. We were closer than sisters. She invited me to go to summer camp with her. I'd wanted to go for years. Daddy said, yes. When I got there it was even better than I'd dreamed. One afternoon Joan asked me to go canoeing with her, but I'd met a boy the night before at the get-acquainted session and I said, 'No, I want to wash my hair.' So she went off alone . . . and she was drowned. I was on the dock when they brought her body in.

"You know about Mom and Dad, of course, but perhaps you don't know that that was one of the happiest days of my life. Everything was perfect. I'd just graduated from high school; won two prizes and a letter. It was my seventeenth birthday. I wasn't supposed to know, but I'd found out that Mom and Dad were going to give me as my present a Siamese kitten I'd been doting on. There were a lot of other things. And then . . . " She fought the tears. "And then pointlessly, needlessly, suddenly they were gone. At the funeral, I remember thinking that after the ceremony I'd go back to the grave and hide in it so I'd be there when they shoveled the earth back in."

Michael said, "More coffee?" to give her time to regain control. She shook her head. He knew the memories were like a knife, thrusting, turning, but he knew too she wanted to go on. And his heart constricted; he knew what was coming.

"Then there was Uncle Harris. It's odd how I took to him. He was a strange man – I never could quite figure him out and Copeland didn't like him at all – but there was a lot of love in him and for some reason he was careful to keep it covered. I think he needed me to put my cheek against his when we saw each other, and it was good for me too. I don't know why. I get lots of love: from Copeland, from you, even from Miss P. – she thinks I'm her chick, or something – but Uncle Harris was somebody I needed for other reasons. We were just getting to know each other."

She looked at him, so involved in her thoughts that she didn't notice his pallor. "Uncle Michael, it's more than residual guilt, it's . . . " She struggled for the words. "I really believe that when I'm happy it's dangerous for the people I love."

Michael was slow to respond, and when he did the nausea had begun to subside. "I don't know, Jennifer, whether the answers I offered you are true or not, but I *do* know that what you just said is untrue. Jennifer, believe me, that's pure superstition. It's voodoo, it's the evil eye, it's witchdoctors and the sticking of pins in dolls. It's a lie!"

She had her head down. Her hair hung like a canopy about her face and from beneath it the tears fell freely onto her hands clasped tightly in her lap.

"Jennifer, darling, what you're really talking about is the risk of loving. When you love you give part of yourself to someone else and the person to whom you give it can hurt you. There is danger in loving, yes, but it's to yourself. Love is an extension of your personality and it makes you vulnerable. When anything happens to someone you love it happens also to you. Look at a mother bending over the crib in which her child lies sick: who's suffering more, the mother or the child? To love is to live dangerously, but to fail to love is not to live fully."

Jennifer hadn't moved nor did she as he paused. He went on, not arguing but gently persuading. "Think a moment, Jennifer. What you said doesn't make sense. Don't you love me, and I you? And hasn't that happiness existed unbroken for years now? You mentioned Miss Pritchard; where has the danger been in that love?

Jennifer, darling, life sometimes deals cruel blows and often there seems no reason for them – there may *be* no reason for them that we can know – but we can't let life be a mere response to those blows. They're grievous, frightening and, it sometimes seems, unendurable, but they're only a part of life."

He paused and said, "Look at me." She did, her eyes brimming. "Life *has* been cruel to you at times," he said, his own eyes wet, "but it has also given you more than a normal share of love. There's that to remember, too."

She got out of her chair and went to him and sat on his lap with her arms around him and her body shaking. He held her and put his cheek against the top of her head and wept with her. He was thinking too of the risk in loving God.

His Eminence,   *May 22*
Michael Cardinal Maloney,
The Archdiocese of New York,
452 Madison Avenue,
New York City, N.Y. 10022
USA

My dear Michael:

The day of miracles is not gone (although I wish I could see more concrete evidence of that) for I have, as you see, put arthritic hand to paper to address myself to some matters that have arisen here and require to be communicated to you.

I am told that when the American army was here it employed a colorful acronym to describe colloquially the condition of army life: namely, Situation Normal; All Fouled Up. (I am not unaware, I might add, that some substituted another verb for the word "fouled.") Be that as it may, the phrase is particularly apt to describe the situation here. Everything is in stasis save for (a) the importunities of the press, (b) the increasing number of inquiries from around the world about His Holiness' health, and (c) the industry with which Benedetti engages in his machinations – of which more later.

Our Lord's commandment: 'Let your Yea be yea and your Nay be nay,' is no longer operative here at the Vatican. Not an hour goes by but what we are forced to bend, twist, disguise, withhold or somewhat maim the whole truth in responding to the press. (What indefatiguable meddlers they are!) The charade has become almost institutionalized. The irony is that they quite obviously don't believe a word of our official statements on the condition of the Holy Father. We know that, and they know that we know, and yet we solemnly dance our daily minuet for the good of all concerned. It having fallen to me to face the jackals from time to time, I simply set aside my dedication to the whole of truth for those few moments and place my confidence in the compassionate understanding of Our Lord. St. Paul's warning that the end of all liars shall be in the lake that burns with fire and brimstone gives me pause, but I comfort myself with the thought that he predicted nothing dire for those who, in the service of God, do not declare their full counsel.

What can I say to you about the Holy Father's condition except that it is worse while remaining the same? I shall not dwell on it, for to do so is to despair. I sometimes watch his fingers plucking at the cover of his bed (I sit with him for an hour each day) and think just so tenuous is his hold on this life. I weep to see him: emaciated — you will not believe it; thinner than when you saw him — a plastic tube inserted into one nostril, plasma leaking through another into a vein in his poor arm, wires leading beneath the bedclothes to his chest, his heartbeat sounding as a squeak and visualized as a pale pattern on the face of one of the plethora of machines that encircle the head of his bed and make me think of the mechanisms that surround an aircraft when it is being serviced. He lies by the hour, staring. No flicker of recognition, no reaction when you draw near. Staring, it would seem, into the void. The doctors do nothing to alter my jaundiced view of their profession: they maunder on mysteriously — sounding sometimes much like theologians — uttering their various prognoses; the sum of what they say being, to use the colloquialism, 'Search me.'

To other matters: I fear you are losing ground in the consideration of many of our brethren as to who shall succeed our beloved Gregory. I wish it were possible for you to be here more often and would urge you to try to be. (It is a common lie that distance lends enchantment and that absence makes the heart grow fonder.) To those who inquire of me, I make no bones about my preference and in some instances press my views on them. However, Benedetti and his little coterie of sychophants are troubled by no such reticence and seem not to rest in their efforts. One hopes, the wish being, perhaps, father to the thought, that his naked and transparent lusting for the prize may be his undoing. Would ever justice be so just! One trusts also in the conviction that the choice is not made finally by the College but by the Holy Spirit. One might, however, be permitted to say without irreverence that we and He are at the moment lagging behind.

I am persuaded from such auguries as I discern and from such soundings as I have made, that your support exceeds his elsewhere. The problem lies here. It must be faced that it would be an astounding break with tradition were the papacy to go to someone not Italian. Some whose minds have hardened with their arteries, find this unthinkable and cannot bear to so much as contemplate the possibility. But there are some less rigid. In them lies the hope of the church.

I, who am not above being occasionally Machiavellian, have in recent days been pursued by a somewhat devious thought. You may remember my earlier counsel in the matter of the contribution being offered by that titled English lady whose name now escapes me. I would change the advice I gave you then. If the lady remains ready to make the gift mentioned in her letter to the Holy Father, is it possible that you could induce her to change her bequest? Rather than make a contribution to your St. Clare's, deserving as it may be, might she be convinced to direct her largesse to the refurbishing of the Vatican? Much sorely needs to be done but there are no funds for it. Were she to see fit so to do, beyond the immediate good that would be done, the receipt here from your hand of the sum proffered could not but impress upon many of our wavering brethren the argument that we must establish closer relations with the United States — from whom all blessings flow. It is unworthy of me to suggest it, but then I am often so. I trust you will find it possible to be equally unworthy and consider it.

Now, if I can release my cramped fingers from this pen, I shall off to such provender as my ulcers and our common table will allow. I salute you across the miles,
in Christ's love

Paolo Rinsonelli

"I thought Copeland was going to join us for dinner?"

"He was, but he's off to Israel."

"To Israel?"

"I drove him to the airport this morning. Some broccoli?"

"I'm fine, thanks."

"They think maybe he can dig up some more facts. The investigation isn't going too well."

"I must say, Jennifer, I'm a little less than happy about this whole thing."

"I can understand that."

"Especially about Copeland being assigned to it. Not very good judgment on the part of his superiors."

"He asked for it, you know. He figured it'd be better than some stranger coming around."

"I can appreciate that, but he almost seems at times to be taking advantage of his, uh . . . his relationships here."

"I'm sure he doesn't mean to do that."

"Miss Pritchard spoke to me. I got the impression he was quite rough on her."

"She's exaggerating. He *did* ask her a lot of questions, but it's his job."

"I know."

"And she was evasive."

"He seems to be – there's only one word for it – suspicious of Dr. Gordon."

"I'm afraid so."

"He's almost obsessive about it."

"Are you ready for your coffee?"

"Thank you."

"The saccharin's in that little covered dish there. It's a new granulated kind."

"Jennifer, this is a bit awkward, but it seems to me that Copeland is pursuing this whole thing with undue zeal. I was going to have a word with him if he'd come tonight. I had a call from Mason's Garage."

"Where you keep the car?"

"From Mr. Jenkins, the manager. He'd had a phone call from Copeland asking whether my car had been used Easter Sunday."

"I don't understand. Why would he want to know that?"

"That's what Jenkins wondered. What happened is, I told Copeland that Harris had asked if he could borrow my car Easter Sunday – which he did, although he didn't use it – and for some reason Copeland called Mason's about it."

"I really don't understand."

"It's the connotation that I don't appreciate. It almost seems that he's checking up on me."

"Uncle Michael, I'm sorry. I'm sure there must be some explanation."

"There may be. But as you can imagine—"

"I'll ask him about it."

"I wouldn't want you to do that."

"No. I'll speak to him when he gets back."

Chapter Four

The great plane swept in low over the flat enamel-blue water of the Mediterranean, unmarred by so much as a wind-ruffle and burnished by the morning sun. Below, all motion seemed suspended save for the swift passage of an occasional gull, wings set, sliding into view and gliding beyond sight. Within the cabin there was a pianissimo of excitement. It had been introduced by the illuminating of the seatbelt sign, had intensified with the request that all smoking materials be extinguished, had swelled with the announcement, "We shall be landing in Israel in a few minutes," and had crescendoed when the driving, energizing rhythms of *Hava negila* burst from the sound system. As one, every head strained toward a window, necks craning, eyes questing for the first longed-for sight of land.

"There it is!" came a cry, and the cry was echoed and elaborated by dozens of voices in dozens of ways. And there indeed it was – *Israel*! But, disappointingly, unlike Israel. More like Florida: a rampart of luxury hotels reared against the sea, stone arms stretched into the water, geometric streets, rectangles of extruded office buildings and apartments, and draped over it all a saffron shawl of smog.

Then the plane swept beyond Tel Aviv and there *was* Israel. Israel indeed! – the vista duplicating a thousand photographs: the parched land, the dusty olive trees, the tattered palms, the terraced, crumbling hills, the distant dun mountains. Even the flat-roofed houses were familiar and oddly satisfying as though remembered from a dream.

The cabin was a Babel, each telling others where to look and none listening. Copeland looked about him and wished he were a Jew. Whether in the black clothes and hat and beard of the orthodox, the restrained flamboyance of Pucchi or the ersatz elegance of Macy's, whether speaking English, Yiddish, Hebrew or whatever, whether young or old, each Jew in the cabin was turgid with emotion. All his lifetime, all his traditions, all his Jewishness had come to focus, and eyes were teared and throats in need of clearing and swallowing came hard. Copeland realized that his own eyes were wet and was glad he'd come to Israel if only for this moment.

Not that it had been easy to arrange. Schultz had opposed the trip from the moment he broached it. "Jesus H. Christ," he'd exploded, "*you* want to go to Israel and *I* can't even get a replacement for my friggin' desk lamp! No way! Now I know why you wanted the goddam assignment. No way!"

Copeland had pointed out the great gaps in his information and emphasized that unless they were filled he could not possibly proceed. Then, feeling gleefully devious, he dropped on Schultz' desk the copy of the *Jerusalem Post* he'd picked up at a Grand Central station newsstand.

"So what's this?" he said disdainfully, tilting back his head so that he might see through the half-moon spectacles low on his nose. "You got a mention in this Hebe newspaper?"

Copeland placed a finger on a three-column heading on the front page:

SUSPECT THEFT OF

DEAD SEA SCROLL

The story quoted the Deputy Minister of the Department of Antiquities and Museums to the effect that what was believed to be an ancient manuscript had been unearthed near Qumran and smuggled out of the country contrary to Israeli law. The find had been made by a United States citizen, reputedly an archaeologist. The reporter, obviously playing the story to the limit despite a scarcity of confirmed fact, made much of a "No comment" by Eleazar Kauffman, the minister, when he'd been asked whether United States government authorities had been contacted in an attempt to effect the return of the scroll. "Meanwhile," the story went on, "the *Post* has learned that an official request for an investigation has gone forward to the District Attorney of the County of New York."

"Son of a bitch!" Schultz gloomed. "If the press has it, the heat'll be on."

"That's what I mean," Copeland said.

Schultz viciously bit off the tip of a cigar and muttered a curse when he saw he'd torn away part of the wrapper. He spat it onto the top of the desk and brushed it to the floor with a sweep of his arm.

"When do I leave?" Copeland said, striving not entirely success-fully to contain the smile.

"Be ready tomorrow morning," he growled. "The tickets'll be at your place tonight. Now get the hell out of here."

Copeland had only left the office when he was returned to the doorway by Schultz's bellow. The captain's head was almost obscured in a swirling nimbus of cigar smoke.

"You better damn well find that scroll," he roared, and then added, grinning, "or I cable the Syrian airforce what hotel you're at!" Copeland could hear him chuckling in appreciation of his own wit as he went down the hall.

Twenty-four hours later he stood on the balcony outside his room on the fourteenth floor of the Jerusalem Plaza hotel looking out over the city. Below and to his right was the modern Jerusa-lem, the traffic fuming and contending in the streets. Off to the left were the walls of the old city, and beyond in the hazy distance, a sequence of rounded mountains falling away to the Dead Sea.

Jerusalem! Sacred symbol to more than a billion Jews, Arabs and Christians, holy city to the world's three great monotheistic religions, center of the world on medieval maps. Has any land on earth been more contested for over the centuries, more coveted by king and caliph, more longed for by expatriates? On this unpre-possessing knoll of rock, some twenty-five hundred feet above sea level, the blood of Babylonians, Macedonians, Ptolemies, Seleu-cids, Romans, Byzantines, Persians, Arabs, Seljuks, Crusaders, Mongols, Mamelukes, British, Palestinians, Jordanians and Jews has stained the stone and seeped into the soil. Has any land seen more hatred and been the object of more devotion? Jews and Arabs alike look back some four millennia to the arrival at this spot of their common forebear, Abraham. It was to a flat rock crowning Mount Moriah, tradition holds, that Abraham took his son Isaac, intending to sacrifice him in obedience to his God. A thousand years later King David captured the site from the Jebusites and brought to it the Ark of the Covenant. Around it, his son Solomon built the first Temple. A thousand years of war and tyranny passed and Jesus of Nazareth walked the streets of the city and preached in the new Temple and died outside the walls. Three hundred years later the Emperor Constantine established it as the heart of Christianity and the center of the world. Later still, from the same sacred stone on Mount Moriah, Mohammed leaped to heaven.

There were other battles to follow and a myriad voices to be raised in anger and triumph and pain and prayer, and much blood to be spilled. And looking down on the city from high above, Copeland sensed the tumult of the centuries.

He went into the room, picked up the telephone and dialed the Department of Antiquities and Museums. Busy. When after three tries it was still engaged, he decided to shower and change. Afterwards, he tried the number again. It rang but there was no answer. He went onto the balcony and was immediately wary.

The sun had set but the skies were bright with twilight. A circle of moon hung above the rim of mountains. Yet, in the few minutes he'd been inside, something essential had changed. A silence had settled. For as far as he could see the streets were empty. Except for a speeding taxi all traffic had disappeared and the sidewalks were deserted. *Air raid,* he thought. But there had been no siren. Perhaps the rush of water in the shower had covered the sound. But why were they not wailing their warning now? He listened intently. Silence except for the distant echoing sound of a dog hysterical over something. He returned to the room and dialed the switchboard.

"Shalom," a voice said.

"Shalom," he said, betraying nothing of the vague apprehension he was feeling. "What's going on?"

"I beg your pardon, sir?"

"What's happening? The streets are empty."

A pause and then a laugh. "Oh, *that.* It's *shabat,* the Sabbath, sir."

"Of course," he said, embarrassed.

"It begins at sundown."

"Yes, I know. Thank you."

Of course; the Sabbath. No work. No travel other than – what was it? – "a Sabbath day's journey." He had a dim Sunday school memory that the limit was a furlong but wasn't sure. The Sabbath: that would mean, of course, that government offices would be closed. Perhaps he could reach Uri Shahak, the press secretary, at his home. He looked up the number and rang it. No answer. He shrugged into his jacket: he'd go have a drink and decide what to do.

At the bank of elevators there was a temporary sign, Shabat Elevator. He pushed the button and after a long wait it came. There had been no operator on duty when he'd gone to his room but there was now, a teenager seated before the panel of buttons. Though Copeland was the only passenger, the boy stopped at each floor on the way down.

In the lobby Copeland bought a copy of the *Jerusalem Post*, descended the broad stairway to the empty lounge, ordered a glass of Avdat, the Israeli red wine, and glanced through the paper. No reference to the theft of the scroll. He wandered about the near-empty lobby, peered into the windows of the closed boutiques, and sauntered through the open door to the entrance patio.

Two Mercedes taxis were parked by the curb, their drivers idling in converation. They eyed him appraisingly as he approached.

"Taxi, sir?" one called out. "The Garden tomb, the Old City, Church of the Holy Sepulchre . . . ?"

"How far to Qumran?" he said.

The driver's face brightened at the prospect of an extended trip on the normally unproductive Sabbath. "It's nothing," he said. "Less than an hour's run."

"Too late today," he said, "Perhaps tomorrow morning."

Beyond, on King George Street, a crowd was gathering in the warm evening air. "What's going on?" he asked.

The driver glanced over his shoulder. "Synagogue," he said simply.

That's why Shahak isn't home, Copeland thought. I'll try him later.

He went for a long walk through the almost silent streets and after dinner called the press secretary. The taxi dropped him at a pleasant semi-detached house on a curving residential street. Shahak's son, a darkly handsome teenager in airforce uniform, shook his hand at the door and after pleasantries and introductions, Copeland sat cupping a brandy glass with Shahak and his wife, she eyes down, crocheting a segment of an afghan.

He liked the press secretary immediately. He was about fifty, had a cherub's face and a high forehead on which there was a cresent-shaped dent accented by a shiny pink scar. (Copeland learned later that a plate had been inset in the skull after a shrapnel wound.) He had thick, brushcut hair that bristled and was obviously resistant to brush or comb. It was his habit to pass his palm lightly over the bristles, obviously enjoying the sensation.

"The truth is," he said, after Copeland had explained his problems, "we don't know what's been stolen. The story in the *Post* is largely speculation. The theft took place at Qumran: *ergo* it's another scroll."

"How did you learn about it?"

"Actually, it took quite a while to come out, and then almost by accident. The curator at the Rockefeller was shepherding a group of British academics on a tour of the Dead Sea area, and as they were leaving Qumran, the ticket-seller there asked what had happened to the new scrolls. The way he put it seemed odd, so Avraham – Avraham Pomerantz, he's the curator – asked why he was inquiring. It developed that, last December, a man who had identified himself as being with the museum, had tramped about the area for ten days, had done some excavating on an outcropping nearby, and had carted something away in a box. Hired an Arab to help him. Avraham asked the attendant why he hadn't challenged him and he said it was because he thought the man was with the department; the first time he'd seen him he'd been driving an official car with the government insignia on the door panel.

"So they did a check on who'd been assigned cars . . . "

"Exactly. There was some trouble nailing down the date but they worked that out. They were able to account for all the cars except for a station-wagon signed out to Dr. Harris Gordon."

"Was he on the museum staff?"

"No, but they all knew him. They'd been on digs together. He'd done a stint with the American School for Oriental Research."

"You know he's dead?"

"Actually, I didn't when we started the investigation. The local papers somehow failed to pick up his obit so we hadn't heard. Avraham wrote him at Albright University and the letters were returned. Finally he cabled the Dean and he wrote that he'd heard Dr. Gordon was in New York City but didn't know his address. So our people got in touch with the District Attorney there."

"What do you think he discovered?"

Shahak turned up his palms and shrugged. "Haven't the slightest idea. The whole thing doesn't make sense. If it was an important discovery, another scroll for instance, the normal thing to do would be to take it to the museum and report it to the department. He'd need some help with it, and where better to get it than there? He'd have been given full credit. Undoubtedly there would have been some remuneration. That's what makes me doubt it was a scroll."

"You say an Arab helped him?"

"Yes, but I don't think we can be of much use to you there. He hired him in Amman. Qumran's on the West Bank, in Israeli-administered territory, you know." He arched his eyebrows. "The Jordanians aren't all that keen to help. We were hoping you people might have the answers."

Copeland shook his head. "We're at a dead end. That's why I'm here. Whatever he took away with him has just disappeared." He rose to leave. "I'll see if I can turn up that Arab in Amman. I'm off to Qumran in the morning."

It could be seen why the ancients spoke of "going up to Jerusalem." Copeland, having been loaned a government car and having nosed his way with many hesitations though the city and onto the highway, discovered that the journey was almost all downhill. Clear of the outskirts, the road coiled about the lower slopes of the mountains, seeking like water the low ground, cutting back and forth over the ancient route in the doing and only occasionally rising to thrust through a ridge or crest a summit. The rainy season had been short and such vegetation as had been able to wrest life from the thin soil was pale from the struggle. The rock itself seemed bleached by centuries of sun. It was mountainous terrain, desert, with no villages along the way. The only evidence of life was an occasional flock of sheep or goats, each followed by a slender Bedouin woman, as agile on the crags as they. There were signs of death though: vultures drifting like kites in a thermal in their constant quest for carcasses other than the rusting skeletons of army tanks and trucks by the sides of the road.

At the turnoff to Jericho, Copeland continued on to the right.

On his left lay the desolation of the Dead Sea, almost thirteen hundred feet below sea level: its shore the lowest point on earth, its surface lifeless under the relentless sun, its deep so saline no life could live in it, its waters so dense they bear a swimmer high, its beaches barren of rush or algae or weed. The Jordan River and a few mountain streams flow into it, but none flow out; the burning sun and the desert air draw off the surplus.

Ahead was a rubbly slope of land rising to a ridge of ragged mountains reaching some four thousand feet into an indigo sky and ranging south along the coast to the horizon. He saw a sprawl of bone-pale rock ahead, and about it, pocking the precipitous side of the russet mountains, caves, and felt an excitement mounting in him. Qumran! The place of the Dead Sea Scrolls. The ancient community in which a renegade band of ascetic Jews had loved their God with inflexible discipline. The area from which had come the most ancient of biblical manuscripts, almost a thousand years older than any known before.

He turned in at a parking area and made his way in the oven heat to an enclosure from which the ticket-seller worked. The man emerged as he approached, and after Copeland had identified himself and explained his mission, they sat together in the shade in a cooling wind sliding up the slope from the sea.

"Yes," the man said, "I remember him very well."

He was an Arab, dark of skin and black of hair and eyes, but dressed in western clothes except for the *kaffiyeh* on his head. He spoke English perfectly with a phlegmy accent.

"He came here every day for about a week last December. Strange little man; like a bird. Spent most of his time over there in the ruins. Later, he climbed all over that rock there." He pointed at a large outcropping which interrupted the surface as it sloped to the base of the mountains. He went on the describe Harris's activities, puckering his lips when a question caused him to rummage about in his memory. He spoke of the day Harris had asked him where he could hire a man with a small truck.

"Did he seem excited?"

"Very. His face was pale under the sunburn. I remember thinking he wasn't well."

"Did you find him a man?"

"I sent him to a friend in Jericho but he wasn't home. He found somebody else."

"Do you know the man he hired?"

"Never saw him before. He was from Amman."

"Remember anything about his truck?"

More puckering and a slow shaking of the head. "No."

"The color? The make? Anything."

"It was, I think you call it, a pickup. Black, I think . . . or blue. Dark blue?"

Copeland wandered aimlessly through the partially reconstructed site, distracted, hoping that somewhere in his brain two facts would connect and fashion a significant conclusion. Within a few minutes he was intrigued by the ruins in which he was walking. He had bought a pamphlet from the attendant and now he began to envision that austere company of men and women who had, for the love of God, withdrawn from their homes to live in this unforgiving burned-out land. He peopled it in his imagination: saw the men rearing the walls and the watchtower against the Romans and other marauding bands; saw them toiling in the sun creating the aqueducts to direct the precious water from the mountains to the settling tanks and into the enormous cisterns hewn by hand from the solid rock; saw them at work in the kitchens, and in the potter's workshop; saw them gathered about the common table, assembled for the Holy Meeting, working silently in the Scriptorium, copying with assiduous care on leather or papyrus – even on sheets of copper – the scriptures, the commentaries and the Manual of Discipline. He felt the fear that gripped the community when they saw that the end was approaching and that the Roman siege was assured of success. He imagined the scramble to hide the treasured scrolls, wrapping them in shawls and linen cloths, placing them in jars and concealing them in caves on the sides of the promontory or the nearby mountains. Standing on the wooden structure erected above the reconstructed base of the watchtower he saw the hated legions storming the walls and breaching them, and then killing, burning, destroying . . . .

Equally vividly he saw Harris Gordon, his face red from the sun and the excitement, scuttling about the ruins, examining stones, fingering inscriptions, gazing off, as he himself was, from the watchtower. For what was he searching? What did he believe could yet be found more than three decades after that Bedouin shepherd lad, in pursuit of a wandering goat, had chanced on the cave in which were the earthenware jars with their precious depository of manuscripts? What remained to be uncovered in an area which had been searched by Bedouins, Israeli soldiers, bands of archaeological students and others? And what, finally, had Harris found out there in that russet heap of stratified rock thrust through the surface many centuries ago by some convulsion of a cooling earth?

He left the complex to traverse the baked gravel surface, toiling up the slope to the outcropping. It was larger than he'd assumed viewing it from the distance, and as he clambered among the boulders, questing in the crevices, he wondered how Harris, some twenty years his senior and with pain pressuring his chest, could have managed. Shortly, he was exhausted. The dust lay on his lips and was gritty between his teeth. The sun seared his shoulders through his shirt and his scalp through his hair and set his brain to wavering. Perspiration dried as swiftly as it oozed and he felt his strength ebbing. Nothing bespoke Harris or any other man. There was no sign that any foot had walked there before his own, no mark of a tool, no cave, no niche, no nook in which anything of consequence might once have been hidden. He scaled and scrambled and searched for another hour, but at the end, nothing. Yet, the attendant had seen Harris's helper carry an empty wooden box to the outcropping and, handling it carefully, put it in a truck and drive away.

In Amman the police were almost obsequious when he introduced himself and presented his credentials. They would be pleased to help, of course, but . . . An Arab without a name and only the barest of descriptions? A dark blue or black pickup truck? There would be perhaps a hundred such. "Lieutenant, even if we found the right one, how would we know?"

He wandered the noisy, twisting, downtown streets, the people eddying about him as he dawdled, some bent under burdens as large as they, some buying and selling with sharp cries: men and women in modern garb and in garments that hadn't altered significantly in millennia; tiny burdened donkeys trotting on tiny hooves among modern cars and trucks. He bought an orange from a street-vendor and stood on a corner peeling and segmenting it, pointlessly noting each passing pickup truck, feeling impotent and testy.

A boy passed, hawking newspapers. Copeland pondered a moment, gulped the pieces of his orange, made inquiries and took a taxi to the newspaper office. The editor spoke cultivated English. Yes, he would be pleased to interview him and carry a story the following day emphasizing the search for the owner of the truck. Where was he staying? At the Intercontinental. Good, he would include that in the story.

The following morning he was interrupted at breakfast in his room by the sharp double ring of the telephone. A man in the lobby wished to speak to him. Would he please come down? The man would not go up nor would he give his name.

In the lobby, ill at ease, black eyes darting about like a captive animal's, was an Arab of indeterminate age, his robe soiled and the coil about his *kaffiyeh* tattered. With him was a lovely dark-eyed girl in a black sweater and short skirt.

"Mr. Jackson?"

"Yes."

"How do you do," she said, revealing perfect and very white teeth in a smile. "I'm Nadia Nassar. I'm with the hotel. This man says you wish to speak to him. Perhaps I can be of service as an interpreter."

"Thank you."

"He says there's a story in the paper this morning instructing him to come to see you."

"That's right. I'm with the New York County District Attorney's office. Does he speak any English?"

The girl asked a question in crisp articulated Arabic. The man shook his head.

"Can we sit down?" Copeland asked. "Over there perhaps," he said, indicating a grouping of chairs in the corner of the lobby.

The Arab began what soon became an animated conversation with the girl. She turned to Copeland. "He wants some money."

He took out his wallet and extracted a five dollar bill. She showed it to the man but kept it and they crossed the lobby and sat. Slowly, painstakingly, double-checking all the pertinent facts, Copeland drew the story from the Arab. He recalled how he had been hired by an American who had accosted him as he waited for a traffic light to change. He had obtained a wooden box for him, a type used for shipping pottery, and they had gone in his truck to Qumran. The American had taken him to a small mountain, had pried aside a boulder and lowered himself into a cave. Had he himself gone into the cave? No. Had he seen what was in the cave? No. The box had been passed out after about fifteen minutes with the top nailed in place. How much more did it weigh then? A quizzical smile and a shrug: "Who can remember such things?" He'd carried the box to the truck.

The Arab now grew excited and there ensued a long and vehement argument with much gesticulation. Nadia gave him the five dollars and turned to Copeland. "He's afraid to tell you any more. He's afraid of what might happen. You're with the police, he says."

"Explain to him that I have no authority here and that what he tells me I will tell no one."

But the Arab was adamant, shaking his head vigorously as she pressed him. "I'm afraid he's not going to tell you anything more," she said.

Copeland took a ten dollar bill from his wallet. He reached across and put it before the man's face and then withdrew it. The Arab, silent, looked at Copeland from the corners of his eyes and at the money. Copeland took out another five. "Tell him I'll add this if he'll tell me what happened to the box and then take me to the cave."

As Nadia explained, the Arab continued to shake his head, but with his eyes on the money. Copeland shrugged and moved to replace the bills in his wallet. The Arab, smiling obsequiously, reached across and gently took the money from his hand.

He and the American, he said, had crossed the Israeli lines at night; even with the money in his hand he was reluctant to say where and Copeland waved that aside. The border breached, he'd driven to Amman, dropped his passenger off at the hotel, this very hotel, and had never seen or heard of him since.

The cave at Qumran was a disappointment. Copeland wriggled his big frame through the opening and crouched in the center, probing with a flashlight. There was nothing but the carved walls, some loose sand and a slight declivity in the center of the floor.

Back in Jerusalem he went to the Rockefeller Museum. The chief curator, Pomerantz, was a intense man in his middle years with a tangle of rusty hair and a beard the color and texture of a welcome mat. He greeted Copeland without ceremony, preceded him into his office, made notes as Copeland, reading from his notebook, reviewed his findings, and promised to send two students to sift through the gravel in the cave in hope of turning up something useful.

"What might Dr. Gordon have found in such a cave as I've described to you?" Copeland asked.

Dr. Pomerantz poked his right auricular finger into an ear and rotated it. "That," he said, "is a rather large question."

"If you will, just speculate," Copeland said. "Bearing in mind that whatever it was, it weighed somewhere around twenty pounds."

As Pomerantz grimaced and continued silently and with some assiduity to excavate his ear, Copeland felt a gloom settle on him and the conviction grow that he was going to return home no wiser than he'd left. He sensed the onset of a familiar quivering anger: that quiet rage which often fermented within him when, for all his persistence, questions wouldn't yield their answers, when facts refused to form patterns and when every trail led to a dead end. His effectiveness as a detective stemmed not from his deductiveness but from his doggedness, and the longer the case the shorter his patience.

"The things usually found," Pomerantz said, "are lamps, cooking utensils, pottery. The fact that the cave is at Kirbet Qumran would lead one to hope that perhaps there would be manuscripts." He sounded disinterested.

"But would manuscripts be that heavy? Twenty pounds doesn't sound like manuscripts."

"On the contrary, especially if they were stored in jars, as were the Dead Sea Scrolls for the most part."

"What else might it be?"

"Bones are a possibility," Pomerantz said without enthusiasm. He added sourly, "I really doubt that this is a profitable exercise – making blind guesses."

Copeland persisted. "But if he'd found a skeleton, wouldn't it take some time to pack the bones in the box? He was in the cave no more than fifteen, twenty minutes."

"It would depend. In some case the removal of bones is an exceedingly delicate operation, taking days, weeks. At other times it's relatively simple."

"What would a skeleton weigh?"

"Recent bone with the marrow intact is surprisingly heavy. Ancient bone, fully dehydrated? A male adult would weigh no more than ten, twelve pounds."

"Then we can't rule out the possibility of a skeleton?"

"I would think that unlikely. If your hypothetical dead man had been a member of the Qumran community, he would have been buried in the common graveyard off to the east of the complex." He paused, drew his brows down, pursed his lips and ballooned his cheeks. After a moment he expelled the breath with a rush of air. "Unless . . . Unless . . . "

"Unless what?"

Pomerantz was puzzling in his mind even as he spoke. "The great incongruity in this whole thing is why Dr. Gordon would risk his reputation for something like a scroll or some other artifacts. The possibility, however, that it might be someone's tomb is intriguing."

He paused, drawing another breath and holding it, cheeks puffed and eyes rolled up in their sockets. Copeland began to feel concern. Suddenly the air was exhaled with a whoosh and Copeland felt a fine spray of spittle on his face. The curator's eyes were blinking rapidly.

"I wonder . . . I wonder . . . " he said.

"You wonder what?" Copeland said. Pomerantz' excitement was infecting him.

"It's utterly improbable," Pomerantz said, speaking mostly to himself, "but then we'd have said that before the discovery of the scrolls — "

Copeland spat out the words: "*What's* improbable?"

The curator's voice was so soft as to be almost inaudible. "This is the maddest kind of speculation," he whispered. "There isn't a mote of evidence, but it occurs to me that Harris Gordon might have found the tomb of the Teacher of Righteousness!"

Copeland felt the hair rise on his forearms and scalp. "The leader of the Essenes," he breathed.

Pomerantz came out of his chair as though launched and began to pace the room. "That would explain it," he said. "Harris would be the last man in the world to smuggle an antiquity out of the country. What would he have to gain? Where could he sell it? And even if he could, it would inevitably be identified as having originated here and there'd be a reckoning with the law, as is happening now. He'd have destroyed himself, and he'd know that."

He paused in his pacing to look out of a window, his hands in his hip pockets, rocking on his heels. Copeland said, "Tell me about the Teacher of Righteousness."

"We don't know his name," Pomerantz said, continuing to look out of the window. "He appears in the scrolls. He's a rather obscure figure and he's been the subject of a great deal of debate. Early on, it was believed by some that he was Jesus of Nazareth, but that's nonsense, the stuff of Sunday supplements: he lived at least a hundred years earlier. Some scholars have seen him as Jesus' prototype – the martyr of God, the resurrected redeemer of the world – but again, that's been pretty well discounted. What he was, it seems, was the leader or at least the chief creative personality of a deeply religious Jewish sect which came into being in the second century before Jesus, the so-called Essenes. They were an apocalyptic group. Shared everything in common. Had strict rules for admission. They developed cells in various parts of ancient Palestine and a headquarters at Qumran. They were persecuted and finally wiped out in an action in the Jewish war against Rome around 70 A.D.

"As I say, there's been speculation about Jesus being an Essene – and it's not unlikely that he spent some time at the community, as, presumably, did John the Baptist – but he certainly wasn't the Teacher of Righteousness."

He turned, the fingers of one hand clenched deep in his beard. "It's entirely possible that his tomb would have been apart from the common burial ground. Yes. And that would explain Dr. Gordon's behavior."

Copeland said, "Forgive me if I'm obtuse, but why would it make sense for him to steal the bones of the Teacher of Righteousness but not a scroll?"

"Because of the enormity of the discovery. Another scroll would be marvelous, but the bones of the leader of the Essenes – especially if there was authenticating data with the bones, which there doubtless would be – would be an international sensation. It would be as important a find as the scrolls, perhaps as significant as the discovery of the tomb of Tutankhamun back in '22. If Harris were to spirit away the bones and the documentation, arguing that he wanted to avoid the circus that followed the discovery of the scrolls and planning to launch the fully researched discovery on the world when he was ready, he'd know he'd be forgiven the theft and be hailed as one of the heroes of archaeology."

He stood contemplating the possibility for a moment and then said in a hushed whisper, "That *could* be it. My God, it could be!"

Chapter Five

After twelve hours non-stop from Lod airport to JFK, during which his large frame was bracketed by two overweight women who brooded over a miscellany of bundles like hens over their chicks, an exhausted Copeland called Jennifer to let her know he was safely back and went directly to his office. He talked to a pre-occupied Schultz who said he'd see him at four, and from a wad of telephone reports extracted a three-day-old Please Call Back message from Dodi Gordon. When she insisted on seeing him, arguing ambiguously that it couldn't wait, he signed out a car from the pool and drove to her flat. There were corrugated cardboard cartons on television set, table and floor, each filled with objects wrapped in newspaper. Dodi, in an obviously new flowered housecoat, greeted him with an odd animal wariness and made only terse, diffident responses to his conversation openers. When five minutes had passed and they were still passing the time of day, he said, "Well? You wanted to see me?"

"Yes . . . " she said tentatively.

"Look, Mrs. Gordon," he said tightly. "I'm here. You wanted to see me. Urgent – remember?"

"It's just that something's happened and I didn't want you to think I was trying to mislead you."

Copeland permitted some irritation to creep into his voice but his interest was piqued. "Look," he said patiently, "why don't you just out and say what's on your mind? I won't bite." She hesitated, frowning. "Is it something you didn't tell me about your husband?"

"Yes," she said slowly, and then quickly added, "It's nothing about what he was working on. Nothing like that."

The air went out of his ballooning hopes. He was suddenly very tired and annoyed at having been brought all the way from town on a fruitless errand. "Mrs. Gordon . . . " he said wearily.

"I told you he didn't leave any insurance," she blurted out. "Well, he did. It was just that I didn't know."

"I see."

"A hundred thousand dollars. I only found out the day after you were here."

He pushed himself erect, preparing to leave, but something tugged at a laggard part of his brain. He said, "Tell me about it."

Dodi was beyond her reticence now, and excitement enlivened her voice. "You remember I told you that the policy had lapsed? Well, it had, so I figured, naturally, that was that. Then Friday I got this call: Would I please come in and see a Mr. Rogers at the Monument Life Insurance office. Didn't say why, just would I come in. I went, of course, and my God, he's the vice president! You should see the office. Anyway, he tells me that the policy had been renewed a couple of months ago and that he needs some signatures. A hundred thousand dollars!" She looked at him. "I didn't know when you were here before. So help me, I didn't."

He was suddenly alert, all fatigue sloughed off. "Let's go back a bit," he said gently, as though the information was a bird that might be flushed and escape. "If I have it right, the policy lapsed last summer?"

"Last July."

"And you got in touch with Dr. Gordon about it?"

"At the time I didn't know where he was. Then I learned he was here in New York, so—"

"So you called him and he agreed to reinstate it."

"Harris? He wouldn't even come to the phone."

"But he did reinstate it?"

"What a surprise! Like, you know, out of the blue there's this phone call. I won't get the money for a few days; there's some paperwork."

"But I thought Dr. Gordon had a bad heart."

"He did."

"And yet they reinstated a policy lapsed by about eight months."

"Guess so."

"But you told me he wouldn't support you, wouldn't talk to you. Why would he go to the trouble and expense of renewing the policy?"

She was fumbling in her purse for a cigaret. "My guess is, Cardinal Maloney got him to."

"Why would he do that?"

"Because I went and asked him to. Oh, not to reinstate the policy, I don't mean, but to get Harris to help us out. He must have spoken to him. The man's a saint, you know. You don't have a light, do you?"

He found a crumpled book of matches in his pocket and lit her cigaret. "You think it was Cardinal Maloney's doing?"

"As if I couldn't figure that out. Three days after I go see him, this young priest comes around. I mean, look, I've been living here for nearly a year and not a soul. And then there's this priest asking how I'm doing. Am I making ends meet, and so on? You know. Then a week later the checks start coming."

"The checks?"

"Fifty dollars a week."

"Who from?"

"The Good Samaritan fund."

"The Good Samaritan fund?"

"Like clockwork."

"No explanation?"

"You don't have to be Einstein. The man's a saint. And me not even a Catholic."

Copeland hadn't realized he'd seated himself and had been taking notes. Now he rose to his feet again. "The vice-president of the insurance company – you say his name is Rogers?"

"Monument Life. On Fifth Avenue." Her face darkened. "You don't think anything could go wrong? I'm planning on moving."

"I'm sure everything'll be okay," he said absently. He couldn't wait to say his goodbyes; his left kidney was signalling like a manic telegrapher.

Mr. Rogers was perspiring and looked unhappy. Copeland's voice was flat and hard.

"You don't seem to understand," he said. "I can get a court

order to examine your records. It'll save everybody a great deal of time and embarrassment if you'll just answer my questions without any more temporizing."

"I'm trying to be helpful, but I have a responsibility to—"

"You have a primary responsibility to answer my questions. Now, again: did Dr. Gordon himself, personally, pay the back premiums?"

"No, sir."

"Who did?"

"Mr. Timothy McGuire."

"And who is he?"

"Mr. McGuire is the treasurer and chief signing officer of . . . of a trust."

"Which trust?"

"Mr. Jackson, I—"

"Which trust?"

"The Good Samaritan Trust."

"The Good Samaritan Trust, you say?"

"Yes."

"Who set up the trust?"

"The monies were paid in confidence and I'd prefer not to—"

"Who set up the trust?"

"The Archdiocese of New York."

"What was the amount of the check?"

Rogers leafed through an open manilla folder on the desk before him. "Two thousand and twenty-eight dollars."

"Which paid the premium to what expiry date?"

"July first."

"What kind of insurance was it?"

"Five-year term."

"You notified Dr. Gordon of this extension, of course?"

"No. You see it was a charitable thing and—"

"Just a moment." Copeland's voice was sharp and his face forbidding. "You insured a man without informing him? That's illegal."

Rogers shifted in his chair and sought surreptitiously to flick away a droplet of perspiration that suddenly coursed from beneath his hair. "It was to be a surprise. We were to hold up notification until he'd been told."

"Was that notification sent?"

Rogers, without much zeal, went through the papers before him. "It seems to have been overlooked," he said, his voice trailing away.

"So he was never notified?"

"It would seem not."

"It has been my understanding that to reinstate a lapsed policy you require a medical."

Rogers' voice lacked conviction. "Actually, all we were doing was extending a policy to its full term."

"You knew he had a bad heart?"

"There's nothing on his record to indicate that."

"You *did* know he was diabetic?"

"We insure lots of diabetics. Our company has been a leader in that field."

"But is it normal procedure here to insure a man without his knowledge?"

"No. But this wasn't a normal situation."

Copeland leaned forward in his chair, his face grim. "Mr. Rogers," he said, "there's a very real likelihood of illegality here. I'll be quite open with you; I'm not interested in that at the moment. What I am interested in is why you waived normal procedures and reinstated the policy of a man sixty years old after an eight-month lapse in the payment of his premiums without requiring a medical, and did so without his knowledge. Now, I'm prepared to overlook the irregularities involved, granted there are no further complications, but I require and I require now to know why you did it."

Rogers arranged and rearranged a number of objects on his desk. In the silence the honking of taxi horns forty stories below sifted through the windows. When he looked up his face was pale.

"Mr. Jackson," he began, and then cleared his throat to begin again. "Mr. Jackson, believe me, there was no wish to do anything irregular. I was given to understand that this was being done for charitable, for Christian reasons. There was no reason to suspect, even for a moment, that any impropriety was involved."

"Mr. Rogers, let me concede that you did what you did for valid reasons, you still haven't answered my question: Why?"

"Because of the person who made the request."

"Who was?"

"Monsignor Jamieson of the Roman Catholic Archdiocese of New York."

Copeland felt the same surge of elation he'd experienced when he pulled the lever on a slot machine in Las Vegas and a freshet of silver dollars had flooded onto the floor. "What reason did Father Jamieson give for wanting to reinstate Dr. Gordon's policy?" he asked, easing back on the pressure.

"Dr. Gordon was living at the residence and, as I understand it, was in financial straits. Apparently his wife and children were suffering as a result, and . . . "

Copeland had all he needed but couldn't resist another pull at the handle. "Would you make such a concession to any priest who came to you with such a request?"

Rogers' eyes were baleful. "No," he said.

"It was because Father Jamieson was from the cardinal's office."

"Mr. Jackson, you must understand: the Archdiocese of New York is one of our largest clients. We carry some twenty million dollars' worth of—"

"It was because Cardinal Maloney, rather than Father Jamieson, was making the request?"

"The cardinal's name was never mentioned."

"But it was clear it was he who wanted to do this favor for Dr. Gordon, to perform this Christian act?"

Rogers' voice was without intonation: "That may or may not have been the case but, yes, that was the understanding I took from the conversation."

At the window in Copeland's apartment, her back to him and the room, the lights of Manhattan swimming before her eyes in the tears that had come though forbidden and would not be gone, Jennifer cursed weeping. Tears had always come to her too readily, and almost always unsummoned. Their onset usually induced anger: they so often obscured an issue, introduced unintended overtones, tainted intentions, twisted meanings. How could one seem rational, *be* rational, with eyes streaming and inflamed, with a nose leaking and in need of blowing, and when sometimes inarticulate for sobbing? Little wonder men read tears as weakness or were angered by them as at an unfair weapon. And there was the added irony that one's frustration at the tears often induced more. *Damn* tears!

On the sofa, his great bulk slumped, forearms on his thighs, hands and head and hair hanging down – dejection's model – Copeland was feeling nothing acutely but resentment. Jet lag had overtaken him. When he moved his head the motion persevered in a momentary vertigo. It was as though his skull had shrunk or his brain had swollen: whichever, thought moved sluggishly and the core of pain at the base of his neck had now radiated to his shoulder muscles and down his arms. He rested his face in his hands and was reminded that after eight hours on the ground he hadn't shaved.

He'd gone from the insurance office to be harassed by an irritated and irritating Schultz who had little interest in hearing of his findings in Israel and had demanded a written report on the trip for forwarding to the District Attorney ("Like, goddammit, on my desk at nine tomorrow morning or I'll have your balls!"), to an infuriating briefing session with a snide FBI agent on the immigration payoffs case. Following that, with no time for lunch, there were callbacks on a dozen of the names on his telephone slips and a phone call to Father Jamieson seeking an appointment as soon as possible with His Eminence, during which Jamieson was noncommittal. Then in the rain to pick up Jennifer at curbside after work, ten minutes late.

The plan had been perfect: they would do some shopping at Gristede's and Jennifer would broil some steaks and toss a salad and give the wine a few minutes to breathe while he showered and shaved and got into a dressing gown. But it had gone awry from moment one. It had been Jennifer's intention to say nothing about her dinner conversation with Michael until the evening was winding down, but the subject had come up inadvertently as they were mounting the stairs to the apartment: Copeland had mentioned that he was hoping to see him the following day, and suddenly they were quarreling. In retrospect it wasn't quite clear what had triggered it, but soon words struck sparks and kindled angers and they began to disdain the restraints of love and reverse the ancient alchemy, transmuting their gold to lead.

"Jen," he said, his voice weary and muted in his hands, "you seem determined to misunderstand the nature of my job. I've been assigned to investigate a theft – you can put a prettier name to it but that's what it is – and I can't turn away from where it leads me. You can't begin a step and then not put down your foot," he finished lamely.

She didn't turn but swallowed carefully to get the tears out of her throat. "But I *do* understand your job," she said, only a trifle huskily. "Of course you have to follow a lead. But that's not what I'm talking about. For some reason you seem to be hearing what I'm not saying. What I am saying is that your job is becoming *you*. You've stopped being a man who works as a detective and you've become a detective. The whole world is suspect. If something seems out of line, you find yourself – and I'm sure it's involuntary; I'm not blaming you – you find yourself questioning it, suspicious of it, reading something into it."

He sat up, flaring: "That really is unfair."

She turned to face him now that she was in control of herself again. In the near darkness of the room she could only dimly see his face. The twilight had faded since they'd entered. The paper sacks of groceries slumped untended on the kitchen divider. She was feeling compassion for him again.

"Darling," she said, her voice stroking him, "try to see what I'm getting at. Think back. Isn't it true that from the moment Harris moved in, your mind has cast up all kinds of dark thoughts about him?"

"Jen, for God's sake – dark thoughts!"

"All right, maybe that's too strong a word. But whatever kind of thoughts they were, they were there: What's he doing down there in that gloomy basement? Why all the secrecy? What wicked deed is being done?"

"But I was right," he trumpeted.

His adamancy jangled her nerve ends and cooled her compassion. "Darling," she said, measuring her words, "you may have been, but you don't know that yet. And even if you were, from what you've told me, what Uncle Harris was doing wasn't all that terrible. If he'd made this incredible discovery and was trying to protect it while he prepared the data for publishing, was that really so terrible? Okay, by the letter of the law he may have been doing something illegal, but do you find what he did so difficult to understand?"

"My function isn't to judge," he said stuffily. "I don't make the law, I just see that it's obeyed. Otherwise you've got a jungle."

She almost blurted out: Oh, for Christ sake, Cope, you sound like Inspector Javert pursuing Jean Valjean through the sewers of Paris for his loaf of bread! But she said instead, "Suspicion can build its own jungle."

He didn't respond but heaved himself upright, walked wearily to the divider and put a hand heavily about the neck of the bottle of wine. "Do you want some of this?" he asked coldly, not looking around, almost resting his weight on the bottle.

"No thank you," she said crisply.

He peeled off the lead foil, pulled the cork, splashed the wine into a tumbler, and without sniffing or tasting it, gulped it down. Jennifer wished she'd said she'd have some but wouldn't ask now. He put his hands on the divider and leaned on them, standing with his head down saying nothing. Jennifer studied him, surprised at how objectively she was doing so. She wanted to have done with the quarrel and steeled herself to speak the words that would close the breech. It was necessary to clear away this disruptive thing that had reared itself between them, and between them and Michael. She walked to him and rested her hands on his shoulders.

"Can't you see, my darling, what this suspicion is doing to all of us? Here we are, quarreling. There you are, chasing half way around the world looking for evidence that will dishonor a friend. You talk to Miss P. and read things into her answers. Even with Uncle Michael . . . You find significance in the exact time he's supposed to have loaned his car to Harris."

He turned quickly and her hands fell away. "That's just the point," he said, "he never *did* loan the car to Harris."

"But did he say he did?"

His answer was unequivocal: "Yes, he did."

She was suddenly aflame with rage but was careful not to let it consume her poise. She looked full into his eyes. Her voice was quiet and precise. "Think a moment, Copeland. Wasn't what Uncle Michael said was that Harris had *asked* to borrow the car? Did he actually say he'd borrowed it?"

Copeland was jolted. In a split second he reviewed the conversation. What had Michael actually said? He certainly had said that Harris had asked about borrowing the car, and it was in the context of the removal of the box from the residence. Certainly that was the impression he'd been left with.

Jennifer persisted. "Well?"

"Well what?"

"Isn't that what he actually said – that Harris had asked to borrow the car, not that he'd actually borrowed it?"

"I don't have his exact words in front of me, but that's certainly what he conveyed." He was being put on the defensive, being pressed about picayune matters when he was at the point of exhaustion, and he resented it. "I'll check the transcript if that's what you want," he added snidely.

Her eyes went wide. "The transcript? You have a transcript of your conversation with Uncle Michael?"

"He knows about it."

In her voice there was absolute incredulity: "He knows you made a transcript of your conversation?"

"I told him before we started that I was taping the conversation."

"And he agreed?"

"It was to save me making notes."

"But a transcript isn't notes."

"Now you're being picky. What's the difference?"

"The difference is—" Her eyes narrowed and she stopped short. "Just a minute. Did you type out the transcript?"

"What do you mean?" he said. His combativeness softened only imperceptibly but she saw it and pressed in for the next thrust. "It's a simple question, Copeland: did you personally make the transcript?"

Now there was bluster in his voice. "What the hell has that got to do with anything?"

The voice was a mother's persisting with a stubborn child about a discovered misdeed. "Please answer me: did you personally make the transcript?"

"You mean, did I type it with my own little hands?"

"I mean exactly that."

"Of course not. I had to get ready to go to Israel."

"Who did type it?"

"It was done at the department."

"By who?"

"What do you mean, by who?"

"Simply, who? What's her name?"

"What difference does that make?"

"You don't know her name, do you?"

"What does her name have to do with it, for Christ sake?"

"You don't know who typed it. Admit it."

"Whether I do or don't is completely irrelevant. She's in the typing pool."

Jennifer slapped her thighs, threw her head back in a gesture of utter disbelief and turned away from him. He stood unmoving for a moment, his fists plunged deep into his trousers' pockets, his brain turbulent. He was half sick in the realization that he had failed to maintain the secrecy of the conversation, but was diverting his discomfiture to her for pinning him to the wall and leaving him with no ground for justification. Downstairs a baby began to cry.

He said: "Jennifer, I've had about enough of this inquisition. And I'm tired of being pictured as the big, bad ogre in the scene. I appreciate your loyalty to your uncle, but shouldn't there be just a little charity for me? I'm tired and I'm discouraged and, to be quite frank with you, I'm disappointed by what I can only describe as your refusal to try to understand what I've been trying to do."

She turned on him, face contorted. "What you've been doing is betraying a trust. You came to the residence as a friend. Everybody welcomed you." The tears were threatening a return. "Everybody threw themselves open to you, and that very openness has been betrayed."

He shouted the word: "Betrayed?"

"Yes, betrayed. Uncle Michael trusted you – do you think he'd have given some other officer the time he's given you – even letting you tape record a private conversation. Then you let that conversation go to a typing pool. You don't even know who typed it! You might just as well stand on the corner of Broadway and Forty-second and play the tape!"

"I've never listened to such garbage," he shouted. "She's full-time in police work. She's used to hearing confessions and interrogations."

Her words were laced with acid. "Copeland, are you trying to tell me she's used to hearing interrogations, to use your word, where the person involved is a priest of God, a cardinal in the Roman Catholic church, a man bound by his vows to hold things in secret?"

He took her by the shoulders. "Jennifer, for Christ sake, will you stop it! You're twisting and magnifying what might have been a simple mistake into a betrayal of friendship and a betrayal of the confessional."

She shook off his hands. "I can just see her, whoever she is, telling her boy friend: 'You'll never believe this, but that dogan cardinal – you know the one; Maloney, at St. Pat's – was hiding a thief in his basement. Would you believe it?' "

"Jennifer, stop it right now. You're getting hysterical."

But by now the pain was too great. Somewhere in her head a voice was crying, "Turn back," but her anger and her hurt had its own inertia and it bore her forward. Her own words had transformed Copeland from the man she loved into the accuser of the man she worshiped, into a callous, indifferent, even malevolent, enemy. She felt herself betrayed, her love betrayed. And the pain pushed her on. Copeland felt his entire nervous system vibrating. There was a lump of fire in his belly and rage behind his eyes. He was feeling aggrieved. His best intentions had been twisted into something ugly, his apology had been disdained, and he needed to strike back. In the apartment below, the baby was squalling and there were loud voices and a banging on the ceiling.

"I'd like to get one thing straight," he said coldly, "and then drop this whole sorry mess. I have tried to act in the best interest of everybody concerned. I have accused no one of anything – not Harris, not Miss Pritchard, not your uncle—"

"But you did."

"I merely said they weren't telling me everything they knew."

"But *that's* an accusation."

"Jennifer, for God's sake!"

"Well, isn't it? You're accusing him of withholding evidence. Earlier you as much as said he lied to you."

"I merely said he wasn't telling me everything."

"May I ask you something, Mr. Sherlock Holmes: Why *should* he tell you everything? He believes in loyalty to his friends. I'm beginning to wonder whether you do."

He raised his eyes to the ceiling and turned away from her. "That's it," he said, his voice choked. "I don't need any more of this kind of shit." He picked up her coat from where she'd thrown it down. "I'm taking you home."

She walked to him and snatched away the coat. "I'll look after myself, thank you."

She struggled awkwardly into the coat, looked about for her purse, picked it up and started for the door. He stepped in front of her. "Jennifer, will you stop!" he said icily. "I said I was taking you home."

She couldn't see his face for the tears that were now filling her eyes and streaking her cheeks. "I can take care of myself," she said, her voice breaking.

"You are *not* going out on the street alone."

"Will you please get out of my way?"

He turned to the clothestree to get his topcoat and she was through the door. He followed her down the stairs, wondering if this could be happening. On the street she strode away in the rain and he followed. At Second Avenue she signalled a cab and it veered to the curb.

"Jen—" he said.

She slammed the door shut and the taxi moved away. He stood watching the tail lights until they were out of sight.

Chapter Six

Jennifer stayed off work the following day ostensibly because she was exhausted and suffering a sick headache but in fact because, when Copeland called, she wanted to be able to talk to him in the privacy of her room rather than from her desk in an open office. Moreover, her eyes were bloodshot and the lids inflamed and swollen. When the switchboard was open she called the office to say she wouldn't be in and to tell the temporary operator to refer all personal calls to her private telephone. She offered her supervisor as a reason for her absence, "a touch of the flu," and there was a sufficient nasal quality to her voice to lend the fabrication authenticity.

But Copeland didn't call.

She stayed in bed through most of the morning (Miss Pritchard brought her a tray and fluttered about), evaluating a variety of responses to Copeland's overtures: How she'd react if (a) he was remorseful, (b) wanted to pursue the argument further, or (c) was grudging in admitting to his lack of understanding. She took some enjoyment from the exercise but prayed that he would come asking forgiveness so that she could immediately clasp the nettle to her own breast and ask his forgiveness. As the morning went on memories of the night before refreshed. She flinched, recalling her almost vindictive pursuit of him; how she'd pounced like a tigress on his admission that he'd had a transcript made. What he'd done had undoubtedly been wrong, but why had she raged so? She couldn't recall having struck at anyone so hard or so persistently.

"Oh Copeland, darling," she whispered, "I'm so sorry. Call me. Call me. Call me."

She got dressed at noon, leaving the bathroom door open as she bathed, with the telephone nearby at the end of its cord. She went to the kitchen to brew a cup of tea and twice raced up the stairs to answer the ringing: friends asking how she was. She ended the conversations as quickly as expedient, fearful that Copeland would choose that moment to call and find the line busy. On the third try, she got the tea made and, her hands trembling, went carefully with it up the stairs. Twice in the next hour she lifted the receiver to reassure herself that there was a dial tone, replacing it carefully in the cradle.

Why didn't he call?

She could understand why he hadn't telephoned during the morning. He'd been away from his office for nearly a week and there would be much to catch up on. But why hadn't he called on his lunch hour? Perhaps the morning had been so busy he'd had to skip lunch. But by the time the clock made its measured way to three, she was alternating between anger and anxiety. Perhaps he'd been taken ill. Perhaps he was lying sick and alone at the apartment. Perhaps he hadn't slept either and the accumulated fatigue had left him vulnerable to some bug he'd been exposed to in Israel. She dialed his apartment, ready to hang up if he came on the line, but the phone rang and rang and rang; she could envision it on the kitchen wall echoing in the empty apartment. So he wasn't ill. He could have called. She felt her nerves grow taut.

At four she dialed the office switchboard. "No calls? Yes, but no personal calls? And no messages either? Thanks. Bye." He hadn't even bothered to try to reach her or to leave a message.

At five the office closed. She knew he knew that, and knew also that it took her perhaps twenty minutes to get home, so she was free of her vigil for a while. She went downstairs to the kitchen to tell Miss Pritchard that she wasn't hungry and wouldn't be at dinner. (She was afraid she wouldn't be able to hear the ring of her telephone over the conversation at the table.) She asked after Michael and was told that he'd left early on a day-long trip upstate but was expected back around seven-thirty. On her way back to her room, she passed Father Jamieson in the hall. How was her cold? "Better, thanks." "You're sure you're feeling all right?" "Yes, I'm fine." "You're sure, now?" "Yes." "I was talking to your fiancé this morning." "Oh . . . ?" "I'm trying to arrange for him to see His Eminence." "Yes, he mentioned that he wanted to." "Doesn't look at this point that it'll be possible before next week unfortunately."

So he'd had the time to call the residence but not to call her! And from what Father Jamieson had said, hadn't even asked after her.

In her room she closed the door and strode about, gloom settling on her and darkening her mind. The inner trembling now spread to her limbs and face. There was no excuse: he surely could have found the opportunity to telephone by now, even if only to say he'd be tied up all day and would call after work. He was being stubborn. He was nursing his anger. He was trying to punish her.

It wasn't just last night: he'd removed himself from her a hair's-breadth since she'd insisted that they delay their lovemaking until after the wedding. The decision had cost her much pain. She'd longed for him, hungered for him, had lusted for the hardness of his flesh, for those moments of abandoned sensuality she'd never believed she was capable of realizing. But although the priest at All Saints had been sympathetic, he'd been firm. "You'll give yourself to your husband for a lifetime," the disembodied voice had murmured. "Make abstinence a part of your penance in the few days remaining as a special gift to your Lord."

But Copeland had pressed her and she hadn't been able finally to summon the will to resist. Afterwards in the darkness his lips had discovered a tear at the corner of an eye, and for all her protestations that it was nothing, and his that he wasn't upset, he'd risen not long afterwards to go to the bathroom, and returning had begun to dress. No, it wasn't just last night: he was trying to punish her for withdrawing a part of herself from him. And here she'd been, loving him, yearning for him all day, for the sound of his voice and for the joy of a reconciliation and he hadn't even troubled to call. Even as she fled from it she was overtaken by self-pity. The tears welled up and she gave them their way.

But wait! Perhaps he'd realized how serious the quarrel had been and knew it couldn't be resolved in the impersonality of a phone call. That would be like him. He'd wait until she had finished work, pick up one of the tiny bunches of violets she loved so much and come directly to the residence. Six o'clock. He'd just have had time to go home, shower and change and come uptown. She set the door ajar so that she'd be able to hear the front doorbell if it rang and went to the bathroom to cup handsfull of cold water to her eyes, to freshen her makeup and to run a comb through her hair.

The hour and a half to seven-thirty went swiftly by and the doorbell didn't ring. When, at eight, Michael tapped tentatively on the door and entered, she was face down on the bed, trembling as with a fever and making small, hysterical animal sounds into a pillow.

Copeland had had one hell of a day.

He'd begun it late, fumbling fuzzily through the near-automatic actions of shaving and brewing coffee, his mind a murk from the combination of fatigue and the sleeping pills he'd downed with a second tumbler-full of wine on an empty stomach. He was conscious of a locus of sorrow at the back of his mind but chose not to recognize it. He had no memory of the alarm chiming at seven, and now going on ten, mounted the stairs and went to his desk expecting the worst. The worst was waiting: a note, "See Schultz soonest!"

As he made his appearance in the doorway to Schultz' office it was obvious that he had nothing in his hands, but Schultz stretched out a hand and with wide-eyed ingenuousness, said, "Ah, you have my Israel report there. Good. May I have it, please." The "please" was the tip-off; Schultz hadn't used the word since he was weaned.

"It's not ready," Copeland said, "I've had problems."

"With problems you go to Ann Landers," Schultz purred. "With overdue reports you come here." He snipped short the snideness and snarled, "Where in hell have you been?"

With Schultz there were no points to be made by tendering excuses or in trying to blunt his lance with explanations. Better to let him take his best shot and get the hell out. "I'll have it for you in an hour," he said.

Schultz addressed the clothestree: "No reasons why, you'll notice. No excuses. Just like butter wouldn't melt in his mouth – I'll have it for you in an hour." He returned to Copeland. "I appreciate your dropping by, Your Eminence. The only thing is, what do I say to the D.A.? He's at a convention at the Waldorf, and already he's been on the blower twice."

"I'd better get to it," Copeland said, edging away.

Schultz was talking to the clothestree again. "He thinks he'd better get to it, he says." He picked up a small desk clock and made an elaborate show of setting the alarm mechanism. "One hour from now? Let me see . . . that'll be 11:05." He placed the clock on the desk and now addressed it. "One hour. That should be just enough time to decide exactly which beat he goes back on tomorrow." He looked into Copeland's face, his grim lips forming what might have been a smile had there been humor back of them. "*Patrolman* Copeland Jackson," he said reflectively. "Has a nice ring to it."

It was exactly eleven when Copeland ventured through the doorway and dropped the report on Schultz's desk. Schultz was on the telephone and didn't so much as glance up, but he did reach across and depress the alarm button on the clock.

Back at his desk, his mind free for the first time that morning, Jennifer slipped the restraints with which he'd confined her and inundated his thoughts. He was immediately desolate. The whole horror resurrected. Eden laid waste. Her face came before him, contorted in an anger he'd never have believed possible; the mouth moist with vehemence, the eyes sparking fire. Why hadn't he reached out to her as he'd thought to do, surrounded her with his arms and simply pinioned her gently until her struggling ceased and the fires of her fury were banked and she was compliant and warm against him? Who could have believed that they – *they!* – could have lifted such weapons against each other?

And that chill moment when, after she'd spun away, he'd stood looking at the crown of her head hating her.

He carried in his wallet a fragrant lace handkerchief he'd asked for and she'd given him. He took it out and hiding it cupped in his hand, brought it close to his face.

He'd say he was going for a coffee, call her from the pay phone downstairs and arrange to meet her for lunch. But there was a man in the booth with a folded copy of the *Racing Form*, talking animatedly, and endlessly it seemed. After glowering and standing about for five minutes he went back to his desk. On a sudden thought he took the transcript from his desk, checked the initialing, climbed the flight of stairs to the typing pool and had JRM pointed out to him. She was skinny, black, in her twenties, wearing a ballooning afro. He went to her, asked for the carbon of his interrogation in the Israel case, took it to his desk and locked it away with the original.

On his desk there was a note: "See Schultz."

The captain seemed to have forgotten their earlier fracas. He had the report and a foolscap pad on the desk before him.

"Problems?" Copeland asked.

"Could be," Schultz said. "I just been on the phone with Mr. Harmon. Not bein' able to forward your report as advertised" – his tone, for Schultz, was only mildly caustic – "I read it to him. He has some questions." He pulled his notes in closer, tilting his head the better to see them. "And so do I."

"Yes, sir," Copeland said.

"I think it's about time you told me exactly what your relationship is with Cardinal Maloney."

The question was so unexpected Copeland stumbled over his response. "Cardinal Maloney? Well . . . he's my fiancée's uncle. He's . . . a friend."

"Does he approve of his niece marryin' a policeman?"

"Yes. Of course. Why?"

"No special reason," Schultz said, dismissing it with a flutter of his hands. "How about you? Like him?"

"Yes."

Schultz peered owlishly over his glasses. "You sure?"

"Yes, I'm sure," Copeland said firmly. Before Schultz could continue, he added, "That's a funny question, Grizz."

"What's funny about it? You're not exactly the catch of the social season. Maybe he don't want his in-law nephew to be a cop and he's let you know."

"Not true," said Copeland, beginning to take umbrage. "We get on fine." Suddenly he was annoyed. "Who wants to know all this; Mr. Harmon?"

Schultz removed his glasses and tilted back his chair, his expression bemused. "Jesus, Cope, even you can't be so dumb as not to see this is a pretty dicey thing, this Israel thing. Let's agree for the moment that this guy Harris smuggled somethin' out. So, okay. But let's face it; he's not your average thief. Besides, he was a personal friend of the top dogan in New York. Even lives in his house. That's problem *numero uno* – right? Then there's the international implications. And there's this report of yours. . . ." He picked it up and hefted it in his hand. "Twice you interrogate the cardinal. You don't like some of the answers. I get the feelin' you're not crazy 'bout him. You think he's holdin' out on you. And some of your questions are better not even raised." He stroked the air with an open hand. "Sleepin' dogs . . . sleepin' dogs."

"Question," Copeland said.

"Schultz shrugged. "So ask."

"Is somebody pressuring Mr. Harmon?"

Schultz let his chair carry him forward, heaved a theatrical sigh and placed his outspread hands on the top of the desk. "Jesus, Cope, at times you are the *dumbest* son of a bitch! What kind of question is that?"

"Just want to know the name of the game, that's all."

"The name of the game is forget it. Nobody's pushin' nobody. The D.A. is . . . shall we say, not anxious to get his nuts in the wringer. Nothin' more than that."

"So I'm still on the case?"

Schultz struck his forehead. "Cope! Honest to God, today you're too much! Of course you're still on the case. You're doin' a hell of a job. All I'm sayin' is; this ain't the Three-I league. Play it cool."

Back at his desk he dialed Jennifer's office.

"Angie . . . ?"

"Angie's off today. Will you hold, please."

He sat with the receiver to his ear for a full minute and then slammed it down. He dialed the residence. Father Jamieson said he didn't think there was much chance of an appointment with Michael before Monday. Cardinal Maloney was upstate until this evening but he'd check with him when he returned. Perhaps Copeland would be kind enough to call back tomorrow morning. He dialed Jennifer's office again and gave the operator Jennifer's local. The line was busy.

He looked at his watch. Eleven-thirty. He'd go have some orange juice and coffee and then wait on the street outside the building in which Jennifer worked, surprise her as she came out, take her to Stouffer's and straighten things out over lunch.

He was outside the main entrance to the building at twelve, poised beside a news-vendor's stand, tremulous as before their first date. There was a sudden engorgement of the entranceway as dozens of workers poured from the building. He strained on tip-toe, searching among them. He heard a voice:

"Hey, Cope!"

A police cruiser had pulled to the curb behind him. The patrol-man in the passenger seat was a friend from his days at the 14th Precinct.

"Jimmy . . . ! How ya doing?"

"Gettin' by. You?"

"No complaints."

"You on a stake-out or somethin'?"

"If I was, you parked beside me would sure help my cover!"

"Stake-out, hell – you're waitin' for a broad."

"So would you get the hell out of here. She doesn't like cops."

The cruiser moved out on the changing light with much lewd guffawing. With a sense of panic, Copeland turned back to scruti-nize the congestion in the entranceway, and to look frantically up and down the street. At twelve fifteen he gave up and wandered around to peer through the window of a delicatessen in which she sometimes lunched. He'd missed her.

He drifted with the crowd on the thronging noontime street, distracted, dispirited, occasionally bumping a passer-by. "Jennifer, I love you," he whispered. The longing for her was so intense it seemed his chest and throat were afire. He saw her face, her hair, shining and heavy on her white shoulders, felt her mouth on his and on his flesh, felt her close. . . . His eyes blurred. He pushed into a phone booth, jammed the door shut, put his face close to the reeking phone and groaned. "Jennifer . . . ! Jennifer . . . !"

He found himself at Fifty-Seventh Street. The subway took him back to the office. There were three telephone slips and a note on his desk: "See Schultz. Urgent!" He checked the telephone slips; none from Jennifer. He went to the washroom, washed his face and hands and went to Schultz's office.

"Where the hell have you been?" Schultz bellowed. "It's past two."

"Working lunch hour," he said.

"Workin' lunch hour," Schultz said sarcastically. "I'll bet! I can guess what you been workin' on. Now, I wouldn't want to stand in the way of you knockin' off a piece of snatch," he said acidly, "but from here on, when you go out you leave word where you can be reached. You read me?"

"I read you," Copeland said, his voice flat.

Schultz subsided. "We," he said portentously, "have got us a problem."

He opened a drawer, pulled out a pad of foolscap, flipped the pages to familiarize himself with the scrawled notes and then returned to page one. "Before we start," he said, "we get one thing straight; we're strictly off the record. Understood?"

"Understood."

"Shut the door."

Copeland did and waited for an invitation to sit down. It didn't come.

"Okay . . . " Schultz began, his eyes on his notes. "I been on the blower three times already with the D.A. I read him your report at 11:13. He calls back at 11:27 and wants it dictated to his secretary. When I get back from lunch at 1:25 there's a message to call him." He looked up at Copeland. "He'd been talkin', would you believe, with the governor, and the governor is not happy."

He paused to let the import sink in and then went on. "Anyways, here's what: you are goin' to write a detailed report on everythin' you've found out, or *think* you've found out, in any way related to Cardinal Maloney. Now when I say detailed, I mean every goddam thing you know. You've talked to him twice – right?"

Copeland nodded.

"Okay. I want as close to verbatim as you can remember, and anythin' else you can think of."

"When do you want it?"

"Mr. Harmon's leavin' for Albany tonight. It's to be in his hands by six. I want to go over it before it goes to him, so your deadline is five at the latest. Use Saleski's old office. Type it yourself. No carbons. Nobody sees it but me. Understood?"

"Understood." He added, "Mr. Harmon's had a complaint from somebody."

"Negative. He's just nervous, and I don't blame him. The governor said your Cardinal Maloney could be the next pope. Well, Mister, you don't fuck around with no future popes!"

Saleski had been transferred to another unit and his office had been gutted; a desk, a chair and a filing cabinet were all that remained. Copeland picked up the phone. Dead. He went to his own desk and gave the switchboard operator Jennifer's local. It rang a half dozen times. The operator came back on the line. "I guess she's on a break," she said.

"Can I leave a message, please?" he asked.

"Sorry. The board's too busy right now. Call back later. Okay?" There was a click and the dial tone.

He lugged his typewriter into Saleski's office, spread out his notes, the transcript and the report he'd filed that morning, put his head down and went to work. The writing did not go well. He had difficulty deciding how to phrase some of his information, knowing whose eyes would read it. He used the transcript for information but took care not to make direct quotations.

At four o'clock Schultz came by. He picked up what had been written and scanned it. "This all you got done?" he asked sourly.

"It doesn't go all that easy," he said, not looking up. "If it's as important as you say, it's got to be right. There's a lot of rewriting."

"Where's the stuff you rewrote?"

Copeland nodded toward the floor beside the desk. Schultz gathered up the crumpled pages, smoothed them and placed them on top of the desk. "Keep all this stuff," he said, "and leave it with me when you're finished. If you go to the crapper, lock the door; the keys are in the center drawer there. How long before you're done?"

Copeland considered: "I'm maybe half way."

Schultz's visage was forbidding. "You listen to me, Mister; you got one more hour. No more. So light a fire under your ass."

He was checking the final page when Schultz returned. It was exactly five. Without a word, Schultz took the sheaf of paper, perched on the edge of the desk and began to read. He read slowly. After a few minutes Copeland said, "I've got to make a phone call." Schultz, without lifting his eyes from the text, said, "Just stay where you are."

Copeland sat shifting in his chair. The afternoon had passed with no further opportunity to call Jennifer. She finished work at five and he wanted to meet her and make a sentimental return to the restaurant where they'd realized they were in love. He looked at his watch and fidgeted. Ten past five. Goddammit! Schultz, you bastard, he muttered silently, will you hurry up!

"Okay," said Schultz, tapping the sheets on his thigh to line them up. "It'll do. Bring that stuff and come with me."

Copeland, cursing softly, gathered the material and followed on. In his office Schultz was all dispatch. He picked up the telephone, pressed a button and said, "Get me District Attorney Harmon at the Waldorf, Room 833," tucked the phone under his chin to free his hands and inserted Copeland's report into a brown manilla envelope. With some awkwardness he licked the flap, sealed it and then stapled it twice. Copeland could see that it had already been addressed and was boldly stamped: DISTRICT ATTORNEY'S OFFICE. OFFICIAL BUSINESS. CONFIDENTIAL. He gestured for Copeland to pass him the untidy pile of rejected pages, stapled them together and placed them in a drawer. As he did, he suddenly came alert and seized the receiver, putting it to his ear.

"Captain Schultz here," he said winningly. "I have the report you requested, sir. Where may I have it delivered?"

God, but he can be obsequious! Copeland thought. A real brown-noser.

Schultz was listening intently, his eyes closed in concentration. "Yes, sir. Yes, sir." There was an extended silence. He bent over the desk, snatched up a pen and made some notes: "Eastern, flight 203 at Kennedy. Right, sir. No, sir, no problem whatsoever. You're leavin' in five? Fine, sir. Detective Jackson will be waiting for you at the airport. Yes sir, I'm sure you'll find the report satisfactory. It's just like you said, sir; very detailed. No problem at all, sir. Good night, sir."

As he put down the phone, Copeland remonstrated: "Goddammit, Grizz, I've got a date."

"You're goddam right you got a date," Schultz said, beaming happily. "At Kennedy." He passed across a pen and a piece of paper. "Here, make a note. Eastern, flight 203. Two zero three." He grinned a tight, tough grin. "You report in late this mornin', you take a two hour lunch – you won't mind workin' a little overtime."

He picked up the phone, pushed a button and snapped, "I want a car at the front entrance in five. Detective Jackson to Kennedy." He put down the phone and smiled up at Copeland. "Be a good boy and I'll even put in for time-and-a-half for you."

Copeland glowered, and when Schultz handed him the envelope, snatched it from his fingers. Schultz's smile faded. "Let me remind you of somethin' buddy-boy: you asked for the assignment so stop the bitchin'. And get your ass out to the airport."

In rush-hour traffic the trip to JFK took an hour and fifteen minutes. Copeland stalked about the check-in desk for another twenty minutes until District Attorney Harmon arrived. He waited without much grace until Harmon had checked his bags, and was then invited to go along to the Departures Lounge. By the time he'd made conversation and the flight was called, it was 7:40. He sprinted to the first bank of telephone booths to find he didn't have change. He loped to the newsstand, and after waiting in line at the cash register, had a surly clerk at first refuse to change a ten dollar bill, doing so only when he flashed his badge. It was five minutes to eight when he punched out Jennifer's number. He let it ring for a full minute, replaced the receiver, and weighted with an infinite weariness, made his way back to the car.

The following morning at eight Copeland dialed Jennifer's private number. He let it ring. There was no response. He dialed the residence. Father Jamieson answered.

"Good morning, Father," he said. "I've been trying to reach Jennifer but there's no answer on her phone."

"Yes. The jack's disconnected. She's resting."

"Is she sick?"

Father Jamieson was slow in responding. "Would you stay on the line a moment?" he said. "His Eminence would like a word with you."

There *was* something wrong. Jennifer was normally up at seven for mass and at breakfast at eight. Resting? She must be ill. And Father Jamieson had been hesitant in his response. Copeland could feel his heart thumping in his chest and a sudden flush of blood to his face.

The sound of a receiver being lifted and another being replaced, and Michael's voice: "Good morning, Copeland."

"Good morning, Your Eminence. What's the matter with Jennifer?"

There was a coolness in Michael's voice and an edge of anger. "She's sleeping. The doctor put her under sedation last night."

"Sedation?"

"She had a very bad day yesterday, Copeland."

"She'll be all right?"

"At the moment what she needs is to rest, and the chance to regain her balance."

"When do you think I could talk to her?"

"I have no idea." Michael's voice was cold. "The doctor's coming in later. We'll just have to wait and see how she feels."

"Will you tell her I called?"

"I'm not sure she wants to talk to you."

"Perhaps when she—"

"To be blunt, Copeland, I'm not sure *I* want you to speak with her. She's very upset."

"I can understand that. I'm sorry."

Michael's voice was intimidating in its sternness. "You may remember, Copeland, that I once told you she's a very vulnerable girl. She's been hurt by someone she thought loved her. She feels betrayed. She waited here all day yesterday and not a word from you."

"But I *did* call! I called her office half a dozen times."

"She checked the office and there were no messages."

"But I *did* call. I called last night, called her there, and there was no answer."

"You'll excuse me," Michael said impatiently, "if I don't involve myself in a discussion as to whether you did or didn't. The point is, whatever your reasons, she didn't hear from you yesterday when she needed to. And that, on top of whatever happened between you two the night before was too much for her. Now, if you'll excuse me, I'm in the midst of breakfast."

Mingled with his concern, Copeland was feeling resentment. He wasn't accountable to Michael and disliked being put in the position where he appeared to be. He spoke slowly. "Would you just tell her I called to apologize and that she can reach me at the apartment."

Michael didn't acquiesce. Instead, he said: "One other thing before I go off the line: Father Jamieson tells me you've been inquiring about a further appointment in the matter of Dr. Gordon. I'm sorry, but I will have nothing further to say on that subject. Among other things, I've learned that you did not hold our last conversation in confidence. I permitted you to record that conversation only after you gave me an undertaking that it was for your ears only. You broke that promise. Beyond that, it has come to me that you have discussed with others private matters having to do with this household and the archdiocese. I must say, Copeland, you have disappointed me greatly. And now I'll say good morning."

Copeland realized that he might not get another opportunity to speak to Michael and almost instantaneously decided to draw a bow at a venture:

"Your Eminence . . ."

"Yes."

"Inasmuch as I won't be talking to you again about Dr. Gordon, I think you should know what I learned in Israel."

He relished the slight delay before Michael responded. "Very well, Copeland, what is it?"

"I found out what was in the box."

It was as though an explosion had detonated within Michael's brain. *Good God, no! Not now. Not after all that had happened. Father, will there be no end to it?* Setting himself for the answer, he said, "And what was it?"

"Bones. A skeleton." (*God! He does know!*) "The bones of the Teacher of Righteousness."

Michael thought he might faint as the tension dissolved and flooded from his body. He took a breath to gather himself.

"Copeland," he said solemnly, "I said a moment ago that I wouldn't discuss the matter with you further, but I will add this one word: you have been down a number of false trails in pursuing this obsession of yours, and once again you are in error. I don't know what your source is, but let me say to you flatly and unequivocally, you are wrong. And now I must go. Goodby."

"Your Eminence—"

There was a click and then the dial tone.

On his desk a note: "See Schultz."

"When are you two going to announce your engagement?" a fellow officer twitted.

Schultz was almost cheerful, but awkward in the unaccustomed role. "Sit down, Copeland," he said.

That's a first, Copeland thought. In his three years with the department he had never been told to sit no matter how extended the meeting. He sat on the edge of the chair, wary. Schultz wiped at an imaginary mark on the top of his desk with a widespread hand.

"Cope," he began, "first let me say you did a hell of a job on that report. I was talkin' to Harmon this mornin' and he says the same."

"Thank you," he said, and wondered: what the hell's coming?

"He asked me to commend you on your work on the case."

Copeland shrugged deprecatingly.

"Now," Schultz said with sudden energy, "I've got another assignment for you. I want you to —"

Copeland straightened. "Just a minute. You mean I'm off the Gordon case?"

Schultz's kewpie-blue eyes were wide and blue and innocent. "Off? What do you mean, off? Your report pretty well wraps it up. Any tag ends, Murray can handle."

"You *are* taking me off."

"Cope," Schultz said reasonably. "I just told you – no. The governor had a word with the Israeli counsel general this mornin', gave him a report, and he's well, satisfied. The wrap-up can be handled by Murray's department; where it should of been in the first place."

So the politicians had the wind up. As Schultz had said yesterday: "Look, Mister, you don't fuck around with no future popes." A big fat cover-up, that's what it was.

There was a red hot coal burning in his belly. He wasn't going to quit without a struggle. "Grizz . . . " he said.

"Yeah?"

"What you just told me is one huge crock of shit. The case isn't wrapped up; it's still up in the air and you know it."

Schultz's jaw snapped shut and color flooded upward from his neck. "Cope," he said, and there was menace in his voice, "I'm goin' to pretend like I didn't hear that."

"Grizz, you know damn well there are a dozen questions without answers in this case. And you know that what's going on is a cover-up. What happened? Harmon heard from Cardinal Maloney? Or from the governor?"

"I'm goin' to pretend I didn't hear that either," Schultz said. As he continued, the old toughness was back and his voice grew vehement. "Now, you listen to me, buddy-boy. You've pushed your luck as far as it goes, so wind it down. Nobody else made the decision; *I* did. I say it goes back to Murray and that's that. And let's not have any more of this crap about a cover-up or you're out in the street on your ass. Understand?"

The first glimmering of a plan began to form in Copeland's mind. He dammed up his anger, put his head down and said nothing. He'd buy time.

When Schultz continued his voice became conciliatory. "Look

. . . To hell with that new assignment. You been workin' too hard. You're tense as hell. Take a few days." He sought to resume his normal bluntness. "Okay, Mister, that's it. I don't want to see that ugly mug of yours till Monday. Get out of here will ya, so I can get some work done."

Chapter Seven

In the end, Schultz had no option but to suspend Copeland from duty. He had become insubordinate, had exceeded his authority, had disdained the chain of command, had begun to have a bad influence on discipline and had grown careless of his appearance. More serious, he had raised complaints, complaints from unnamed VIPs, complaints that were lodged at the highest levels, from whence they descended with great impact on Schultz's head in the form of brief telephone calls or terse memoranda.

Copeland's decline began the morning after Schultz notified him that he was being reassigned. Schultz arrived at his desk to be informed that Copeland was in Saleski's office and had been there half the night. He went to have a look. Copeland was indeed there, with the door closed, hunched over the desk. Notebooks and papers were spread untidily about. Schultz started the door open and put his head in.

"I thought I told you to take till Monday."

Copeland looked up. His eyes were puffy and bloodshot. He needed a shave. "I'm off," he said. "I was just using the office."

Schultz entered, craning his neck. "What's that there?"

"Where?"

"There – what you're readin'."

"Oh, this. A transcript."

"Like, a transcript of what?"

"An interrogation I did."

"With?"

"Cardinal Maloney."

"I told you you were off that."

"I know. I am."

"Then what are you doin'?"

Copeland shrugged. "Just . . . curious."

Schultz frowned. "You mean there's a transcript of your interview with Cardinal Maloney? You never said nothin' about a transcript."

"I promised not to show it to anybody. I was just checking it out before I shredded it."

"The hell you're shreddin' it." He held out a hand. "Give."

Copeland's tone toughened. "Will you just leave me alone to finish it? Okay? I won't be five minutes."

Schultz decided there was no percentage in poking a sleeping bear and said grudgingly, "Five minutes." He paused at the door. "Then get the hell out of here. You're off duty, you're off duty someplace else."

With Schultz gone, Copeland folded the transcript, put it in an inside pocket, went to his desk, put the other notes in a drawer, removed the carbon copy of the transcript and put it in another pocket, told an officer at a nearby desk, "If Schultz is looking for me, tell him I had an urgent call and had to blow," and went quickly down the stairs to the street.

The city seemed asparkle. There had been an all-night rain. It had washed the air clean and now the day was hung out to dry in the sun. Invigorated, Copeland took the subway to Forty-Second Street and walked the dozen blocks to Madison and Fiftieth to stand half-hidden in a doorway across the street from the residence. There was no evidence of life in the great house. No one came or went. No light was visible. In a few minutes he walked slowly toward Fifth Avenue, glancing up at Jennifer's window as he went. It was impossible to be certain but it seemed the drapes were drawn. He stood for perhaps ten minutes in the doorway to Sak's Sport Shop, watching, lighting a cigaret from another. At one point he thought he saw one of the lace curtains on the ground floor drawn aside, but decided it was his imagination. He went down the street to a pay phone at Sak's and dialed Jennifer's number. It rang without response. He called her office: "Sorry, she isn't in today."

Back at the apartment he cleared the kitchen table, found a pair of shears and cut sections from the transcript. With transparent tape he attached a sheet of typing paper to the bottom of each segment and printed the word ANALYSIS at the top. Then he sat down to study them.

He went first to the section of the transcript that had led to the exacerbation of his quarrel with Jennifer. What in fact had Michael said?

A – Perhaps this might help. He asked if he could borrow my car that day. Perhaps it was to move his things.

ANALYSIS: Jennifer right. Michael hadn't said Harris borrowed car, only asked if could. But statement irrelevant. Also misleading. Conveys impression Harris borrowed car. Why did he volunteer the information and suggest it might help? Harris hadn't borrowed car so how could it help? QUESTION: Jenkins at garage says car ordered for 6.30 delivery. Pickup ordered at 7.15 A.M. Monday. Why left overnight? Possible explanation: confusion after Harris's heart attack.

Q – The box was delivered here?
A – So I understand.

ANALYSIS: Seems deliberately ambiguous. Didn't *understand* box delivered, *knew* it was. Says later, "It wasn't a large one." Knew size so must have seen it.

Q – Did Dr. Gordon tell you what was in it?
A – I gather there were some artifacts.

ANALYSIS: More ambiguity. In next response admits knew what was in box.

Q – He was no more specific than that?
A – Indeed he was. He said something about a scroll and some fossil remains.

ANALYSIS: If Harris had told him what was in the box, why say, "I gather there were some artifacts"? Avoiding specific responses, hoping subject not pursued. Note evasive phrases: EG. "So I understand," "I gather," "He said something about." Such responses common practice: leave room to back off if necessary.

Q – I believe you were the first person to go into the workroom afterwards?
A –Yes.

Q – There was no sign of the box or the artifacts?
A – Well, I didn't take a careful look, but . . .

ANALYSIS: Says later went to workroom to remove manuscript. Able to find manuscript but doesn't notice if box there. Unlikely. More evasiveness. Why?

Q – Do you feel free to tell me the subject matter of the manuscript?

A – I'm afraid not. I haven't read it nor do I intend to.

Q – Did he discuss it with you?

A –Yes.

Q – But surely if he discussed it with you there'd be nothing improper in telling me.

A – I'm afraid so. When the book is published it will be very controversial and it would do a great deal of harm to a great many people if it were to be released prematurely.

ANALYSIS: Knows enough of subject matter to say, "very controversial" and "would do a great deal of harm," yet says hasn't read it. Says Harris discussed it with him. How possible to discuss it without reference to (a) what was in box, and (b) subject matter of manuscript?

A – Dr. Gordon told me things which I consider to be of the nature of a confession. They touch on his book. You must realize that, as a priest, I am bound not to divulge anything of what he told me.

ANALYSIS: Strange extension of secrecy of confessional. Harris avowed agnostic. Might tell things in confidence but certainly not as confession. Perfect cop-out. Can admit awareness certain facts but cut off questions when wishes to.

He went from the table to wander about the living room and then went to the window to stare unseeing at the city. There could be no doubt that Michael was being less than open. Hadn't he said on the telephone only yesterday – "flatly and unequivocally" – that the box didn't contain the bones of the Teacher of Righteousness? How could he be certain unless he knew what was in the box? The obvious conclusion was that, for reasons yet obscure, Michael didn't want Harris's discoveries published and was using his position and his priestly privilege to stonewall any inquiry. Copeland let out a small bitter laugh: it was a better device than Richard Nixon's subterfuge of protecting national security. Not even a Senate inquiry could violate the confessional!

But more important were the questions raised by Michael's evasiveness and (to call it by its name) his lying. He would not deliberately lie, Copeland knew, except under extraordinary circumstances or for a very good reason. What could Harris have discovered that would be sufficient to induce Michael to deal in falsehood and dissimulation? It could only be something that posed a threat to his personal interests or could put the church in jeopardy. Whatever it was, the incongruity of Michael's reactions was the measure of its importance.

At 5.30 Copeland went again to Madison and Fiftieth and stood about on the corner watching the front door of the residence. At seven he saw the day maids leave. Shortly afterward, lights went on in Father Jamieson's and Father Carroll's rooms. Ten minutes later the drapes were drawn in Michael's study. At 8.05 Father Carroll left by the front door and hailed a cab. As he got in he glanced at Copeland. Copeland wandered slowly along Fiftieth Street to where he could see the window of Jennifer's room. It was dark. He continued on to Sak's, dialed her number and let it ring. He hung up and phoned the residence. Father Jamieson answered. He hung up, made his way back to Madison Avenue, bought a packet of cigarets and stood lounging in the shadows of the old Villard Mansion across the street from the residence.

He was suddenly alert. Someone leaving: Father Jamieson. Pulling on a topcoat, he crossed the street and came directly to Copeland.

"Good evening, Copeland."

"Good evening, Father."

Jamieson pointed toward Fiftieth Street. "Will you join me for a drink?"

Copeland shrugged and they went to a restaurant, a hole-in-the-wall delicatessen. Father Jamieson ordered a beer and Copeland shrugged assent. Nothing was said until they were served. When Father Jamieson took a long draught and said, "Drink up." Copeland did.

"This isn't the ideal place," the priest said, "but I thought perhaps we should have a talk."

"Okay," Copeland said noncommittally.

"You're behaving very badly, you know."

"No, I don't know."

"What do you hope to achieve, standing outside here all day?"

"I haven't been here all day."

"You know what I mean, Copeland."

"You said I'd been here all day. I merely said I hadn't."

"You do realize that Jennifer's not there?"

"Could be."

"Believe me, she's not."

"Where is she then?"

"I'm not free to tell you that. You must understand that she's not well. She's under the doctor's care."

"Part of the reason for that is she's been kept from seeing me."

"She is not being kept from seeing you. I'm sorry to tell you this, but she doesn't want to see you right now. She's just not able to handle it."

Copeland raised his glass and took a long pull at the beer, looking over the rim with cynical eyes. "Believe me, Copeland," Father Jamieson said.

"In a word," Copeland said, "I don't."

Father Jamieson's eyes went flinty. "There's no call to be rude. I'm only trying to help."

Copeland didn't respond, nor did he lower his eyes.

Father Jamieson made a patient and understanding voice. "Copeland, this is a bad time for you. I know that. You and Jennifer are having problems. There are problems at your work. You're under great pressure. You've lost your sense of proportion . . . "

"Why don't you tell me where Jennifer is?"

"The truth is—"

"Don't talk to me about the truth. That place over there's filled with lies."

"Copeland, that will be enough of that!"

"Well, it's true."

Father Jamieson had finished being reasonable. "My son," he said sternly, "you will listen to me. I'm warning you, not asking you, to stop all this—"

Copeland had pushed back his chair and was gone into the night.

He stood out of sight until he saw Father Jamieson cross Madison Avenue and walk north to the parish house. Then he made his way to the back of the residence and rang the door bell. Miss Pritchard's eyes widened when she saw him.

"Why Mr. Copeland . . . !"

"May I come in?"

"Of course. Of course."

She followed him into the kitchen, flushed, poking an errant strand of hair into place. There were some used dishes on the table, and despite his remonstrances she removed them, wiped the seat of a chair with a dish towel and asked him to sit down.

"Goodness sakes," she said. "You at the back door! Give me a start, it did. Will you be havin' some coffee?"

"No, thanks," he said. "I promise not to keep you."

"You'll have a wee cup." she said. There was a pot of coffee on the stove, and in a sequence of sure, swift movements it was in a mug and steaming before him on the table. She seated herself opposite, absently making cleaning motions with a part of her apron on the shining enamel surface. "You know Miss Jennifer's not here?" she offered.

He said, "I wanted to see you."

"Not more about Dr. Gordon?"

"Just a couple of things."

"Mr. Copeland . . . " There was exasperation in her voice. "Sure 'n I've told you everythin' I know."

"Miss P.," he said, finding and holding her eyes with his, "I'm sorry, but I don't think you have."

Color flooded into her neck and then to her face. She was about to respond and then didn't, but just sat there. "You know what Dr. Gordon was working on, don't you ?" he said.

He didn't miss the almost imperceptible blink of her eyes. As she drew breath to reply, he said, "Miss Pritchard, do be careful. I'm your friend but I'm here as a policeman."

She looked at him levelly, to his surprise quite self-possessed. "Mr. Copeland," she said, "you're not bein' fair to me. In one breath you say you're my friend and in the next you accuse me of lyin'."

"I didn't mean that. It's just that you have certain loyalties and—"

"Wouldn't you expect me to?"

"Of course. It's just that . . . " He shifted in his chair and a small note of pleading entered his voice. "Miss Pritchard, I have a job to do."

Her voice was patient. "Mr. Copeland, you're still not bein' honest with me. You're not on the case no more."

"Who told you that?"

"Isn't it true?"

"Not officially, perhaps."

"His Eminence has told you he'll not have another word to say on the subject, and here you are in me kitchen tryin' to worm somethin' out of me. Is that bein' a friend?"

Copeland looked at her then dropped his eyes. There was no hostility in her face and her voice was a mother's. In the silence the refrigerator motor clicked on.

"Mr. Copeland, I'm terrible sorry about you and Miss Jennifer. She's like one of my own and I feel for her. She's takin' it very hard. Poor darlin', her feelin's is always so close to the surface. But the way you're carryin' on, what you're doin' is only makin' things worse. I can understand your feelin's, too, but for the life of me I can't figure out what you're tryin' to prove. Dr. Gordon's dead and gone – God rest 'im – why not let 'im be ?" Her brows knit. "Sometimes . . . " she said slowly, "sometimes I wonder why 'tis you keep goin' on so. I'm not sayin' for a minute it's true, but sometimes I get the feelin' you've got somethin' against His Eminence. It's not true, of course."

"Of course it isn't."

"Of course not."

"For goodness sake, Miss P., I'm a Catholic. I try to be a good one."

"Of course you do."

Copeland subsided. Miss Pritchard looked at the top of his head. "There's one thing I don't understand," she said. He looked up. "Why is it you keep worryin' away at this?"

"I told you; I'm a detective."

"But the detective's been taken off. It's the man who keeps goin'. And for the life of me I don't know why."

Copeland felt a rasp of irritation. He was getting quite fed up with everybody taking it on themselves to lecture him on his responsibilities. Goddammit, he knew better than they what needed doing! It was his job. Now here was a goddam housekeeper telling him what his duty was. And before her there'd been Father Jamieson with his smooth talk, and Michael with his lies, and Schultz with his cover-up, and the D.A. – even the goddam governor of the state! And Jennifer, too. Why were they all so anxious to get him off the scent? Didn't matter: they were all wrong. Every one of them. There *was* something rotten in Denmark. All his instincts confirmed it. And they weren't going to stop him now, not when he'd come this far.

He looked at Miss Pritchard again; his voice was overly precise. "Miss P., I'm making an investigation for one reason and one reason only: Dr. Gordon is guilty of theft and smuggling. That's one thing. Beyond that there are other questions, and I regret to say, a lot of covering up. It's my duty to—"

He broke off. She was watching him compassionately. "I'm sorry," she said softly.

"There's no need to be," he said gruffly, getting out of his chair and going to the back door.

"Mostly, I mean, for you and Jennifer," she said.

Mr. Jenkins wasn't being cooperative. He was debating with himself whether flatly to refuse any more information to the hulking and disheveled man standing over him, but was deterred from that by the possibility of police harassment. He'd had an experience of that: standing on his rights only to find that when you operated a garage in midtown Manhattan the police had ways of leaning on you. He wanted no more of that. This same Detective Jackson had come by a few days earlier to ask questions about Cardinal Maloney's car. He'd reported the visit to Father Jamieson and hadn't had to be too perceptive to recognize that the priest was not pleased. He'd thanked him and asked to be informed of other inquiries. And now, leaning over his desk again, pressing him, was the same officer.

"I'm not trying to give you a hard time, Detective Jackson," he said, his voice conciliatory. "Perhaps if you told me what it is you're looking for, I could help you. But, I mean, it's Cardinal Maloney's car and, well, you can understand—"

"Look," Copeland said, bearing down. "I've seen the car, now I want to see your records. Keep on stalling and I'm going to wonder whether maybe I shouldn't send in the IRS. What's the problem, two sets of books?"

Jenkins caved in. He rose from his grimy desk, went to a filing cabinet and removed and passed to Copeland a manilla folder. Copeland sat at the other side of the desk and opened the file.

Jenkins, needing to regain some face, said, "I'll have to report this to Cardinal Maloney, you know."

Without looking up, Copeland skidded the telephone toward him. "Be my guest," he said.

Jenkins sat slouched and sullen and silent while Copeland leafed through the file. The records were detailed, listing dates and times, specifying mechanical work done, gasoline added, oil changes, washes, even the hours and costs of labor. With a forefinger, Copeland ran down the dates until he found:

April 12. Wash $2.75. Gas (Premium) 10.3 gals, $7.35. Oil checked. Tires checked. Delivery ordered 12.44 P.M. Delivered 6.21 P.M. Mileage out: 57,322.4.

April 13. Pick-up ordered 7.28 A.M. In garage 7.47 A.M. Mileage in: 57,506.6.

Copeland's pulse quickened. The car had been driven approximately 184 miles Easter Sunday night or the following morning. Perhaps Harris *had* used the car. Of course not; he was dead before it was delivered. Who, then? Michael?

He looked across at Jenkins. "When you deliver the car, where's it parked?"

"In the parking area in front of the old Villard Mansion."

"Across the street from the residence?"

"Yes."

"What do you do with the key?"

"It comes back here." He gestured with a thumb over his shoulder at a board untidy with tagged sets of keys. "We have our own set."

"At the residence, who drives the car?"

"Cardinal Maloney. It's his car."

"I know that. Who else?"

"I wouldn't know. Why don't you ask him?"

"I may do just that," Copeland said, tossing the file onto the desk and rising.

Emerging into the sunlight he heard his name called.

"Cope! Over here!"

Double-parked in an unmarked car was a shirtsleeved Schultz. He's come straight from the office, Copeland thought. He walked slowly to the car and leaned in the window on the passenger side. "How are you, Grizz?" he asked amiably.

"Get in," Schultz said. "You and I are gonna talk."

He got in. Schultz burned rubber and bulled his way into the traffic flow, raising an angry hooting. "I'm heading for my place if it's not out of your way," Copeland said lightly.

"Let's skip the smartass routines," Schultz said, wheeling into a parking space and turning off the engine. He swung around in the seat. "Okay, Mister," he said, "what the Christ do you think you're doin'?"

Copeland shrugged, a small smile at his lips. "Nothing," he said.

"What were you doin' at the garage there?"

"Just checking something out."

"Like?"

He was suddenly infinitely weary of Schultz and his unremitting bully-boy macho manner. Almost as though disembodied, he looked out from behind his eyes and watched the ugly wet mouth spitting out words, noticed the yellow tobacco stains on the crooked teeth, saw the dark pores on the nose and the stiff, black bristling hairs jutting from the flared nostrils, and turned off the sound as though on a television set. His brain seemed filled with an aqueous substance in which a single thought was kicking like a struggling swimmer: 184 miles. Where would 184 miles take you to ? Where might Michael want to go on Easter Sunday night or early on a Monday morning that was 184 miles distant? But wait, it wouldn't be to a point 184 miles distant – that was the total mileage – it would have been a return trip to a place 92 miles from New York. What was 92 miles away? To the south? Atlantic City, perhaps. Or Philadelphia. Princeton? Possible: Michael and Harris were Princeton graduates. But Princeton wasn't that far away. Heading north he'd end up somewhere around Hartford. Heading east he'd get into Pennsylvania. Allentown or Reading, perhaps. The Poconos. . . . My God, yes! The Poconos! *The Cottage*! Of course, it was almost exactly 90 miles. But why would Michael drive to The Cottage that late at night only to return the next morning before 7.30? Not merely to be by himself; there had been no one else at the residence. Perhaps to remove the manuscript to a place of safekeeping. Maybe even the box. Perhaps Dr. Gordon *had* intended to borrow the car. Perhaps he'd even loaded the box and the manuscript into it, planning to take them somewhere now that his work was done. Perhaps the effort had brought on the heart attack and Michael had suddenly found himself faced with the fact that his friend was dead and the controversial box and manuscript were in his car. What to do? He wouldn't want to return them to the basement, so he'd taken them to The Cottage. Of course. It all came together like the pieces of a puzzle. That was why Michael had been evasive under questioning: *the box was at The Cottage!* There was one question remaining, however: Why hadn't he waited until the following day? Why had he made the drive in the night? What *was* in that box?

" . . . so you're suspended till further notice." The sound was back on. "Copeland, you hear me?"

"Yes, I hear you, Grizz. They can hear you on Staten Island. Now, if you'll excuse me."

He opened the car door. Schultz had turned purple. "Goddammit, Copeland, I'll have your badge!"

"Yeah, Grizz," he said and closed the door of the car.

The Cottage was reached by leaving Pennsylvania State Highway 119 and turning into an abandoned logging-road which meandered through a mature deciduous woods, a pleasant mix of birch and beech and maple and oak, to the western shore of Round Lake. The turn-off effected an immediate transition to another world in which urban ugliness could only dimly be remembered and the air had bouquet and the spirit opened as a blossom to the sun. Years earlier Michael had had the underbush and the lower limbs of the trees cleared away and the forest floor had never returned to its primeval tangle. The trees thrust straight as columns for the sky, arching their uppermost boughs to create cathedrals and permitting the sun access only to dapple bush and wildflower and fern. Duncan Maloney had bought The Cottage at the depth of the depression – "Stolen it," he insisted; taking perverse pleasure from the willing confession of unchristian rapacity. It had been named The Cottage inappropriately and by default when, having been required to, no one in the family came up with a name that found consensus. Duncan had proposed Duncanscroft but that had been shot down as nouveau riche and soon forgotten.

The Cottage was actually a one-hundred-year-old nine-room house perched atop a rock outcrop at lake's edge. Built entirely of wood, with many Victorian curlicues and much scrollwork, it had a steeply pitched, gabled roof. The sides were sheathed in cedar shakes which had been permitted to weather to a dignified old age. At one corner, on the water side, there was a squat round-tower surmounted by a rococco cupola, above which Michael flew the Stars and Stripes or a Vatican flag when in residence. It had become Michael's study: "An inevitable mistake," he often said. "You can't possibly say no to it, but there are a thousand distractions outside the windows."

From a deck cantilevered over the water, a set of sturdy cedar steps ran down to a wharf which tiptoed on slender stilts into the lake, coming to rest on a log crib. Nearby there was a boathouse, a sagging clapboard box, and back of the house, a garage. In an earlier time the garage had served as a stable. There were still three stalls along one wall, and above them an open hayloft reached by a ladder which ascended two vertical uprights.

At Michael's invitation, Copeland had twice visited The Cottage with Jennifer, and he had no difficulty finding his way there this morning. He parked behind the house out of sight from the water, and while removing his jacket, looked about while considering where to begin his search. There was little likelihood of being interrupted: the highway was a quarter of a mile distant but the site was screened by the woods, and although there were two runabouts snarling through the waters of the lake and a sailboat fluttering to attract a breeze, it was known locally that Michael came to The Cottage for privacy, and natives and nearby cottagers had learned not to drop in.

He decided to begin his search within the house and easily gained access by slipping the bolt of the lock with a credit card. There would be no need to rummage about: how many closets or corners could contain a box as large as the one he was seeking? In ten minutes he had concluded his tour, even checking the unfinished basement floor to see if there had been any recent excavating done. He went next to the boat house but needed barely to put his head within to know the box wasn't there. In the stable he checked each stall. The cubicle that had once been the harness room but now contained a lawn mower, a variety of garden and other tools and a clutter of fuel cans seemed a likely place, but proved not to be. For a moment he thought he had come upon the hiding place: a feed bin, large enough, and closed with a hasp secured with a piece of wood. But when he raised the hinged top it was empty.

He climbed to the loft. Dusty, faded hay was banked against the three walls. A pitchfork stood on its tines resting against an upright. He took it, and wading in the hay began a systematic probing, tossing the dry grasses aside and in the doing creating bars of shifting light where the sun, having slipped inside through knotholes, was betrayed by the dust.

In a corner the pitchfork twanged short of a full thrust. The impact leaped like electricity from the handle to his hands and through his nervous system. He went to his knees, pushed the hay aside and saw the white pine and the tattered waybill. Carefully, he lifted the box from its nest, carried it to a clear space by the ladder, set it down and crouched beside it.

There it was! The object of his search halfway around the world, looking almost familiar, he'd imagined it so often. He was almost overcome by an inundation of emotion and gratification. After a moment he roused himself and tried to raise the top. It had been carefully secured. In the harness-room he found a pry bar and, despite much protesting by the nails, gently levered the boards free. The box was filled with glistening bundles of pliofilm. He carefully unrolled one. Cocooned within absorbent cotton he found what he took to be the bone of a human forearm, beige and burnished with age. He rewrapped it carefully and replaced it in the box. There was a cylinder of pliofilm wedged along one side. He removed it, sat with his feet over the edge of the loft, placed it on his lap and began slowly to unroll it. Sandwiched between sheets of plastic was an ancient scroll, dun-colored and dark at the edges. Gently he returned it to the box. At one end, on its side, was a cardboard carton. He picked it up and saw that it bore the inscription, *REGAL. America's Finest Bond Paper.* Within, filling only half of the space, was a typed manuscript. The title page read:

THE TOMB OF
JESUS OF NAZARETH

being an account
of my discovery of the grave
and the bones of Yeshuah ben-Yoseph,
known as Jesus Christ

HARRIS G. GORDON
Ph. D., Litt D., M.A. Oxon.

The blood drained from Copeland's head and he was overtaken by a sudden riving terror. He sat as though stricken; motionless, only barely breathing, numbly reading and rereading the words on the paper. After perhaps five minutes he stirred, drew an unsure breath, placed the title page upside down within the cover of the carton and began to read. When he was finished it was dark in the stable.

Michael came slowly through the front doors of the residence looking very tired. Father Jamieson, waiting, having caught the sound of the key in the latch, came downstairs and took his raincoat. "It's nasty out there," he said in a clucking mother-hen way that required no response. "How is she?"

"The doctors seem pleased enough," Michael said, "but I don't know." His voice was flat and without vitality.

"When will she be coming home?"

"Tomorrow morning, they say. I'm to pick her up around ten."

"Being here will make a big difference. Miss Pritchard's all sixes-and-sevens not being able to look after her."

He shook his head. "She seems too subdued, too amenable." A heavy sigh. "Worries me. She's talking about going up to The Cottage on the weekend. Wants to get away." He deliberately changed the subject. "Any messages?"

"Only three of any importance. Copeland again."

"Not again. I'd hoped that had ended."

"He's called three times. I've told him there's no point but he still calls back. I don't like the sound of him."

"Oh?"

"He sounds distracted. I didn't recognize his voice the first time."

"Did he say what he wanted?"

"To talk to you. I asked if there was a message, but no. He insists on calling back tonight."

"What else?"

"Lady Hambleton. She was returning your call."

"Yes."

"She said she could be reached until midnight." He looked at his watch. "It's eleven there now."

"What was the third?"

303

"Cardinal Rinsonelli from Rome. Urgent."

Michael turned toward the study and stopped at the door. "Three things: tell Miss Pritchard we'll eat at seven. Get Cardinal Rinsonelli on the line for me. I'll take it in here. I'd like you to talk to Lady Hambleton for me. Tell her I hope I haven't inconvenienced her and so on, but the reason for my call has passed. You might also tell her that her lawyers and ours completed the transfer of funds to St. Clare's this morning. Express my appreciation and tell her I'll be in touch in a few days."

Copeland was drunk. For four days he had slept only in brief snatches and in that time had eaten little – opening some tinned beef to leave it untouched, and spooning into his mouth only a few dollops of cold pork and beans. He had drunk many cups of coffee and smoked packs of cigarets, replenishing his supply from a carton in the kitchen cupboard. On the Friday, as night fell early and an east wind keened and flung sheets of rain against the house in fitful pique, he was set upon by a dark dread, and when it deepened, sought to exorcise it with a tumbler filled with scotch from the liquor cabinet in the living room.

For four days he hadn't bathed or shaved and had sometimes been disoriented. He had prowled the house and the woods, head down, hands in pockets, kicking at objects in his path, much of the time oblivious to his surroundings. Perhaps a half-dozen times a day he went to the garage and climbed to the loft. On the first morning, he had hesitated at the door, had gone slowly to the ladder and had paused before ascending. Since, he had gone without wariness or hesitancy. After making the sign of the cross, he would drop to his knees before the box, almost reverently clear away the hay with which he'd covered it and sit looking at it for hours.

It never occurred to him that the bones could be other than Jesus'. The style of Harris's manuscript was scholarly, replete with technical terms and references and heavy with footnotes, but the recounting of his search was straightforward, and Copeland saw no reason to doubt a detail of it. He was only dimly aware of the ramifications of the fact that, apparently, Jesus had not been resurrected. He realized, of course, that it touched on his deity – just how was unclear – and that it would take some getting used to. Easter would have to be seen differently, that was obvious; but Jesus' teachings and the fact of the crucifixion remained true, didn't they? He puzzled about how Harris's discovery would affect the Eucharist but gave up on it: he'd leave that to the church fathers: they'd know the answers.

He found himself praying to the box. He wasn't accustomed to extemporizing prayers and the words came awkwardly, slowly. Mostly, he sought help in deciding what to do. On the day he'd discovered the hiding place he'd tried to reach Michael by telephone but had given up when it became clear that he wasn't going to be permitted to speak to him. It had occurred to him to broach the fact of his discovery to Father Jamieson as a means of getting through, but he'd refrained and had made the decision to tell no one until he's come to a better understanding of all that was at stake.

He spent hours puzzling over Michael's actions. For how long had he known what was in the box? If he'd known from the beginning, what were his reasons for bringing Harris to live and work at the residence? He recalled his own suspicions, the formless feeling that something was awry, and found satisfaction in the knowledge that his intuition had been vindicated. He went back over each visit to the residence and reviewed everything that had been said by either Harris or Michael. He understood now those puzzling asides by Harris that night when he'd entertained with the story of the man who'd been crucified. He reviewed the conversations he'd had with Michael and especially the two interviews, and was appalled in the realization of how often and how skillfully Michael had lied to him. He wished he had that damn transcript of their second conversation with him here: it would be fascinating to examine each response in the light of what he now knew. He found himself growing bitterly resentful of Michael: of his interference between himself and Jennifer (probably because he perceived Copeland's suspicions and felt put in jeopardy by them) and of his intruding into the investigation. He had no doubt that Michael had put pressure on the governor and had been responsible for his being removed from the case. He could understand why he'd want to hide the facts, but he'd done more than that. Apparently, he'd laid careful plans to spirit away the box and its contents on the night of Harris's death and had had the car sent around for such a purpose.

But wait a minute! Michael had called the garage shortly after noon; how could he possibly have known at that time that Harris was going to die? Copeland sought to bar entrance to the terrible thought but it persisted. How *could* Michael have known that Harris would die that evening? Perhaps he didn't. Perhaps the car was there for another reason. That must be it. But was it only coincidence that Harris had died on the one day in months when Jennifer, Miss Pritchard and the two priests would be absent and the residence empty? He shook his head to dislodge the idea. It was unthinkable! How could he even for a moment contemplate the possibility that Michael could have known in advance about – could possibly have *planned* – Harris's death? He rejected the thought but it nagged at him, badgered him and was sometimes the stimulus that drove him from the loft or from his bed on the sofa at night to wander the woods or to stalk about the house.

Finally, he could no longer leave the question unresolved. He called the Medical Examiner's office in Manhattan, identified himself and asked to have the file on Dr. Harris Gordon read to him. Cause of death: cardiac arrest following upon ventricular fibrillation induced by insulin shock. Had an autopsy been done? No, there'd been no reason to. The deceased's physician, Dr. Raymond, had signed the death certificate. He was familiar with the deceased's medical history. He had noted on the certificate that the deceased had been diabetic, that he'd been on regular insulin twice daily, and that he'd suffered chronic angina. There had seemed no need for an autopsy. Was he suggesting that there should be one now? No, nothing like that: just a routine inquiry.

So that was that. And yet . . .

What was Michael planning to do with the bones now that they were in his possession? For the moment the hiding place was ideal. No one ever went to the loft. There would be no children or grandchildren to chance upon the box in the midst of a game. The stable was dry and secure and the box would undoubtedly remain undiscovered for years. But was it right to keep it hidden? Michael had told him that publication of the manuscript would do great harm and had spoken of postponing it for ten years, but how would the passage of the years alter matters? What circumstance would be different then? (It had probably been another of his lies.) But surely so important a discovery demanded to be published? Was it not presumptuous arbitrarily to decide that it should be withheld? Would the consequences be all that grievous? Would they harm the church that much? Perhaps, but putting the question to himself, Copeland decided that his own faith was in no way diminished.

He feared the bones. Having nailed up the box he wouldn't open it again. When clearing away the hay each day he was careful not to touch it, and before burying it each evening he crossed himself. Sometimes, sitting contemplating it, a shiver would travel his body and there were moments when, sitting alone in the silence, the hair on his forearms and on the back of his neck would suddenly come erect. He wouldn't go to the loft at night and at times would pull aside the kitchen curtains to peer through the darkness, half expecting to see a glow from the place where the bones lay.

Now, drunk, he stumbled from the house and went to the stable. The moon was at the full but was intermittently obscured by roiling black clouds. In the darkness he stumbled twice, falling each time to his knees. He was wearing only a shirt, trousers and shoes and was wet to the skin before he reached the double doors. Within, the stable was stygian. He felt his way to the ladder and climbed it, pausing as his eyes reached the level of the loft, and then continuing on. He fumbled in his shirt pocket for the book of matches he kept there. The matches were damp and his fingers clumsy; the sulphur sputtered and flared but would not flame. He struck another and another until one lit. Two tiny rubies glowed and abruptly disappeared, and there was a scurrying in the hay. In the feeble light he went on his knees toward the box. The match burned his fingers and he dropped it. He lit another and with one hand cleared away the hay.

He stayed so, on his knees, for some time and then was suddenly very tired. In the darkness he lay down beside the box, his brow inches away, the fingers of his right hand lightly touching it.

The wind was mourning in the eaves, the rain was beating in a soft fury against the roof and there was a sound of water trickling. But all that was outside the center of peace in which Copeland lay, and he was soon asleep.

In the morning, renewed, he bathed and shaved, ate breakfast, and went to the typewriter in Michael's study:

The Cottage
Friday Morning.
Your Eminence:

I have tried a number of times to reach you by telephone but Father Jamieson protects your privacy well. It is now obvious that you will never agree to meet me face to face. I expect that as usual you'll be coming here for the weekend. I considered waiting but concluded that doing so would only lead to a confrontation in which I'm sure I'd never get to say everything that's on my mind. Therefore I'm writing this letter. I've made a carbon and will leave it for you at the residence. I'm sure the chance to see you there is nil.

As you will have surmised by now, I have discovered the box in the hayloft and have seen the Bones and the scroll. I have also read Dr. Gordon's manuscript. I knew all along that something important was being hidden in Dr. Gordon's workroom but I had no idea, of course, that it was the bones of Our Lord. You can imagine the shock when I opened the box.

I have spent the past four days trying to decide what my responsibility is and have come to the following conclusions:

(1) I regret to say this to a leader of my Church and a priest of God, but your actions in this matter have been dishonorable from the beginning. I can no longer accept your word on anything. You have lied not once but dozens of times. You have lied to me, to Jennifer, to Miss Pritchard, to the police and to the governments of the United States and Israel. You have aided and abetted a criminal act and have used the power and the prestige of your office to do so. And you have done this apparently without any concern for the fact that you have been responsible for destroying the happiness of your niece, not to speak of myself. Our Lord may forgive you, I doubt that I ever can.

(2) I presume the reason you hid the box was because you felt that the disclosure of the contents would harm the Church. Neither am I prepared personally to take the responsiblity of telling the world that Our Saviour's bones have been found. It is not for me to decide such important things. On the other hand, I am not prepared to leave the matter in your hands alone. I insist on knowing what you plan to do. I certainly am not willing to have His remains left in a cheap wood box in a hayloft. (Never mind any other possibility, have you considered the danger

of fire?) It is now six weeks since Dr. Gordon died and you have done nothing to provide a better resting place for His remains. I will expect you to inform me about what you have in mind when we meet.

(3) There are some questions I intend to ask you about Dr. Gordon's death. I am not making any charges at this time but I will be expecting straightforward answers. There has been enough lying already.

(4) Finally, I realize that I can't report my findings to my superiors. That would raise too many serious problems. It might also lead to charges being laid against you. (Although I'm not sure the Powers-That-Be would proceed.) But for the sake of Our Lord and the Church I can't take that chance. However, the matter must not remain as it is. I have given it a great deal of thought and have prayed for guidance. Here are my proposals:

(a) Return the Bones and the scroll to Israel anonymously and let the Israeli government decide what to do. After all, it is their property illegally removed.

(b) Alternatively, arrange to transport them to Rome and leave the decision on what is to be done to the Holy Father.

(c) In the meantime, transfer Dr. Gordon's manuscript to a place of safekeeping (after personally making a xerox copy) until such time as either the Israeli government or the Holy Father, whichever is the case, has decided what should be done. At that time a decision can be made about the manuscript.

I will be at my apartment. I will expect to hear from you by no later than Monday noon. In the meantime, you might do something to repair the quarrel between Jennifer and me, for which your actions have been largely responsible.

Sincerely
Copeland Jackson

He placed the letter face up on Michael's desk, let himself out, checked that the door was locked, got in his car and drove away.

He parked on Fiftieth Street and, trembling, went to the front door of the residence and pushed the bell-button. Jeannie came to the door, pulled aside the curtain, looked out and turned back into the house. In a moment there was a sound of heavier footsteps and Father Jamieson opened the door.

"What is it now, Copeland?"

"I'd like to see His Eminence, please."

"He's not here."

"There's no need to lie to me, Father."

"And there's no need for insolence. He's in Rome as you must surely know."

"How would I know that?"

Father Jamieson looked at him closely. "You do know the Holy Father is dead?"

"Dead?"

"Since Monday. How could you possibly not know – it's been in the papers and on the radio and television."

Copeland was smitten with a sudden sense of being bereft. He felt drained, impotent. "I've been away," he murmured.

"Cardinal Maloney left for Rome Tuesday night."

The Holy Father was dead. He felt a need to weep but restrained it. There would be no point in leaving the letter now. He put it in the pocket of his jacket. It occurred to him: perhaps with Michael away he could see Jennifer.

"Would you tell Jennifer that I'm here and that I'd like to see her?" he asked humbly.

"She's not here either."

Copeland looked at him abjectly. "Father, please. I promise not to bother her. I love her."

Father Jamieson's face softened. "I'll do this," he said. "She's gone to The Cottage for the weekend, but I'll be speaking to her tonight and I'll tell her you called."

How he reached the turn-off to The Cottage without police pursuit or without spinning out on a curve is not readily explained. It may have been a result of two years driving a patrol car or because the police were busy elsewhere. However that may be, he had not turned into the logging-road more than one hundred yards before he saw the three police cruisers clustered at lake's edge, their red lights flashing, and the ambulance attendants coming from the water.

Chapter Eight

From twenty-one countries on five continents and the islands of the sea, the members of the Sacred College of Cardinals had converged on Rome, and the city was again for a few days the center of the world. Not surrounded by the perquisites of power as once they'd come, flanked by aides, personal physicians, secretaries and retinues of servants; but simply, by commercial aircraft, railroad train and automobile. Sixtus V had set the maximum number of the College at seventy and so it had remained until John XXIII and Paul VI had increased it to 145. But thirty-three of that number were not in Rome: nineteen, having passed the age of eighty, were ineligible to participate in papal elections, six were too ill or infirm to travel and eight offices remained unfilled after the deaths of the incumbents.

From the moment of arrival, the cardinals had been secluded in monasteries and ecclesiastical colleges, scrupulously avoiding contact with the hundreds of journalists running in packs about Rome and the Vatican State, sniffing about as for carrion. Even when meeting with members of the Vatican diplomatic corps, the cardinals did so in mass audience lest there be any suggestion that they were influenced in their decision by political considerations.

Gregory XVII lay buried in the crypt beneath St. Peter's, and with his interment the mood of the city had subtly changed. Mourning yielded to anticipation, sobriety to contained excitement. Though the city was lovely in summer dress, she still wore some black and moved to the tolling of bells from a hundred towers. But as plans for the election of the new pontiff proceeded, rumor ran the streets, darted into every hotel lobby and restaurant and bar and stimulated every conversation. The Apostolic Constitution required that "not less than fifteen nor more than eighteen" days after the death of the pope, the College be convened, and that date having been set by the *cardinal camerlengo*, every preparation was under way. On that date, the 112 cardinals, having presented their credentials and having been bound by an oath sworn under pain of reserved excommunication, having put off their garments of mourning and having robed themselves again in the scarlet of princes, would proceed in solemn single file through the halls of the Vatican palace to the Sistine Chapel to a special mass of the Holy Spirit. The great bell in the courtyard of St. Damasus would sound, warning unauthorized persons to leave, and the Prefect of Ceremonies would lead the procession to the Vatican where they would be sequestered until a new pope was elected. They would by no means be alone but would live as part of a small, self-sustained community in makeshift accommodations, seriously lacking in sleeping and bathroom facilities. In addition to the Prefect of Ceremonies, doctors, secretaries, carpenters, plumbers and even firemen would remain with them to deal with emergencies as they might arise. Their food would be prepared outside their quarters by the Sisters of Santa Marta – an order not celebrated for its culinary skills – and passed through a revolving section installed in a door.

The Prefect of Ceremonies and the Architect of the Conclave, with two electronic technicians, would then make a ritual search of the area to be sealed off. The windows would have already been whitewashed, all radio and television sets removed and all telephones disconnected. They would make a tour of the building, looking in every corner and closet, peering behind every drapery and poking into every hiding place. The search would be traditional, the presence of the two technicians new. In 1975 Paul VI had ordered that the strictest precautions be observed to prevent electronic eavesdropping or filming of the deliberations. The order was understood to have stemmed from two events: the proliferation of listening devices and their use by government officials and agencies, but perhaps more immediately, by a scandal in the early 1970s when two Italian journalists, a man and a woman, had published a book entitled *Sex in the Confessionals*, consisting of their tape-recorded confessions to priests, in which the journalists claimed that, having been given detailed and specific accounts of their sexual activities, the priests then sought to draw them out. The pope, enraged, had excommunicated the authors.

The search completed, the Swiss Guard would march out, followed by the Marshall of the Conclave, and the great door of the chapel would be swung shut. The Marshall would turn his key on the outside, the Prefect of Ceremonies would turn his on the inside, and the door be secured so that none might pass in or out and no messages be transmitted until after an election was achieved.

To choose a new pontiff the cardinals would cast a series of ballots, each secret. The voting would continue until one candidate received an electoral majority – two-thirds. After each vote the ballots would be burned in a small pot-bellied stove, its flue passing through a small window and visible from St. Peter's Square. If a vote was inconclusive, wet straw would be added to the fire to produce a dark smoke. When a consensus was reached, only the ballots would be burned, and the white smoke, the famed *fumata*, would signal to the world outside that the See of St. Peter was no longer vacant.

Paolo Rinsonelli's days were excitement. The weight of years had been put aside and arthritic pain disdained. His office had become a command post from which orders went out and to which reports came in his battle to win support for Michael's candidacy. "The time for decorum has passed," he roared, "let the battle be joined." No cardinal arrived in Rome whose predilection was not known within the hour and to whom, if he was uncertain, uncommitted or malleable, some appropriate advocate was not assigned. But for all this activity there was little evidence of it and Rinsonelli moved at the heart of his storm, serene at its center even as he induced it.

At his own request, Michael had been quartered at the North American College in the room he had occupied during his years of graduate study, and was almost reclusive. To Rinsonelli's fuming impatience, he refused to see visitors or attend receptions except where it was mandatory. His meals were sent in, and apart from taking long walks in the city, he spent his days and evenings in the room, reading – histories of the church, lives of the popes and devotional classics – praying, or looking from his window over Bernini's colonnade to St. Peter's Square and beyond to the Vatican.

On the Friday, having clumped with much complaining up four flights of stairs to reach Michael's room (the elevator being out of service), Rinsonelli banged on the door, and when Michael opened it, collapsed heavily onto a chair.

"Give me a moment to catch my breath," he said, puffing heavily, his face flaming. "I bring you good tidings of great joy."

Michael smiled at him affectionately. "Such a zealot!" he said.

"One of us must do God's dirty work," Rinsonelli said, producing a great handkerchief and proceeding to mop his face and neck. "It's all very well to play the reluctant bride here atop the hill, but without the marriage-broker may not the swain's ardor cool?"

"They also serve who only stand and wait," Michael smiled.

Rinsonelli was now able to get on without too much gasping, and rummaged in a battered valise. Michael could sense his excitement. "What's the word your press barbarians use?" Rinsonelli asked, pulling out a sheaf of papers. "A sampling, yes? Well, we have taken a sampling of our own and . . . " he scrutinized one of his papers, " . . . and, with 96 of 112 contacted (disregarding regional first-ballot preferences) here are the results."

"You sound like an old Tammany ward-heeler."

"Then God bless Tammany ward-heelers," Rinsonelli said, no whit intimidated. "As I was saying, here are the results: Kalumbulu 8, Castonguay 6, Meyer 2, Della Chiesa 17, Benedetti 33, Maloney 30." He looked up, triumph making his eyes to dance.

Michael was doing some mental arithmetic. "I'm not sure I understand the reasons for your elation," he said. "Together, Della Chiesa and Benedetti have 50 votes to my 30, and 76 are needed to elect."

"I begin to wonder whether my energies might not better be employed in another cause," Rinsonelli said. "Permit me to explain the facts of life. Benedetti has nowhere to go. Not one of Kalumbulu's supporters will go over to him and only three of Castonguay's. Meyer's are beyond shifting. So, even if you apportion him half of those we haven't made soundings about (which is generous) he can't achieve the requisite number. The sentiment against him and the Italian dominance is quite astounding. I think we can attribute that to Paul's intransigience and the perception that Benedetti is cut from the same cloth. Mark me well: it will take no more than four or at most five ballots!"

Michael stood looking down at his friend, his face grave. "Have you nothing to say?" Rinsonelli demanded. "You look as though you're ready to kill the messenger."

Michael went to the window to look out with unfocused eyes, oddly calm. There was silence in the room except for Rinsonelli's breathing. It was broken by the sound of running on the marble floor of the hall outside, distant and then coming closer to climax in a loud knocking. Michael crossed and opened the door.

"I'm sorry to trouble you, Eminence, but you are to come to the telephone. A Monsignor Jamieson is on the line from New York. He says it's urgent."

"Ashes to ashes. Dust to dust . . . "

The morning was incongruously beautiful: the greens of grass and tree lush, the air fragrant, the birds skipping like stones from bush to bush to pipe their tiny tunes, and overhead the sun: a shepherd surrounded by his flock at rest in a field of blue. Bishop Kelley's voice was strong in the silence of the cemetery: "I am the resurrection," Jesus said. "If she believes in me, even though she dies she will live. And she who lives and believes in me will never die." He had adapted the ancient promise to Jennifer, giving it a particular poignancy. Now, away from the ugly gash in the earth, alone in the limousine waiting for the hearse to pull away and permit departure, the words repeated like a litany in Michael's brain and the tears that had not come, came.

As the limousine moved forward he saw Copeland walking ahead, his great bulk unmistakable. Michael had looked for him but had not seen him either at the service or the cemetery. But there he was now, stooped, alone, heading for his car which Michael saw some distance down the road. As he drew abreast, Michael spoke to the driver and lowered the window.

"Copeland . . . "

He turned, started from a reverie. The face was drawn, thinner. The eyes were puffed.

"Will you get in for a moment?" Michael said.

Copeland looked at him, his expression blank. Then he opened the door and got into the car.

To the driver Michael said, "Pull off and park."

They sat encapsulated in silence, neither looking at the other, the car insulating them from the world outside.

"I want to tell you how sorry I am," Michael said. "I can't say how sorry I am." When Copeland didn't respond, but continued to stare ahead, he said. "How swiftly tragedy changes our perspective. I see now how wrong I've been. I failed Jennifer. I failed you, Copeland." There was no response, not so much as a glance. "I can't think of anything to say except that I'm sorry."

He went on. "Father Jamieson tells me you were there when they found her. Were you able to speak to her before she . . . ?

Copeland shook his head slowly, numbly.

"Do you know why she did it?"

Copeland reached into his jacket, brought forth an envelope and passed it to Michael. Michael saw that it was addressed to him, tore it open and began to read. When he was finished he put it in a pocket.

"Did Jennifer see this?"

He nodded. "I left the original on your desk. She burned it; I found the ashes in the fireplace." He was silent for another moment. "I killed her," he said softly, and then turned to look at Michael for the first time since entering the car. "We killed her," he said, his voice almost inaudible.

He put out a hand and opened the door. "Where are you going?" Michael asked.

"I don't know," he said.

He got out and walked to his car. Michael waited until he had driven off then nodded to his driver.

Epilogue

Cold . . . . *Was it the winter of the spirit?*

He was forever cold now: toiling in the fields high on the mountain; in the evening in meditation in the cloister; through the night beneath the rude covers; in the morning, putting his feet over the edge of the pallet on which his elbows now rested — bare feet on the chill stone floor — getting into the scapular, clasping his hands tightly beneath, burying his head in the hood and, eyes down, going quickly in the pre-dawn darkness to his place in the choir stall. In the first few days — how long ago it now seemed! — he had almost begrudged the chanting: it seemed only right that having lived by words he should not speak them for a time.

Had he done well to come here? Does one draw near to God more readily in a monastery than in a cathedral? Do prayers rise more surely to heaven if they spring from a barren cell? Does discomfort commend one to God? Is He impressed by austerity, by rigors, by mortifications, by wildernesses? It would seem so: was not the promised land into which He led the children of Israel very much like a wilderness; did He not succor Jesus in a wilderness?

But, with God, how could one know? "How impossible," the apostle said, "to penetrate His motives or to understand His methods. Who can know the mind of the Lord?"

Perhaps striving to understand was itself sin. Perhaps he should simply trust. But surely not, for the commandment is in part: "You must love the Lord your God with all your mind . . ." If one is com-

manded to love with the mind then the failure to think must surely be sin. So he must continue to seek understanding, to learn wherein he had erred.

But did he not already know? Had he not been tripped up on that source of all sin, pride? Was not the measure of his undoneness the length and breadth and depth, the heart and mind and bone and marrow of his pride? For all his disclaimers, for all his piety and prayers, had he not in truth lusted to ascend to Peter's throne and to wear the Fisherman's Ring? True, he had sought God's guidance, but when the answer had been silence he had read that silence as acquiescence. In his pride he had come to believe that God had called him, Michael Maloney, to save the church. What delusion — the church of God dependent upon a man! What was God's church, a sapling beneath the woodsman's ax that it might be so easily toppled?

Together, he and Rinsonelli had decided what remedy was called for: Rinsonelli for whatever his reasons, and he for his own. They had denigrated Benedetti and dismissed Della Chiesa. (How had Paolo spoken of Della Chiesa that night at dinner? "An old man. A cipher. At best a caretaker-pope.") But God had chosen to set the cipher on the papal throne. Not Benedetti, not Maloney, but Della Chiesa . . .

Innocent XIV.

What was God saying in elevating this quiet old man? Was He saying that what was needed at this moment (with the godless at the gate, with strife within the very walls, with the old order passing) was not the brilliant mind or the strong arm but, even if for only a few months or years, a caretaker, someone who in humility and love could be trusted to take care?

Surely what he had already done with the bones had demonstrated such thoughtful wisdom. There they lay at the heart of the Vatican, resuming their interrupted rest, while the Congregation of Rites, whose responsibility it is to examine those proposed for canonization, began their quiet deliberations. Sometimes the examination (or the trial — for that is what it is) takes decades: surely this even more important task will require as long. The church moves slowly in such matters as well it should, "for with God a thousand years is as a day and a day a thousand years."

Yes . . . pride. Undoubtedly, pride. His sin was ever before him.

318

But what was Jennifer's sin? Was it that the sins of the fathers had been visited on her? Was that what had brought her to turn her hand against herself in that most terrible of acts; the usurping of the prerogative of God, the negation of His creativity, the denial of the gift of life? Or was her failure simply a failure to trust His love? Was she broken, frail reed, by her lack of faith?

And Copeland . . . How was he ensnared? Did the Enemy sow the seed of resentment in the fertile soil of his love for Jennifer? Was there a meanness in his spirit that would not permit her affection from anyone but himself? Was that why he had hounded Harris beyond the grave and why he almost welcomed the spoor leading to the residence? Or could it be that his doggedness, his stubbornness had unwittingly become the instrument to accomplish God's design?

And Harris . . . . Old friend, friend of his youth. Were you a liar, Harris? Did your need for recognition in a day that esteems it so highly entrap you? Did you, too, lust for eminence and the praise of men? Were you fabricating one final enormous hoax, Harris? Whose were the bones, Harris? Whose ?

Not many days now and the summer would be over. The penance he had imposed on himself completed, he would return from his personal wilderness. Humbled? Wiser? He would not speculate about that now: that would begin to be seen when he resumed his duties in the crucible of New York and Washington and Rome. The Trappists with whom he had been living took no vow of silence – remaining free to speak or not to speak – and he knew that whatever vows he might or might not make, he would remain free to be his own man or God's.